GINGER, LORETTA AND IRENE *WHO?*

Books by George Eells:

THE LIFE THAT LATE HE LED:
A Biography of Cole Porter

HEDDA AND LOUELLA

GINGER, LORETTA AND IRENE *WHO?*

GINGER, LORETTA AND IRENE *WHO?*

by George Eells

G. P. PUTNAM'S SONS
NEW YORK

SBN: 399-11822-5

Library of Congress Cataloging in Publication Data

Eells, George.
  Ginger, Loretta, and Irene who?

  Filmography.
  Includes index.
  1. Moving-picture actors and actresses—United
States—Biography. I. Title.
PN1998.A2E35   791.43'028'0922   [B]   76-20806

PRINTED IN THE UNITED STATES OF AMERICA

For
George, Bess,
Donna and Sandy

Acknowledgments

Grateful acknowledgment is made to editor Harvey Ginsberg; researcher Alys Aker; Tom Clapp, Richard Lamparski, Aurand Harris, Mrs. Alfred Stern, Natalie Schafer, Bess Schmidt, Joan Blondell, Jean Howard, George Cukor, Marie (Baby Marie) Osborne, Stanley Musgrove, Nick Lucas, Jack Gordon, Becky Morehouse, Billy Hallop; Michael, Christianne and Tom Hopkins; Grady Sutton, Stanley Gordon, Ruth Waterbury, DeWitt Bodeen, Stratton Walling, Therese Lewis, George Leigh, Warren Brown, Barbara Myneder, Eddie Shaw, Mrs. Everett Chase, Robert Mayberry, Lee Wallace, Allan Brandt, Fredric March, Florence Eldridge, Royce Pitkin, Mary Loos, Ben Pearson, Ben Stroback, William Dozier, Phil Berg, Pat Harris Liberman, William Keighley, Charles Higham, Blossom Seeley, Joe Kallahan, Helen Steig, Frances Goodrich, Albert Hackett, Pat Newcomb, Ray Daum, Frith Banbury, Hope Williams, Mrs. Ambrose Chambers, Robert Lord, Allan Davis, Allen Vincent, Eva Patton, Jered Barclay, Richard Sale, Bill Ramsay, Annie Laurie Witzel, John Vivyan, Irving Berlin, Lynn Unkifer, James Hemingway, Betty Bentley, Hilda Coppage, Perry Leiber, Mrs. William Anthony McGuire, David Graham, Claudia Hatch Stearns, Jack Hamilton, Robert Raison, Alex Tiers, Donna Ganshirt, Robert Friess, Paul Rawlings, James C. Madden, Hasse Nyborg, Sandra Simon, Jack Langdon, Lee Silvian, Robert Ullman, Madeline P. Smith, Violet Alderman, Arnold Weissberger, Raymond Rohauer and Larry Michelotti. *(Continued on next page.)*

Dr. Robert Knutson and Mrs. Alvista Perkins, Special Collections, Doheny Library, University of Southern California

Paul Campbell, Fort Worth Library

Department of Film, Museum of Modern Art, New York

Maris M. Vlack, Public Library, David City, Nebraska

Ted Fetter, Marion Spritzer Thompson, Bill Richards, Mary Merrell, Wendy Warnken, Dolly Hecht of the Museum of the City of New York, Virginia Wright, Missouri Valley Room, Public Library, Kansas City, Missouri

Paul Myers, Betty Wharton, Dr. Roderick Bladel, Maxwell Silverman and Brigitte Kueppers, Theater Collection, Lincoln Center Library of Performing Arts

James Powers and Rochelle Reid, American Film Institute, Los Angeles

Mildred Simpson and staff of the Motion Picture Academy of Arts and Sciences, Los Angeles

Fine Arts Division, Dallas Public Library

Mrs. Ford Hubbard, Daughters of the American Revolution.

Office of Commandant, United States Marine Corps

American Society of Composers and Arrangers

Social Register Association of New York

Elizabeth Krakeur, Goddard College, Barre, Vermont

Muriel Campbell, registrar, Cathedral School of St. Mary, Long Island City

Barbara B. Lyons, alumnae director, Katharine Gibbs School, New York

Ray Olsen, radio station WOW, Omaha, Nebraska

Hetti Arlith and staff of the library of the *Fort Worth Telegram*

John Drap, library, *Kansas City Star*

Leonard Maltin, *Film Fan Monthly*

Films in Review

"Movie Star News"

"Ron's Now and Then Memorabilia"

"Cinemobilia"

Brian Rust and Allen Debus' *Complete Entertainment Discography*

Miles Kreuger, Theater and Movie Musical Historian

Special thanks to Samuel Stark for indexing the book.

TABLE OF CONTENTS

INTRODUCTION
New Year's Eve – 1933!

GINGER ROGERS
MIRIAM HOPKINS
RUTH ETTING
KAY FRANCIS
LORETTA YOUNG
IRENE BENTLEY

Each has her name on a movie marquee in the Times Square area. **STANDING ROOM ONLY** signs are posted at every theater,* and each of the six faces 1934 confidently.

Stars are photogenic.

Movie fans consider most leading ladies so picture-book pretty that it seems incredible they are real flesh and blood, not Vargas calendar girls. A few sophisticates may complain that Hollywood makeup men have powdered, painted, tinted and tweezed until sometimes a girl's individuality is endangered. (A fan magazine is running a layout of Irene Bentley sporting six "looks" ranging from Garbo to Janet Gaynor to Norma Shearer.)

---

*Although movie attendance was down from a high of 110 million weekly in 1930 to 60 million in 1933, the New York *Times* reported Broadway's movie houses were filled to capacity on this gala night in the midst of the Depression.

Stars have personality.

Each one expresses some facet of the aspirations and ideals of millions of fans. And these are fans—not students of the cinema, who will emerge years later. In spite of the physical remodeling, the changing of names and the altering of biographies, each retains her uniqueness.

Stars have talent.

In addition, all have something beyond—that indefinable presence that is often unnoticed in personal encounters but is a necessity in front of a movie camera.

Stars flourish in the limelight.

As celebrities they are expected to live their private lives in public. Although it may ultimately result in alienation, it is a price that they are expected to pay. There is room for only one Garbo.

Stars are idealized.

Fans demand it. They hunger for the exploits of such goddesses as Loretta, Kay and Miriam play onscreen. Moviegoers unselfconsciously subscribe to the cliché that life is grim enough without plunking down a hard-earned two bits to see their own problems on the screen.

In 1934 intellectuals are concerned with political developments in Spain and Germany. They discuss James Joyce, Gertrude Stein and Virginia Woolf or Oswald Spengler's *The Decline of the West*. They relax working Double-Crostics or playing croquet. The rich and sophisticated prefer Eugene O'Neill, Elmer Rice, Maxwell Anderson and Cole Porter to films.

Movies still belong to the masses, and scores of Hollywood publicists apply their ingenuity and fertile imagination to fabricating witticisms, eccentricities and anecdotes to help familiarize the public with the players. Grace Kingsley keeps her readers informed on sweet-faced little Irene Bentley's "tired of it all" world-weariness. Ed Sullivan limits his reports on the six to casting news.

Jimmy Fidler apprises radio listeners of their triumphs and failures. And the queen of gossip columnists, Louella O. Parsons, snipes away at Ginger's lack of style and dancing ability while she plunders Roget's *Thesaurus* to find new ways of trumpeting praise for "lovely Loretta Young." All six receive reams of publicity. Even Irene Bentley, the least recognized among the group, is customarily identified as "the girl Fox Studios believes in."

In a society made more thing and money conscious by the Great Depression these lucky girls are smashing successes whether or not they are artistes. At a time when most Americans are grateful for shelter, food and meager wages these high-flying beauties are living in style and taking home hundreds, if not thousands, of dollars each week.

If the rewards are enormous, so are the pressures. But on this gala New Year's Eve the difficulties are forgotten. For the six are, in Garson Kanin's rendering, "moooooooovie stars." Privately, every star and starlet reflects the combined efforts of moguls, producers, writers, cameramen, film cutters, lighting experts, hairstylists, publicity men, still photographers, costume designers, agents, lawyers, accountants, business managers, dialogue directors, lovers, mothers, fathers, husbands and/or friends. As Jesse Lasky once observed, "It takes more than talent."

Some project an inner essence that catches the public fancy. Others just happen to be at the right place at the right time. Colleen Moore got nowhere as a saccharine ingenue, but when she was cast as a hoydenish flapper, she became the silent screen's top star. The lucky ones who can cope with celebrity prosper. The unlucky or difficult who find fame a burden turn to liquor and pills, become bitter, embrace religion or left- or right-wing politics. Is it because of guilt they experience in receiving four-figure salaries for mediocre work? Or is it to wipe out the sense of what they really are in comparison to what they are supposed to be?

On New Year's Eve, 1933, the lucky six seem to have risen beyond the insecurities of the rat race. Their secret vices and sorrows are skillfully suppressed from a public that doesn't want to know about such things anyway. For the moment, these are superwomen who act out the fantasies of the masses, living supposedly stress-free lives unobtainable to mere mortals. They are personifications of Horatio Alger's pampered sister, Hattie.

There is GINGER ROGERS. As 1933 turns into 1934, she is appearing at Radio City Music Hall in *Flying Down to Rio*. The nominal stars of *Rio* are Dolores Del Rio and Gene Raymond, but billing be damned. Everyone is talking about a new dance team—feather-footed Fred Astaire and vivacious Ginger Rogers. The acclaim that greets their dancing, especially "The Carioca," reassures Ginger about her future. Unlike the qualities that set her RKO rival Katharine Hepburn apart, Ginger's appeal lies in the fact that she seems a spectacular version of her contemporaries. She is at once sweet, sexy, tough, sentimental, hard-boiled, warmhearted and wisecracking. She is easy for a girl to identify with. She suggests the fabled "million dollar baby at the five-and-ten cent store" that any fellow in the audience can dream of finding.

At the Times Square Paramount (whose lobby was inspired by L'Opéra), MIRIAM HOPKINS is the attraction. She portrays the sparkling Gilda in Ernst Lubitsch's bowdlerized version of *Design for Living*, which, as screenwriter Ben Hecht boasts, has retained only one line of Noel Coward's dialogue.* Since bisexual chic is not to be publicized by newsweeklies for another 40 years, the leading players in the film, unlike their counterparts on the legitimate stage, keep their bed switching off limits and settle for platonic relationships. Miriam, who is considered Hollywood's most versatile actress, plays the pal of cronies Fredric March and Gary Cooper. Her desire, in Hecht's words, was simply to be a mother of the arts. Ironically, in view of Hecht's mutilation of the Coward play, numerous critics will complain that neither Miriam nor her co-stars possess the requisite style to manage Coward's witticisms and epigrams.

Simultaneously, Miriam is appearing in person at the Ethel Barrymore Theater as Julie in Owen Davis' *Jezebel*. Whether she is better suited to the vixenish Southern belle Julie than to the glib, globe-trotting Gilda is a matter of debate—as her interpretations of all roles are destined to be. Even in 1973 one respected director shouted in response to a description of her as a "good actress," "Good? What do you mean, 'good'? She was great!" Another, even more illustrious director dismissed her as a "blond pickaninny."

Not far from the Paramount is the Rivoli Theater at Forty-ninth Street and Broadway, which is showing Eddie Cantor in *Roman Scandals*. Receiving billing second to Cantor is the celebrated RUTH ETTING, star of night clubs, vaudeville, records, radio and the prestigious Ziegfeld Follies. But her followers are in for a surprise. She has only one song. The canny Samuel Goldwyn is simply using Ruth's enormous popularity as box-office bait. Her martinet of a husband, "Colonel" Martin Moe "The Gimp" Snyder, is determined to turn her into a full-fledged star of movie musicals. He is confident that once the public has been heard, "the little lady" will have producers on their knees, begging for her services. Ruth, for her part, is unperturbed, resigned to

*"For the good of our immortal souls."

14

the fact that worldly success is meaningless as her private life is miserable.

Two blocks north of the Rivoli with its classical white Greek columns stands the French-style Hollywood Theater. There the name KAY FRANCIS dwarfs the title of her latest extravagantly emotional vehicle, *The House on 56th Street*. As usual, Warner's has taken a script rejected by another star and counted upon Kay Francis' idolaters to make it a commercial success. The assumption is that her following is indifferent to the quality of the story as long as the raven-haired, limpid-eyed Kay Fwancis (of the intriguing lisp) looks soignée, casts her magic spell and suffers nobly. Ever since the studio stole Kay from Paramount and elevated her from featured player to star, it has been presumed that "the best-dressed woman on the screen," cast in a woman's story, automatically guarantees a box-office bonanza. But after several failures the pragmatic Kay is beginning to wonder.

Loretta Young's film *A Man's Castle* is showing at the Rialto Theater at Broadway and Forty-third Street. LORETTA YOUNG, who began as Gretchen Young doing extra roles at four, launched a second career as a leading ingenue opposite Lon Chaney in 1927, then made the transition to "squawkies," as detractors called them, with ease but little distinction. Yet, because of her haunting photogenic quality and her bulldog determination, her studio persisted in nurturing her. Darryl Zanuck, her mentor at Warner's-First National, cast her opposite one popular male star after another, and by 1933 she has a fan following. Critics also begin to take notice. For the first time, reviewers mention something other than her wardrobe and her eyes when she appears in *Zoo in Budapest*. And in *A Man's Castle* (perhaps because of her offscreen love affair with Spencer Tracy) she generates enough emotional heat to promise developing into a leading woman—or even a top star.

On New Year's Day pert, perfectly featured, diminutive IRENE BENTLEY, purportedly a New York socialite, has her second film, *Smoky*, reviewed in the New York *Times*. Since out-of-town reviewers have already acclaimed *Smoky* as the best horse picture ever made and Irene plays the only female role in it, she may be mildly disappointed to find her work not even mentioned by the critic of the leading metropolitan daily. But she may take heart from the advertisements in which her billing is second only to that of Victor Jory's.

Heterogeneous as this group seems—from neophyte Irene Bentley to Broadway star Ruth Etting—its members share tenacity, physical stamina, good luck and a luminous quality that sets them apart—at least for powerful movie executives—from the hordes of would-be stars. They are also, in varying degrees, beautiful, sought after, individualistic, sexually emancipated, pampered and, compared to other Americans, affluent.

One will prove to have only a momentary glow that vanishes mysteriously, three will become victims of the wastefulness inherent in the big-studio system, one will voluntarily retire at the politic moment, and one will emerge as the ultimate survivor.

This is a story of triumph and defeat, of the advantages and disadvantages of fame—individually and generally. It is six stories, and it is one story of six women who, on New Year's Eve, 1933, had every reason to be optimistic.

GINGER ROGERS

The Survivor

Ginger Rogers' career was progressing at such a pace as 1933 turned into 1934 that the realities of the bank holiday, street-corner apple salesmen and studio retrenchment hardly penetrated her consciousness. This euphoria remained as late as 1975, allowing her to tell a reporter complacently, "The thirties were such a pretty time. I know it was bad for an awful lot of people, but not for me. I remember the whole atmosphere, the ambiance of the thirties with a glow because success was knocking at my door. I got to California in thirty-two,* just in time to do *Gold Diggers of 1933*, where I sang 'We're in the Money.' It was a whole new life for me, and I was excited about it. It was happy and beautiful and gay and interesting. I was surrounded by marvelous people, all the top people in our industry. I was playing tennis and wearing slacks considered too wide today and shorts that are considered too long. And there were polo games that don't exist anymore.

"Today, it's a wild, kind of crazy, thoughtless, selfish society."

Indeed, Ginger's greatest luck occurred in the final weeks of December, 1933. On December 23 *Flying Down to Rio* opened as the holiday attraction at the Radio City Music Hall. Astaire and Rogers, as hardly anyone remembers, rated fifth and fourth billing following Dolores Del Rio, Gene Raymond and Raul Roulien, a name that rates inclusion in *Variety*'s "Who dat?" category. Audiences were only mildly stirred by

*Actually in 1931

17

Dolores Del Rio's familiar classic beauty or the main plot, which concerned her romantic entanglement with Raymond and his assumption that Roulien was her suitor, not her cousin. Yet apple-cheeked Ginger, with the common denominator personality, and the elegant Astaire of the thin face and matchstick physique had neatly wrapped up the picture as their own even before they slithered into "The Carioca."

Had Ginger been insecure, she might have worried that the December 26 premiere of the straight comedy *Chance at Heaven* at the Rialto might diminish her triumph in the musical. As it turned out, she had little to worry about. Reviewing the short-lived new film for the New York *Times,* Mourdant Hall had little good to say for the offering, but there were kind words for Ginger: "Ginger Rogers, who dances so nicely in *Flying Down to Rio*, the Radio City Music Hall picture, assumes here the role of Marje," he wrote, "and she acts the part better than it deserves."

Ginger's career was shifting into high gear.

In 1933 Ginger had three great advantages over other actresses. She had herself, her mother and God in her corner. Her mother, also known as Lela, Lee-Lee and Mommy, was a devout Christian Scientist who never gave Ginger any cause to question her loyalty. She also saw to it that even as a little girl Ginger equated what was good for her with what God wanted for her.

At the time Ginger made *Flying Down to Rio*, she showed few indications of developing into the ultimate survivor she has become. Most people must have regarded her as merely another vivacious, even-featured, friendly, none-too-well-educated performer, but as Lela said in 1975, "People didn't realize she had more than one cell to her battery." Indeed, she did. She could sing in a small pleasant voice, dance expertly enough not to handicap Fred Astaire, time a comedy line precisely and—although no one but Lee-Lee, Gee-Gee and God believed it then—play dramatic roles. She was also beginning to exhibit a mysterious cinematic quality that exists apart from talent and even though beyond precise analysis, is instantly recognizable to moviegoers.

"Whatever I am, I have to be me first," is a Rogersism that allowed Ginger to indulge in the actor's ultimate egomania while shoring up her behavior with her two great supporters.

Ginger's devotion to Lee-Lee and Lee-Lee's to Gee-Gee demonstrated that two heads are better than one in show business. While Lee-Lee has never fitted the classic stage-mother stereotype any more than

Ginger has always heeded her advice, there can be no question that the two of them sometimes rushed in where Ginger alone might have feared to tread. Not that this rashness has always been unwise. Certainly during Ginger's half century as an entertainer, she and her mother have traveled along side by side, scoring many triumphs and engaging in few serious disagreements.

In 1965 Ginger discussed her celebrated parent with an English journalist, telling him, "You should see my mommy! She's a card. Tiny, turned-up nose, tiny hands, tiny feet—the cutest little female you ever saw. But bright! She'd mow us all down. Knows everything, reads everything—mention a subject, and Lee-Lee will tell you about it. First I call her Mommy—then Mother—then Lee-Lee. And she answers to all of them. Oh, she's a wonder, you'd get a boot out of her. She's had the time I'd love to have to sit down and study and read. My life hasn't been conducive to study of any kind. . . . Mommy's an avid reader. You name it, she will have read it, she will know all about it and she will tell you about it. Best talker you ever saw—talks a blue streak! I'm the silent one. Could be I'm intimidated by her! A really wonderful woman—great sense of humor, great courage, wonderful foresight!"

That foresight stretched back to the 1930s when Lela unsuccessfully attempted to persuade Ginger's agent Leland Hayward to demand 5 percent of the television rights to Rogers pictures. He refused, a decision Ginger has been unable to forgive him even unto the grave.

If Ginger's bitterness appears mean-spirited, coming from a woman who proclaims that God is love and that she has lived with Him since she was a small child, Ginger explains that achieving perfect love is as difficult as attaining perfect harmony in music. She believes that hellfire and brimstone are here *now* and heaven is, too. "When I'm a bitch, I say to myself, 'Ginger, there is no God in this,' and I try to stop." Ginger has said that she doesn't know what she would do without her religion and explained that religion is glorifying God in whatever way one has. "It's doing your work marvelously to the best of your ability," she says.

No one can accuse the girl who used to rehearse dance routines until her pumps and stockings were bloodstained of being a slacker. And she attributes her long career to three parts hard work and one part inspiration.

A few years ago, after attending a retrospective showing of ten of her films at Manhattan's Gallery of Modern Art, Ginger observed, "It ain't really me up there. Just images and shadows. Me's here."

But who or what is—or was—*me*?

Greta Garbo, Claudette Colbert, Katharine Hepburn, Bette Davis, Joan Blondell, to cite only a few, worked within easily defined images, but superficially, Ginger was a girl of many faces and diverse talents and characteristics. "I believe in flexibility. You have to be a chameleon of many colors" she has said. Yet whether she was a flapper, a gold digger, a fraudulent café singer, a white-collar girl, a fake nymphet, an accused murderess, a Broadway star—whatever—nobody better projected the comforting illusion that any reasonably ambitious, hardworking girl could achieve similar success; and that any man could, with a little luck, find just such a captivating creature as Ginger for a wife.

What did she represent? A screen divinity or a caricature? An original or a cartoon? Or a little of each? Like most major stars, she dances on the razor's edge between originality and universality. She has maintained her star status at who knows what price? Happy marriages and easy everyday relationships that ordinary human beings enjoy have been sacrificed to the discipline that her career has dictated. Her reward has been that she is one of the survivors.

Whether the rewards have compensated for the sacrifices, only she knows. But how that career was achieved is her story.

Lela, one of the five pert Owens sisters of Kansas City, Missouri, was strongly motivated from the beginning. After finishing eighth grade, she immediately enrolled in business school and, by the time she celebrated her fifteenth birthday, was working as a stenographer. On the day she turned eighteen, which was Christmas Day, she married electrical engineer Eddins McMath but from the first showed no intention of turning into a housewife.

After their first child died in infancy, Lela hired out as a newspaper reporter in Independence, Missouri, and blithely moved to 100 Moore Street, leaving her husband to follow when he could free himself from his obligations. Lela's newspaper career was interrupted—officially in 1911, although some longtime friends insist the year was 1908—by her second pregnancy and the birth, on July 16, of Virginia Katherine McMath.

For this second child Lela began to feel special regard during her pregnancy, as if she foresaw the unborn infant had been touched by a special grace. Unsure whether or not to believe in prenatal influences, Lela nevertheless exposed herself to great paintings, ambitious musi-

20

cal compositions and literary masterpieces. In a time when women believed in "marking" children by traumatic shocks Lela saw to it that her unborn child was exposed only to the most harmonious forces.

A few months after Ginger, as a small cousin called her, was born, the McMaths left Independence. Not, however, before Lela had taken the first step in establishing Ginger as a public personality. A photographic portrait of the two of them was so suffused with tenderness that an enlargement of it was hung in the Missouri State Building in Jefferson City, where it was titled "Modern Madonna and Child."

When Ginger was not yet a year old, the McMaths turned up in Ennis, a small Texas town. By this time the extent of the marital mismatch was obvious. Lela's sunny appearance—the halo of honey-colored hair, the upturned nose, the saucy blue eyes that crinkled around the outer edges when she laughed—belied her plucky individualism. And her husband, who appeared to be the most ordinary of men, turned out to be an uncompromising adversary.

The marriage failed, and Lela moved Ginger into a hotel while divorce proceedings were instituted. McMath was granted liberal visitation rights, but one day he impulsively kidnapped Ginger. Lela promptly tracked him down and hauled him into court, where the judge sharply curtailed his visits. Enraged, McMath again kidnapped Ginger and took her to Missouri. This time Lela was forced to hire detectives to locate and return her child. After that episode Ginger rarely saw her father during the eight remaining years of his life.

Referring to her childhood, Ginger once said that the early years, like most people's, were all mixed up. But Ginger's were more chaotic than most. Lela's peregrinations after the divorce were so complicated that later even she sometimes became confused about the sequence of her career. Following her divorce, she probably returned to Kansas City, where she worked either for the Kansas City *Post* or for Montgomery Ward at less than $10 per week. While so employed, she won a short-story competition sponsored by an amusement park and was asked to convert her entry into a screenplay. She went to Hollywood in 1916, leaving Ginger in the care of her parents. For professional reasons she adopted the pen name Lela Leibrand and wrote or helped write scripts for such silent stars as Gladys Brockwell, Theda Bara, Baby Marie Osborne, Gloria Joy and the Lee Kids. Free-lancing at first, Lela later joined the staff writers at Diando Studios, then transferred to the Fox Company, which sent her to New York.

Lela's desire to serve her country during World War I culminated in her enlistment as one of the first marinettes. As Sergeant Lela Leibrand* attached to the Publicity Department of the Marine Corps, she wrote for *Leatherneck* and other publications, but, as she now recalls, her main contribution was in motion pictures. "In Washington I was working day and night, processing and cutting film for the Marines and the Navy and the Army because I was the only one in the darn town who knew anything about film. I made a training film, *All in a Day's Work* and turned out a lot of newsreel coverage that had been sent back from the front," she says. She also appeared in some of the footage shot around the nation's capital.

Ginger still remembers the evening when her grandmother announced that they were attending the theater to view Lela's film. "I hadn't seen my mother for a long time, and I was beside myself when she appeared in her little Sam Browne belt, perky overseas cap and all. She looked so natty. When it was over, everybody applauded, and Grandma said, 'All right, now we can go home.' And I said, 'No, I want to wait here for my mother.' I wasn't a terribly bright child. I thought my mother was back there somewhere behind the screen, and that she was coming out."

Ginger was obviously painfully homesick during Lela's stint in the service. From her later comments it is obvious that she feared the temporary separation would turn out to be permanent, as the one from her father had. Lela, for example, recalls getting such a barrage of "Dear Mother" letters that the other marines nicknamed her Mother, and she also remembers that when she was ill, she received an emotional plea not to die until Ginger could repay the $3 she had borrowed. Some friends contend that Ginger has spent her life unconsciously bribing her mother to remain at her side.

Lela was discharged from the service, and Ginger got what she wanted: her mommy back in Kansas City. There Lela quickly recovered from her illness, got a job, and resumed an interrupted romance with an old suitor, John Rogers. Following their marriage in 1919, John Rogers adopted Ginger, and the family moved to Dallas, where Daddy John conducted his insurance business and Ginger enjoyed a year of homelife that came closer to being normal than any that she was to know. The Rogerses moved to Fort Worth in 1921. As Ginger later wrote: "Life began . . . [in] Fort Worth, Texas, where we had a home on Cooper Street."

*Asked why the U.S. Marine Corps allowed her to enlist under a pen name, Mrs. Rogers snaps, "They didn't know the difference."

22

At this point Daddy John began to slip out of focus and was gradually to disappear altogether. But not before writing "Cowboy Cabaret," a Western ballad celebrating Fort Worth's history, which he and Ginger, wearing six-shooters and cowboy chaps, sang and hawked on the streets at 25 cents a copy to defray cost of publication.

Lela had not been in Fort Worth long before she began promoting the arts, founding the Symphony and acting as its first business manager, as well as writing about amusements for the Fort Worth *Telegram*. Her earnings initially merely supplemented her husband's, but as the couple's relationship deteriorated, Lela worked longer hours so that her increased earnings made her independent of him. Her newspaper assignments made frequent backstage visits a necessity, and Ginger enjoyed accompanying Lela. Ginger also delighted in mingling with the vaudeville headliners who congregated at the Rogerses' home. Although she took dancing lessons at the Elizabeth King Studios and played the ukulele, no one guessed that either she or Lela harbored stage ambitions for her.

"I doubt that kids were sharp enough in those days to spot latent talent," Ginger's first boyfriend, Charles Cartwright (nationally known for his comic strip "Church Chuckles"), says. "She was attractive, with a great personality and boundless enthusiasm and energy, but as far as we were concerned, she was just 'one of the Cooper Street gang.' From the standpoint of classic beauty, Florine McKinney, two doors down on Cooper, probably would have been more blessed. However, Florine, who was helped into the movies by Lela Rogers, had a brief career.

"We had a one-horse neighborhood orchestra, with yours truly on saxophone. I don't recall Ginger singing with us, but she wore out the rugs and floors of our house doing the Charleston before she ever thought of entering any contest."

Ginger's theatrical activity was limited to pageants written by her mother for various fund-raising projects. One, *The Birth of Music**, traced song and dance from their beginnings to the 1920's, with Ginger playing Jazz Dancing, or Evil, and Florine McKinney Classical Dancing, or Good.

If the general impression Ginger created was that of a happy-go-lucky child with no strong will of her own, her behavior on a couple of

---

*It proved so successful that in 1937 a physical education instructor repeated it—with Lela Rogers bringing the music and dances up to date.

occasions provided clues to single-mindedness in achieving her ends. For instance, when she reached middle school, she encountered an English teacher, Ruth Browning, who influenced her greatly. Years later Ginger was to say, "She's an absolutely adorable woman, and I had very good taste because I chose her as my ideal and she is a living doll. Even today there isn't anything she can't do. She can make a lampshade. She can make the most marvelous fudge. She can decorate a room. She has a green thumb. So I wanted to emulate her." Ginger wanted the inspiration of her teacher not only during school hours but also at home. "One day," says Ruth Browning Zant, "Ginger came up and said she wanted me to come and live at her house, that her mother would come to see me. Which she did. And she said she had heard that I was going to come live with them. I said, 'That's what Ginger tells me.' So that afternoon they came to my apartment and moved me to Cooper Street. And I lived there for two years."

Ruth Browning and Ginger became best of friends, even devising a special lingo which only they could understand. "She was a completely beautiful child, always cooperating with me in every respect," Mrs. Zant recalled in 1975. "Yet never leaving the impression that she might have been teacher's pet. She had great sense of fitness."

Ginger's determination to have her way manifested itself in a more important way, too. When the Interstate Vaudeville Circuit announced a series of Charleston contests in various cities, Ginger was determined to enter. Lela opposed the idea. She had given the contest at Fort Worth's Majestic Theater a big publicity buildup in the *Record*. Should Ginger win, Lela feared people would think competition had been fixed. She also wanted her gangly, freckle-faced daughter to finish her education before going to work. But Ginger enlisted the help of those associated in presenting the exhibition. They applied pressure on Lela, who finally agreed to allow Ginger to enter and sat up all night sewing brilliants on a white crêpe romaine dress for her daughter to wear.

Ginger was chosen as the Fort Worth representative by audience applause. Then in the state finals, which opened the new Peacock Terrace Roof Garden at the Baker Hotel on December 4, Ginger was named the "feet-up, hands-down" winner over 100 other contestants. The prize was a booking of four weeks at $100 a week on the Interstate Circuit, which included Texas, Alabama and Arkansas. Lela, who had orginally been so opposed to the move, quit her jobs and began organizing an act.

24

Response to Ginger's appeal and talent at that time was varied. Frank O. Starz, head of publicity for Interstate, said, "She was just a swell kid who could do the Charleston better than the one who invented it."

Terry Browne, later a Fort Worth restaurateur and oilman, who performed a comedy Charleston in blackface, said he wasn't at all impressed with Ginger or her Charleston. "Of course, I'd already been to Hollywood and thought I was a man of the world, and she was just a freckle-faced kid. But I guess she danced okay."

Mrs. Doris Shelton, a neighbor of the Rogerses, said, "I can still see her with two little braided pigtails and that homemade glittery white dress bouncing about on her bean-pole frame. But she could really Charleston, I can tell you that!"

For her part, Lela's pride in her offspring didn't cloud her judgment. She realized that Ginger was an unseasoned amateur and hired two other contestants who had been runners-up to form an act, "Ginger Rogers and Her Redheads."

Ginger was to say in 1936—following two marriages, playing major roles in Broadway musicals and making several films with Fred Astaire—"Winning that contest was without too much doubt the happiest day in my life." Her triumph marked the end of Ginger's education and her ambition to become an English teacher.

Two and a half weeks after winning the Charleston championship, Ginger opened in vaudeville, and John Rosenfield, Jr., who was to gain a national reputation as arts critic for the Dallas *Morning News*, reviewed the turn. Although he later admitted he would rather have been at the Palace listening to the symphony orchestra, he felt bound to file an honest—if brief—report: "Ginger Rogers of Fort Worth, diminutive state champion of the eccentric Charleston, assisted by Earl Leach and Joe [sic] Butler,* 'Dancing Redheads,' takes this week's Majestic audience by storm. Capacity audiences Sunday just couldn't get enough of Ginger's own personality and slender grace."

Later Rosenfield deflated the assumption that Lela Rogers was one of those jungle mothers such as June Havoc and Gypsy Rose Lee had. Lela Rogers, he said, was too involved in newspaper work and symphony subscriptions to think seriously of a career for her sixteen-year-

---

*Earl Leach and Josephine, not Joe, Butler soon quit the act, married and eventually opened a dancing school in Buffalo, New York.

old daughter, whose only notable characteristics seemed legs "as fast as lightning" and "a sweet, tractable disposition." Lela, Rosenfield said, was thought a little too genteel to hold stage aspirations for her offspring. But, he reported, once Ginger had drunk deeply of public applause she was "irreparably stage-struck. You couldn't do a thing with her except let her sing and dance at every opportunity, large or small."

Ginger and the Redheads did so well on the Interstate Circuit that they were offered a spot on the Publix chain, where success went to the Redheads' heads and they struck out on their own. Lela took the opportunity to return to Fort Worth, thinking that Ginger would reenter school, but Ginger was having none of that. "I believe, and believed then, that parents should let children alone to enjoy the natural things in life. Ginger wanted to go into the theater. I couldn't have prevented it," Lela sputtered to reporter Rosalind Shafer. "Now people say she had no childhood. Well, neither did I. I started work at sixteen, but it's better that way if you're trying to get started in some special line."

Having accepted Ginger's dedication to show business, Lela attempted in every way to help her daughter succeed. "I wrote her baby-talk monologues. I wrote songs. I made clothes. I even carried a sewing machine. I was a regular Madame Rose. Exactly—*except* that I did it by cooperating with the circuit, cooperating with the managers, making them see that what's good for Ginger is good for them." Lela transformed them into silent partners, devoted to making a success of the act. And she went out of her way to do little favors for other performers on the bill, counting on occasions that might arise when those performers were in a position to return the favor.

None of it was easy. Gee-Gee and Lee-Lee spent two years of constantly moving up and down and across the country. They accepted engagements in clubs, on the radio, on the variety chain known as the Junior Orpheum Circuit and on another, known among performers as the Death Trail of Vaudeville. Ginger filled in as a "disappointment act" and worked glorified amateur contests. She sang without compensation over the Dallas *Morning News*' radio station WFAA in return for publicity. When things got particularly grim, Lee-Lee donned one of Ginger's costumes, and they appeared as a sister act.

Name any backwater town, and Ginger is likely to have played it. But after two years her luck began to change. She was booked to appear with Fred Lowry in St. Louis, billed as "The Original John Held Jr. Girl." Audiences were enthusiastic about her loose-limbed dancing

26

and her chirruping baby talk—so much so that the management held her over for thirty-two weeks, during which she and Lee-Lee were able to reassemble their assets and polish Ginger's act.

Everything was proceeding smoothly, with mother and daughter seeing eye to eye on professional issues, when Ginger ran into a young man she had known in Texas as Jack Culpepper. Now, as Jack Pepper, he was working as a hoofer in vaudeville. Ginger fell wildly, uncritically in love and during a three-week layoff in 1928 married Pepper in New Orleans, despite Lela's opposition. Husband and wife teamed as Ginger and Pepper. But the act met with little success, and the marriage foundered in less than a year. Not, however, before it served Mommy notice that, devoted daughter though Ginger might be, she was her own woman.

Ginger returned to the road as a single following the collapse of her marriage, hitting a professional peak when she played the Oriental and North Shore theaters in Chicago. At the Oriental, she worked with Paul Ash, one of the most gifted men in the presentation of variety shows. "As a matter of fact," Ginger told television host Irv Kupcinet in 1975, "Chicago was one of the places I was 'held over,' quote, unquote, which is one of the thrilling things that happens to you when you're beginning a career."

Ginger was then relying heavily on Lela's baby-talk monologues, popular songs of that type and her expertise as a Charleston champ. Paul Ash was impressed enough with her work to offer to take her to New York with his show, but Lela advised Ginger to get more experience. Ginger reluctantly agreed and was chagrined when another performer, Helen "Boop-Boop-a-Doop" Kane became a national rage with the same type of delivery she had been using.

When Miss Kane moved on to bigger and better things, Ginger accepted Ash's renewed offer, playing the Times Square and Brooklyn Paramount theaters. At the Brooklyn Paramount she attracted favorable attention doing what ironically had come to be known as a Helen Kane act. She was, in fact, invited to audition for *Whoopee* but failed to get the role. Yet even her failure is transformed into oceans of prestige in the retelling. Speaking of her stint with Ash, she ingeniously manages to interject two other stellar names plus two Broadway hits. "I didn't realize that this [working with Ash] was my first big break," she says. "Eddie Cantor saw me at the Paramount. He was unsuccessful in getting me a part in *Whoopee*, produced by Florenz Ziegfeld, but this contact finally resulted in my getting the comedy lead in *Top Speed*."

27

Cantor, Ziegfeld, *Whoopee*—none had anything to do with her getting the part of Babs Green in *Top Speed*. Charlie Morrison, an agent who later operated a Hollywood nightclub, saw Ginger with Ash and recommended that librettist Guy Bolton and songwriters Bert Kalmar and Harry Ruby, who had formed a company to produce their own musical, look at her. They liked what they saw, and Ginger was hired.

The show opened at the 46th Street Theater on December 26, 1929, and Ginger's hoydenish humor suited audiences much better than the cloying sweetness of dimpled Irene Delroy. It also moved critic Brooks Atkinson to make his oft-quoted observation that "an impudent young thing, Ginger Rogers carries youth and humor to the point where they are completely charming." Ginger sang "Keep Your Undershirt On" with Lester Allen, the much-admired featured comic, and then led the chorus kids in "Hot and Bothered."

In the theatrical profession some of Ginger's contemporaries found her less accomplished than her notices would have led one to believe. She was admired for her Charleston, but her tap dancing left something to be desired. A casting director who covered *Top Speed* for Paramount filed a report on her saying, "Just another Charleston dancer. She can't act, but she's cute and plump and pretty and would do all right for a flapper role."

Still, Ginger registered strongly with those in a position to give assignments. Like many young actresses, she appeared in a few short subjects, including *Campus Sweetheart* with Rudy Vallee, *A Night in the Dormitory* and *Office Blues*. Walter Wanger, who was familiar with the shorts, signed her for the film version of Katharine Brush's *Young Man of Manhattan*, in which she played Puff, a society girl, who uttered a line that became a national catchphrase, "Cigarette me, big boy. Well, do it!"

Ginger and Lela gave up their suite at the Piccadilly Hotel and rented a Long Island house before Ginger began acting in *Young Man of Manhattan* in the daytime and appearing in *Top Speed* at night. The studio provided a limousine and a chauffeur to pick up Ginger at 6 A.M., and each morning she'd tumble into the backseat and fall asleep until delivered to the make-up department at Paramount's Astoria studios.

Filming finished for the day, she would again pile into the limo and fall asleep on the drive to the theater. "I just had time to change from movie into stage makeup before going on," she later recalled, but she thrived on the routine. The performances didn't bother her, she said, likening them to parties—the only drawback being that the same guests appeared at every one.

When the show closed, Paramount proposed sending Ginger to Hollywood. She and Lela were tempted. Ginger had registered well on screen in *Young Man of Manhattan*, in which she outshone Claudette Colbert, in *The Sap from Syracuse* with Jack Oakie and *Queen High* with Bill Boyd and Charlie Ruggles. But when Ginger was offered the part of Molly Gray, the leading ingenue role in George and Ira Gershwin's *Girl Crazy*, Gee-Gee and Lee-Lee decided to remain on Broadway.

Ginger introduced "Embraceable You" and "But Not for Me" at the October 14, 1930, opening of the show. But once again the comedienne overshadowed the straight ingenue. Ethel Merman, belting out "I Got Rhythm," outshone Ginger in this production, just as Ginger had outdone Irene Delroy in *Top Speed*.

During the run of *Girl Crazy*, Ginger made two more films, *Follow the Leader* and Dorothy Arzner's *Honor Among Lovers*, both with Charlie Ruggles. In the latter, Miss Arzner had no intention of using Ginger, but when the determined young actress begged for a part, the director gave her the script and asked her to read it and indicate the part she thought best suited her talents. The next day Ginger appeared and named a character whom the scriptwriter had described as a tall, dark, slim and sophisticated gold digger. Miss Arzner pointed out the author's conception of the character, and Ginger improvised a flashily dressed dumb-Dora type who hung on her hero's arm and followed him around, staring up into his face with rapt admiration. Miss Arzner was as amused at Ginger's determination as at her inspiration and agreed to have the part tailored to Ginger's specifications. This refusal to take no for an answer would serve Ginger well as her career progressed.

When *Girl Crazy* closed, Ginger and Lela decided it was time to move on to Hollywood. While Ginger would always continue to work on the stage, it was obvious to both of them that Ginger's small voice and conventional prettiness were better suited to the screen than to the legitimate theater.

Having ended her association with Paramount, Ginger accepted a contract from Pathé and left New York on the Chief in 1931 (not 1932, as she sometimes says), bound for California. During the trip Ginger became acquainted with Harold Ross, editor of *The New Yorker*. Ross, who liked fresh, fun-loving, not overly intellectual girls, was immediately taken with Ginger. In California Ross was met by a movie mogul who wanted to hire him as a story editor. Ross mischievously introduced Ginger as Elizabeth Dupont, an heiress on her way to Honolulu. The executive immediately invited the supposed socialite to a party he was giving in Ross' honor that evening. She accepted, and even though she had already appeared in half a dozen films, no one recognized her except the Marx brothers, who eagerly joined in perpetrating the hoax. The tycoon, for his part, kept urging "Miss Dupont" to take a screen test, but she declined, explaining that her heavy social schedule precluded tying herself down to any extensive obligations. Thereafter, as Ginger's star rose, Ross and the Marxes would periodically wire the executive, inquiring when he would be testing Elizabeth Dupont.

Ginger never lost a childlike delight in disguising herself. She would also constantly change her type for business reasons. She began as a dark-haired, spit-curled vamp, became a wisecracking blonde and from then on would vary her appearance again and again to keep abreast of the times. Said an acquaintance, "She's had almost as many looks as she's had hometowns or husbands."

In Hollywood the Rogerses discovered that Ginger's Pathé assignments were to be strictly on a B-picture level. Her first, *The Tip-Off*, with Robert Armstrong and Eddie Quillan, made few demands on her. Nor did *Suicide Fleet* in which she innocently led three sailors—Bill Boyd, Robert Armstrong and James Gleason—to believe she loved each of them. In *Carnival Boat* she played a singer on a showboat who becomes involved with lumberjack Bill Boyd. Pathé dropped her option after that film, and Ginger considered everything about it—including herself—so ludicrous that she obtained a print of it which she sometimes showed to friends for laughs at her own expense.

While making *Carnival Boat*, Ginger put out feelers in the press for a Broadway role, but when no offers materialized, she agreed to play foil to star comedian Joe E. Brown in a film version of George S. Kaufman's hit play *The Butter and Egg Man*, retitled and reworked as *The Tenderfoot* at Fox. With nothing better in sight, she snapped up the female lead in *The Thirteenth Guest*, opposite Lyle Talbot, at Monogram and then hied herself back to Fox for *Hatcheck Girl*, even though it meant demoting herself to the wisecracking pal of leading woman Sally Eilers.

"It may not seem that she and Lela were planning her career," says Talbot, "but they weren't in a position to pick and choose then. The picture we did was an independent made by a guy named M.H. Hoffman. Everybody in Hollywood loved him. He used to make these six-day wonders on poverty row. We worked Monday through Saturday and long days because the Screen Actors Guild hadn't taken hold yet. Hoffman rented an old house from Universal for the exteriors, but the interiors were made right at the old Chadwick Studio at Sunset and Gower.

"The director was Bill Ray, a nephew of the old silent star Charles Ray. And he was a fast director. He'd set up shots and hit them so fast that we all had to be dedicated. We came in knowing our lines and prepared, so he never had to bother with that sort of thing. Characterization wasn't too important.

"Ginger had to have done her homework, and Lela probably helped, because she was always on the set. But she never interfered. She wouldn't have had a chance, really, because by the time she'd have objected to something, it was already wrapped up and in the can.

"But Lela ran things. While we were working, Ginger and I dated. It was no big romance or anything, but we dated. Ginger and Lela and Ginger's cousin, Phyllis Fraser, lived together. Phyllis married the publisher Bennett Cerf and then, after he died, Robert Wagner, who'd been mayor of New York, you know. Anyway, I'd go to pick Ginger up at home. One night I asked where she'd like to go. There was this talented comic who worked in a club that was located in the basement of the old Christie Hotel. Jean Malin. He was a brilliant entertainer, a very funny guy, but risqué. And Ginger said, 'I don't know whether my mother would approve, but I'd like to see Jean Malin.' I told her her mother didn't have to know everything she did, and we went. But I knew then that Lela really ran things.

"Ginger was wonderful to work with then, and again the following year, when we did another cheapie, *A Scream in the Night*. At the time of *The Thirteenth Guest*, she was just going from picture to picture with no seeming progress."

During that period, Ginger began dating director Mervyn LeRoy, whom she had met in New York during the run of *Girl Crazy*, and Talbot feels that LeRoy joined Lela in giving Ginger's career direction. "Something changed Ginger," he says, "because we were good friends while working together. Then some years later, after she'd become successful at RKO, I was on the lot one day, and I got from Ginger one of the first brush-offs I'd ever gotten in my life. I've had my ups and downs, but at the time I was doing quite well. It wasn't one of my low spots. I couldn't believe it. From Ginger of all people. I said something about it to a friend who was under contract at the studio, and his reaction wasn't one of surprise. More, 'Oh, Ginger . . . well, yeah.'" Despite the refrain over the years about God and universal love, Ginger was developing a pattern of behavior in pursuing her career: she expended her energies charming those who could help her and conserved them the remainder of the time.

Upon completion of *The Thirteenth Guest* and *Hatcheck Girl* Ginger began working for First National and Warner's. Her first assignment was once more to serve as a foil to Joe E. Brown in *You Said a Mouthful*. When the company went to Catalina on location for two weeks in September, 1932, Louella O. Parsons reported that Mervyn LeRoy "tagged along to keep an eye on his girl." Others suspected he was giving her private tips on making the most of her scenes without offending the cavernous-mouthed comedian, who felt the only person audiences came to see in a Joe E. Brown picture was Joe E. Brown.

Ginger's first real chance came in *Forty-second Street,* when it was decided that Joan Blondell was too well established to play Anytime Annie, a character who got her nickname because the only time she ever said no was when she didn't hear the proposition. It was a small but colorful role that called for Ginger to affect a British accent, carry a cane, wear a monocle, lug around a Pekinese dog, crack wise and sing "Shuffle Off to Buffalo." Mervy LeRoy urged Ginger to accept the part, predicting that it would be built up. It was, and it gave Ginger the most memorable role she had had since *Young Man of Manhattan.* Even now her duet with Una Merkel, singing "Shuffle Off to Buffalo," remains fresh in the memories of those who have not seen the picture in forty years.

When the film opened in 1933, most critics concurred with Louella Parsons, who after heaping praise on Ruby Keeler and Dick Powell, refrained from her customary sniping at Ginger, writing, "This isn't a one-woman or one-man production. Ginger Rogers is excellent as the affected chorus girl."

At the post-premiere party, Ginger excited gossips by showing up with the then gregarious young millionaire Howard Hughes, with whom she had an on-again, off-again romance during the next few years.

Mervyn LeRoy, recently married to Doris Warner, Harry's daughter, nevertheless cast Ginger in *Gold Diggers of 1933.* Although her role was less important than those of Aline MacMahon, Ruby Keeler or Joan Blondell, Ginger's pig latin rendition of "We're in the Money" later became a camp classic. It has since been used to help evoke the early 1930s in *Bonnie and Clyde* and in the documentary *Brother, Can You Spare a Dime?*

The place that chance plays in any career is neatly illustrated by

"We're in the Money." As Ginger recalls, she and the rehearsal pianist were working on a dark, deserted sound stage when she indulged in her trick of turning a lyric into pig latin. Suddenly she saw the end of a lighted cigar, and knowing that meant Darryl Zanuck, the head of production at Warner's, was approaching, she stopped. Zanuck asked what she was rehearsing, and she told him a song for the picture. He requested that she sing it again, and she began to perform the number as written, but he stopped her and ordered that it be done exactly as she had been doing it when he arrived. After Ginger finished, Zanuck grunted, puffed on his cigar and vanished. She was sure that she was going to be sacked, but shortly word came down that Zanuck wanted her to perform the song in the film just the way she'd done it for him. "And so it really was a quite outstanding thing," Ginger says. "It happened, and everyone who saw the show remembers the sound."

With LeRoy married, Ginger left the Warner lot, going to RKO to make the unpretentious *Professional Sweetheart* with Preston Foster. The script offered some good satiric thrusts at radio sponsors, false piety and commercialized Puritanism, and Frank Nugent of the New York *Times*, who had never before shown much interest in Ginger, noted that she had rarely been so entertaining.

At this time RKO decided to place Ginger under a nonstarring contract, but not before she had returned to poverty row for *A Shriek in the Night*, her second film with Lyle Talbot. Despite the loss of stature in accepting a "six-day wonder" with its stringent budget, the picture turned out better than anyone had a right to expect, and both Ginger and Talbot were rewarded with favorable notices for their portrayals of rival newspaper reporters.

Earlier, while *Gold Diggers of 1933* was in production, Ginger had attended a party at Una Merkel's home and there had met an attractive, introspective young actor whose career was not developing in the direction he had hoped after his brilliant beginning. He had come into films at the end of the silent era, giving Garbo a kiss in *The Kiss*, and then had scored a resounding success in *All Quiet on the Western Front* with a performance that would earn him a permanent place in the annals of film history. His name was Lew Ayres, and he was in the process of being divorced by Lola Lane. The introverted Ayres was immediately attracted to the vivacious, outgoing Ginger, and the day following their meeting he called and arranged to take her tea-dancing at the Biltmore Hotel. After that they were frequently seen together, and the romance intensified when Ginger went to Universal to play opposite Ayres in *Don't Bet on Love*. While the picture was a business-as usual venture for Ginger, it was another disappointment for fans who recalled Ayres' earlier sensitive work and were waiting for him to receive the opportunity to demonstrate his range and depth of artistry again. In *Don't Bet on Love*, all they perceived was a definite chemical interaction between the two leading players. Nevertheless, Ginger insisted to the press that she and Ayres were merely good friends. She continued to see other well-known and sought-after bachelors.

Lela, meanwhile, planted stories with obliging fan writers explaining that Ginger was so valuable as box-office insurance that RKO had insisted on giving her a nonstarring contract, that Ginger was being hailed as "the greatest little picture saver in Hollywood" and that she enhanced any star's appeal whether he happened to be a "crooner, romancer, wisecracker, dumbbell comic or dancer."

Ginger chimed in, explaining that when she first arrived on the West Coast, her agent had advised her to put on an act to attract attention if she expected to get anywhere. "He said I'd have to do things to make them want me," she said. "I refused to be anything but myself. But Hollywood apparently didn't know I was alive." So Ginger began announcing that she wanted to play Joan of Arc. As she intended, her statement earned attention from columnists and fan magazine writers. Who'd have thought that this singing, dancing comedienne who had played foil to Joe E. Brown and Jack Oakie took herself seriously? Like Marilyn Monroe's assertion that she wanted to make *The Brothers Karamazov*, Ginger's ambition to be seen as the Maid struck people as hilarious.

Paramount's *Sitting Pretty* with Jack Haley and Jack Oakie was a far cry from Joan of Arc, but Ginger, cast as a fan dancer, scored with her rendition of "Did You Ever See a Dream Walking?" Then she returned to RKO for her eighth film that year, her thirteenth film since arriving in Hollywood—and the one that represents the turning point in her career.

The film, of course, was *Flying Down to Rio*. Dorothy Jordan, who had originally been scheduled to dance with Astaire, instead married Merian C. Cooper, and Ginger was assigned the part three days after the film went into production.

Partially because of the magnitude of the Astaire-Rogers triumph and partly because of persistent rumors that they were mutually antagonistic, both of them have adopted patently bogus stories about their relationship. They claim that they first met in New York. Sometimes Ginger says that she was taken backstage by Ross of *The New Yorker* to meet Fred and his sister, Adele. On other occasions she and

Fred have stated that he was asked to help choreograph, according to him, "Embraceable You," according to her, "But Not for Me," during rehearsals of *Girl Crazy*. Astaire goes even further in his autobiography, *Steps in Time*, relating that he often dropped in on Lela and Ginger to discuss show business and whisked Ginger off to Central Park to dance to Eddy Duchin's music at the Casino.

Astaire says that he was pleased to learn that Ginger had been cast opposite him in his first film at RKO since she was camera wise, but that he was afraid she wouldn't be happy because her previous pictures had not been musicals. This statement doesn't hold up since her two most resounding recent successes had been supporting roles in *Forty-second Street* and *Gold Diggers of 1933*. What undoubtedly was true is that Astaire welcomed as a partner another perfectionist, whom he later described as "the hardest-working gal I ever knew."

Both Fred and Ginger agreed that there was insufficient rehearsal for the dance sequences. They realized that their physical appearances complemented one another, but neither regarded the execution of "The Carioca" as particularly outstanding.

Neither Ginger nor Fred foresaw that they were about to score a hit that would turn a run-of-the-mill ingenue-comedienne and a thirtyish, none-too-handsome stage performer into the most popular and stylish dance team ever to grace the screen. Even though the studio was optimistic about their potential, Ginger was eager to get back to playing leads, worrying that her ninth and final film of the year, *Chance at Heaven*, would further type her as a friend of the leading lady. But by the end of 1933 the results were in. Ginger and Fred were on their way to becoming stars of the first rank. Their success was to color permanently Ginger's recollections of the 1930s as a glorious decade.

The Astaire-Rogers series, exhaustively analyzed over the years, is almost entirely based on the hoariest of stage-musical formulas: the entanglement and escapades of two couples, one romantic, the other comic.

In their first co-starring picture, *The Gay Divorcée*, they were given romantic leads, but in *Roberta* they might easily have represented comic relief had their dexterous footwork not overshadowed the poorly written romantic relationship that existed between the characters played by Irene Dunne and Randolph Scott. With *Top Hat* they reached the apogee of their power as darlings of the gods, quite untouched by any mundane problems of daily existence. To avoid creating a sense of *déjà vu* in *Follow the Fleet*, the writers elevated types usually relegated to best friends of the hero and heroine and made them leads. The increasingly familiar situations were partly camouflaged by deglamorizing the surroundings, setting the story in a tacky dance hall, on a battleship, in a modest apartment, etc. Ginger became a vaudevillian *cum* dance hall hostess, and her former partner, Astaire, a gob in the U.S. Navy. *Swingtime*, as Arlene Croce points out in her definitive *The Fred Astaire and Ginger Rogers Book*, is about the "Fred and Ginger myth," which encompasses both the imaginary world of nighttime frolics and the ordinary working world of the audiences. "It is the world of top hats and empty pockets," Miss Croce says, pointing out that "Never Gonna Dance," the climactic number, "is a dance of parting, its mood one of frustration and defeat."

By the time the sixth film, *Shall We Dance*, was released in 1937, director Mark Sandrich was complaining that reviewers had the habit of referring to the "Astaire-Rogers formula." This caused the New York *Times* critic to twit the director for being "one of the few people in history who ever have objected to being told they have found the recipe for success." However, in an attempt to disguise the familiar plot in *Shall We Dance*, writers Allan Scott and Ernest Pagano made Astaire a Russian ballet star who falls in love with a ballroom dancer—played by—who else?—Ginger Rogers.

Despite the film's success, fifteen months elapsed before the next Astaire-Rogers teaming. The picture, *Carefree* (1938), was an impossibly broad spoof of psychoanalysis. Were it not for *Carefree*, one might argue that any libretto would serve as long as the stars were given numerous dance interludes, but this leaden film dispels any such misapprehension. Nor did it augur well for Ginger's future that *Carefree* was essentially her picture, rather than Astaire's.

The cycle was running out, and early in 1939 the last of the RKO-Astaire-Rogers films was released. In *The Story of Vernon and Irene Castle** Fred and Ginger interpreted the lives of the Castles, who had revolutionized ballroom dancing in the early 1900s. This salute to the most popular dancers of one era by the most admired in a later period was a felicitous swan song for Fred and Ginger, even though many critics would have preferred seeing them in a lighter vehicle.

---

*Irene Castle, who had a contract guaranteeing her right of approval in all areas, gave Ginger and costume designer Walter Plunkett some difficult moments. She objected to Ginger, many felt, because she wanted to play the part herself. And she coined a new synonym for any scene, performance or gown that she considered dreadful by saying, "It's rather plunketty, isn't it?"

What word best describes the response that these dazzling, diverting and highly profitable films aroused in the co-stars?

Resistance.

One of the ironies of the entertainment world lies in how frequently performers strenuously resist the role or the song or the scene that ultimately brings them enduring recognition. Such was the case with Ginger and Fred. Both were personally ambitious, and neither had desire to be held in check by what he or she regarded as the other's limitations.

Recognizing the pair's box-office potential, financially troubled RKO proceeded with unprecedented caution. Studio executives allowed eleven months to pass before the team's first co-starring vehicle was released to cash in on the success of *Flying Down to Rio*. During that time Lou Brock, who had produced *Rio*, developed *Radio City Revels*, whose caliber was judged not high enough to ensure maximum response to the new public favorites. Instead, Pandro S. Berman acquired *The Gay Divorcée*. Astaire, who had starred in the musical on Broadway, was appearing in Allan Scott's revamped stage version in London's West End. Since Astaire was busy, the studio was compelled to find employment for Ginger.

While flooding the papers with phony publicity about their search for a more dignified name to replace the flip "Ginger," RKO cast her in two mediocre films on the home lot: *Rafter Romance* with Norman Foster and *Finishing School* in support of Frances Dee and Beulah Bondi. The management also lent her to Fox for an indifferent film, *Change of Heart*, which reunited the popular team of Janet Gaynor and Charles Farrell; to Warner's for Ben Hecht's *Upper World*, so murky a melodrama that none of the principals, including Mary Astor, Warren William or Ginger, would make anything comprehensible of it. Her best release between her first and second teaming with Astaire was First National's *Twenty Million Sweethearts*, with Dick Powell and Pat O'Brien.*

Since Merian C. Cooper was ill and Lou Brock had wisecracked that he could blow a better script out of his nose than *The Gay Divorcée*, dynamic little Pandro Berman, who had risen from the ranks of film

---

*The plot called for Ginger, an established radio favorite, to come to neophyte Powell's rescue during a broadcast audition when he faltered while singing "I'll String Along with You." During filming, Ginger, who was never adept matching action in long shots and close-ups, could not time taking over the song. After she failed to hit the cue on the twenty-fourth take, songwriter Harry Warren stalked out in disgust.

cutters to the head of production at the studio, personally produced the film, assigning Mark Sandrich to direct.

Their first decision, according to Berman, was to ignore complaints from both their new stars. "Fred unquestionably was the best dancer of his type in the world—yet he might never have been recognized as anything more important than a ballroom dancer if we hadn't teamed him with Ginger, "Berman says. "As Katharine Hepburn said at the time, she gave him sex and he gave her class.

"Fred didn't want her for the part in *Gay Divorcée*, because he said—and rightly, too, from his point of view—'How can you expect her to play an English lady?' And I said, 'I don't expect her to. I expect her to play Ginger Rogers playing an English lady, and nobody will give a good goddamn.' Audiences don't have to believe people playing parts in this kind of mistaken-identity farce. All you have to do is entertain the public. The dancing took care of that. So I made him do it against his will, and from then on I forced them to make every picture they did together.

"She didn't especially want to do the films either. She didn't really want to be a dancing comedienne. She had ambitions of her own—to be a Katharine Hepburn or a high-class comedienne like Carole Lombard. Besides, she didn't like the billing. She'd had a lot more experience than Fred, and she wanted to be first-starred. Here she was playing a secondary, co-starring role and getting second billing.

"I tell you there's no question that these two people were forced by circumstances to work together against their wills. But as head of production I couldn't be concerned about what they wanted. My big job was to let them know that we were going to go on making Astaire-Rogers pictures. Period. And if they didn't like it, they could lump it."

Extraordinary concessions were granted for *The Gay Divorcée*. Instead of winging it, RKO allowed a full six weeks to rehearse the choreography for Con Conrad's "The Continental" and "Night and Day," the only song retained from Cole Porter's Broadway score. The latter number was always to rank as one of Ginger's favorites. If in these routines she seems to be a superb athlete substituting skill and coordination for natural grace and solid training, the flowing gowns designed by Walter Plunkett go a long way in camouflaging her weaknesses. Plunkett, who designed Ginger's clothes in both *Rio* and *Divorcée*, says he soon learned to make it a rule to be present whenever a new dress was to be photographed. "Otherwise she'd add a crepe paper orchid or a string of beads or some goddamned feathered thing," he says. "She just never could resist little improvements."*

When, after all the delay, *The Gay Divorcée* opened in October, 1934, it scored an instantaneous hit. Even though "The Continental" failed to catch on in ballrooms as "The Carioca" had, audiences were dazzled by Fred and Ginger's virtuosity. As *Flying Down to Rio* turned December of 1933 into a celebration, *The Gay Divorcée* furnished Astaire-Rogers with a happy ending for 1934.

In 1935 and 1936 there were two co-starring films each year. Jerome Kern's *Roberta*, which had enjoyed mild success on Broadway, was rewritten by a team of writers including Allan Scott. Scott, who was involved in scripting many of Ginger's successes, recalls that RKO originally had been interested in *Roberta* as an Irene Dunne vehicle but did not make any commitment until Pandro Berman suggested that Astaire be cast as a character based on the two roles played by Bob Hope and George Murphy. "It wasn't too difficult to tailor the part for Freddie," Scott recalls, "but what the hell to do with Ginger was a problem. The obvious part for her was a foreign countess, but Ginger was apple-pie American. So what we did was to make a phony out of the character. By making Ginger an American pretending to be a countess in order to obtain work as a Continental café singer, we added a dimension to her performance." As Lizzie Gatz-Countess Schawenka, Ginger had a role only peripherally connected with the plot, but that very fact allowed her the widest scope to utilize her comedic talents.

The team's next effort, and Ginger's fourth film of the year, was *Top Hat*. Judged as one of the best pictures of 1935, it remains a delight today—one of the reasons being that the "flimsiest of plots," as some reviewers complained then, now seems just inconsequential enough to blend perfectly with such Irving Berlin tunes and such Astaire-Rogers routines as "Isn't This a Lovely Day to Be Caught in the Rain?" "Cheek to Cheek" and "The Piccolino."

The dance routines of the next five Astaire-Rogers musicals are all of remarkable quality. Consider the position this placed Ginger in. As

---

*Nor was her private taste reliable. On one occasion Plunkett saw her at a party done up in feathers, flowers and baubles and, despite the comments of others, said nothing. Finally, Ginger asked why he hadn't complimented her. He told her she was a pretty girl but she was smothering herself and suggested they talk about it. He invited her to dinner, and when she showed up, she wore a simple gingham jumper, little makeup and pigtails. "She was breathtaking," he says. "But, of course, she couldn't stick to it."

several writers have commented, the phrase that best describes her personality is "fiercely competitive." She had always been driven to excel, whether playing championship-caliber tennis or mixing supreme ice-cream sodas. Yet here she was forced to appear in dance-oriented films opposite a man who was generally acknowledged to have no peer. Early in the series, various critics lamented that she was not in Astaire's class and suggested replacing her with Jessie Matthews, Gertrude Lawrence, Margo or—by some magical means—his sister, Adele, who had married into royalty.

Ginger's reaction was complicated. While she battled to free herself from the partnership, she also dedicated herself to the futile attempt to outdo—or at least equal—her choreographer-partner.

After finishing *Follow the Fleet*, Ginger granted an interview in which she described to Bosley Crowther of the New York *Times* the excruciating regimen and endurance required to produce the smooth-flowing, seemingly effortless perfection of an Astaire-Rogers scene: Crowther wrote:

Of all the hardest workers in Hollywood Miss Rogers has been known to dance before the cameras for eighteen hours in order to film a sequence that lasted exactly four minutes on the screen. Little things, such as her dress whirling in the wrong direction, may cause the whole scene to be discarded. Her director, Mark Sandrich, has a theory that the more tired she and Astaire are, the better they are likely to be; he spends hours just wearing them down, reducing the couple virtually to a state of automation.

When the cameras stop clicking, leaving her tired and disheveled, the torture doesn't end; it merely changes. At the cry of "cut" about eight persons move in firmly upon her; the wardrobe mistress with pins in her mouth; a man to wipe off her shoes which always must be new and painful; a cleaner to remove possible spots; a hairdresser to rearrange her coiffure, putting in pins or calmly breaking off a hair that protrudes, catching a highlight; a make-up person, who carefully swabs perspiration from her forehead; an assistant director coming in with an idea of what she should do in the next scene; the director, who may want to discuss the last scene, and a personal maid, to see if she wants a drink of water or anything.

In addition, it's likely as not that the cameraman will come over to make a suggestion, and perhaps a bright-faced script girl will bounce in with the reminder: "Remember, Miss Rogers, you had your purse in your left hand when you finished and the flap was out!"

Following the finish of each film Ginger's doctor would order her to bed to recuperate and regain lost weight. She once only half-jokingly wisecracked that she'd like to take a vacation digging mines.

Under the circumstances a great deal of tension was generated between the two unwilling partners, who found themselves almost as hopelessly linked as Siamese twins. In the "Smoke Gets in Your Eyes" sequence from *Roberta*, Sandrich pushed them to repeat their routine over and over until their nerves were frazzled and their bodies exhausted. Then, when the perfect take seemed within their grasp, at the climactic moment of the dance, during which Ginger dropped back on the exhausted Astaire's arm, he let it fall a fraction of an inch too low, destroying Ginger's balance, and she went down on her head. Ginger laughed about it at the time, but years later two wardrobe women who worked with her in the post-Astaire years told how she used the accident to illustrate her point that she had always had to be alert for her partner's weakness or else risk being dropped on her face.

Then, during the filming of *Top Hat*, the famous feather-dress feud erupted. As Ginger tells it, designer Bernard Newman asked whether there wasn't a dress she had always dreamed of having created for her. She said there was—a blue dress with feathers which would move gracefully with her body during the dance. For one reason or another, neither the director nor the producer seems to have okayed the design. Ginger rehearsed in slacks, and the first time anyone but Ginger saw the dress was when the wardrobe woman walked it across the sound stage. Astaire was aghast, asking the director whether Ginger was going to wear *that*. The director said he guessed so. She soon was apprised that she was going to have to find a substitute in wardrobe. She inquired what was wrong and was told Fred didn't like the gown.

"I disagree completely," Ginger recalls saying. "Because I think it's one of the loveliest dresses I've ever had."

With that the director called a lunch break. Afterward Ginger sulked in her dressing room and Astaire in his. "So the president, the treasurer, the whole thing of RKO came down on the set," says Ginger, whose speech tends to be imprecise, "and here I was, a lone woman holding out against them. So I got on the phone and I dialed mother. 'Mother, would you please come over. I need some help because they're trying to take my dress away from me!' So she got in the car and whizzed over, and I explained the problem to her. And she said, 'What's the matter with everybody? That's a beautiful dress. I'll tell you what, if they don't like it, why don't you tell them to get a new girl?' So we both headed for the door."

The result was a compromise. The dance was filmed in the feather gown, but it was agreed that if it proved unphotogenic, a substitute would be found. The next morning in the screening room the dress and Ginger were vindicated. By way of apology, Astaire says in his autobiography, he and choreographer Hermes Pan concocted a parody of the "Cheek to Cheek" number in which she wore the gown:

Feathers—I have feathers—
And I never find the happiness I seek
With those chicken feathers dancing
Cheek to cheek.

Ginger remembers that several days later a box arrived from Fred containing a gold charm in the shape of a feather, inscribed "Dear Feathers, I love ya', Fred," and afterward, he often kiddingly referred to her as Feathers.

Her wardrobe annoyed him throughout the series. He could never understand why she insisted upon wearing new shoes and was often irritated to find her attempting to slip spike heels past him. In *Follow the Fleet*, she appeared in the "Let's Face the Music and Dance" routine wearing a dress with heavy-beaded sleeves which proved to be dangerous weapons during quick turns. He absentmindedly went along with it, but during the first take one sleeve clipped him on the side of the face, partially stunning him. He kept on dancing, however, and at the finish, when Sandrich inquire if it was okay for everyone, Astaire explained what had happened and asked for another go at it. They spent the entire day trying to get an acceptable take, then the next morning in the screening room learned that the first one had been perfect.

Contributing to the tension were Ginger's mother, Lela, and Fred's wife, Phyllis. While Lela seldom spent time on the sound stage, Astaire saw her fine hand at work behind the scenes. And Ginger was visibly affronted by the appearance of Mrs. Astaire whenever a scene involving physical intimacy was to be shot. Ginger also complained about being condescended to by her co-star, who orginated the dances and recorded his own taps while hers were dubbed by choreographer Pan; and while she sang her own songs in RKO films, another singer was brought in to dub high and low notes that Ginger had trouble hitting.*
The tension was further heightened by the conflicting views on what

---

*To her credit, she studied and later learned how to use her singing voice effectively in subsequent films and in the theater.

was or was not in good taste. So throughout this series of musicals of unprecedented popularity Ginger was agitating to be allowed to prove herself in a dramatic role, and Astaire was keeping an eager eye on box-office returns, hoping to detect a falling off in receipts presaging a demise of the partnership.

In 1937, after much pressure from both stars, there was a brief interruption of their co-starring vehicles. Then they were reunited for *Carefree* and their final RKO film, *The Story of Vernon and Irene Castle*. By that time, Fred was awaiting the expiration of his contract and planning to go elsewhere, and Ginger had become the undisputed queen of the RKO lot.

Upon parting, there was no regret on either side, but thirty years later Ginger told an English magazine writer, "I love Fred so, and I mean that in the nicest, warmest way. I have such an affection for him *artistically*. I think that experience with Fred was a divine blessing. It blessed me, I know. And I don't think blessings are one-sided. We had our differences—what good artistic marriage doesn't?—but they were unimportant."

The multifaceted relationship between Ginger and Lela transcended that of mother and daughter. They were, according to Ginger, very good friends. Yet there is no question that Lela was the dominant force. By inclination a friendly, uncomplicated, high-spirited young woman, Ginger would on cue from her mother suddenly begin to speak, as Lela did, of the necessity of cultivating universal love of humanity to develop the magnetism an actress needed to draw audiences to her. At her mother's urging she increased her vocabulary until her sentences were no longer means of communication but obstacle courses. Left to her natural impulses, she could be impish and amusing, but counseled by Lee-Lee that stars were a thing apart, Ginger gradually became aloof and detached.

Yet in many ways the two of them treated themselves to the childhoods they had missed. They planned and built a shingle-stucco-fieldstone home high up on Beverly Crest Drive. This "typical farmhouse," as they called it, was equipped with a working drugstore-size soda fountain, a projection room, and all-blue and all-beige bedroom suites for Ginger and Lela, respectively. There was a library with leatherbound copies of the scripts of all the films Ginger had appeared in. The pool was Olympic-sized, and the tennis courts were covered with a special, fast-drying surface.

It was a suitable domicile for a movie queen who often lapsed into baby talk, a girl who after being introduced to producer David Lewis at a boring party exerted enough charm to persuade him to go out ringing doorbells. Lewis was amused by her ingenuousness, and for a few weeks they frequently dated. Then one evening he arrived at Ginger's dream house directly from an exhausting day at the studio. As he disappeared into the guest bathroom to freshen up, he called out that he was desperately in need of a drink. When he reappeared, the teetotaling Ginger had lined five ice-cream sodas along the counter. "There!" She beamed. "That ought to hold you!" It did. They never spent another evening together.

Even as an established star Ginger continued her childlike love of masquerading. For no good reason she once borrowed a provocative gown from wardrobe, applied dark makeup, false eyelashes and a black wig and had herself taken around the studio and introduced as Marcelle Brown, a French chanteuse. Unrecognized, at least as far as anyone let on, she was granted an audition at which Oscar Levant volunteered to play for her. In addition to getting a couple of propositions, she was elated to be offered a small part in a Ginger Rogers picture before turning her back and having her legs recognized by a studio executive.

She found a more purposeful use for her love of disguising herself during the period when she was campaigning for dramatic roles, around 1934 or 1935. Garson Kanin tells how she pleaded with director John Ford to allow her to play Queen Elizabeth to Katharine Hepburn's Mary Queen of Scotts. According to Kanin the studio had been thinking of Katharine Cornell, Judith Anderson or Ruth Gordon, but Ginger coveted the role so passionately that she offered to test for the part. "Using her considerable influence," Kanin wrote, "she forced the issue and made the test. I have seen it—a surpassing achievement. Her self-effacing makeup, new voice and fearless approach might have carried the day were it not for the fact studio policy ruled against her.

" 'Hell,' said one of the executives, 'Nobody will know it's her and if they do, they'll be waiting for her to crack wise or get up and do a number!'

" 'Nobody with the name of Ginger can play a Queen,' said another categorically. 'The public won't stand for it. Do I have to tell you how fussy they are?'

"Ginger gave up the battle, ruefully," Kanin concludes. "She had been victimized by the power of her personality."

However discouraging RKO executives were to Ginger's dramatic aspirations, Lela was always supportive, constantly working with Ginger at home and keeping her eyes open for a good showcase. Lela definitely wanted something better for her offspring than the chorus girl who befriended the immigrant Francis Lederer in *Romance in Manhattan*. "No great show was made of it," says one former RKO publicist, "but in the background the old lady was always manipulating. In retrospect, I have a sneaking affection for her, despite her Neanderthal politics, but I didn't feel that way then. She didn't openly interfere. But there was no doubt who pulled the strings. Ginger was a very obedient daughter about her career. And she minded the old lady about being a good Christian Scientist and not drinking or smoking. Men were something else. The old lady didn't have much influence until after Ginger married them. I've heard she broke up the first one, to Jack Pepper, and I know she was dead set against Lew Ayres."

For this reason insiders were surprised on November 1, 1934, when Mrs. Lela Rogers sent out formal announcements of the betrothal of her daughter Virginia Katherine to Lewis Frederick Ayres. Shortly afterward, at a press conference on the set of the film Ayres was making, Ginger described theirs as "the perfect romance." On November 14 at the Little Church of the Flower in Glendale, Ginger became Mrs. Ayres.

A reception was held at the Ambassador Hotel, at which several members of the press entertained themselves by laying side bets on how long the marriage would last before Lela found a way of breaking it up. The portents for survival decreased when reporters heard that the bride and groom would only go to Lake Arrowhead for a brief honeymoon since Ginger was needed at the studio for rehearsals of *Roberta*.

Eyebrows were raised a few weeks later, at which time the story was circulated that Ginger's chief gift to her intellectual young husband that Christmas was an electric train set from FAO Schwarz. Still, Ginger made an attempt to change, taking up painting, sculpting and reading books to please Ayres rather than going on the town as had been her custom.

Upon completion of *Roberta* Ginger made two more films, *Star of Midnight* with William Powell and *Top Hat*; then the Ayres left for Hawaii on a delayed honeymoon. Two days after their arrival in Honolulu the studio called Ginger home to begin preparations for a solo-starring musical, *In Person*, with George Brent. In it she played a movie star who develops agoraphobia and flees to a rural area where she falls in love with the bucolic Brent. Written to order for her by Allan Scott, the film turned out to be too frail to increase her fame. But it demonstrated that the common-denominator quality in Ginger's personality was powerful enough to put across material that better actresses with less magnetism would have failed with.

At the time Ginger worked in *Follow the Fleet*, rumors of a rift between the Ayreses began to circulate. Ginger's name was again linked with oilman and producer Howard Hughes, who had given Jean Harlow an opportunity to become a star by casting her in *Hell's Angels*. The association would have been attractive for almost any ambitious actress. Finally, on May 9, 1936, RKO issued a statement in behalf of the Ayreses announcing an amicable separation. Ginger was going home to mother, but no divorce was contemplated.

On July 30 the *Hollywood Reporter* named Astaire-Rogers as the top box-office attraction in films. With Ginger once more living at home, she and Lela continued their machinations to propel her to superstardom. Their togetherness was so complete that when either spoke, it was almost invariably "us" or "we," seldom "I." Because of the closeness of their association, Ginger felt little need to make friends with employees, as so many stars did. "She kept her distance between her secretaries and stand-ins and herself," one of them says. "The only exceptions were Eddie Rubin, who got her publicity, the girl who fixed her hair and her still photographer. And the advantage of those associations is easy to understand."

As a single woman and a top star Ginger freely exercised her prerogative of carrying on romances with young men about town, including Jimmy Stewart, Cary Grant, Burgess Meredith, Alfred Gwynne Vanderbilt, Greg Bautzer and others. But the romance with Stewart fizzled because he found her too self-involved, and the one with Grant withered when he took to sending her home alone in a chauffeur-driven car.

In later years Jack Carson told with some amusement how, as an ambitious young man, he had unsuccessfully pursued Ginger, feeling that she could open doors for him. Finally, the two of them happened to spend a weekend in New York and became very close. So close that Carson smugly felt he had it made—only to discover, upon returning to Hollywood, that when he tried calling her, he couldn't even get her to come to the phone.

Ginger wasn't the only one who could be high-handed. During her relationship with young Hughes he showered her with gifts, including a new station wagon. After their affair had ended, Ginger went out to the garage one morning to find the automobile missing. She assumed it had been stolen and reported the theft to the police. She was chagrined shortly afterward to learn that the auto had always been registered in the name of the Hughes Tool Company—which had had it towed away. "You could always tell when Ginger had a new romance going," says one co-worker from the Astaire-Rogers days. "She'd come on the set in the morning and announce, 'There's something radically wrong with this scene.' It took almost a year for everyone to discover what was 'wrong': Ginger had been out the night before and hadn't had a chance to learn the lines. The scene improved miraculously after she hurriedly studied her speeches while the director and writers wrestled with the scene. Finally, she found something 'radically wrong' once too often. Everyone on the set exploded into laughter." She learned to discipline herself, however, and only on rare occasions during later years did she allow herself such self-indulgence.

The incident most often recounted by former RKO cohorts occurred when Lela undertook to break up the affair between Ginger and director George Stevens. Ginger had been married twice and was well past a quarter of a century at this point. "It was generally assumed that Ginger—and many other stars—had had affairs with their directors," says a source who prefers to not be identified. "But the way Lela came charging into the studio and onto the set, you'd have thought Ginger was a virgin and Lela was going to charge George with statutory rape and sue the studio for contributing to the delinquency of a minor. Or blow up the place."

Pandro Berman, who never socialized with Ginger or Lela, exept for visiting their home to see the soda fountain, recalls: "Mrs. Rogers' intervention put me in a very awkward position. The director* was a married man, and Mrs. Rogers became a problem because one day she made an appointment with me. I was flabbergasted when she marched in with Ginger and this director in tow. She sat them down in my office and said in effect: 'This man is destroying my daughter. He's going to cause her to be thrown out of the film business, and you've got to put a stop to it.' Now here were these two adults listening to all this. It was a very embarrassing moment because I didn't give a good goddamn about it. But she was protecting her daughter because this guy was married, and I believe she was quite right. But I don't think she managed to end it. I think it ended in its own way, naturally, eventually."

Studios, according to Berman and contrary to popular assumption, refrained from interfering in star's private affairs unless the behavior

---

*Berman discreetly never revealed Stevens' identity in recounting the incident.

was likely to explode in scandalous headlines that would wreck a career and harm an investment. Especially, Berman might have added, those stars who were in their ascendancy.

Ethel Barron once wrote that if ever an Academy Award for the Mother Who Knows Best were given, Lela Rogers would win hands down. Lela would have agreed that with God's guidance she deserved it. "She'd never have got there without that help," Lela said in 1975. "Nobody gets there alone. Yes, I was always there. One book said I was like a mother hippopatamus protecting her young—and that's not true. Yes, I had arguments, but they weren't knockdown. It was: 'This is not good for the studio any more than it is good for us. So we won't do it.' I was stern. I knew what I wanted. I knew Ginger would thrive by developing all sides. She already had vaudeville and Broadway under her belt. She was in the movies now, and we saw to it that eventually she could do anything. She could do musicals. She could do dramas, heavy dramas, tragedies. She could do slapstick, light comedy. Whatever they wanted her to do, she could do it.

"Now Irene Dunne was hard to cast. All she could do were light comedies and musicals. The same with the others. They were one-celled amoebas. But between every dancing picture Ginger made a straight comedy or drama while Fred went off to Europe on vacation.* She never took a rest. We worked and developed. That's why she survived."

By late 1937 Ginger and Lela were becoming more insistent in their demands that the studio give Ginger an important role in a major straight film. Since she and Katharine Hepburn were the two important young stars on the RKO lot—Hepburn a prestige star, Ginger a box-office attraction—someone conceived the idea of casting them together in a film, thereby bringing out the hidden competition between them and spelling big profits.

With this in mind Pandro Berman made a trip to New York, where he attended George S. Kaufman and Edna Ferber's *Stage Door*. After the performance he astounded Allan Scott, who had accompanied him to the play, by announcing that he was buying it as a vehicle for Ginger and Katharine Hepburn and by asking Scott whether he wanted to write the screenplay. Scott didn't, but Berman acquired the property†

---

*Actually, Astaire spent the time working out choreography for the next Astaire-Rogers film while Ginger made the nonmusical pictures.

†Playwright Kaufman waspishly suggested retitling it *Screen Door*.

and hired Morrie Ryskind and Anthony Veiller to rework the plot, tailoring the two leading parts to obtain maximum impact from Rogers' and Hepburn's personality traits. Hepburn played the wealthy patrician idealist, while Ginger was cast as a flip, slightly cynical pragmatist. As director Berman assigned Gregory LaCava, who, legend has it, improvised lines for characters just before filming a scene. (Scott, who worked closely with LaCava, claims that the director had a theory that the short rehearsal time allotted a movie scene killed the initial spontaneity, so he had alternate lines prepared on each scene. When he felt the actors had gone stale, he sprung some of the alternate lines on them.) Whatever his technique, it worked so well that the New York *Times* spoke for critics and audiences alike, observing, "Miss Hepburn and Miss Rogers, in particular, seem to be acting so far above their usual heads that, frankly, we hardly recognized them."

Stage Door marked the beginning of a dazzling climb for Ginger without Fred. She sparkled again in *Vivacious Lady*, playing a flashy café singer who marries Jimmy Stewart, an academic from an academic family, and proceeds to wreak havoc on the staid campus life. This screwball comedy was directed by George Stevens, and it was no coincidence that about the time Ginger made the picture Lela decided her daughter should be on her own and departed for New York to try to arrange a production of a play, *Funny Man*, that Lela had written. While *Vivacious Lady* seems anemic and slow-moving today—except for Beulah Bondi's timeless performance—it was an enormous success for Ginger when it was released. So much so that the Aryanized version of Arthur Kober's borscht-belt comedy about Jewish summer camps, *Having a Wonderful Time*, with Douglas Fairbanks, Jr., failed to dull Ginger's steadily rising star.

Ginger, deprived of Lela's guidance, almost made the mistake of her life when she high-handedly wrote a note to Pandro Berman refusing to appear in *Bachelor Mother* and returned the script. Berman tried to reason with her, but she remained adamant, and he placed her on suspension to bring her into line. Under Garson Kanin's understated direction, Ginger and David Niven, as a salesgirl and the son of the department store owner, struggled vainly and hilariously to persuade an unusually talented group of comedians that neither was Niven the father nor Ginger the mother of a child she appeared to be abandoning on the doorstep of a foundling home. Once the picture was shown, Ginger was at last recognized as one of Hollywood's very special comediennes. Berman waited in vain for a note of apology for refusing the script or for a note of thanks for forcing her to do it. Ginger's only recorded comment was to Fred Astaire, regretting that she had put her rejection in writing.

Her final picture for the year was *Fifth Avenue Girl*, a comedy Allan Scott again tailored to her talents. With it Ginger held the ground she had already won, even if she did not advance perceptibly.

In 1940 Ginger instituted significant changes in her life. Lela came roaring back to Hollywood after her eight-month New York stay and leaped into the fray, protecting and promoting her daughter as if there had been no interruption. When Sheilah Graham wrote in her column that Ginger was the "Miracle Girl of 1940" who had arrived in Hollywood with "bad skin . . . ditto hair . . . a crooked leg . . . an atrocious lisp" and little poise, Lela took the columnist to task, insisting Ginger's skin had always been perfect except for a brief time when she contracted makeup poisoning after making four pictures in a row, that the lisp in *Queen High* was not a speech defect, but characterization and—well, that Ginger had always been and continued to be God's 100 percent perfect work. She didn't even concede being responsible for developing Ginger, so great was her indignation. "If she hadn't had it, all the training in the world would have been useless," Lela told Sheilah. "As a matter of fact, when Ginger won the Charleston competition in 1926, I said, 'One day she will occupy the position in Hollywood that Mary Pickford does today,' and everyone laughed."

Ginger also divorced Lew Ayres in 1940. She charged mental cruelty, but the marriage had long run its course and was simply over. Ayres, always the gentleman, told reporters that Ginger had matured enough to be independent of both him and her mother. Although he didn't deny that Lela's constant presence had affected the relationship between him and his wife adversely, he assumed his share of the blame, saying that his irritability at the lack of progress in his career had contributed to the collapse.

Rumor had it that Ginger had instituted the proceedings because she would wed Howard Hughes, but when asked about that, she parried, "Who's Hughes?" Still, in his autobiography* Hughes executive Noah Dietrich claims Ginger caught Hughes in bed with another girl and ended their relationship.

At the studio her prospects continued to brighten. In *Primrose Path* Ginger played Ellie May Adams according to Buckner and Hart's

---

*Written with Bob Thomas.

Broadway version, a third-generation prostitute—unlikely casting for a devout Christian Scientist. Ginger however, not only accepted the part but for many years chose Ellie as her favorite role; for in the film version of the Broadway hit Ellie is a virgin who is a victim of guilt by association with her own family and comes to a happy end in the arms of a hamburger-stand clerk who recognizes her purity and marries her in spite of her sleazy background. Still, incredible as it may seem today, the film was rejected as unfit for the Radio City Music Hall and finally found a home in the more raffish Roxy.

Director Gregory LaCava said then that he was presenting a new Ginger Rogers, "a glamour girl, dancer turned actress." Scott later explained that there had been no problem in getting Ginger to accept the part. "She seldom questioned situations, but she'd question a word or a line. It got so I put lines in for her to cut out." Ginger's portrayal was mentioned as worthy of an Academy Award nomination, and while none materialized, she had proved beyond doubt that her aspirations to become a dramatic actress were to be considered something more than a joke.

Buoyed up by reassurance of success, Ginger found a story written by Sacha Guitry which she urged Allan Scott to read. He read it without much enthusiasm, but undeterred Ginger went to the front office. The story was bought, and since Scott was not otherwise occupied, he developed a treatment which turned out so well that it intrigued Ronald Colman. Playwright John Van Druten was hired to work with Scott on the script, and the prestige director Lewis Milestone was assigned to it. "Suddenly this little magazine story was turning into an A-picture," Scott says, "and to give credit where it's due, it all started with Ginger." The picture was *Lucky Partners*.

Ginger was exhausted and preparing to go away for a rest when producer David Hempstead brought her yet another script. She read it and said she wasn't interested. It seemed like a silly soap opera to her. Hempstead suggested that perhaps she was tired and should take a rest before she read it again. Ginger finally agreed, and upon rereading it, according to her, she cried like a baby and immediately called Hempstead, begging to be allowed to do it.

It was based on *Kitty Foyle*, Christopher Morley's best-selling novel about a white-collar girl's business life and love affairs. The script by Dalton Trumbo, with additional dialogue by Donald Ogden Stewart, sentimentalized and romanticized both the milieu and the characters, but the film turned out to be an enormous success. The white collar

Ginger wore in the film was manufactured and sold to American women who thought of themselves as "white-collar girls." It became a symbol of the new, proud American workingwoman.

In January, when RKO arranged for Ginger to attend the annual stenographers' ball in New York a couple of weeks after the film opened, she was met by 1,500 fans in the main rotunda of Grand Central Station, including 100 stenographers whom the studio had provided with banners hailing her as their spokeswoman.

When she alighted, she was swathed in a mink coat, a mink-trimmed hat and gold earrings. Beneath the coat she wore a brown suit with the famous white collar, on which Ginger had pinned an enormous diamond broach. She was immediately given a scroll by the Queen of the Stenographers for 1940, who was somewhat at a loss for anything to say since she had not seen *Kitty Foyle*.

Scroll in hand and questions answered, Ginger waved good-bye to all the stenographers, ducked into the waiting Cadillac town car and took off for the Ritz Towers.

The nominees for the best actress of 1940 included Ginger, Katharine Hepburn, Bette Davis, Susan Hayward and the heavily favored Joan Fontaine. At the Academy of Motion Picture Arts and Sciences Dinner on March 1, 1941, Ginger emerged as the surprise winner.

Her first picture after her triumph was *Tom, Dick and Harry*, in which she played a telephone operator who manages to get herself engaged to three men at the same time and can decide which one she wants only because he's the one who makes bells ring when he kisses her. Although Women's Liberation would undoubtedly excoriate writer Paul Jarrico's view of women's emotional stability and logic, under Garson Kanin's direction Ginger emerged at her most beguiling. Discussing their collaboration on *Tom, Dick and Harry*, Kanin commented, "The director-player relationship is frequently as complex as the renowned husband-wife one. It, too, calls for patience, adjustment and compromise. It feeds upon exchange and give-and-take. If one party or the other comes to dominate, rare opportunities are lost. Ginger Rogers never directed me, but it is fair to say that like all fine players, she occasionally directed my direction."

Ginger's contract was up for renewal in 1941. With her success both as a musical and dramatic star she was in a position to talk RKO into the increasingly popular nonexclusive pact. Not surprisingly, since few stars have ever resisted typecasting as vigorously as Ginger, she chose a role that moved her 180 degrees from the business girl heroines she had recently been playing. In the title role of *Roxie Hart* at Twentieth

Century-Fox Ginger created a bold cartoon of the featherbrained flapper, complete with windblown bob, beauty mark and chewing gum. Nunnally Johnson fashioned his script from Maurine Watkins' farce about Chicago in the 1920s, when notorious characters became instant celebrities and, often as not, vaudeville headliners. Using the device of having a reporter recall those wild and woolly days, Johnson hoped to suffuse the events in nostalgic charm. But William Wellman bore down so hard for laughs that Ginger's amusing characterization was criticized as unsubtle and the finished product pleased neither Johnson nor the critics—although it was a box-office hit.

This willingness to experiment, while not always successful, supplied Ginger with a way of surprising audiences that kept her free from the dangers of overexposure.

Her stardom was not without its price, however. Newspaper writers who had customarily described her as a warm, friendly girl or a direct, honest-to-a-fault young actress now began noting that while Ginger rode the wave of success, she was far from being the most popular star with co-workers. And Ginger herself admitted that in achieving success, she'd changed. "I was trying to accomplish something, and you can't accomplish things without changing. That's the first rule of progress, isn't it?"

When a writer informed her that a bit player had said, "It's ducky to have fame and success develop you, but if I had the sense of humor that kid sported in *Gold Diggers of 1933*, I wouldn't trade it for a hundred Oscars. She doesn't have time for laughs anymore." Ginger responded that the writer should tell the bit player to come over some morning before she had her hair done at 6:30 A.M., and they would have some laughs.

Moreover, she worked continuously. She finished *Roxie Hart* just in time to spend Christmas week at the 1,035-acre ranch which she had bought twenty miles from Medford, Oregon, and which she now regarded as home. By New Year's she was back at Twentieth Century-Fox to film her sequence of *Tales of Manhattan*, an omnibus of short stories in which she appeared in a romantic segment opposite Henry Fonda.

Then, after only a week's rest, she reported to Paramount for the first of a three-picture deal. Billy Wilder, at the time known in the United States as one half of the Brackett-Wilder scriptwriting team, recalls their professional association as one of his most pleasant. "I'd always wanted to direct in America, but nobody would let me. Then Charlie Brackett and I came up with the notion of *The Major and the Minor*, and Ginger, of course, was the ideal casting," he says. "The only trouble was, at that time she was at the height because of the Fred Astaire pictures and the Academy Award she had gotten for this serious picture, *Kitty Foyle.*

"Well, to get her to be directed by this dilettante—which I was then—this is like saying they're going to put a brand-new jockey on Secretariat. So we told the problem to Leland Hayward,* and he got her to agree, and she just went. And I'd like you to know in all those forty years since, I've never worked with anybody more professional than Ginger. She was an absolute delight. She is on time. She comes prepared for this tiny little dance. She thought about it; she rehearsed it. And everything was—I wish life would always be like that."

The Major and the Minor gave Ginger the opportunity to express the duality of character at which she was always so expert. She played a homesick young woman who, through economic necessity, posed as a preteenager to scrape up the train fare home.†

Nor was Ginger ever more appealing than as a scrubbed-faced innocent, wearing pigtails and attempting to hide her shapely figure beneath a middy blouse and skirt. Through plot complications she met a handsome major (Ray Milland) stationed at a boys' military school and took refuge in his stateroom for the night. The film was laden with double entendre and barely hidden perversity—all made acceptable by the assumption that a child is per se innocent and incorruptible.

"It was in the days of censorship, and behind the back of the Breen Office we actually did *Lolita.* They didn't know what they'd okayed for us," Wilder says. "It worked very well, because of the grown man's plain attraction for the little girl, and secondly, what worked for us were the corps of masturbating cadets being driven crazy by the child because she seemed so mature. She had to stave them off, and all the while she's falling in love with Milland and doesn't want him marrying the other woman. So it was shades of *Lolita,* I might say, twenty years before Mr. Nabokov."

*Their mutual agent.

†Later, when she arrives home and the major pursues her, her role turns into a real tour de force: she pretends to be her mother, while Lela, her real and reel mother, assumes the identity of her grandmother.

In addition to cashing in on Ginger's success by appearing in the film, Lela also wrote and published *Ginger Rogers and the Riddle of the Scarlet Cloak,* described as "an original story featuring Ginger Rogers, famous motion-picture star, as the heroine." One memorable line ran: "Ginger Rogers was not the 'usual' telephone operator because the Seaview Arms was not the 'usual' hotel. Built in 1926 by Madame Millicent Dulhut. . . ."

Ten days after finishing the Wilder film, Ginger returned to RKO for Leo McCarey's *Once Upon a Honeymoon*, in which she co-starred with Cary Grant. McCarey's attempt to set a whimsical romance against the backdrop of Hitler's conquest of neighboring countries offended audiences. In a period before anyone had defined the absurdist point of view or made dark comedy popular, McCarey and company were accused of simple bad taste.

Then Ginger went back to Paramount. Considering the ease, tranquillity and general good feeling that suffused making *The Major and the Minor*, it remains difficult to understand the tension and recriminations that were generated when Ginger returned to the same studio to co-star once again with Ray Milland in *Lady in the Dark.* Apparently no one but Ginger had faith in the film or in her ability to play the fortyish-and-frigid fashion magazine editor who suffers an identity crisis that drives her to a psychoanalyst's couch. Certainly director Mitchell Leisen was unenthusiastic about the project. He told his biographer David Chierichetti* that he threw out the script and wrote another himself. He said he knew before starting the picture that the role "was not up Ginger Rogers' alley," claiming the task of putting the film together took ten years off his life. He accused Ginger of being so prudish about showing her legs that he had to sneak close shots with a telephoto lens. He said she was unbelievably bad at matching shots, having difficulty recalling at what point and how she had performed a bit of business. Worse still, in such a hostile atmosphere this supremely disciplined actress developed the habit of holding up production by consistently being late. He said that on the day he had scheduled shooting "Suddenly It's Spring" she kept 165 electricians waiting from early morning until she appeared at 3:30 P.M.

"In those psychoanalytical scenes on the couch she didn't know what the hell she was talking about. I'd go in quietly and try to explain to her what the whole thing meant and pull it out of her. And I mean really pull," he said.

In her constant attempts to broaden her range Ginger had got beyond her emotional depth. Leisen, unable to cope with the situation, soon abandoned the dramatic development of the film, focusing his attention on those things he knew best—sets, costumes, lighting and special effects.

Nor was he the only one who despaired. Dialogue coach Phyllis

Hollywood Director, Popular Library

Loughton Seaton described Ginger as "a lovely person, but she was a star with a capital S. . . . I was more stage manager on that picture than dialogue coach."

Even Ray Milland, who had worked so happily with her in *The Major and the Minor*, grew disenchanted when Ginger suddenly stopped production for her third marriage.

"One day we were doing scenes on the couch, and she blew take after take until I thought I'd go out of my mind," Leisen told Chierichetti. "Finally she said, 'I'm sorry. I just can't keep my mind on this because I'm getting married tomorrow.'"

On January 15 the engagement was announced. The following day Ginger and twenty-two year old marine private John Calvin Briggs II, former bit player at RKO, whom Ginger had dated fewer than ten times, were married at the First Methodist Church in Pasadena. After telling the press, "He's everything I've ever dreamed about—companionable, intelligent, a grand sense of humor and a six-foot, two-inch, brown-haired, brown-eyed American," Ginger left with him for a short honeymoon. (Newspapers said it was two days; Leisen claimed two weeks.) When Ginger returned, filming on *Lady in the Dark* resumed. Another delay occurred on February 19, when Ginger was overcome by carbon monoxide fumes as she and partner Don Loper danced atop seven tons of dry ice in one of the movie's spectacular fantasy sequences. The studio doctor was called, and Ginger was sent home for a day or two.

At last, however, *Lady in the Dark* was finished. For a full year it languished on the studio shelf as wartime audiences jammed theaters, lengthening runs from the customary two weeks to several months. Finally, Leisen, fearing the costumes and hairstyles would become dated was successful in getting it released in February, 1944. It grossed $4,500,000, and uncritical audiences were carried away with its sumptuous sets and costumes, but in the end it damaged the reputations of both Leisen and Ginger, marking the beginning of her decline from superstardom.

Hollywood was puzzled by the sudden Rogers-Briggs nuptials. Since Briggs had been under contract to RKO and played a bit part in *Tom, Dick and Harry*, people assumed that they had met then. Actually, Briggs had been assigned as her marine honor guard when Ginger had gone to Camp Pendleton to entertain for the USO. Afterward the young marine had asked press agent Eddie Rubin for her telephone number. When Ginger learned Rubin had refused to divulge it, she said that if Briggs asked again, Rubin was to provide it. Briggs did, and Rubin did, and shortly Briggs and Ginger were married.

Some acquaintances felt she had married Briggs to gain a respite, however brief, from the problems confronting her in *Lady in the Dark*. But Helen Seitz, who was in RKO's editorial department for thirty-three years, says Ginger just fell in love. "When she was making a picture at Paramount, she would bicycle over to her dressing room at RKO to use the facilities," Miss Seitz says. "And when I'd see her, I'd call out, 'Hello, Mrs. Katz,' which was Jack's stepfather's name, and it tickled her. She'd just glow. Then one day she stopped and showed me a bracelet he'd given her—the kind you could win at a carnival. It said, "To Mommy," and she was as thrilled with it as if it had been set with diamonds.

"And later she went to Camp Pendleton and cooked and loved keeping house until he was shipped overseas. After the war they went to the ranch she'd bought, and he tried to run it, which the foreman objected to—and that was a problem. But the marriage lasted as long as any of hers. With Lew Ayres his career didn't progress as fast as hers, and that made it difficult. But he was such a nice person. Of course, in all her marriages there was always a little too much mama."

Ginger had no releases in 1943, but two, *Lady in the Dark* and *Tender Comrade*, in 1944. Neither Ginger nor Lela seems to have detected any questionable political messages in *Tender Comrade*, a sudsy drama about war wives, written by Dalton Trumbo and directed by Edward Dmytryk. In fact, they were enthusiastic about the picture, envisioning that it would provide Ginger with a topical box-office hit. When it failed to fulfill their best hopes, Ginger and Lela read scripts and novels for independent production, but none of the projects materialized. Nor did RKO have anything for the star. Finally, she agreed to replace the rebellious Joan Fontaine in David Selznick's *I'll Be Seeing You*, even though Joseph Cotten's role was obviously bound to elicit the most profound response from audiences. But neither Cotten nor Ginger registered as well at the sneak previews as ex-child star Shirley Temple. It was another straw in the wind.

Nor was the trend reversed by MGM's *Weekend at the Waldorf*, a remake of *Grand Hotel*. Undertaking the role of the world-weary movie star (originally a ballet dancer, played by Greta Garbo), Ginger was disappointing to critics.

Her salary of $292,149 again put her out front as the industry's highest-paid star, and she ranked just behind General Motors' Charles E. Wilson as the eighth-highest-paid individual in any industry in the United States. But her career was on the decline. With *Heartbeat*, a Gallic trifle in which she definitely looked long in the tooth, she earned guffaws when she testified on the witness stand that she was eighteen years old. In this dismal fashion she wound up her contract at RKO. Having attempted the role of clear-eyed ingenue once too often, Ginger now tried playing a mature, pseudo-historical character, Dolley Madison, in Universal's *The Magnificent Doll*, opposite David Niven. Granting the film's visual beauty, *Time* magazine's review noted that Ginger looked "far too regal ever to have been Fred Astaire's hoofing partner," which may have accounted for the box-office apathy.

With film offers coming in less frequently, Ginger flirted with the idea of running for a congressional seat on the Republican ticket. Lela, on the other hand, was cutting a swath as a self-styled expert on Communism. Testifying before the House Un-American Activities Committee, she described herself as "the manager of my daughter's affairs and a writer of sorts" and as one of the original members of the Motion Picture Alliance for the Preservation of American Ideals. Between 1938 and 1945 she had served as an assistant to Charles Kerner, vice-president in charge of production at RKO. She had read properties for him, ferreting out hidden Communist propaganda. Asked for an example, Lela told how Mr. Kerner had given her *None but the Lonely Heart*, which someone had suggested for Cary Grant. Lela had realized immediately that it was "filled with despair and hopelessness" and therefore subversive, only to be told that Kerner had bought it thirty minutes earlier. Producer David Hempstead quickly signed Clifford Odets to write and direct the film. Odets, she said, was a Communist. How did she know? She produced a January 8, 1936, column by O. O. McIntyre naming Odets as a Communist. "I never saw that denied," she stated—as if that settled the matter.

Asked if Odets had been successful in slipping subversive material into the film, she produced the *Hollywood Reporter*'s review, which described the picture as "moody and somber throughout, in the Russian manner," adding later that it "takes time out for a bit of propaganda preachment whenever director Clifford Odets, who also wrote the script from the Richard Llewellyn novel, felt the urge." She cited the film as a splendid example of the type of propaganda Communists liked to inject in motion pictures. Later she amplified her views: "As a free people we had no experience with such intrigue and conspiracy. Our executives were no more asleep than were our people or our government or the whole world, in fact. The Communist propagandist is a trained propagandist, highly disciplined. . . . His ways are devious and not easy to follow."

Robert Taylor and Robert Montgomery had told the committee that they had refused to act in films with or by Communists. Had Lela and Ginger ever objected to or turned down scripts because there were lines for Ginger to speak that were un-American or communistic?

They had. Lela recalled rejecting Theodore Dreiser's *Sister Carrie* because it was "just as open propaganda as *None but the Lonely Heart*."

At another time she told investigators that Ginger had refused to speak the line "Share, and share alike—that's democracy" in *Tender Comrade* whereupon it had been given to another actress. She identified Dalton Trumbo as another Communist.

She also went to great pains to spell out that perhaps only 1 percent of the people associated with films were Communists; but that was enough, she added, coming up with the startling information that only 2,000,000 of 200,000,000 Russians were Communists. When a committee member questioned one of her assumptions, she checked him, "Sir, you are thinking like an American."

She did not mention that because of her allegation in a Town Hall radio broadcast that Emmet Lavery and his play *The Gentleman from Athens* were red-tinged, she had been sued by Lavery and producer Martin Gosch for $2,000,000. At the end of her testimony, committee member John McDowell paid what may have been a more accurate tribute than he intended, calling her "a disturbed lady who in the course of her activities in Hollywood has stumbled across the fingers of this conspiracy against the American government" and stating that "she has become, in my opinion, one of the outstanding experts on Communism in the United States, and particularly in the amusement business."

The shameful truth is that such nonsense was taken seriously, ruining many lives and suppressing *None but the Lonely Heart* for several years.

Why, if she had been such an expert, had Lela not sniffed out the insidious message that Dalton Trumbo, by her definition, must have smuggled into *Tender Comrade*? Says a former RKO producer, "Ginger and Lela didn't have the slightest idea either Eddie, or especially Dalton, was an avowed left-winger. They were thrilled that Ginger had a good dramatic part."

An ex-RKO publicity man says that the more often Lela saw her name in print, the more outrageous she became. "The old lady was definitely hurting Ginger's popularity with her charges, most of them hearsay," he says. He recalls refusing to release one such blast, telling Lela that if she had complaints, to make them to his supervisor, and that, as far as he could see, she had no firsthand knowledge of what she was saying. "And I think Ginger finally privately told her to knock it off. As for Ginger, I don't think she was interested in anything except a good role. She might have talked about running for Congress, but if you'd asked her, I doubt that she could have told you the difference between the Republican and Democratic parties—if there is one."

Ginger's age, financial demands, declining box-office appeal and controversial image combined to keep her off the screen for another year. After Jack Briggs' return from overseas early in 1947, he and Ginger went to Quakerstreet, New York (population-190), where they helped his grandparents celebrate their sixtieth wedding anniversary. They were accompanied by a *Look* editor and a photographer. The editor slyly reported in her story: "A neighbor who had expected to be awed by movie-star glamor said delightedly, 'But she's so ordinary. And so nice.' "

The Briggses said that Ginger would make *Wild Calendar* for Enterprise Pictures and that Briggs would serve as associate producer on the film, but the project foundered, and Ginger did not have another film in movie theaters until December, 1947, when she appeared in Columbia's *It Had to Be You*, a picture Bosley Crowther excoriated by accusing the producers of suffering from "arrested development."

There were no appearances during 1948. Ginger and Briggs divided their time between the 4-R ranch in Oregon and her Beverly Hills home. Ginger read novels, short stories, plays and scripts, searching vainly for a role that would bring her back to public favor. She also sculpted and painted, fished, went skeet shooting, swam, played tennis and golf, read *Science and Health* and kept herself at a physical and mental peak, awaiting the opportunity that she never doubted would soon present itself.

After five years of marriage the relationship between Ginger and Jack Briggs luckily showed few signs of strain, and with Ginger's career in the doldrums it appeared that she might slip into retirement without actually realizing what was happening.

But Lela had trained her daughter never to overlook any possibility, however remote. This turned out to be invaluable. When Ginger heard that Arthur Freed was following the popular *Easter Parade* with an as yet untitled Fred Astaire-Judy Garland original, she wrote Freed a letter, ostensibly congratulating him. That Judy's emotional and physical health were a matter of concern to the Freed unit was no secret, and there were some, Arthur Freed among them, who suspected Ginger was reminding him of her availability.

It was a shrewd move and a key to Ginger's professional longevity. Only two days before production on *The Barkleys of Broadway* was to begin MGM executives were notified by Miss Garland's doctor that she had suffered an emotional collapse and would require at least three months to recover.

Freed immediately contacted Ginger at 4-R. She agreed to read the script, which arrived on Saturday night, and on Monday morning she was at MGM for costume fittings and first rehearsals for the six dance routines. She was to receive $125,000 for the picture and was obviously as pleased to be working again as were the 5,000 fans who wrote within a week to welcome her back.

Judy Garland was not happy about being replaced, and knowing about the fine-as-peach-fuzz facial hair on Ginger's cheeks that gave cameramen so much trouble, she maliciously sent Ginger a floral arrangement in a gigantic shaving mug. Whether Ginger got the point or not, she never batted an eyelash as she displayed the flowers and told everyone how sweet it was of Judy to wish her well.

Shortly after shooting of the picture started, "there was," according to Arthur Freed's biographer Hugh Fordin, "a big kabob between Ginger and Judy. Judy walked on the set while Ginger was working and let it be known—like, who was this amateur taking her role? She began drinking coffee with Oscar Levant and causing a fuss. Ginger retreated to her dressing room and wouldn't come out until Judy left. Judy wouldn't leave. Finally Chuck Walters, the director, practically had to have Judy carried off the set."

There were other problems, too. Shades of the past, an open dispute developed with Astaire over the height of her heels and another about the use of weights in her sleeves. He privately referred to Ginger as Miss Wasp—a reference to her social values as well as her increasingly less than sunny disposition. Ginger also argued with producer Freed over whether it was his or her idea to reprise "They Can't Take That Away from Me" from *Shall We Dance* as the *Barkleys'* theme song. Nor was she happy to lose a couple of songs that Judy had been scheduled to sing.

But given the circumstances under which Astaire and Rogers had been reunited, the end results were pleasing. If Ginger appeared—as a number of critics couldn't resist saying—to have reverted to being the superb athlete of the early Astaire-Rogers films rather than the polished dancer of later years, the sentimental glow that enveloped the occasion more than made up for any loss of esthetic appeal. And the film placed as one of MGM's top five money-makers of the year.

With her career rejuvenated, Ginger and Jack Briggs spent more and more time in her Beverly Hills home and started drifting apart. During the shooting of *Barkleys* she often worked late, and when she arrived home, Briggs would be absent. He would return long after she had had to retire in order to be up early and on the set next morning.

By the time she finished the film and signed for Warner's *Perfect Strangers* she and Briggs virtually fit that description. He left for Oregon to assess their deteriorating relationship, and Ginger told Louella Parsons that even though they were separated, she still believed they would reconcile. But on September 6 Ginger filed for an uncontested divorce, making all the familiar charges to avoid revealing the real trouble.

Perfect Strangers co-starred Ginger and Dennis Morgan, but this tale of an aborted love affair between a divorcée and a married man who serve on a jury together failed to interest the public. Still, Ginger had ingratiated herself sufficiently with producer Jerry Wald* and director Stuart Heisler for them to hire her when Lauren Bacall preferred suspension to appearing in *Storm Warning*. Although now over forty, Ginger played a young New York model tyrannized by her brother-in-law and the Ku Klux Klan and forced to testify against them by her conscience and the pressures brought by District Attorney Ronald Reagan.

But if *Storm Warning* was a mechanical reproduction of the social problem dramas that Warner's had made a specialty of tearing from the headlines and turning into important picutres, *The Groom Wore Spurs* was a witless farce that caused Bosley Crowther to begin his review by asking readers to pity poor Ginger Rogers and to end it by announcing that the only funny thing about the movie was that it was called a Fidelity Film.

Ginger's—and by extension Lela's—judgment seems to have been clouded by their eagerness to reestablish her. After finishing the two Warner's films, Ginger told Hedda Hopper, "The whole picture [*Storm*

---

*Semi-immortalized as the heel-hero in Budd Schulberg's novel about a no-talent Hollywood opportunist, *What Makes Sammy Run?*

Warning] is strong meat. My part is certainly off the beaten track for me. I play a very ordinary girl who accidentally becomes involved with the Ku Klux Klan. I followed *Storm Warning* with a light comedy, *The Groom Wore Spurs,* with Jack Carson.'' She also told Hedda, ''At this stage of my life I simply have to give the public what it wants in the way of pictures.''

Following the unveiling of these two films, Ginger's career was in need of another *Barkleys of Broadway.* With none in sight, she made a trip to New York to appear in a fund-raising gala for the American National Theater and Academy, singing an inaudible version of ''Embraceable You'' and doing a comedy dance with Paul Hartman.

After her return to Hollywood Ginger was approached by French playwright Louis Verneuil who had provided Celeste Holm with a frothy comedy, *Affairs of State*, in which Miss Holm had won ecstatic notices. Now he proposed to do the same for Ginger with *Love and Let Love.* When Verneuil read the play to Ginger and Lela over lunch, they thought they saw the opportunity for Ginger to score anew. Verneuil proposed to direct and play the part of the mature diplomat—one of the two men between whom the plot had the glamorous star choosing. Producer Anthony Brady Farrell—a former chain manufacturer from upstate New York who had been lured into theatrical production by a sexy dancer who later become one of Errol Flynn's wives—was glad to leave artistic decisions to the Rogerses and Verneuil. Ginger and Lela hired designer Jean Louis to do the gowns. Overlooking nothing, Ginger sent flowers from her garden to show him the exact shades she desired and even asked the set designer to duplicate the tone of green on her living-room walls in the stage setting.

For her convenience rehearsals were held in Beverly Hills, even though in her high expectations for success she had signed a long-term lease on a New York apartment. After an uneventful period of rehearsals Ginger and Lela came to New York in a state of euphoria. But soon after arrival Ginger learned that her playwright-director-leading man had suffered a heart attack and that she would have to open in New Haven opposite the understudy. Still undaunted, Ginger, Lela and the management began searching for a suitable replacement and succeeded in persuading Paul McGrath to take over the part in time for the Philadelphia premiere six days later. In that city Verneuil showed up with a new speech that pleased him and displeased Ginger.

After that there was little they agreed upon. In Washington, reviews were bad; audiences, cold; and relations between Ginger and Verneuil, frigid. She insisted that she needed a new director and that the play required a doctor. There were discussions about closing the show out of town, but theater tycoon Lee Shubert assured Ginger that an audience awaited it in New York, so the production staggered on to Boston.

The feud broke into the newspapers when Ginger granted an interview to critic Elliot Norton, telling him that Verneuil seemed to think the only thing wrong with the play was her. She said she'd never considered the script a great play, but that she still thought it could be an amusing trifle. Meanwhile, Sally Benson had been called in and was busily dictating fresh scenes to a typist. The minute they were finished the assistant stage manager snatched them out of the typewriter and delivered them to the newly imported director, Bretaigne Windust, who began staging them. By the time the play finally arrived in New York on October 19 Ginger estimated 48 percent of it had been rewritten. Even so, everyone had pretty much given up hope for it. The emphasis now was on showing off a real-life movie queen in a series of startlingly beautiful gowns. And on opening night when receiving an ovation, Ginger milked the audience response by prancing around in a circle like a little circus pony.

The next day all critics turned thumbs down on the play, but many had kind words for Ginger, and when *Life* magazine ran a story on her tribulations in getting the show to Broadway, she said she'd stick with it as long as the audiences wanted her. "Regardless of what critics say, I'll always be glad we came to New York," she said. "We could have gone on touring around the country, possibly playing to packed houses and getting our money back on the show. But I'd rather be a sitting duck on a big pond."

Despite the play's resounding failure, it did what Lela and Ginger had gambled on. It made her newsworthy again. *Time* reported that the only fresh thing about a National Association of Manufacturers' convention in December, 1951, was Ginger Rogers' call for women to get into business.

Moreover, while the play failed, Brooks Atkinson's tribute—"she is beautiful and alive and has a sunny sense of humor. She can also act with bounce and animation. . . . . No one that gorgeous can be entirely overwhelmed by a playwright's dullness"—did her no harm in Hollywood.

During 1952 she made three films for Twentieth Century-Fox. The first was Nunnally Johnson's *We're Not Married.* (The premise concerned the effect on five couples of the sudden discovery that they are not legally wed.) Ginger and Fred Allen* were cast as a husband-and-wife radio team who ladle out sweetness and light on their daily breakfast show and spit venom the rest of the day. Many considered it the high point of the picture. In *Dreamboat* she played a silent screen star who embarrasses her conservative former co-star, turned college professor, when she resurrects their old films on television. It was a run-of-the-mill comedy, but Ginger and Clifton Webb were praised. And in *Monkey Business* Ginger, Cary Grant, Marilyn Monroe and Charles Coburn made a one-joke script about a middle-aged couple (Rogers and Grant) who drank a youth-reviving elixir and became downright childish popular with audiences, no matter what devastating things critics said about it.

On February 7, 1953, six months to the day after they were introduced by actress Evelyn Keyes in Paris, Ginger married Jacques Bergerac in the private chambers of Judge Eugene Therau in Palm Springs. In a line of unsuitable husbands Bergerac, a handsome French boy of twenty-four, stood out. Even experienced press agents were hard put to apply a cosmetic gloss on the match. They subtracted from Ginger's age and added to Bergerac's. Depending upon whose word you took for it, Bergerac was: (1) a lawyer; (2) a law student; (3) a hotel desk clerk; (4) a part-time hotel desk clerk; (5) a photographer; (6) a jai alai player; (7) an actor. And when Ginger had returned to the United States after their meeting: (1) Bergerac had followed to woo her; (2) she had brought him to California where (a) an MGM talent scout had arranged a screen test and (b) Ginger had persuaded MGM bosses to put him under contract to groom as a successor to Fernando Lamas.

At Christmastime, 1952, Ginger, Lela and the young Frenchman had spent some time in Oregon at the 4-R ranch. Despite his aversion to country life (Ginger was never again able to persuade him to visit the place), they decided to marry. Although he spoke little English, he was a well-coordinated young man who played a smashing game of tennis, danced well and is reported to have a knack for pleasing Ginger by knowing when to be attentive and when to fade into the background.

Naturally, gossip columnists and reporters dwelled upon the difference in the couple's ages and status in the world. Both bride and groom

*Allen had written the sketch and played it several times before on radio and TV opposite Tallulah Bankhead.

tried to dismiss all the chatter. Ginger even announced that while she might be the star in the family, he was the boss.

Bergerac waved aside the question of age difference, saying, "I think I was first attracted to Ginger by her niceness. She seemed so genuine. Age is not the most important thing. Of course, the way a woman looks makes a difference. She is very pretty." And when a woman columnist cattily informed Bergerac that she had known his wife before he was born, he wisely bit his tongue and said nothing. For her part, Ginger said she had never understood what the fuss was about. "The important thing is we're in love. I wanted to find a husband who was intelligent, sympathetic, charming and handsome. I wasn't interested in when he was born."

Ginger seemed so genuinely unconcerned about their ages that during 1953, in *Forever Female*, she agreed to appear as an aging star fighting to snare the ingenue role and the callow playwright (William Holden) away from a real ingenue (Pat Crowley). While Holden and Pat Crowley were adequate, Ginger brought an old pro's know-how to playing the part of the over-the-hill actress—proving that if she were so inclined, she could gracefully slip into character roles and continue her screen career indefinitely.

But for some reason—friends hint it was because she often supported husbands and other relatives—Ginger suddenly accepted a number of unsuitable parts. Although Nunnally Johnson admired her portrayal of an adder-tongued actress* in his feeble thriller *Black Widow*, hardly anyone else did. *Twist of Fate*, made in England, was no more suitable for her. Ginger did it only to provide Bergerac with a showcase role after his option was dropped by MGM. When the picture was released, even so lenient a critic as Dorothy Manners complained about Ginger: "The veteran actress is far from her best in the new British production." Having unsuccessfully attempted to combine her private and professional lives, Ginger abandoned her dream of establishing a wife-husband acting partnership. "Jacques and I have decided it's better for our careers if we don't make any more films together," she said.

Jacques said nothing publicly, docilely accepting the television roles obtained for him by the agent his wife had provided. He did confide to one executive that he was being driven out of his mind by Ginger's

---

*Originally written for Tallulah Bankhead, who talked and talked and talked herself out of it.

boundless energy, enthusiasm and best-of-all-possible-worlds optimism.

Perhaps sensing his restlessness, Ginger suggested a trip. Discussing this "second honeymoon" with a columnist, Ginger conceded, after two and a half years of marriage, that Jacques was not the perfect husband, but added that since life would be impossible with the perfect man, she was more than satisfied.

They were only on the first leg of their trip when a call came that clearly illuminated the priorities Ginger assigned to her private and professional lives. Agent Sam Jaffe phoned to say Twentieth Century-Fox wanted her for the mother role in *Roomful of Roses*. Without a moment's hesitation Ginger forgot about the "second honeymoon" and booked passage on the first Hollywood-bound plane.

Back in Los Angeles, she began preparing for the film, which the studio had retitled *Teenage Rebel*, in an obvious attempt to cash in on the popularity of *Rebel Without a Cause*. The finished product, which depicts the problems that arise between a divorcee and her teenage daughter when the mother remarries, provided Ginger with an opportunity to demonstrate that fading youth had not diminished her talent.

But like so many star personalities, Ginger was not content to slip gracefully into character parts. Forever mindful that a switch from musicals to straight comedy and then to drama had led to an Academy Award, Ginger attempted to repeat the plan, hoping to revitalize her career by changing her physical appearance. She explained that playing a murderess in *Black Widow* and a mother in *Teenage Rebel* had been experiments. Next she checked in at RKO for *The First Traveling Saleslady*. This script had been developed for Mae West. But Miss West had dismissed it as having too many female companions to suit her, wisecracking, "I've said it before, and I'll say it again. When I make a movie, I play opposite a man, not a woman."

Ginger accepted the part, and by the time filming began the cast included Carol Channing, Jim Arness, Clint Eastwood, James Brian and Barry Nelson, even though the rewrite of the screenplay was unfinished. The picture was such a disaster that it was never shown in New York.

Ginger's next performance, in Nunnally Johnson's *Oh, Men! Oh, Women!*, was overshadowed by the flashy farcical playing of Dan Dailey and Tony Randall in this burlesque of American dependence on psychoanalysis.

Predictably, as Ginger concentrated on her career again, her marriage fell apart. Although she assured Hedda Hopper in late April, 1956, that she and Bergerac were completely happy, they separated less than a month later, and on July 10, 1957, Ginger was granted an interlocutory decree on grounds of mental cruelty.

Fancy-free, Ginger concentrated on her career. Ignoring the fact that she had long looked down her nose at nightclubs, she agreed to open a new room in a hotel being built in Havana and signed to tour in the national company of *Bells Are Ringing.* Both moves signaled that motion-picture offers had stopped coming in, even though Ginger claimed these live engagements not only offered huge compensation but also offered an opportunity to polish her stage technique far from the critical eyes of Hollywood and New York.

She finally, decided to go into television, too. In 1951, when she had been in New York with *Love and Let Love,* Bill Dozier had approached her with the then revolutionary idea of filming a TV series. Ginger had seen the possibilities and agreed to do it, but the project failed to materialize. In 1954 she had starred in three one-act plays selected from Noel Coward's *Tonight at 8:30.* But not until 1958 did she actually make a pilot for a regularly scheduled show.

She finally decided to go into television, too. In 1951, when she had scheduled the same week as the sensationally successful *An Evening with Fred Astaire.* Ginger's hour also starred Ray Bolger and the Ritz Brothers. In her review Harriet Van Horne, then TV critic for the New York *World-Telegram* let Ginger down gently, paying tribute to her past accomplishments: "Miss Rogers is a beautiful, slim, ageless woman who danced divinely. We watched her a hundred times in the darkness of the temples of our youth. We remember her airy as a sprite in the arms of Fred Astaire. We remember her in slapstick comedy and heavy dramas full of sin and suffering and too many sequins. On TV, she is naturally welcomed as an old friend, but she never reaches us as Mr. Bolger does."

In the New York *Daily News,* Ben Gross was blunt. "Ginger and Ray appear in a merely so-so show," he wrote. When the Trendex rating came in, Ralph Edwards' *This is Your Life* had crushed Ginger with a 23.4 rating to her 13.6. Nor were the results any happier with her NBC pilot.

During this period Ginger signed with producer Paul Gregory to star in a play with music, envisioning appearing on Broadway at night and making her TV series during the day. When NBC failed to sell the show, Ginger promised to grant them extra time, but nothing ever came of it.

Hurrying to the West Coast, Ginger rehearsed for Leslie Stevens' *The Pink Jungle,* in which she co-starred with Agnes Moorehead. When this play with music opened in San Francisco on October 14, it had a cast of fourteen, an orchestra of fourteen, four songs and eighteen stagehands. By the time it reached Boston by way of Detroit, the cast and orchestra had increased to twenty-two each. There were ten songs and thirty-three stagehands. There was also monumental dissension involving Miss Moorehead, Ginger and Lela, the playwright, the director, the choreographer, Gregory and his co-producer, Sherman S. Krellberg. The play closed in Boston on December 12, 1959, with the producers' announcement that they were adding six additional songs and were searching for a new director, a new choreographer, a new cast (with the exception of Ginger and Miss Moorehead) and a play doctor.

Fifteen years later Gregory recalled the trauma with humor. "Ginger Rogers? She's one of the reasons I left show business," he said. "The only other people I dealt with that were amost as rotten as she was were Claudette Colbert, Charles Laughton and Raymond Massey. She's a totally manufactured commodity. We'd give her a new scene, and she couldn't remember the lines. She couldn't sing and, surprisingly, she couldn't do the dances. And all through the horror of it she was smiling and grinning and unreal. There's no denying her appeal to the public. That's what makes her so dangerous. She almost smiled me into bankruptcy. God knows I don't mind her being a Christian Scientist. I just wish she'd put a little more emphasis on the Christian. But time is a great healer, and I can look back on it all now and wish her well."

So despite the $350,000 advance, the show closed for rewriting, recasting and general reworking. It was scheduled to reopen in April, 1960, but nothing more was ever heard of it.

There were no films between 1957 and 1964. After the Boston closing of *The Pink Jungle* Ginger accepted a few television engagements on variety shows, but she concentrated most of her energies on polishing her rusty stage technique in the relative privacy of stock. She was determined to survive, and she began by touring in the surefire *Annie Get Your Gun.* Given a role with audience appeal, she could win enthusiastic approval from so astute a critic as Elliot Norton, who traveled from Boston to Framingham, Massachusetts, to see her performance and wrote, "Miss Rogers has to force her voice to fill the Carousel, which is almost as big as Fenway Park. The important point is that she does it. You get the strong and exhilarating feeling that there is nothing she wants to do on stage that she can't or won't do. She has the skill, the force, the personal charm and the terrific sense of professionalism—which involves obligation to an audience—that are irresistible.''

Others were not so kind, but audiences as always poured out their love and their money as she played *Annie, Bell, Book and Candle* and, eventually, *The Unsinkable Molly Brown* and *Tovarich.*

While touring in *Bell, Book and Candle*, she and actor-producer-writer William Marshall, whom she had first met while making *Kitty Foyle*, began a romance which brought the customary announcement by Lela on February 22, 1961; Ginger and Marshall would wed. On March 17, Ginger, for the fifth time, and Marshall, for the third, were married at the First Methodist Church of North Hollywood.

After a mild career as a Hollywood actor, Marshall, a big, handsome man, had at 43 already married and divorced French actresses Michele Morgan and Micheline Presle. Through them he had been connected with Euopean film production but after his last divorce had returned to the United States, where he undertook a number of promotional schemes while also appearing in stock.

Ginger met Marshall at the precise moment in her life when she was vulnerable to a vital, fast-talking, seemingly shrewd businessman. ''Each thought the other had clout. She needed a strong shoulder to lean on, with no big-time offers coming in,'' an associate who asked not to be identified says. ''She and Lela would have seen through Bill in a jiffy if she hadn't been really scared. The key to that relationship is in her statement to some reporters that they'd just drive up the coast for a honeymoon. They were too busy with business plans to get away long. Does that sound like sexy Ginger got carried away by her head or her heart?''

Another old friend of hers, Allan Scott, who approached her with a play in which he hoped she would star on Broadway, suddenly found himself writing a picture for Ginger which Marshall was to produce. Marshall, Scott said in 1975, was the one part of Ginger's life he wouldn't presume to discuss with her.

In any case, while rehearsing for an appearance on *The Red Skelton Show* on TV in late March, 1963, Ginger anounced that she and Marshall were deserting Hollywood to form a partnership with the Jamaican government, producing films at studios being constructed in Kingston. They were to produce pictures and to receive a percentage of other features shot there. Ginger was particularly excited because she envisioned an opportunity for a woman to have a voice in operating a studio. "The movies have become more and more of a financial hazard, and the men who control them think that only other men understand business," she told reporter Joseph Flannigan. "So they deal mostly with male stars because they speak the same language.

"It's like trying to break into a political caucus for a woman to get into those smoke-filled rooms. You just can't. Women don't operate in the same way as men."

If Ginger's thinking on women was muddled, so were her personal values. For one way or another she committed herself to playing, of all things for Ginger Rogers, a madam in *Confession*. The script was based on a story supposedly written by Marshall. Through a series of wiles and impassioned pleas she secured Ray Milland as the male lead, Scott for the script and William Dieterle as director.

When they left for Jamaica, Scott had only forty pages of completed script. Worse still, they arrived to find sound stages unfinished. Electrical current was insufficient to light available interiors, so scenes had to be relocated out of doors, using natural light. To complicate matters further, when *Confession* was finally finished, the agreement between the government and Marshall was challenged. The film was seized and after four years' delay passed on to new owners. It was first retitled *Seven Different Ways* and then *I'm Having a Baby*. Mercifully, it received only a few scattered bookings.

Milland, Dieterle, Scott and many of the rest of the company found that each had agreed to make the film because he had been led to believe the others had committed themselves. All were disenchanted. Yet in June, 1964, when Ginger was appearing in *Tovarich* opposite TV's *Mr. Lucky*, John Vivyan, she still had faith in the picture and claimed that Jamaica was the perfect place to make movies with locales resembling Italy, Arizona, the Mediterranean and Missouri.

Marshall was not to be Ginger's rescuer. Judy Garland, however unintentionally, was. Judy had been cast by producer Bill Sargent to play Carol Lynley's mother in the Electrovision version of *Harlow*. As director Alex Segal recalls it, Judy agreed to do the part only on the condition that her young husband, Mark Herron, be given a role and when Herron wasn't, Judy suddenly grew too ill to appear. So Sargent thought of his neighbor Ginger Rogers. Ginger listened to the offer and accepted it. Once again her capacity to lose herself in an assignment, however unpromising, emerged. Not only did she act the role, receiving the best reviews in a bad lot, but she also made a cross-country trip to promote the film. Affectionate and nostalgic pieces about the veter-

71

an star rekindled producer David Merrick's interest in signing her to replace Carol Channing, who was leaving *Hello, Dolly!* after a run of 652 performances.

Envisioning a dancing Dolly, Merrick approached Ginger, who accepted his offer. Upon her return to the West Coast, leaving nothing to chance, Ginger engaged voice coach Harriet Lee and began working with director Gower Champion* three hours a day. Three months after the opening of *Harlow*, Ginger appeared as Dolly Gallagher Levi at the St. James Theater on August 9, 1965. Her fans gave her a tumultuous standing ovation before she uttered a word.

While reviewers found her less overpowering than Miss Channing, they conceded that Dolly was the kind of part that allowed an actress to remold the character in her own image, and Rogers' fans clearly loved her. What did it matter that members of the company were expressing surprise that she wasn't actually a singer and, more astoundingly, that she hadn't been unduly modest over the years when she had said she was essentially not a dancer.

As usual she proved herself a hard worker. "We called her our most efficient Dolly," someone connected with the show said. "She was always on time. She took a shower and looked immaculate onstage. She kept her costumes better than any of the other Dollies. She fixed herself up and came out like a movie star, and she added a lot of éclat.

"What's more, no one knocked on her dressing room door after half hour because she was running through her lines. And she ran lines for the second act during intermission. She even rehearsed that 'spontaneous' curtain speech—'You've given an actress the most precious thing in the world tonight'†—until one chorus gypsy performed it as his party trick.

"She's not easy to know. She was not close to the company. Now

---

*A dispute arose during rehearsals, causing Champion to walk out. A widely repeated story, perhaps apocryphal, has it that the disenchanted choreographer-director met Hermes Pan on the street and moaned, "Hermes, why didn't you tell me?" to which Pan responded, "But, Gower, I thought you knew!"

†She customarily would introduce a celebrity from the audience or, if none was there, her mother. Once she gave a big buildup to Betty Grable, who held a grudge against Ginger for "the rotten treatment" Betty and other chorus girls had received while working some of the Astaire-Rogers films, and when the spotlight hit the seats Betty and a friend had occupied, the chairs were empty. Another time, on tour, someone interrupted and flustered Ginger in the middle of her speech. She dried up. Then, after an agonizing pause, she started over from the beginning again.

whether that's because she wanted it or she comes on too strong or she just wasn't comfortable with the company I don't know. But she knew she was a star, and she didn't let them forget it either. Or maybe Mama and RKO drilled it into her that that was the way to protect yourself."

Realistically, much of the resentment can be traced to Bill Marshall, who saw to it that she was a capital S star. The chorus gypsies were at first inclined to laugh when the Marshalls rented the mansion that had belonged to Katharine Cornell and Guthrie McClintic and temporarily renamed it Rog-Mar, but the humor wore thin.

"He wasn't popular with the company," one of the singers said. "He showed his disdain by ignoring the fact we were there. The only thing we could ever figure out was that he must have been great in bed. Why else would she have let him get away with the things he did? Or why would she play a madam in his picture? That's not the general type character associated with her. And then there was that novel that had to be an embarrassment to her."*

Probably the most resentment arose from Marshall's treatment of Ginger's standby, Bibi Osterwald. "Ginger got blamed for things that weren't her fault," according to a Merrick staff member. "Everyone says she wouldn't let Bibi wear her costumes or use her dressing room. That wasn't Ginger. She wasn't even there. It was Bill, who came roaring in and said, 'Those are Ginger's costumes, and this is Ginger's room. Get out!' and Lucia Victor, the production stage manager, very nicely said, 'Mr.'—whatever his name was—'this is the theater, and this is the way we do things. Tonight Bibi is the star, and this is her room.' And he left."

Rumor has it that he had the dressing room fumigated, although why he would have done so is a mystery since Ginger doesn't believe in germs.

"I don't know Miss Rogers socially. She didn't allow it," Bibi Osterwald says. "I said 'good evening' when I came in and 'good night' when I left, and that's all. I think I knew Miss Merman a little. I think I knew Martha Raye very well. Phyllis Diller has become a fast friend. And Carol Channing, of course, is one of my dear friends. Betty Grable was warm and sweet. And Dorothy Lamour lent me her costumes before she'd worn them herself. She's a warm, sweet woman, but

---

*The Deal by Marshall was described by an English magazine writer as "mainly concerned with the misadventures of a glamorous male star who wears an artificial 'dong'; were it written by anyone else, Ginger would consider it unnecessarily vulgar."

she's not as big as Miss Rogers. So maybe Miss Rogers is doing something right.

"I must say she is not my idea of Dolly, but to be fair, I will tell you on the plus side, she sold every seat in the theater everywhere she played. She's a big box-office girl. But she stands alone. Nobody else gets close. Maybe that's why she is where she is today."

After eighteen months on Broadway Ginger took a brief vacation and then joined the national company of the show. This company, made up of players from the Mary Martin and Betty Grable troupes, rehearsed for a week before Ginger's arrival. On the big day they were ordered to line up on each side of the rehearsal-hall door and applaud as Ginger entered. When she came in, the company manager announced, "Company, this is your star. Miss Rogers, your company."

"Ginger acknowledged it graciously," says Robert Hultman, a singer and the Equity deputy. "But we'd had Betty Grable, and when they pulled the 'company, this is your star' stuff, Betty's first word was 'Help!' and everyone loved her."

Hultman and many of the others resented the fact that Ginger never troubled to learn their names. "After nine months working with somebody eight times a week and still not to have them know who the hell you are can be a little disconcerting. I think it was her Hollywood training. The studios shielded her from any real personal contact with people. You hear how outgoing she was as a young girl, but I think her mother probably said, 'Honey, stars don't act that way.' But I ended with ambivalent feelings toward her. After we got to Vegas, where Dotty Lamour and Ginger both played Dolly, she saw how Dotty, who is a warm, interested woman, could be friendly with the company without sacrificing their respect. So gradually Ginger began to warm up and act a little more friendly."

Hultman's second reevaluation occurred long after the touring company had closed and he was working in the New York production. Having become interested in helping paraplegics, he arranged to bring groups from Philadelphia to attend the Broadway show. In this way he met a Special Services Officer who eventually remarked that she was surprised that she hadn't met him when Ginger's company played Philadelphia. Invited to visit the hospital, Ginger ordered and paid for a Polaroid camera to provide each patient with a photographic memento of her visit. She also brought along fifty pounds of Hershey chocolate kisses which had been presented to the *Dolly* company when it had played Hershey, Pennsylvania. "Not only hadn't she popped all those chocolates in her face, but she went back several times to visit while we were there. And Tina, the special officer, told me there was one triple amputee who hadn't responded to any treatment. So Tina was going to steer Ginger past him. But the kid reached out with the one arm he had and grabbed Ginger and pulled her down close to him. Tina was going to try to get Ginger loose, but Ginger looked up and signaled to be left alone. And she stood there for forty-five minutes talking to that boy. He was crying. Ginger was crying. Even Tina, who didn't know what Ginger was saying, was crying. And from that time on the boy responded to treatment. There's no doubt there's sometimes a lack of warmth, but in that particular crisis the warmth was there. And it changed my thinking on Ginger."

Bill Mullikin, who played Cornelius in *Dolly*, sometimes had supper with Ginger after the performance. From the first he had called her Miss Rogers. Then, testing her at one point, he called her Ginger, excused himself and emended it to Miss Rogers, and she let it stand.

As a performer Mullikin found Ginger easy to work with since she laid down the rules and everyone knew what to expect and what was expected in return. "If you're a disciplined actor, that's easy," Mullikin says. "It may not be thrilling, or it may not be stimulating or goose bumps—but easy."

One night after the matinee and evening performances Ginger attended a party in the hotel suite of the orchestra conductor. As always at such gatherings, she drank 7-Up from a champagne glass, and she volunteered to do her "famous champagne trick." Thereupon, she placed the glass on her forehead, leaned back without touching anything with her hands and gracefully lowered herself to the floor in about twenty-five seconds. Those present cheered and applauded, but Ginger said, "Wait, I haven't finished yet. I get up." Then, without removing the glass from her brow, she rose to a standing position. "Superlady," says Mullikin. "I mean, strength. And that's what you met as your boss—because she was the boss of our show. And she was the boss because we assumed she had it in her contract that she had final approval on every word, every thing, every body—every gesture."

On the strength of Ginger's superstardom, nostalgic appeal and recent success in *Hello, Dolly!* she was offered a precedent-setting contract. She was to receive $12,000 per week for fifty-four weeks to headline *Mame*, the largest amount ever paid an actor in London's legitimate theater. Ginger signed and then startled the management by immediately asking for the best place to obtain ice cream, explaining, "While there's life, there's got to be ice cream."

75

As befitted a superstar of the thirties and forties, Ginger arrived in Southhampton with a husband, a 1940s hairdo and 118 pieces of luggage—crammed with paintings, mohair blankets, tennis balls, sundae syrup plus other necessities—and the attitudes of a former teen queen intact. Waiting for her was the press corps, ready to board a private four-coach Ginger Rogers Mame Express bound for London. In her private car Ginger received various star reporters while lesser members of the press feasted on Roast Turkey Mame (prophetic!) and Ginger Rogers Delight (mocha ice cream) and drank champagne while viewing a vintage Astaire-Rogers film, *Top Hat.*

Ginger assured reporters she was not in the least awed by her astronomical salary, that she hadn't been out to set any records but had only wanted a fair week's pay for a hard week's work. And, as the press agents pointed out, there was already an advance sale of $600,000, a month before the opening. Furthermore, Ginger assured everyone that hers would be a different kind of Mame. Pressed for details, she prattled, "I want to make the part my own. But don't ask me how I'm going to play it. That's like asking Richard Burton or Laurence Olivier how they're going to play *Hamlet.*"

When a reporter inquired about her film career, Ginger made it plain that she had been offered many roles but had turned them down because they were "tasteless and vile." She cited family pictures such as *Daddy Longlegs* and *Good-bye, Mr. Chips* as the type of films she would enjoy appearing in. "It's not my place to find fault," she told one reporter, "but you'd never get me undressing in front of a camera. I'd scream or die before that."

In a lengthy session with Helen Lawrenson at the Savoy, where Ginger was stopping, Miss Lawrenson interviewed—or attempted to interview—the star on her current interests. Asked about reading, Ginger confessed she didn't have much time for books. But when she did read, she liked science fiction ("Are you ready for that one?" she asked as if she had got off a snapper) and biographies of painters. Who was her favorite painter? She laughed merrily and named herself. Her favorite painting, she finally recalled, was "One Sunday Afternoon." "It's by the one who does all the little dots—now *what* is his name?" Miss Lawrenson moved on to pop music. Ginger liked "American Big Band sounds" and "would be interested to hear" folk songs. Did she like Dylan? "Who, dear?" She said she had not seen *Hair* because "the unwashed" were not her generation. Asked to name a person, living or dead, whom she admired, she replied, "The Master." This time Miss Lawrenson asked, "Who?" "The Master," Ginger repeated, and the interviewer suddenly thought Ginger surely couldn't mean the Maharishi. The Master? "Yes," Ginger said. "The Master. Jesus the Christ." When Miss Lawrenson admitted weakly she had said anyone living or dead, the undaunted Ginger replied, "Yes, you did. And Jesus is certainly a leader you can admire."

Admirers of Ginger did not include most of the critics who covered the February 21 opening of *Mame*. The *Guardian*'s man said, "I must be candid and say I do not think Ginger Rogers is really good at the big loud wisecrack." The *Daily Mail*'s man found her as eccentric as a pillar of the ladies' luncheon club, and the *Daily Telegraph*'s reviewer assessed the performance as "less Mame than tame."

Near the end of the show's run the highest paid of all stage performers in England committed a faux pas that was widely reported in the British press. For Christmas she presented the twenty-eight-piece orchestra with one seven-pound jar of chocolate limes, labeled "A Sweet Treat from Auntie Mame." The outraged musicians sent the treat to a children's hospital and muttered about being insulted. On that tinny note she ended her stay in London.

Returning from England in 1971, Ginger found herself with a marriage on the rocks. Whether she and Marshall were or were not divorced she was unsure, but the marriage was over. There were bitter private charges and countercharges. But publicly she maintained a dignified silence, claiming she regretted neither this nor any of her other four marriages. She even refused to predict that she would never marry again.

Her first move was to tour in the road company of *Coco*, playing the role originated by her old RKO rival Katharine Hepburn, but she insisted upon deleting a four-letter expletive that had earned Hepburn an enormous laugh. "I don't use those words," she told columnist Earl Wilson. "Our world morality has so weakened that youngsters think evil is good and don't know they're doing wrong. Adults should teach that there is a morality and a decent vocabulary."

In the same year she began representing the J. C. Penney Company's nonrun Gaymode Pantyhose—although the Los Angeles *Times'* Bella Stumbo found her more like a missionary than an emissary of Penney's as Ginger proclaimed, "God is LOVE. Evil is nothing more than a false concept of good. If we strive for it, we can all learn God. We can make our lives perfect LOVE." But eventually she got around to saying she had taken the job because Penny's was a "nice, dignified, decent outfit, founded on the golden rule." And wherever Ginger went, whether it was Los Angeles, Dallas, Kansas City, Boston, New York or somewhere in between, women turned out en masse, so that in 1972 Penney's expanded her role as a representative of the company. Why? "I'm Mrs. America," Ginger explained. "I think the ladies identify with this American apple-pie face." And she was as indefatigable at whatever she did as she had been in her palmiest days at RKO.

She went on working now because she had learned that discipline and nothing else satisfied her. The point was not that art was her life or that she felt she had to create; she needed to work to fill her time.

After the expansion of her association with Penney's Ginger ran into a member of David Merrick's staff at Sardi's Restaurant. "Oooooh!" Ginger called out. "I'm sooo thrilled about my new career." Asked what it entailed, she trilled, "I'm designing a whole new line of clothing for J. C. Penney's, and I'm so thrillllled! It's so fulfilllling!"

"Of course, she was with a J. C. Penney man," the Merrick staffer said. "Isn't that heaven? She's a real phony, if you know what I mean. She's not a phony phony—and there's an enormous difference. I don't mean it in a derogatory way. I mean she believes every bit of her phoniness. Her mother wouldn't let her stop."

Between 1972 and 1976 she has appeared as the stage manager (usually played by a male) in a student production of *Our Town*, which opened the $2,000,000 Ida Green Communications Center at Austin College in Sherman, Texas, has performed in a production of *No, No, Nanette* (making it a point to do more dancing than Ruby Keeler), could be seen in both winter and summer productions of *Forty Carats* and has prepared her first nightclub revue. In this revue, with the help of a young Ginger Rogers impersonator, a comic and four dancing boys, Ginger produces a ninety-minute nostalgic tour of her career. Ignoring the fact that Fred Astaire has pointedly refused to share joint tributes with her, she kisses a top hat and sighs, "Good night, Fred." And on opening night at the Waldorf she made her customary thank-you speech to cheering patrons, telling them, "You are beautiful people. I love you. I'd like to can you and send you to my mother."

In March, 1976, Ginger granted a joint interview with the new man in her life. Love, they admitted, was wonderful, but they couldn't say anything definite about marriage. The Man is George Pan, a Greek actor-dancer, who said Frank Sinatra had given them his blessing. Ginger, sixty-eight, claimed to be sixty-four, and Pan, about twenty-eight, gave his age as forty-one. Their description of the relationship produced a sense of *déjà vu* as the name Jacques Bergerac and press clippings of a quarter of a century ago came to mind.

Through it all, fans remain faithful to this survivor. At one Eastern engagement of *Forty Carats* in 1975 an especially devoted pair—brother and sister—bought seats and two copies of Arlene Croce's *The Fred Astaire and Ginger Rogers Book* well in advance. They enjoyed the performance enormously and presented themselves at the stage door, where a doorman took the books to Ginger's dressing room for autographs. He returned to say he was sorry, but the star would not sign the books because they were unauthorized biographies. Determined to have a memento, the brother shoved their programs into the doorman's hand and implored him to have them signed. Shortly thereafter a commotion out front made it apparent that Ginger was leaving by another exit. Desparate now, the young man raced to the street and seemed about to fling himself in front of the limousine into which Ginger was scrambling. Suddenly, from the depths of the interior, a voice commanded, "Be polite. Sign! Be thankful they still remember you!"

The voice belonged to Lela.

MIRIAM HOPKINS

The Maverick

On January 1, 1934, Miriam Hopkins was already a controversial figure in Hollywood. Ernst Lubitsch, who had directed the film version of *Design for Living* which was playing at the Paramount Theater, was convinced that she was developing into the greatest actress on the screen. On the other hand, Emanuel Cohen, head of production for Paramount Pictures, felt she wasn't worth a wooden nickel at the box office and was letting her option drop.

But Miriam wasn't worried as she puttered around her suite at the Hotel Pierre. She thrived on trouble. It stimulated her. Besides, the Forces were with her. She had the assurance of her astrologer that the planets were favorable, no matter what the fate of *Jezebel*, the play she was starring in. Her numerologist had analyzed the addresses of the theater and hotel, plus the number of her suite and other pertinent figures, and had confirmed the astrologer's calculation. Although Miriam ordinarily avoided carnival-type fortune-tellers, even the tea-leaf reader at the Gypsy Tea Room concurred with the astrologer and the numerologist.

Throughout her career Miriam was often rumored on the verge of signing for a part that she ultimately did not play. Sometimes she would read and reject the script. More often her astrologer or numerologist advised against the project. Or if either warned against travel at the time the film was scheduled to go on location, she would turn down the role, no matter how attractive the inducements offered.

These eccentricities affected not only her career but also her personal comfort. She refused to live at an address that added up to an unfavorable figure. While traveling, she often rejected the best suite in favor of a less desirable one to avoid living in a "two" or a "four." Although highly intelligent, she would go to extraordinary lengths to fool the Fates—or herself. Sometimes the solution was simple: for example, simply changing the numbers on a door. In other cases she interpreted the figures to suit her needs. Being born on October 18, 1902, pleased her because the month, the day and the year added up to 22. "That's a power number," she observed. When a friend asked whether the 22 didn't add up to a "four" or a box, Miriam indignantly informed her: "Of course not. You don't add twenty-two."

She was serious about astrology and numerology, and she believed in ghosts, but she amused herself and others by reading cards and palms at parties. On one such evening she volunteered to read the hand of actor and carnival barker Peter Garey. Garey resisted, explaining that he had been told by a carny mitt reader that he would die young, and that, while he didn't believe it, he didn't want another reading. The more he resisted, the more Miriam insisted. Finally, he extended his hand. After studying the palm for a few moments, she said, "Stop worrying! You're not going to die. You may have an accident that will leave you paralyzed from the neck down, but you'll live to a ripe old age." Afterward Garey could never decide whether she had been serious or putting him on.

Even in the early 1930s, when her career looked promising, Miriam, or Mims, as her friends called her, had an ambivalent attitude toward motion pictures. "That's because I'm a Libra," she explained. "We vacillate." On another level, she felt the stage-trained players' condescension toward a "bastard art form," and although she would seldom admit it, she harbored doubts about her photogenic appeal. Her face was not as exotic as Garbo's, as boldly theatrical as Joan Crawford's, as patrician as Katharine Hepburn's or as saucy as Mae West's. Designer Edith Head considered her stunning, but others thought her mouth too unusual and her eyes too close together for the camera.

Miriam was a diminutive woman. Only five feet two inches tall and weighing 102 pounds, she wore size 4½ shoes and gloves designed for children. A woman who admired and sought out the company of intellectuals, she might have been expected to put more emphasis on intelligence than on physical beauty, but she took a Southern belle's pride in the daintiness of her hands and feet. "I inherited the Cutter foot," she said, referring to her distinguished maternal ancestors. "Small, thin and difficult to fit." Her figure was shapely, but like her contemporaries, she emphasized her legs and minimized her breasts. She had small, cerulean-blue eyes, a halo of naturally curly, taffy-colored hair, a peaches-and-cream complexion (lightly tinted, with a few freckles across the bridge of her nose) and a highly individual mouth.

Despite her tiny proportions, when she was excited or angry, her head would go up, her strong chin point the way, and she would transform herself into an imposing figure. Her staccato speech pattern was normally softened by traces of a Georgia accent, but when she threw one of her "scenes," she was capable of unleashing a terrifying amount of aggression. Even such an experienced infighter as Bette Davis was moved to observe, after appearing in two pictures with her, "Miriam is a perfectly charming woman socially. Working with her is another story."

Both socially and professionally, Miriam's nervous energy kept her on the move. She went from the legitimate theater to films and then from studio to studio and back to the stage again, just as she moved from house to house and from man to man. She bought houses that had once belonged to Garbo, John Gilbert and John Barrymore, remodeled them and usually sold them for a profit.

She was even more casual about men than houses. Some relationships were fleeting, some long-lasting, but of her many lovers she married only four—perhaps because each of those she did wed cost her a mint. She was a *femme fatale*, a Southern belle who flirted as naturally as she breathed. She enjoyed the intrigue, but she was inconstant in her affections. When John Gilbert, suspecting her of infidelity during their affair, reacted to her noncommittal response to his accusations by putting a bullet into the wall above her head, Miriam coolly confiscated the gun. One evening when she decided she was tired of playwright-scenarist Edwin Justus Mayer, she impetuously seized a glass of scotch and threw the liquor in his face, ordering her bewildered lover out of her sight.

Paradoxically, while she almost always abandoned her lovers, three of her four legal husbands left her. Yet most of her ex-lovers and all of her former husbands except the one whom she left remained friendly with her afterward. In later years she did not enjoy talking about her career, but she relished discussing her romances. "When I can't sleep, I don't count sheep. I count lovers," she said. "And by the time I reach thirty-eight or thirty-nine I'm asleep."

Miriam was a complicated woman, a mixture of thistledown and steel wool. She had wit, warmth and charm. Strangely though, an observation that would amuse her on one occasion would turn her into a foot-stamping, ashtray-throwing, door-slamming virago on another.

These outbursts, plus her relentless attempts at scene-stealing—especially when she thought the director untalented or weak enough to allow her to get away with it—quickly earned her a reputation for being temperamental. But as fan magazine writer Delight Evans put it at the time, "Hollywood likes dangerous women," and Miriam enjoyed a reputation in 1934 for being one of the screen's most difficult and dangerous actresses.

In the autumn of 1933 Miriam decided to return to Broadway in Owen Davis' *Jezebel*, starring in a part originally written for Tallulah Bankhead. When Tallulah fell ill, Miriam took over, confident that she could turn Davis' ramshackle melodrama into a tour de force. In Julie, the central character, Miriam was acting her favorite role—a fascinating bitch who reveals unsuspected nobility during the third act. As a real Southern belle Miriam felt she could draw upon her past to bring values to the play that were lacking in the manuscript.

Miriam's roots extended beyond the Confederacy to the very founding of the United States of America. On her mother's side—the only side that counted with Miriam, as with so many actresses, including Ginger Rogers—a relative had signed the Declaration of Independence. And Miriam's great-grandfather combined his plantation with those of three other owners to incorporate as Bainbridge, Georgia. His daughter Mildred married Ralph Cutter, and they became the parents of twins Ellen and John. After attending the New England Conservatory in Boston, Ellen married Homer A. Hopkins, and they settled in a brick house on Gordon Street in Savannah, Georgia, where a first child, Ruby, was born in 1900 and a second, Ellen Miriam, on October 18, 1902.

The diminutive Ellen Cutter Hopkins had a powerful personality and a dominating nature that caused trouble in the marriage almost immediately. After each row Ellen would gather up Miriam and Ruby to make the short trip to Bainbridge and Grandma Mildred's.

When Miriam was seven and Ruby nine, the visit became permanent. Homer Hopkins vanished from his daughters' lives. How deeply this rejection affected the seven-year-old no one realized. But once in old age, during a moment of insight, Miriam told her agent that in looking back it seemed that all her nonstop talking, all her achievements as an actress, all the houses she had bought and furnished had been unconscious attempts to show Daddy what a marvel she was and to bring the family together again.

"Mims was the prettiest child you could ever imagine. Golden hair, very pink cheeks and blue-blue eyes. She was like my private doll. She was so cunning-looking the other kids would pull her curls and things, and every time they touched her I'd go over and knock them down," Ruby recalls. "It got so mothers wouldn't allow their children to have anything to do with me. Some people said Mama ought to send me to reform school. Mama blamed Mims, but it was really Mama's fault for dressing Mims in all those dainty dresses with sashes and bows like that."

Miriam's memories were different. She recalled singing in the boys' choir at St. John's Episcopal Church and climbing Spanish-moss-draped evergreens to watch the blacks stage their baptisms in the Flint River, and she remembered palling around with Clara Murphee and Caroline Battle. With their help she launched her theatrical career by writing, staging and acting in plays in the woods behind Massey school.

By the time Miriam was thirteen Ellen Hopkins' twin brother, John, had accumulated $1,000,000 and willingly assumed support of the Hopkinses. So Ellen packed up the children and headed north. They soon arrived in Syracuse, New York, where Tom Hopkins, Homer's brother, headed the Geology Department at Syracuse University. "Mother was very ambitious for us to go to the university," Ruby recalls. "So we went on this visit to meet Uncle Tom and Aunt Bess. Uncle Tom played the fiddle, and Miriam and I thought he was adorable. We were both so lively I guess we got on Aunt Bess' nerves—because she began to find fault all the time. So even though Uncle Tom wanted us to live with them and Mother thought it was a lovely idea, Aunt Bess didn't think it would work. She was very frank about that."

Taking her cue, Ellen packed her offspring back to New York, where Ruby joined the World War I farmerettes and Miriam, much to her chagrin, enrolled as a junior in public school. Near the end of the year she suffered an attack of appendicitis and was operated on. Returning to school, she fainted twice while climbing the stairs. When her mother turned up to request that Miriam be allowed to ride the elevator, permission was denied. A terrible scene followed, ending with Miriam and her mother stamping out, vowing never to set foot in that terrible place again.

Because of the fainting episodes and the scene with the principal, Miriam spent her senior year at Goddard Seminary, a private preparatory school in Barre, Vermont. At Goddard she was one of three girls to sport windblown bobs, which scandalized more conservative students. "Miriam stood out," says a former classmate, now Mrs. Everett Chase. "She was a little spoiled, a little vain but very attractive.

She had bright blue eyes and wore her blond hair loose. She had a green dress and from the back looked like a full-blooming dandelion walking down the street.''

Characteristically, in addition to the regular academic course, Miriam signed up for piano and voice as part of her self-improvement program. Also characteristically, she cast about for the likeliest-looking young man and chose as her boyfriend Royce Pitkin, who was later to return to Goddard as president, after the seminary had been converted into a college.

At Goddard Miriam concentrated on extracurricular activity. Early on she entered a public-speaking contest and won the $2 first prize. "The girl who got second was my roommate," Mrs. Chase recalls. "She felt it unfair for a newcomer to turn up and carry off the prize." To make matters worse, Miriam also snagged plum roles in the senior class play and Goddard's Fifty Year Pageant. In the latter she took the part of the Girl Graduate—representative of the school's finest flower. In the former—a comedy with the title *The Fascinating Fanny Brown*—she played the feminine lead, Dorothy Dudley. The play was a variation on *Charley's Aunt* in which Dorothy's boyfriend invents a rival for his affections, said Fanny Brown, to make Dorothy jealous. Dorothy confounds him by persuading her brother to get into drag and impersonate the nonexistent Fanny. The *Goddard Record* noted, "Miriam Hopkins acted the part of Dorothy Dudley, and it could not have been done better."

In her official biographies Miriam claimed that after graduating from Goddard, she studied writing at Syracuse University. The registrar's records show no evidence that she ever attended college, but the story probably grew out of her earlier visit to her uncle Tom.

It was another uncle who played the most important part in her choice of career. His name was Dixie Hines, and he ran the International Press Bureau at 1400 Broadway. He was a tall, gangling man, whose flowing hair, bow ties and horn-rimmed spectacles were his trademark along Broadway.

His dust-ridden office was cluttered with autographed photographs, press clippings, stacks of old newspapers, scrapbooks and posters, and his clients were some of the most glamorous names in entertainment— actors, dancers, singers, designers and writers. For Dixie Hines, in spite of his company's grandiose name, was a well-known Broadway press agent.

Since Dixie was a bachelor, he often invited Ellen Hopkins and her vivacious offspring to enliven his dinners. He also frequently included them on the guest lists for his parties. Ruby, by this time, was working at Macy's, demonstrating toys. Miriam held a series of short-lived jobs which she acquired through bluff and promptly lost through ineptitude. Both girls were interested in theatrical careers, but Dixie assured them it was no place for ladies.

Dixie, who was a renowned soft touch, had a number of clients who neglected to pay him. When he complained of this one evening, Miriam piped up to suggest, "Why not let Ruby and me take it out in trade?" Thereafter the girls were clothed by a famous theatrical designer. Miriam took acting and diction from a Shakespearean actress, Roselle Knott. Both girls studied at Vestoff Serova's Russian Ballet School.

In 1920, when Miriam announced she was going to try out for a Broadway play, Dixie lectured her and Ruby, saying he'd rather see them dead and buried than on the stage, that it was a terrible life for well-bred young women and that if he had had any idea either of them would consider an acting career, he would never have allowed the lessons. "In Uncle Dixie's mind there was no thought we'd use this training," Ruby says. "To him it was just nice for gentle-born Southern girls to develop their—their little assets."

When Miriam defiantly began making the rounds, she received chilly receptions wherever Dixie had passed the word to discourage her. Finally, in 1921, she heard of a production with songs by Irving Berlin that Hassard Short was about to stage at the new Music Box Theater. So Miriam put on her prettiest dress, betook herself to rehearsal and told the man at the door that Short had told her to come around.

Inside, Miriam waited while a man she assumed was the dance director moved the girls around the stage. When he called a break, Miriam bounced up to him and announced Hassard Short had sent her. "He grinned from ear to ear," Miriam recalled later, "and said, 'Well, you're kind of a cute-looking little trick, young lady, but I've never seen you before in my life. I'm Hassard Short.'"

Using her most flirtatious manner and a voice dripping with a Georgia accent, Miriam explained Uncle Dixie's attitude. "It's not fair," she said with a pout. "He doesn't think a lady should go on the stage. But since I'm here, won't you at least see what I can do?"

Short agreed. Miriam talked a song, performed a little ballet and demonstrated some tap steps. "Lord knows how long I'd have gone on if Mr. Short hadn't stopped me," she said later. "He was charmed. And that's how I became one of Irving Berlin's Eight Silver Notes, at forty dollars a week."

Almost at once she caught the eye of a young-man-about-town, Bennett Cerf, who was beginning to make a name for himself in publishing circles. Cerf gave her a big rush, and soon the two were inseparable. Ellen Hopkins looked upon her daughter's career with a benign eye, but she viewed Miriam's suitor with alarm. As a daughter of the Old South she felt little more kindly toward Jews than toward blacks. But Miriam had escaped the South early enough to deride her mother's objections to the charming young Cerf.

She had not left early enough, however, not to develop a lifelong aversion to obscenity. And since she customarily wore navy-blue frocks with white collars and cuffs, the other chorus girls referred to her as Miss Priss, delighting in shocking her with dirty talk and jokes.

One evening one of the chief offenders, whom Miriam had told off frequently, showed up early in the communal dressing room. She was obviously in great discomfort. Miriam was already there, and the new arrival confided that she had come directly from the recovery cot of an abortion mill because if she missed a performance, she would be fired. Miriam, to the girl's astonishment, offered to accompany her home to stay the night and also suggested telling the company manager that the girl had pulled a ligament in her leg and ask him to allow them to switch places. It was done, and at that performance Miriam gave it her all from down front, stage right, instead of the back row. "So you see," Miriam said in telling the story, "it wasn't entirely altruistic."

Because Miriam regarded her early years in the theater as boringly average, she seldom stuck to the truth. She claimed to have fallen downstairs during the senior play at Goddard and sprained her ankle so badly that she had to finish the performance sitting down. She also invented a story about being hired to head a South America-bound ballet company. On her way to the passport office, she said, she tripped, fell and broke her ankle, which ended her dancing career. Another fabrication was that she had been a promising writer, a client of Elizabeth Marbury, the well-known literary agent specializing in Continental playwrights.

Actually, Miriam played stock at $100 a week for George M. Cohan and joined a Shubert unit—vaudeville plus a tab musical-comedy production—touring to the West Coast and back. When that was finished, she signed to support May Tully in a vaudeville sketch. Her first tentative step in establishing herself as a vivid personality on Broadway came when she appeared as Juliette in Harlan Thompson's musical *Little Jessie James* at the Longacre Theater on August 15, 1923. It ran for 453 performances. Miriam's reviews were complimentary enough, but as was often the case, her offstage personality left the more lasting impression on associates. Harlan Thompson's widow, Marian Spitzer Thompson, who among other accomplishments wrote the theatrical history *The Palace*, recalls, "She had the most charm when she wanted to of anyone I've ever known. When I read *Gone with the Wind*, I immediately thought of her. She was Scarlett before the book was written.

"Every man was crazy about her. She had this charm and then, in a very special way, a great deal of sex appeal. Men felt that she was kind of unreachable—and I think that's one of the most alluring, magnetizing things there is. That's always a big challenge, and somehow the challenge often turns into enormous desire."

Despite the attention Miriam received in her first musical comedy role, she aspired to straight drama. Nothing could be a better illustration for opportunities in the theater at that period than her career during the remainder of the 1920s. She played in seventeen Broadway shows, one London production, was fired during out-of-town tryouts at least a couple of times and made a number of appearances in stock. Not until 1925 did she make her dramatic debut on Broadway. In March of that year she replaced Claudette Colbert during the out-of-town tryout of *Puppets*. The show, which opened late in the month, earned her personal notices of the kind usually reserved for fictional heroines. In the *Telegram*, for instance, Bernard Simon wrote, "A slim little girl with a head of thick blond hair, thin legs and a beautiful voice—whose previous experience on Broadway had been confined to musical shows—came onstage at the Selwyn Theater last night and ran away with the show. The girl was Miriam Hopkins." Nevertheless, the play collapsed after fifty-seven performances. Yet there were so many Broadway productions then that before the end of the year she had managed to appear in both *Lovely Lady* and *The Matinee Girl*.

In the same year Miriam met the first of her four husbands. He was leading man Brandon Peters, who had made his Broadway debut in 1925 with William Farnum in *The Buccaneer* and had spent the summer with the famous George Cukor-George Kondolf Stock Company in Rochester, New York. Peters was a good-natured, uncomplicated young man who was overpowered by Miriam's forceful personality.

They were married on May 11, 1926, and had barely set up housekeeping before Miriam was selected for the plum role of Lorelei Lee in the dramatization of Anita Loos' best-selling *Gentlemen Prefer Blondes*. Very shortly, trouble developed. Miss Loos and her husband, John Emerson, concluded Miriam projected too much logical intelligence for the flibbertigibbet Lorelei and fired her. Miriam turned her failure into a lucky break: she almost at once landed the part of the socialite Sondra Finchley in *An American Tragedy*, which ran for 216 performances. Through her performance she recruited the first members of the Miriam Hopkins cult.

Her marriage—no more satisfactory than her mother's had been—had a shorter run. Peters, unable to obtain a Broadway engagement, was seldom home. When he was there, Miriam paid the bills. "It was an impossible situation, because she was such a practical little thing," Miriam's sister, Ruby, says. "I remember her telling that on her birthday he came home with this big box of American Beauty roses and she asked where he got them. He said, 'Well, dear, I got them at the florist's.' She asked whether he'd charged them, and he said yes, and she told him, 'Well, that account is in my name, and believe me, we're so broke now I cannot afford to send myself American Beauties, so take them right back.'" The unfortunate Peters did just that, but soon afterward accepted another stock engagement, and both understood the marriage was over.

Separated from her husband, Miriam quickly became involved with dramatist Patrick Kearney, who had adapted Theodore Dreiser's *An American Tragedy* for producer Horace Liveright. Kearney was the type of man Miriam found fascinating. An unpredictable Irishman, he shared her love of poetry, theater and high drama in private life. An Ohioan, he had arrived in New York in 1920 to work in Famous-Players Lasky's publicity department. His friends included Eugene O'Neill, novelist Floyd Dell, producer-publisher Liveright and other literary and theatrical figures. In his spare time Kearney wrote one-act plays for the Washington Square Players and had also written a full-length original play, *A Man's Man*, which had been produced on Broadway. By the time he fell in love with Miriam he had had two unhappy marriages. She found his conversation about Yeats and Joyce and other Irishmen fascinating. She was infatuated and became, in her phrase, "his spiritual echo." "We led a hectic literary life," she said. "On Thursdays we sat around Theodore Dreiser's, chewing the toughest rags a youngster ever set her teeth in. On Saturdays we went to novelist Ernest Boyd's to discuss the Irish Renaissance." On some Mondays they met and talked theater with Eugene O'Neill. Miriam loved Kearney, but she had no intention of marrying him. They continued their relationship after she left *Tragedy* to appear in Zoe Akins' *Thou Desperate Pilot* during the spring of 1927. After it closed, she accepted an engagement at the Four Cohans' Theater in Chicago, where she secretly filed suit to divorce Peters, a fact she kept from Kearney.

She liked to be able to point to a husband whenever Kearney begged her to marry him.

Upon her return from Chicago she decided to break up with the playwright, and Kearney, who had been drinking excessively, terrorized her with a razor, insisting that he was going to slash her throat and then his own. Kearney's threats and her anguished pleading aroused neighbors, who summoned the police. Before the officers arrived, Kearney passed out, and Miriam managed to break away. She went directly to a friend, writer Ward Morehouse, who unaccountably chose to hide the distraught girl in a maternity hospital in Harlem. She remained there until it was time for her to entrain for Rochester, where she had been engaged to play leads with the reorganized and renamed Cukor-Kondolf Lyceum Players.

By the time she returned from stock she was set for the short-lived *Garden of Eden* (twenty-three performances), then went into one of her bigger successes, *Excess Baggage*. In this play the heroine, having to decide between becoming a star and being a dutiful wife, chooses the latter. Miriam, too, had faced such an alternative with Brandon Peters. "For me to make that choice took real acting," she remarked about her role in *Excess Baggage*. (In later years, she denied ever having been married to Peters. Her adopted son was to learn of the marriage only when he read her obituary.)

Miriam met the love of her life—Austin Parker, whom everyone called Billy—in 1928. Parker had come to New York in 1916, starting his career as a reporter on the New York *Tribune*. During World War I he had enlisted in the French Army, become a much-decorated sergeant pilot in the Lafayette Escadrille and flown for the sultan of Morocco against the Riffs. Along the way Parker had married short-story writer Phyllis Duganne. Upon his return to the United States he had taken a job as a reporter on the New York *World*. During his work for that paper, his short stories had begun to appear in the *Saturday Evening Post*, *Cosmopolitan* and *Liberty*. At the same time, he had started to try his hand as a playwright.

Like many men of his generation, Parker was influenced by F. Scott Fitzgerald's achievements and life-style. Parker's adventurous background and his Fitzgeraldean affectations made him seem highly sophisticated to Miriam. Since he was several years older than she was, their romantic attachment was buttressed by a surrogate father-daughter relationship that made her speak kindly of him all her life.

Their marriage provided colorful news copy. Miriam, for reasons not altogether clear, had filed suit to divorce Brandon Peters in Chicago instead of New York. Then, on June 2, 1928, disregarding her attorney's warning not to wed until the decree was signed, she and Parker impetuously drove to Newark, New Jersey, where they were secretly married by a justice of the peace. Or so they thought. The story broke in the Newark *Star Eagle* four days later. Before they sailed on the *De Grasse*, Parker was forced to confirm the news. Her rashness caused the Chicago divorce judge to threaten to withhold the final decree, and the Hearst press ran a cartoon showing Miriam being torn from the arms of her bridegroom upon their arrival in France.

The Parkers, unperturbed, spent four glorious months in Europe, where, according to friends, Parker formed Miriam's mind and taught her to appreciate good paintings, excellent wines and great literature. "He opened the world to her," her sister says.

By the time they returned to the United States in October, the issue of her divorce from Peters had still not been settled. But Miriam and Billy Parker took a lighthearted view of such mundane matters. Speaking for both (probably one of the few times the voluble Miriam allowed anyone to talk for her), Parker said, "Thank heavens we are not lawyers. Thank goodness we have nothing to do with the law—that is, any more than is necessary. Our marriage is quite all right so far as we are concerned. We are satisfied. Who should care?"

They moved into a picturesque stone house in Greenwich Village and proceeded to found a salon for good talk and general merriment. There, in the third-floor studio, Miriam scattered persian rugs and black-and-silver floor cushions to supplement the deep-cushioned divan and low armchairs. On the far side of the room she placed a grand piano especially for their friend Ernst Lubitsch, who would sit, cigar in mouth, in front of the keyboard, playing Chopin for hours at a time. Not far away there was a backgammon set. At the time Miriam told a reporter she'd rather play backgammon than breathe.

During their first months on Waverly Place Miriam, unemployed, with her savings spent during their honeymoon, was forced to live on her husband's earnings as a short-story writer. Once a week their bootlegger called to deliver gin for the parties. Sensing money was tight, he confided on one occasion that he had "something special, real special—sparkling Burgundy."

Parker fixed him with a cold eye and snapped, "Sparkling Burgundy! We wouldn't wash our dog in it!"

Not that the regular guests—Lubitsch, Dorothy Parker, Alan Campbell, Anita Loos, Ben Wassan, Theodore Dreiser, George Oppenheimer, Beatrice and Don Stewart, Bennett Cerf, Katharine (later Kay)

Francis—or most of their other friends would have minded what they served. There was always exciting talk about politics, acting, writing and art—and there was gossip. In this milieu Miriam's interests were deepened and developed.

In February, 1929, she secured a brief engagement in *Flight*, of which the breathless reviewer for the New York *American* wrote, "For sheer daring, her statement that she was not aware which one [of her lovers] had summoned the feathered visitor has seldom been equaled on the American stage." Even so, audiences were small, and the play quickly collapsed. Miriam at once went into rehearsal for the Theatre Guild's *The Camel Through the Needle's Eye*, which opened April 16 and eked out seventy-two performances.

She then returned to Rochester to help Cukor and Kondolf launch their new company at the Temple Theater by re-creating her Broadway success *Excess Baggage*. (Bette Davis was in the supporting cast.)

In September Miriam was off to London to appear opposite C. Aubrey Smith in his starring vehicle *Bachelor Father*. "It was decidedly Miss Hopkins's evening, and if *Bachelor Father* draws expected crowds, hers will be the greatest share of the glory," the New York *Sun* correspondent wired.

Miriam didn't tarry long. By February, 1930, she was again on Broadway, this time in *Ritzy*, opposite Ernest Truex. While appearing in it, she was offered the part of Kolonika in *Lysistrata* at $700 a week. Miriam read the play and was disappointed in Aristophanes. Despite hard times and curtailed production, she told the management, "This is a tiny part. Why don't you give it to the girl who's the leader of the chorus, cut me out entirely and save my salary?" They persuaded her to accept the role and enlarged it by taking speeches from other characters and inventing comedy business for her. "It's actually all been written by Aristophanes, but rearranged for my benefit," she explained.

Critics generally praised star Violet Kemble-Cooper, who, they said, dominated the proceedings except when Miriam took over. In those moments Miriam's sheer joy in playing the role communicated itself to the audience.

"I try to be simply natural," Miriam said of her approach to the characterization. "For I figure she's a very real girl with strong impulses. . . . It's a lot of fun playing a hoyden because it's a comedy role. And in so many productions I've been in heavy parts, usually roles in which I was about to become a mother and was going around yelling and having hysterics for the second act curtain."

During the run of *Lysistrata* in New York Miriam's acting aroused the enthusiasm of a Paramount Pictures representative, and on June 25 she signed a contract with Paramount Publix Corporation to begin filming *The Best People* (subsequently retitled *Fast and Loose*) at $1,000 a week for four weeks plus $500 a week for participating in advance "rehearsals and/or tests of vocal recording and photography."

Miriam filmed during the day at the Astoria studios and played at night in *Lysistrata*. Among others, Claudette Colbert, Ginger Rogers, Carole Lombard and Fredric March were already at work on the Astoria lot, and Miriam was not about to arrive at the gate in Billy Parker's beat-up old car. "I hired a taxi driver to be my chauffeur the first day," she once told columnist Erskine Johnson. "I was going to do this thing in style. We rolled up to the studio, and the dear boob didn't even know enough to hop out and open the door for me. I had to tell him with the gateman listening."

Miriam hid her insecurity and embarrassment by immediately informing everyone up to and including studio head Adolph Zukor that she wasn't sure she was interested in working in the movies. Zukor mildly replied to wait to see how she registered on film before worrying about that. But from the first she hated rising at six in the morning in order to be on the set by nine, as well as other rigors actresses were expected to undergo. Her distaste was reinforced on the first day's shooting. She and leading man Charles Starrett appeared in a swimming scene. Miriam promptly caught a cold and developed an ear infection. Recovered, she finished the film during the last week in August and gratefully concentrated on the stage, beginning rehearsals for *His Majesty's Car*, which represented a personal success for her but lasted only briefly.

Her film debut in *Fast and Loose*, in which Carole Lombard also appeared, earned mixed notices. "*Fast and Loose*," Al Hughes wisecracked, "was born in Long Island and died all over the country." Mourdant Hall of the New York *Times* praised the picture as "an amusing feature, with competent direction and clever acting. . . . Miss Hopkins is most pleasing as the impudent and charming Marion." Irene Thirer told the mass circulation audiences of the New York *Daily News* that Miriam combined the features of Esther Ralston with the hair of Greta Nissen. "But her voice and pantomimic ability are what will earn more screen roles for her. She certainly has a comedy flare [sic]!" *Variety*, assessing her national appeal, concluded, "This stage artiste plays tic-tac-toe with the camera, sometimes winning, sometimes losing, but the merit of her performance will be universally obvious." All in all not a triumph, but not a bad beginning either.

In a year when most Americans were wondering where they could find any kind of work Miriam was besieged with job offers. She signed with producer Bela Blau to appear as the little chorus girl who is jilted by her protector in *The Affairs of Anatol*. The play, which requires five distaff stars, opened on January 15, 1931, to a friendly reception but proved too costly for the Depression-deflated box office. Miriam's rewards were a glowing set of reviews and a lifelong friendship with producer-director Henry C. "Hank" Potter, who was then Blau's stage manager.

The failure was no hardship on Miriam since Paramount at once offered her $1,500 a week to appear in both the English and French versions of *The Smiling Lieutenant*, in which she would work with that master of light comedy Ernst Lubitsch, playing the ugly-duckling princess whom Maurice Chevalier accidentally marries. Miriam hesitated. She still felt an allegiance to the stage, and she worried whether her French accent was good enough to match those of two French-speaking stars, Chevalier and Claudette Colbert. "But zey weel think eet charming," Chevalier assured her, and she was persuaded to try. "You never feel lack of an audience when Mr. Lubitsch directs you," she bubbled to an interviewer during filming. "For he will, if he likes what you're doing, call the electricians, the prop boys—anyone within hailing distance—and say, 'That's fine. Clap hands.' "

Her marriage to Billy Parker had at this time begun to come apart, partly because of Chevalier's advances, which she found irresistible. As for Parker, he realized that he had been more accurate than he knew when he had compared her to good champagne. Now he added that like champagne, too much effervescence gave a man a headache. At this point he had been hired by film producer Walter Wanger to combine his stage play *Week-End* with a film script about the Wall Street crash which Lois Long, of *Vogue* and *The New Yorker*, had written.

"We soon discovered his play had nothing to do with the crash, so we got full of champagne and started blocking out a new script," Miss Long recalled many years later. "That's when I met Miriam. I thought she was a bitch. She went around saying—I was married to Peter Arno and was getting beaten up for nothing—saying, wasn't it nice Billy was having an affair with such a nice girl! Oh, my God, I thought Arno would hear about it. He was trying out a play in Philadelphia. She kept repeating it. Then at Tony's, the night before Billy left for California, he said, 'You know, we're getting all the credit from Miriam for having this affair. What about it?' I said I couldn't, I was faithful to Arno in New York, but I would be coming to California a couple of months later. He said that was no good. He had someone there. So the next day he left on the train, and shortly I got a wire, 'Meet me in St. Louis.' "

Before leaving New York, Billy Parker, who had had so much influence on Miriam's development, talked over their marital situation with her, and they decided to end the marriage. "I remember the day they split," Hank Potter says. "Miriam called me from the Algonquin and said, 'Come around, because I'm feeling blue and we're all here drinking champagne.' I went over, and half a dozen people had flocked to her immediately. I think Billy left her. That's why Billy's analogy to champagne is quite accurate, because it bubbles like crazy and when it goes flat, you throw it away. It happened to her more than once. I think she exhausted her husbands. I don't mean sexually, it was just too much vitality to live with."

Miriam's initial giddy, high-spirited reaction to Hollywood in May, 1931, is preserved in a letter she wrote to Ward Morehouse, who included it in his book *Forty-Five Minutes Past Eight*.

Well, I'm here. I never knew sunshine could be so gloomy, or people so funny, or architecture so grotesque. ———— has an Italian villa glued to the side of a mountain with two dining rooms and five baths and one of those cathedral effects for a living room. Every time I enter I feel like dropping to my knees and saying prayers. There are forty-three electric lights in the living room (I just counted them). Every time I see them lit I think of Bee Lillie's line when she was riding up on the hill and looked down at all the Hollywood lights and said: "Yes, they're beautiful but I can't help thinking some day they'll all run together and spell Marion Davies."

I haven't been to the studio yet. Nobody seems interested. They called up and said greetings but fortunately I wasn't in and I've forgotten to call back. The pay checks continue every week plus two hundred extra for California expenses. . . .

That young actor we were talking about is a great success and is going to live here forever. He owns one polo pony, a darling brownish one, and is buying four more. Every afternoon John Cromwell, Jimmie Gleason, Will Rogers (what is the matter with this typewriter? It must have gone Hollywood like its owner) and a bunch of them play polo at the country club. The house—pardon, villa—is filled with mallets, helmets, etc. Then, of course, there is the tennis and the golf—oh, we're just too sporty for words.

The other day I went to a typical beach party. A little French girl named ――――― slapped ―――――'s face five times. He picked her up by the seat of the pants and threw her out of the house on the beach. ――――― sat about in nothing but trunks, tiny ones, and he has five rolls of fat about his middle. He helped give Mamoulian a swimming lesson. Mamoulian is going back in a couple of months to direct a play. He is interested in three. One is the something or other in Vienna that the Lunts are going to do and one is a new one by Sam Behrman. And at that beach party, June Walker sat around looking healthy and feeling frail. Jeffrey (Geoffrey Kerr) came in from tennis and was very attentive. They call each other Lovey. After supper we wandered over to Selznick's and sat down in the private bar. Sam Behrman said he's going back soon. Dashiell Hammett, long and slim with silvery gray hair, sat about all evening but I never heard him speak. They call him Dash.

――――― flirted all evening with a cute little trick who was all eyelashes. In the center of it all were ――――― and his wife on a sofa with terrified looks on their faces. When things got a little quiet ――――― rushed out on the beach and rolled in the sand in her pink lace pajamas, screaming at the top of her voice. I went out to her but got bored and left her, but even at the bar I heard her crying, "I'm a fool, I'm a fool." The last I saw of her a drunken juvenile in flannels was carrying her out in his arms. He collapsed and reached to open the screen door but something happened and he dropped her. And at that point I fell off the wagon and had a large brandy and soda.

Despite her amusement at Hollywood, Miriam herself soon adopted some of its behavior patterns. Buoyed up by her initial success in films, and realizing that if it hadn't been for the advent of sound, no studio would have considered signing a twenty-eight-year-old, she was alternately arrogant and terrified. Before the West Coast premiere of *The Smiling Lieutenant*, fearing those who had not seen her on Broadway or in *Fast and Loose* would think her as homely as the princess she played,* she suggested abrogating her contract. Scoring even better than Claudette Colbert at the premiere, she instantly became the self-assured new girl in town.

She leased Garbo's Santa Monica beach house and announced on July 28 that she and Billy Parker were separating. "We've been off again, on again for the last year. We couldn't make it," she said. "Quite naturally, we just had to call it off. We're still very good friends, and neither of us plans any divorce business."

*Ignoring the fact that she was pretty and charming by the end of the movie.

Paramount, simultaneously, began building up her name. Items about her flooded fan magazines and newspaper columns. Fillers were cranked out. Fashion spreads were set up and shot. Interviews were arranged. Paramount revealed that she would work with Lubitsch again. Although Miriam's name was in the papers almost daily, nothing was definitely set.

After five weeks of leisure Miriam could no longer tolerate inactivity. She went to director Marion Gering and auditioned for the role of the nightclub singer in *24 Hours* with Clive Brook and Kay Francis. In the midst of her second song, "Don't Blame Me," she forgot the lyrics and burst into heartbroken sobs. The startled Gering complimented her, saying he had never witnessed such a display of raw emotion. The role was hers. The film, released in the fall of 1931, was undistinguished.

By insisting upon making *24 Hours*, Miriam committed a serious error. Paramount had under contract a small group of stars, including Marlene Dietrich, for whom vehicles were written to highlight their assets and conceal their weaknesses. Originally, Miriam was included among the elite. The studio intended to stress her versatility and to assign her only to directors of the calibre of Lubitsch and Rouben Mamoulian. But by volunteering for the commonplace *24 Hours*, Miriam demoted herself. If she was willing to play Rosie Dugan, Paramount could reasonably expect her to accept their assembly-line casting practices. Like Kay Francis, Carole Lombard, Claudette Colbert and other promising contractees, she must be ready to step in wherever she was needed.

But that fall Miriam made a film that helped rectify the harm she had done her reputation. Producer-director Rouben Mamoulian called her in and said he had a part for her in *Dr. Jekyll and Mr. Hyde*. He gave a script to her and told her he wanted her to play the cabaret singer, Ivy. She returned next day to say that she preferred Muriel, the conventional good girl. "I told her I was sorry about that; that she would make no impression as Muriel," Mamoulian recalls. "But I have never found it acceptable to force an actor to play a part against his will. An actor must have enthusiasm for what he is going to do, or you cannot get a good performance. So I said, 'Fine, if you want to play Muriel, you have Muriel. But Ivy would have made you a star.' She said, Thank you, and started to leave, then she came back. 'Let's talk,' she said. 'I don't want to talk,' I told her. 'I'll have no trouble finding an actress for Ivy. Any actress can make a big hit in it.' She asked if I really thought so. I assured her I did, so she said, 'All right, I'll do it your way.' "

By doing it Mamoulian's way, Miriam heightened the impression upon release of *Dr. Jekyll and Mr. Hyde* in January, 1932, that she was an actress of unique quality. Two weeks later she was seen in *Two Kinds of Women*, the screen version of Robert E. Sherwood's *This Is New York*. In this film, Miriam was miscast as the South Dakota senator's daughter who gets entangled with gangsters, and she reinforced the impression that she was an uneven performer with her negligible contributions to *Dancers in the Dark* and *The World and the Flesh*. But in November she was teamed with Herbert Marshall and Kay Francis in Ernst Lubitsch's *Trouble in Paradise*. Miriam and Marshall played two fanciful crooks who work as typist and personal secretary to handsome widow Kay Francis, whom they intend to bilk out of her fortune. This frothy story with its stylized characters presented Miriam at her most engaging. It was Lubitsch's favorite among his directorial efforts, and the fact that the sophisticated German director regarded Miriam so highly and elicited such a polished performance from her erased memories of her mediocre work in her previous three pictures.

The most important man of all entered Miriam's life about this time. Early in 1932 Miriam, who was single again, visited the Evanston Cradle Society in Illinois, quixotically taking along the hard-drinking Dorothy Parker as a character witness, and made arrangements to adopt a child. She chose a five-day-old boy whom she christened Michael Hopkins. When all the problems involved in arranging for a single parent to obtain the child had been solved, Miriam, in a typical Hopkins gesture, called Ben Wassan, a writer's agent who was a devoted friend, and asked if he would run out to Chicago to pick up the infant for her. Wassan did.

Much to Miriam's amusement people noted Michael's blond hair and blue eyes, so much like hers, and concluded that she was his natural mother. Nor did her answers in the press do anything to quell the rumors. Questioned as to her motives, Miriam turned off queries by contending she didn't know *why* she had adopted a child. "There was no sense of Mission in Life attached to it," she said. "I'm not passionately maternal. I didn't yearn for the patter of little feet. I wasn't lonely. I don't have time to be lonely. I just felt, I suppose, that it was nicer to have a baby in the house than not to have a baby in the house. . . . So I adopted a baby."

Such statements, calculated or not, gave her a growing reputation for eccentricity. Among actors she had become increasingly notorious for her "little tricks" of upstaging her fellow players. Even her good friend Kay Francis complained that in one episode she had been forced to eat almost two dozen eggs before the director could get a take with her face toward the camera—and it was supposed to be her scene. Writers on Miriam's pictures were bombarded by notes suggesting alterations in plot and dialogue. They called her Helpful Hopkins behind her back. Many directors were overwhelmed by her suggestions— which, when rejected, could cause Miriam to throw a tantrum that ended with her stalking off the set and retreating to her beach house until whatever displeased her had been rectified.

Her flights from Hollywood were both impulsive and compulsive. While removing her makeup after finishing the final scene of *Dr. Jekyll and Mr. Hyde*, she was seized by an overwhelming urge to visit New York. Without pausing to think, she phoned B. P. Schulberg, head of productions, and said she must see him. Told by his secretary that Schulberg was free for a few minutes but then would be busy all day, she rushed to his office, still wearing character makeup, her hair screwed up like an Irish washerwoman. "I've got to go to New York," she told him, "if only for a few days." The astonished Schulberg granted permission without question. "I think he was so taken by surprise by my weird appearance that he couldn't say anything else," she explained.

By late 1932 Paramount was reeling from the Depression, in addition to complicated internal problems. The result was that Schulberg was replaced as production head by Emanuel Cohen. With the disappearance of Schulberg, who had brought Miriam and other New York actors, including Sylvia Sidney, Claudette Colbert and Ruth Chatterton, to the lot, her insecurities increased. It was then that she began building a reputation as "the town's most ferocious tigress."

Miriam made four pictures for Paramount and one on loan-out after Cohen's arrival. In May, 1933, she was seen in the title role of *The Story of Temple Drake*, a free translation of William Faulkner's *Sanctuary*. As the wild society girl who scorns a proper dance to go riding with a drunken playboy and who inadvertently becomes involved with a sinister gangster, Miriam gave a multifaceted performance, suggesting both a horror of and an almost subliminal enjoyment of her degradation. In the 1930s the film received mixed reviews and earned its profits because of attack on it by professional bluestockings. Yet it did much to establish Miriam as an emotional actress.

In her second film that year she was lent to MGM for *The Stranger's Return*, in which Phil Stong seems to have attempted a naturalistic retelling of King Lear set in rural Iowa. It did little more for Miriam than she did for it. Her third release was *Design for Living*, which united her with Lubitsch for the last time. Afterward Lubitsch repeated his opinion that Miriam was on the way to becoming the greatest actress on the screen. Thirty-five years later, upon Lubitsch's death, Howard Thompson of the New York *Times* quoted her: "Ah, Lubitsch . . . there was only one of him. . . . No, he didn't help my career. . . . He made my career."

Design for Living, highly regarded by film buffs today, opened at the Criterion Theater on November 23, 1933, on a two-performances-a-day schedule, but movie patrons waited for it to come, at popular prices, to the cavernous Times Square Paramount—which is where it was to be found on January 1, 1934.

During 1934 Miriam's last two films under her contract were released: *All of Me*, in which she appeared with Fredric March and George Raft, and *She Loves Me Not*, with Bing Crosby and Kitty Carlisle. They stand as an example of what can happen to an actress working out contractual obligations. The breaks were given to Raft, Crosby and Kitty Carlisle, performers whom the studios were building, while the erstwhile golden girl was carelessly photographed and shunted to the side—even at the expense of the form of the films. Looking back, assessing this first phase of her career, Miriam commented, "When I started, I was so excited with myself—making fifteen hundred dollars a week and not knowing what to do with it. I think I was self-centered and selfish, but it was a natural youthful thing."

At the time, however, she could hardly wait to return East to appear in *Jezebel*. It opened out of town in rough shape. *Bone.*, in *Variety*, observed, "In her present vehicle, these assets [vivacity and sparkle] register 'No sales,' partly due to the remoteness of the stage from the audience and partly due to the use of half lighting which had her reading lines in the shadows. Aside from this, Miss Hopkins does a first-rate job."

The technical problems were quickly remedied, and Miriam's hopes were high as the show moved to New York for previews. Response in Manhattan was dour. At one preview, during intermission, Donald Ogden Stewart bet Miriam's and Ginger's agent (and Miriam's lover), Leland Hayward, a case of champagne that the melodrama wouldn't last a week. Hayward, for whatever reason, unwisely reported the wager to Miriam. After the performance, when Stewart, his wife, Beatrice, and George Oppenheimer arrived in Miriam's dressing room to take her to dinner, they found a termagant, staging a scene none of them would ever forget. In the midst of a long, long tirade about their theatrical obtuseness there was a knock at the door. "Who's there?" Miriam demanded, and Stewart quickly interjected, "The man with the champagne." Stewart's wit triggered one of the changes of mood for which Miriam was notorious, and after a good laugh the foursome were off to supper.

Brooks Atkinson spoke for most reviewers when he described her as "rhapsodically beautiful," adding, "When she cannot outdazzle an awkward line or scene, every honest votary of beauty is ready to lay the blame on Mr. Davis's wan doorstep." The play lasted thirty-two performances.

During its run Miriam began rehearsing the scene she had played in *The Affairs of Anatol* for personal appearances at the Paramount Publix theaters in greater New York. As her director she chose Hank Potter, stage manager of the 1930 production. "It was a great example of jumping off a diving board into an empty pool," he says. "We didn't hoke it up. We were reverent enough to do Schnitzler's play justice, but we broadened it so that the kind of audiences that came to see movie stars doing five a day could appreciate it.

"Still, I had doubts. Schnitzler wrote for intimate theaters, and these were enormous barns of places. But audiences ate her up and thought she was the funniest thing since Jack Benny. I traveled with her for three days. And with her movie experience, where she'd been expected to begin acting at nine A.M., she was just as good at the first show at ten thirty in the morning as she was at the fifth show that night."

While Miriam was busy on Broadway, her West Coast agent, Myron Selznick, negotiated with several studios. The best offer came from Samuel Goldwyn. Goldwyn, who had recently broken with other members of United Artists, ordinarily developed his own stars, but he had been impressed with Miriam's prior stage and screen work and was convinced that what she needed were stories especially created to showcase her offbeat talents. He shared Lubitsch's optimism that, given this careful handling, she could gain recognition as the most versatile actress in Hollywood.

Goldwyn was notorious for the iron will with which he ruled his players. Why either Miriam or her agents thought that she could be happy with or would be capable of submitting to his dictatorial ways is a mystery. She had not yet left New York to meet her employer when she succeeded in arousing his ire by buying the house at 13 Sutton Place that had belonged to literary agent Elizabeth Marbury. Before taking off for Hollywood, she persuaded Donald Oenslager, a leading theatrical designer whose stage settings and costumes had included those for *Jezebel*, to decorate the house for her. "I'd never done such a thing before and never wanted to," Oenslager recalled. "But Miriam said, 'Don, I'm going to go out on the Coast to do films, and you don't have to send me anything for approval. I don't want to see anything until I come back to New York, and then I want you to take me through the house.' I was fond of her and respected her, and so I said all right."

In Hollywood Miriam was summoned by Goldwyn, who angrily demanded to know why she had bought the New York house. She knew, he said, that he wanted his stars to live and work in Hollywood. He insisted she get rid of it. "Sam, I'm going to die in that house," was Miriam's reply. Despite her outward bravado, Miriam always suffered from insecurity. Now, by openly defying the man who was in a position to propel her career to new heights, she gave herself an excuse for failure, should their pictures turn out to be disappointments.

Her ambivalence toward film work was to become more and more apparent as time passed. "What's the use of being in the movies if we can't have champagne?" she used to ask—as if champagne were the only reward. She traveled now with the Santa Barbara-Pasadena social crowd, and tempestuous love affairs with rich playboys followed one after another.

If her romantic relationships were stormy, there were two men in her life to whom she was loyal: Michael, her child, and Billy Parker, her ex-husband. "Michael's arrival was a turning point like A.D. and B.C.," a friend observes. And Billy Parker was her best friend, now that they weren't romantically entangled. They remained extremely close, and Miriam was at his bedside when he died in 1938. According to his wishes, instead of holding conventional funeral ceremonies, she presided over a champagne party at the mortuary where his body rested in an alcove. The highlight of the occasion was Ronald Colman's reading of Billy's farewell letter.

Since Goldwyn had no project on tap that fitted Miriam's talents, she was lent to RKO for Norman Krasna's *Richest Girl in the World*, in which she played Dorothy Hunter, a Barbara Hutton-Doris Duke type who switches places with her secretary to ensure she's loved for herself, not for her money. If Dorothy was a far cry from Lavinia in *Mourning Becomes Electra*, a role Miriam yearned to play, her performance in this screwball comedy went a long way in countering the poor impression she had made in her last two releases.

When the film was finished, she flew to New York to inspect her new home. Oenslager had left two rooms untouched—one done by Elsie de Wolfe and a paneled room with special Oriental paper. "In the big stair hall, where she had a piano, I used an enlarged nineteenth-century Bi-

bienne stage rendering on the wall. These were very baroque things, and I turned that hallway into a kind of theatrical setting.

"On the top floor I did Michael's room with a soldier-and-drum chandelier—a typical kid thing. I did her bedroom in a kind of old beige and yellow with an elaborate, rich dressing room-bath. Then I thought about her quality and air and hair, and I did the main living room in a kind of cobalt blue. You might say I did the whole thing as if I were doing a stage set, with her as the leading person. When she came back, I nervously took her through it one morning. She was more astonished room after room and, I must say, very pleased.

"In Hollywood Miriam was constantly moving from one house to another. While she was there, she would rent her Sutton Place home, accumulate a little money and then come back to occupy it. But she always kept it as a kind of nest egg. She also had paintings—first-rate ones, including a Matisse and a Monet. But those paintings and the house she thought of as investments—unlike the first editions, which she would never part with."

In December, 1934, since Goldwyn still had failed to turn up a property for her, she was lent out again. This time to a company called Pioneer Pictures, Inc., which had been formed by John Hay "Jock" Whitney and his cousin Cornelius Vanderbilt "Sonny" Whitney to produce films in the new three-dimensional depth Technicolor process of which they owned 15 percent. For the initial film they chose William Makepiece Thackeray's *Vanity Fair*. Lowell Sherman was signed to direct and Miriam to play Becky Sharp. Production began. One third through filming Sherman developed pneumonia, collapsed and died. The Whitneys hired Rouben Mamoulian to replace him. Mamoulian immediately scrapped Sherman's work, and early in January, 1935, filming began anew.

Whatever their other production problems, there were none of the scenes that were becoming a part of Miriam's reputation. Mamoulian felt she was a perfect trouper. "She knew her craft. Now she did have definite opinions, and a person like that can be difficult with someone she feels knows less than she does." he says. "Some actors and some directors may say she was difficult. I did not find her so. The difficulties, if there were any, came from the fact that she was a born actress, and the minute she got into a scene, she was rearing to go. Others couldn't keep up easily. Miriam had a quick temperament—which is not to be confused with temper. She could evoke an emotion in a fraction of a second without giving the other actresses a chance to warm up.

"She was tenacious, but when she discovered that someone could give her something better than she had thought of, she became pliable, and you could get all kinds of things from her that are unavailable from more malleable actresses. And it became a delight because she was so sensationally good."

Yet in the final analysis, both the screenplay and the character of Becky Sharp were insufficiently developed. While the picture was recognized as a watershed production—and Robert Edmond Jones' color direction remains a treat to the eye—the breath of life seems to elude the characters. Still, by starring in the first Technicolor film, Miriam secured for herself a niche in cinema history which her better performances would never have gained for her.

When Miriam returned to Goldwyn, the producer, contrary to all talk of special handling, had nothing for her except Ben Hecht and Charles McArthur's brawling *Barbary Coast*. He had originally announced that Anna Sten and Gary Cooper would star. Now he assigned Miriam, Joel McCrea and Edward G. Robinson the leading roles.

In his candid autobiography*, *All My Yesterdays*, Robinson squares off by calling Miriam "a horror." She was, he says, "puerile and silly and snobbish." He reports that she "complained bitterly about every line, used every trick to upstage me. But when Miss Hopkins refused to stand on her marks, those little triangles of masking tape that set the actor within proper range of the camera, it was too much. What was really too much was that Miss Hopkins, in period costume and headdress, was taller than I. When we did a scene together, Miss Hopkins wanted me to stand on a box. I refused, not only because it was undignified and made me self-conscious, but because I was unable to play with any sincerity high on an insecure perch. My suggestion was that Miss Hopkins take off her shoes. When I think of it now, I suspect she could not play with any sincerity in her stocking feet."

Eventually, Robinson told Miriam off in front of the crew. As it happened, the following scene called for him to slap her. He suggested rehearsing so he could fake it, but Miriam told him, "Eddie, let's do this right. You smack me now so we won't have to do it over and over again. Do you hear me, Eddie? Smack me hard."

"I followed her instructions. I slapped her so you could hear it all over the set. And the cast and crew burst into applause."

*Written with Leonard Spigelgass.

"Miriam was disenchanted, but when a performer was under contract to Goldwyn, if he said, 'Here's a script, you start Monday,' filming started Monday. I was at Goldwyn when she was, and I think she quickly became bored," Hank Potter says. "And he was disappointed, too. *Barbary Coast* was successful, but it wasn't the greatest. Then he assigned her to *Splendor* opposite McCrea, directed by Elliott Nugent. She had to do it because she was under contract, but she didn't like it. She was discouraged and uninterested."

For all his promises, Miriam felt Goldwyn was providing even skimpier opportunities than she had had at Paramount. She complained that she was appearing opposite McCrea so often that the public must be tired of seeing them together. Nevertheless, Goldwyn again cast the two of them, along with Merle Oberon, in *These Three*. Luckily, this brought Miriam together with director William Wyler, who was to use her more often than any other director in future years. Wyler was almost as mercurial as Miriam was. "Willie loved her one minute and hated her the next," says a friend. Wyler, not as communicative as Lubitsch and Mamoulian, seemed unable to verbalize his intentions in a scene. And Miriam drove him to distraction with endless suggestions until, in desperation, he took to maneuvering her onto his deaf side, where she could chatter away and he could solve his problems undisturbed. Sometimes he would shoot a scene as many as fifty times. This repetition would drive her into a temper fit, and the two of them would battle it out. When he had eventually worn her down and had secured the interpretation he wanted, they would fall into each other's arms, carried away with their achievement.

These Three, Lillian Hellman's screen version of her play *The Children's Hour*, was, in deference to censors, not concerned with lesbianism. Instead, the malicious lie concocted by the neurotic child pertained to free love. The picture was well received. Miriam got excellent reviews, but not better than those of Merle Oberon and Joel McCrea. Generally, the two little girls, Bonita Granville and Marcia Mae Jones, were accorded the most enthusiastic praise.

Many at the studio felt that after having provided her with this third opportunity, Goldwyn lost faith in his assessment of Miriam's potential. "I was under contract there at the time, so I saw a good deal of what was happening," Potter recalls. "Miriam was great in *These Three*, but I wouldn't say the picture was a blockbuster. It got admiring, intelligent reviews, but it didn't appeal to the lowest common denominator. And when the critics and public saw Miriam's portrayal, they didn't say, 'Here's the new Jean Harlow or Marilyn Monroe.' Because it wasn't that kind of part. But you knew there was a sense of disappointment around the studio at her reception.''

Upon completion of *These Three* Miriam packed up Michael and set off for a European vacation, during which she acted in a negligible British film, *Men Are Not Gods*, for Sir Alexander Korda. During the eight months abroad she met the kind of people she enjoyed. She dined with Rebecca West, Noel Coward, G. B. Stern and King Edward VIII—shortly before the furor over Wallis Simpson broke. In Paris she visited that great expatriate guru Gertrude Stein, in Munich she was entertained by the American ambassador, in Budapest she cavorted for ten days with friends of Ernst Lubitsch, and in Venice she arrived in time to be appalled by Mussolini's announcement of his conquest of Ethiopia. "I wouldn't take anything for those experiences," she said. "Some were stimulating and some terrifying. I felt I had a front seat at history in the making.''

Aboard the *Normandie*, returning to the United States, she met Russian-born director Anatole Litvak. Litvak had already established a reputation in cinema in Berlin and Paris (notably for his direction of Charles Boyer in *Mayerling*). It was love at first sight for the perennial bachelor and the divorcée who had grown used to playing the field.

They were inseparable on the ship and constantly together in New York. By the time they arrived in Hollywood, Tola, as Miriam called him, had convinced her that she was the only woman to play in his picture *The Woman I Love*.

In Hollywood, when Litvak was not in Bel-Air helping furnish the house Miriam had bought from her ex-lover John Gilbert, he was on the set of her film *Woman Chases Man*. And when they worked together on *The Woman I Love* and Litvak had to go on location sixty miles away for scenes in which Miriam did not appear, she drove to the site each day to spend time with him.

Neither *The Woman I Love* nor *Woman Chases Man* turned out to be the film to restore her tarnished prestige. Although Miriam, in the throes of infatuation, had compared Litvak to Lubitsch and Mamoulian, her personal relationship was clouding her judgement. Neither she nor Paul Muni could rise above the clichéd situations and the hackneyed dialogue of *The Woman I Love*. Nor were critics in 1937 taken with the Dorothy Parker-Alan Campbell-Joe Bigelow script for *Woman Chases Man*, although Miriam, Joel McCrea and Charles Winninger were held blameless.

On September 4, 1937, Miriam and Litvak eloped to Yuma, Arizona, honeymooned in Coronado, California, and returned to Los Angeles where, after having spent all their time together while single, she took up residence in her Brentwood mansion and he lived in a house at the beach. Their excuse was that Litvak was allergic to the foliage on the grounds, but truth to tell, two such individualists could not dwell under the same roof.

On the one hand, Litvak's European charm fascinated Miriam; on the other, his assumption that the man of the house made decisions went against the strong egocentric streak in her personality. In the beginning she submerged her distaste for nightclubs and accompanied him on his rounds of the Clover Club, the Trocadero and Ciro's. Her parties, which had customarily been small and composed of personalities who enjoyed exchanging ideas, were abandoned for spectacular affairs where conversation was all but impossible. Cost was no deterrent to the showmanly director, and Miriam helped pay for things she didn't enjoy.

If she and Litvak were mismatched, she could take comfort in the fact that he was excellent with Michael. This was important to Miriam. Initially she had hoped that Billy Parker would take a fatherly interest in the child, notwithstanding the divorce. Because of his continuing friendship with her, Parker, whom Michael called Uncle Billy, had made a number of ineffectual jabs at establishing a relationship. But his commitment had never reached far beyond bringing the boy a silver baby cup engraved "It's a long time between drinks."

As Michael grew older, Miriam saw to it that he received instruction from outstanding teachers. She sent him to a series of private schools beginning with a boarding school in Tucson, Arizona, continuing with Riverdale High School and Valley Forge Military Academy and culminating in four years at Lawrenceville before he enlisted in the military service during the Korean war. Being single during much of his youth, she took responsibility for being both mother and father. She persuaded Big Bill Tilden to provide tennis instruction and José Iturbi, piano lessons. Because Michael was interested in planes, she arranged for Igor Sikorsky to instruct him on air power. When Michael began making inquiries about sex, Miriam assumed responsibility for enlightening him. She warned him that the worst thing a man could be was a bad lover. Michael pondered this statement and finally inquired what she did when a man was a bad lover. "I kick him out of bed," she responded.

After her marriage to Litvak she made the final picture in the second phase of her association with Hollywood. It was called *Wise Girl* and

107

was filmed at RKO. *Wise Girl* was an attempt to mine the type of screwball comedy generally associated with Carole Lombard. The result: a mildly entertaining, uneven picture, which would have ended most actresses' Hollywood careers. After all, Miriam was now thirty-six years old and, in the eyes of movie moguls, had twice had the opportunity to establish herself. In their judgment she had failed. So once again Miriam sold her home and left for New York.

There Miriam signed to play the female lead in S. N. Behrman's *Wine of Choice* for the Theatre Guild. In his book *The Magic Curtain* Lawrence Langner reported that the Guild was doing the play simply because it did all Behrman plays—good or bad. Alexander Woollcott played a sarcastic newspaper correspondent and Leslie Banks, a senator from New Mexico, "while the boss's daughter," Langner writes, "was played by Miriam Hopkins, one of the most versatile actresses of stage and screen, with a gift for rapid-fire dialogue both on and off stage. Miriam, whose acting I admired greatly, was not at all happy in her part and had no hesitation in saying so. Neither was Leslie Banks. Nor was Alexander Woollcott. . . ." Langner continues:

> There was a good deal of revision under way, and each morning Sam would appear at the theater with his few sheets of paper which contained the rewriting which had been agreed upon the night before. At the termination of each rehearsal, I was visited by Leslie Banks who remarked, "Really, Lawrence, I see from the way this is being rewritten that you don't need me in this play. You can replace me easily with a hundred-dollar-a-week actor." Miriam would invite me to discuss the rewritten pages over the supper table, and together with her husband Anatole Litvak would comment until the small hours of the morning on how unfavorably her part had been affected. Alec Woollcott, on the other hand, scorned to criticize where he thought he could create. His method of showing his dissatisfaction was to take to his typewriter and rewrite all his scenes using his own dialogue—which, considering how light and limber was his usual conversation, was angularly heavy and repulsive.

Finally, during the Pittsburgh engagement in January, 1938, Miriam turned in her notice, and the Guild replaced her with Claudia Morgan.

About this time, when everyone from Norma Shearer to Paulette Goddard, from Tallulah Bankhead to Katharine Hepburn was being touted for Scarlett O'Hara, Miriam let it be known that she was available. Although this overture fell on deaf ears as far as producer David Selznick or George Cukor (who was originally scheduled to direct the production) was concerned, Miriam was the choice of readers in polls conducted by the New York *Daily News* and *Photoplay.*

Earlier, when Miriam had been about to finish her Goldwyn commitments, she had issued a statement saying she no longer wanted to be tied to any studio, much as she liked the security of such an arrangement. But by September, 1938, she had apparently changed her mind. Exercising her considerable magnetism, she helped Litvak get a job at Warner Brothers, and before she was finished with that, she had also secured a two-picture contract for herself from Jack L. Warner. In announcing it to the press, she seemed under the impression that she had the privilege of script approval and went out of her way to underline the fact, saying, "If you don't like my pictures from now on, you can blame me." Considering that she had turned down a starring part in the stage hit *Broadway*, had rejected *Twentieth Century* (which proved a big success for Carole Lombard) and had dismissed *It Happened One Night* (which earned an Academy Award for Claudette Colbert) as "just a silly comedy," Miriam's assuming responsibility for her vehicles seems foolhardy at best.

For her first assignment, Miriam agreed to appear with the Queen of Warner Brothers, Bette Davis, in *The Old Maid*, receiving second co-star billing. The story centered on the struggle between two sisters for the affections of an illegitimate child. "The Old Maid," played by Bette Davis, had borne the baby out of wedlock, and her sister, played by Miriam, was rearing the girl as her own. Both parts were good, but Miss Davis played a sympathetic character while Miriam portrayed a flashy bitch. When word spread that Miriam proposed to vie for acting honors on the Warner lot with Miss D, one columnist observed that it was a feat that ranked with volunteering to show the Houdini family card tricks.

Queen Bette herself commented to costume designer Orry-Kelly, "She'll be trouble, but she'll be worth it." The remark proved accurate on both counts. Half of her prediction was fulfilled on the first day of shooting when Miriam appeared, dressed in a duplicate of one of the costumes Miss Davis had worn in the film version of *Jezebel*. In her autobiography Miss Davis wrote:

Miriam used and, I must give her credit, knew every trick in the book. I became fascinated watching them appear one by one. . . . When she was supposed to be listening to me, her eyes would wander off into some other world in which she was the sweetest of them all. Her restless little spirit was impatiently awaiting her next line, her golden curls quivering with expectancy.

Once in a two-shot favoring both of us, her attempts to upstage me almost collapsed the couch we both were sitting on. She kept inching her way toward the back of the couch so that I would have to turn away from the camera in order to look at her. If her back had been a buzz saw that allowed her to retreat beyond it, I wouldn't have been the least surprised.

Nor were Miriam's insecurities and resultant aggressions limited to the set. At home, relations with Litvak had become increasingly disturbed. "I knew the marriage was over," she said later, "when he came home from the studio one night and said he had found a marvelous property. 'It's going to make a wonderful movie for Bette Davis and a radio play for you.'

"Fortunately," Miriam said in telling the story, "it was *All This and Heaven Too*, which didn't make a very good movie."

In July, when Miriam went to New York to give pre-opening interviews for *The Old Maid*, she and Litvak were estranged. And while she was in Manhattan, the notorious incident involving Litvak and a rising glamor girl is reputed to have occurred under the table at Ciro's. Undoubtedly sensing that it would become a chapter in the oral history of Hollywood, Litvak called Miriam and cautioned her not be believe what she heard.

Miriam had little time to think of her disintegrating marriage. The picture opened to good reviews and enormous popular acclaim. It was, as had been planned from the beginning, Bette Davis' picture, but there was enough glory for each. And in her interviews Miriam batted her blue eyes, smiled innocently and told reporters how perfectly ridiculous it was to think there had been a feud. Feuds, she said, were generally concocted in publicity departments. Hadn't she demonstrated her amiability by working peacefully with Kay Francis, Merle Oberon, Claudette Colbert, Carole Lombard and other female stars? Then, contradicting her first statement, she added that feuds generally were begun by other actresses.

On August 23, 1939, Litvak arrived to effect a reconciliation, but the attempt failed. Miriam, with Michael and Kay Francis in tow, took off for Nevada. Upon arrival in Reno Kay was amused to find herself and Michael shunted into the background while Miriam made a star exit from the plane to accommodate waiting photographers. Establishing residence in Lake Tahoe, she filed for divorce, charging irreconcilable differences. Litvak counterfiled, alleging cruelty, then dropped his suit, and by mid-October Miriam was once more a free woman.

Upon return to Hollywood she was astonished to find that, script approval or not, she had been assigned to appear in *Virginia City* with Randolph Scott and Errol Flynn! Flynn felt the same way about her.

Designer Orry-Kelly says in his unpublished memoirs that Miriam aroused murderous feelings in him. He then tells how at a final fitting she threatened to make his costumes appear so ridiculous that director Mike Curtiz would have to delay the picture and she could get the script rewritten. True to her word, when Curtiz came to the wardrobe department to inspect Kelly's work, Miriam let her shoulders slouch and stuck out her rear. Kelly, fearing Jack Warner and Curtiz would accuse him of inferior work, straightened Miriam up with a jerk. "This lady just wants the script rewritten," he announced. And to Miriam's complaint that he was hurting her he replied, "Not half as much as you're hurting my reputation." Eventually the truth about her misbehavior emerged. "Miss Hopkins' spiteful behavior with her co-workers dimmed a potentially brilliant career," he concludes.

Her bitchy interviews about the quality of *Virginia City* before its release could scarcely have endeared Miriam to Warner's. "If you want to see me look tragic, you must take a peek at my new picture. I just finished—whoof—and came to New York for a few days' breath. I worked in it for almost twelve weeks. Why I was cast in it I shall never know," she told New York *Post* reporter Michael Mok. "I had to do all the things I can't do. I had to sing, and I can't carry a tune. I had to dance, and I hadn't taken a step except on a nightclub floor in ten years. . . . I'm a brave pioneer woman. Oh, it's a honey! I even do a love scene with Errol Flynn on the edge of the Grand Canyon. It's got almost as much in it as *Gone with the Wind*—I start with Jefferson Davis and end with Abraham Lincoln."

The self-mockery and the bitterness toward the studio system continued and were echoed by reviewers when the film was released. Critics described the script as cliché-ridden and Miriam as wooden. Nor did she fare any better in *The Lady with Red Hair*, in which she played Mrs. Leslie Carter for Warner's. The film was short on biographical facts about the celebrated actress and producer David Belasco but was long on unbelievable invention. This time the director, Curtis Bernhardt, beat Miriam to the gouge. Even during filming he announced that she was uncooperative. In the final analysis the script was flawed, the direction unimaginative, and Miriam exerted little effort to breathe life into the flamboyant Mrs. Carter.

Publicly Miriam assumed an I-don't-care attitude. Privately she admitted frustration and humiliation. Judging by the scripts offered her, the studio was eager to drop her option. Columnists who had toadied up to her in her golden days sniped at her. Hangers-on began to slip away. And in line with the gratuitous cruelty the public bestows on erstwhile favorites the editors of the *Harvard Lampoon* selected her as the woman with whom they'd least like to be marooned on a desert island.

Once more Miriam went to New York, intending to appear in a summer stock production of Molnar's *The Guardsman* with Italian-born leading man Tullio Carminati. When she excoriated Mussolini, Carminati walked out. The producer threatened to sue. And the Actors' Equity Association, surprisingly enough, fined not Carminati but Miriam $1000. She was learning that a reputation for being temperamental could be costly.

About this time she read a script by an as-yet-unrecognized playwright which so captured the rhythm of her Georgia-accented speech that she might have improvised the lines. It was Tennessee Williams' *Battle of Angels,* which was to be produced by the Theatre Guild. Miriam was signed to play the sexually driven central character. She was enthusiastic about the manner in which the playwright combined a poetic approach with sexual frankness, but according to Lawrence Langner, she was not backward about suggesting revisions. And on one occasion she worked herself into such a state that she threw the script at the producer's head. Luckily, he said, he knew Miriam well and was prepared to duck.

As rehearsals progressed, everyone was working at cross-purposes. By opening night in Boston nerves were frayed. Miriam's periodic invitations to the young stud to accompany her to the back room drew laughter from Guild subscription members. Some banged up their seats, shook their fists at the stage and noisily stomped out. Then, during the big fire scene, the smoke machine malfunctioned. Fumes rolled over the footlights, converting the disaster into a rout of the choking audience.

In a newspaper ad two days after the opening the Guild reaffirmed its faith in Williams but apologized to their membership for presenting this particular drama. A decade and a half later, theater patrons had caught up with Williams' advanced view of human nature, and *Battle of An-*

gels, rewritten and retitled *Orpheus Descending*, became a commercial hit.

Now, with two undistinguished pictures to her discredit, as well as a play that had closed out of town, Miriam became increasingly insecure. After turning down several scripts, she agreed to appear opposite Brian Donlevy in United Artists' *A Gentleman After Dark*. Why she chose this oft-filmed story—the first screen version had appeared in 1920, and there had been several subsequent ones—is hard to fathom. The budget was small, and Miriam's performance teetered precariously on the brink of self-parody.

Fortunately, Warner Brothers had purchased John Van Druten's Broadway play *Old Acquaintance* for Bette Davis. Although there was controversy about its artistic merits, this woman's story had demonstrated its box-office strength. It told of two female novelists—one serious, one popular—who remained friends over the years despite the latter's consistently selfish behavior. Bette Davis played the artist, who was noble to the point of seeming almost simpleminded. Miriam played the hack, so bitchy she could hardly be accepted. When Warner's offered Miriam the role, the studio executives stirred her mounting anxieties by asking her to take billing below the title, something she had never done before. Still, it was an A picture, a prestige production, and she accepted.

When she arrived on the lot, she attempted to let bygones be bygones. She was soon disabused of that idea. Dashing to wardrobe for a costume fitting, she gaily flung her arms around Orry-Kelly and kissed him on the cheek, crying, "Dar—ling!"

"Please, Miriam, we don't like each other," Kelly recalled saying. "I'll do my best to dress and please you, but no kissy-kissy, please." Said Kelly, "She suddenly became Becky Sharp. 'Aren't I awful, Orry-Kelly?' Now what are you going to do with a belle like that? Difficult or not, I think she was an exceptionally fine actress."

Miriam simply ignored the past and attempted, somewhat unrealistically, to achieve the impossible—steal the picture from Davis. Ignoring the fact that the studio had protected its valuable investment in Miss D, Miriam's quixotic behavior quickly stirred up trouble. None of those involved was about to allow Miriam to distort the script. And the publicists lost no time in circulating rumors of an all-out feud between the stars, even going as far as working up a composite of two boxers squared off to do battle—with Bette's and Miriam's heads superimposed.

Insiders who knew the shooting schedule appeared on the set when the scene in which Miss Davis was required to slap Miriam was to be filmed. Miss D, however noble on the screen, was a formidable brawler in her own right. Many expected Miriam to toss the script out the window and fight back. They were disappointed. After many takes, when the director was finally able to keep Miriam from going limp as a piece of spaghetti or moving out of camera range, she accepted the slap. But as Bette Davis later wrote, Miriam's eyes filled with tears of self-pity—useless since her back was to the camera.

In the hostile atmosphere she had created Miriam proceeded to lose eleven pounds. She was now forty years old—too mature to play romantic heroines, too young for character parts. In the past she had alienated so many executives, directors and co-stars that she could hardly hope for any considerations that would prolong her career. So when the picture was finished, she sold her California house and left for New York, claiming that she never wanted to return. "I'd told too many directors how to make pictures," she said later. "They wanted to shut me up. I wouldn't. But I could have gotten away with it if I'd batted my eyes and spoken as if honey wouldn't melt in my mouth."

Director Vincent Sherman claimed Miriam had told him she felt he was protecting Bette Davis. "Miriam, if my own mother was playing a scene, I wouldn't protect her," he had said. "I'm protecting the picture." That attitude was one Miriam never understood.

Interestingly, in the 1940s popular opinion had it that Bette Davis far overshadowed Miriam, but in 1975 Howard Thompson articulated the 1970s viewpoint when he wrote in a capsule TV review in the New York *Times*, "Highly entertaining over-the-years witchery and bitchery. Bette wins the sympathy but Miriam has the juice."

Back in New York, Miriam settled down at 13 Sutton Place and, against the advice of friends, signed to replace Tallulah Bankhead in *The Skin of Our Teeth* at $1,500 a week. Considering the magnitude of Tallulah's personal triumph, it was tantamount to putting her head in a lion's mouth and daring him to bite. Under the circumstances her notices were satisfying. While no one felt she outshone her predecessor, the consensus was that on her own terms she was a satisfactory substitute.

Her social life, too, was more to her taste. California offered tennis and sunshine; New York, intellectual stimulation. She engaged in a hectic romance with writer John Gunther and traveled in a group that included Vincent Sheehan, Lord Stanley, Leland Stowe, Henry Luce,

Margaret Bourke-White, Grace Moore, Marcia Davenport and Eve Curie. The Gunther romance fizzled, but the friendship remained.

Gunther was succeeded by Ray Brock, a foreign correspondent for the New York Times who eventually wrote *Nor Any Victory* (an account of his life in Belgrade) and *Blood, Sand and Oil,* a book about the Mideast. Friends tried to warn her away from the hard-living Brock, but Miriam ignored them. "I have a little weakness for newspapermen. And I think foreign correspondents are the world's glamor boys. I do like the slouch hats and the wonderful stories they tell," she confided to a reporter.

Not that she always allowed the correspondents to tell what they knew. At the time she began seeing Brock she invited Muriel King and George Oppenheimer to dinner. Meeting her guests at the door, she quietly said, "I've got a little man you're going to meet who knows all about Yugoslavia. He's absolutely fascinating. Now when I give you a little signal at dinner, ask him about Tito." At dinner when Oppenheimer felt a kick, he brought up Tito. Miriam leaped in at once and talked about Yugoslavia for half an hour without giving Brock an opportunity to utter more than half a dozen interrupted sentences. "Brock was furious," Oppenheimer says. "But that was Miriam. She didn't know a goddamn thing about it. She was just quoting him."

They were married in the fall of 1945.

Professionally, the next five years were lackluster. Miriam starred in *The Perfect Marriage,* a play by Samson Raphaelson, who had written so many Lubitsch films. Her leading man was Victor Jory. Each thought the other miscast. There was talk of replacing Miriam with Constance Cummings, but Miriam put a stop to that. "As the curtain went up on our tenth wedding anniversary, we were supposedly having champagne and dancing," Jory recalls. "After ten years, we didn't care for sex anymore, but we were trying to recapture lost romance. As we'd rehearsed it, I let my hand slip from her waist to her bottom and she patted my hand. But on opening night, as the curtain went up, she whispered, 'Victor, I'm going to faint,' whereupon she went limp and all I could do was to carry her to the bed and ad-lib until she came round. It killed the scene.

"Now an amazing thing happened. We later found out that she had sent wires to a number of the critics apologizing for not giving her best performance because she had been ill and fainted. It was shrewd thinking, and any person who attains a certain plateau of success has to fight to maintain it. But she'd sent the telegrams before she came to the theater—*before* she fainted. It was a little too much. I have worked with actors who have upstaged their co-workers so far that they upstaged themselves. Miriam did." The play folded after ninety-two performances.

As Miriam's insecurity increased with each failure, her behavior became more erratic. The following season, buoyed by his success in producing *The Glass Menagerie,* Eddie Dowling hired Miriam to star in *St. Lazare's Pharmacy,* opposite the French-Canadian favorite Fridolin. After the first reading Miriam suggested Fridolin's role be played by two actors, and when Dowling rejected the proposal, she boycotted rehearsals for two days until he threatened to have her called before Equity on charges of unprofessional behavior.

The production opened in Montreal on December 6, 1945. Ken Johnstone of the Montreal *Standard,* who moonlighted as a stringer on *Variety,* described Miriam's performance as hammy. His review had hardly appeared when he received a wire from *"Variety,"* warning that Chicago critics were ganging up to pan Fridolin. Johnstone reported receiving the wire, adding that the comedian had also received three similar wires, and that there appeared to be a plot afoot.

Johnstone's indirect accusation stirred Ray Brock to write an open letter defending his wife and blasting the article as "shockingly vicious . . . slanderous . . . filthy and cowardly." Brock closed, "You are a fourth-rate cub, Johnstone, and I strongly advise you to mend your manners."

At the theater the new director of the play called a cast meeting and told Miriam publicly, "With your interpretation of the role the play will be slaughtered in New York. You are not trying." And when, several days later, he criticized her acting after a performance, Miriam screamed so that the audience, which had not yet left the premises, could hear that she was "tired of taking criticism from a second-rate son of a bitch."

The entire fracas, reported in detail in *Newsweek* as "Miriam Acts Up," did nothing to diminish her reputation as a stormy petrel whose performances no longer compensated for the problems she created.

In 1946 she toured in Hunt Stromberg Jr.'s national company of *Laura* with star-crossed Tom Neal as her leading man, and in 1947 she appeared on Broadway in *Message for Margaret* for five performances. That summer she toured in *There's Always a Juliet,* and the next winter in the national company of Anita Loos' *Happy Birthday.*

Out of the blue, in 1948, she received a call from William Wyler, who, though he didn't tell her so, had heard that on Christmas Eve of

1947 she had tripped and fallen, injuring her back. She had spent seven weeks in the hospital and four more confined to bed at home. Friends were also concerned about her relationship with Ray Brock, a heavy drinker who encouraged her to drink along with him and who was not averse to her paying the bills.

Wyler announced that he was about to make the film version of *The Heiress* and told her that she was his first choice for Aunt Lavinia. As their forty-five-minute conversation progressed, Miriam became enthused. Like Norma Desmond, the faded silent star in *Sunset Boulevard* who constantly recalls what Mr. De Mille had once said, Miriam kept telling friends that this was the kind of part that her first important director, Ernst Lubitsch, had advised her to play. "'Never play just nice girls. Always try to get parts that are a little off-center,' he said. " She added that Aunt Lavinia was like that, not just the broken-down, shawl-over-the-shoulders aunt.

Thus, in 1948 both Miriam and Ginger returned to Hollywood after extended absences from the screen. Ginger was starring opposite Fred Astaire for one last time, but Miriam was now a character woman. No longer striving to steal the spotlight, she was acting under the supervision of a director whom she trusted. The result was a touching performance. Bosley Crowther described her in the New York *Times,* as "delightful," and she assumed there would be heavy demand for her services.

Before the film opened, however, she returned East to tour the summer circuit in the title role of the play, as if to serve notice that, though she might accept character parts in films, onstage she was still a leading lady.

The Heiress opened at Radio City Music Hall on October 6, 1949, and drew large crowds. Olivia de Havilland was awarded an Oscar for her performance. Miriam not only did not draw a nomination but also had no single job offer during 1949 and 1950. Finally, in 1951, Mitch Leisen brought her back to Paramount to play Gene Tierney's mother in *The Mating Season.* Unluckily, Miriam's role was less originally written and acted than Thelma Ritter's. Miss Ritter dominated the screen. Still, enough kind things were written about Miriam so that she was hired for *The Outcasts of Poker Flat* with Anne Baxter and Dale Robertson. Although she received third billing as Duchess, a lady of the night, her one-diminsional part gave her little opportunity to shine.

That same year she divorced Brock, much to the relief of her friends. "He cost me a mint—like all of them, except Billy," she said. "I don't know why I married him—except he wanted me to so much."

117

As for the future: "I just haven't found the right man. I'm still waiting for him to come along. Men with money don't especially appeal to me. Nor young men. But I am interested in intelligent men."

Professionally, the 1950s seemed to drift by. Miriam capitalized on her 1939 film by touring the summer circuit in *The Old Maid*. She played the title role, while Sylvia Sidney appeared in Miriam's old part and Miriam's niece Margot Welch, Ruby's daughter, made her debut as the girl. Miriam was so eager for Margot to succeed that she overwhelmed the girl, and the director finally forbade her to make any suggestions; but she still stood in the wings, mouthing the lines and unnerving Margot.

Since Miriam's mother and sister were both dominating personalities, Miriam didn't spend a great deal of time with them, nevertheless, she remained a dutiful relative. Whatever her excesses, she had breeding that instinctively caused her to do the decent thing—as long as it did not conflict with her career—and one of the decent things was to be nice to your family. Although she had not managed to accumulate a large amount of money, she spent freely on her family. She provided her mother with a Fifty-Seventh Street apartment and a generous allowance.* She suggested placing Ruby on her payroll, and when Ruby refused, Miriam instructed her lawyer to advance her sister money should an emergency arise. On one occasion a minister contacted her to report that her father, whom she hadn't seen since she was seven years old, needed expensive dental care. She immediately wrote out a check. "I barely resisted writing across it, 'Daddy, here I come!'" she said.

Her generosity to her family, including occasional checks to Michael—who had disappointed her by becoming a career man in the Army and who now had a wife and a son—plus her openhanded attitude toward less fortunate friends made it necessary to sell an occasional painting. She rented out her Sutton Place home. "I'm the only landlady on the street," she said gaily and leased a penthouse apartment with a large terrace at Forty-Ninth Street and Third Avenue. When a friend worried about unpaid bills, Miriam counseled, "Just send each creditor ten dollars. It shows willingness to pay. You never have a problem then."

Except for work in stock and an occasional guest shot on television

---

*Upon her mother's death she is alleged to have buried her in a fur coat, maintaining, "Mama always wanted a mink. Now she's got one."

118

there were no offers until mid-1958, when playwright Ketti Frings called to ask Miriam to replace Jo Van Fleet in *Look Homeward Angel*. By this time little was left of Miriam's once-substantial reputation, and even her old friend and longtime supporter Ward Morehouse privately told his wife, Becky, "She won't be as good as Jo Van Fleet." But when she appeared in her gray wig and gray makeup, Morehouse was astonished—not so much by the controlled performance that sacrificed glamor to the demands of the role as by the fact that she had discovered depths of character that had eluded Miss Van Fleet. Nor was he the only critic to be impressed. In the New York *Post* Richard Watts wrote that some of the replacements in the cast were reproducing the performances of the originators and added, "But not in the case of Miriam Hopkins, who has the role of the mother, originated by Jo Van Fleet. Miss Hopkins is giving a brilliant portrayal, one of the ablest of her career, and nothing stands in the way of her force and will."

Miriam continued in the part until the play closed in New York and then agreed to undertake a bus-and-truck tour. John Drew Barrymore was set to play Eugene Gant, the role originated by Tony Perkins, but Barrymore and Miriam clashed. "She knew the play so well, she was propelling him around the stage," says her friend Florence Sundstrom, who played "Fatty" Perk. "Barrymore didn't like it, and he had good reason because the director didn't have much control over Mims.

"One day Barrymore didn't show up, and the director called me to ask whether he could locate John, did I think Mims would stay home for a few days until he could break the kid in and make him a little more at ease. I called her, and, of course, she got highly incensed. And I said, 'Look, honey, you were pushing him around the stage, and he resented it.' She spluttered but finally agreed to stay away for a few days. But when she came back, the same thing started happening again. She was playing his part for him, and he really walked. What it amounted to was switching the play around to be her vehicle. I told her that this was a Pulitzer Prize play, a Drama Critics Award play, and it detracted from its value. I don't know why she took it from me, but I could let her have it with both barrels. I was closer to her than to my own sister, and I think she knew I was trying to help.

"But she was so mercurial. I'll never forget when we were to open in Chicago. We were having drinks together, and she said, 'I can just visualize the review that acidy Cassidy will give me. She's going to say, "Miriam Hopkins, with eyelashes that swept the floor and a bouffant wig, was more Madame Butterfly than Eliza Gant." '

"So I said, 'Well, Mims, if you can foresee what Claudia is going to say about you, why don't you get rid of the eyelashes and use the straight wig, the good one, and she won't pan you?' 'No,' she said, 'I wouldn't give her the satisfaction.' But on opening night she wore the gray wig, and the eyelashes were gone. And Claudia Cassidy gave her a good notice. Then the next night I arrived at the theater, and here was Mims in the bouffant wig and the long eyelashes again.

"She liked the status quo. She wanted to remain the glamor girl, the Southern belle. One time the scenery and costumes got lost when we were playing Alexandria, Virginia. That night she played Eliza with her blond hair flying and wearing a perky little black dress, and she loved doing it that way because she was pretty. She was good as Eliza, but she didn't like being the stern matriarch."

When the tour closed, there was no more work until 1962, except for infrequent television jobs. Miriam was content to relax in her East Side penthouse, reading and tending flowers on her terrace. Finally, a call again came from William Wyler. Wyler was remaking *The Children's Hour* as it originally had been written, with Shirley MacLaine playing Miriam's old role, and he wanted Miriam for the aunt. As always when she worked for a director she respected, she curbed her trickery and turned in an affecting performance.

Her unique style impressed a young producer, Stanley Raiff, who thought her perfectly suited to play the leading roles in two one-act plays he was producing under the title *Riverside Drive*. Each play had only two characters. Basil Rathbone had already agreed to act the males. Miriam read the scripts and became enthusiastic. When Rathbone withdrew, she assumed a proprietary interest in the project. She began by proposing minor word alterations to make the lines easier to deliver but eventually suggested changes in plot and motivation. She questioned the suitability of director Douglas Seale and nagged Raiff to dump him. She urged hiring Mamoulian, who, she assured Raiff and playwright John Donovan, would "direct me doing a tap dance on my hands with my drawers showing." She turned up with a list of male stars, volunteering to call them. All were polite, but afterward several called Raiff to warn that he had a tough baby to control.

In the fall an agent submitted Donald Woods, and Miriam agreed with Raiff and Donovan that he was a suitable choice. Woods arrived from California, and on Christmas night, 1963, the company gathered for the first cast reading. "Right there I made a fatal mistake," Donovan says. "She announced she should be looking at the New York *Times* instead of the *Daily News*. I tried to reason with her, pointing out it was a character part, and she said, 'But I would never buy the

Daily News,' and I told her, 'This is not *you*. I know you would never buy the *News*, but this woman would. She no longer will make the effort to read the *Times.'* And this became such a problem that the read-through came to a standstill. From there on it was all downhill."

Problems mounted as Miriam immobilized everyone. Although young Raiff had spent countless summer evenings cueing her, when rehearsals got under way, she insisted on carrying her sides. Day after day she clung to them. Nor was this the only problem. If the call was for 11 A.M., she would show up at noon. At evening rehearsals she sometimes would have been drinking too much. Most alarming, she insisted on rehearsing only the comedy and resisted the second play, which was concerned with an emotionally overwrought woman who drank excessively, destroyed her husband and made a mess of her life.

Set designer Leo Kerz, who had worked with Miriam previously, warned Raiff to watch her or she would never learn her lines. When Kerz's set was erected, Miriam unnerved Seale and Woods by drifting about the stage, improvising scenes in which she envisioned that they would find that the doors wouldn't work or they would trip over furniture and fluff lines. "But don't worry, dear,'' she reassured Woods. "I'll take care of you."

Woods began to break out in rashes, and Seale, presumably sensing disaster, turned in his notice. Raiff called off rehearsals and mollified Seale. The next morning, three days before the first preview, Miriam called in ill. The following day she contracted Raiff to ask if he minded her accepting a television assignment. He did, and that night she appeared for rehearsal—still carrying her sides.

Previews were postponed, but after two days she again failed to show up, and it became clear that she was not ready to open. Raiff called her agent, who also represented Sylvia Sidney, and told him that he wanted to replace Miriam with Sylvia. The agent conscientiously alerted Miriam, and she arrived at the theater within the hour.

She was smiling and as gracious and charming as she had been during the pre-rehearsal days when she had introduced Raiff to friends as her "producer and protégé." After greeting everyone present, she suggested getting started. Donovan and Seale drifted away, leaving Raiff to tell Miriam that she was sacked. She declared that that was ridiculous, that there was no reason to fire her. Raiff then pointed out that after three weeks of rehearsal she didn't know her lines and they had no idea what the plays sounded or looked like. Labeling that a ridiculous declaration, she went down the darkened aisle to the stage, where only a dim work light burned, and proceeded to recite both plays word for

121

word—not only her own lines but those of her co-star as well. At the conclusion she peered through the gloom and shouted, "You can't fire me from some tacky little off-broadway theater. Don't you realize who I am? I'm *Miri*am Hopkins!" then she stamped offstage.

It was a heart-breaking moment. Raiff waited for her to reappear. Finally, he went to her dressing room to tell her the theater was being locked and to offer to find her a taxi. She ignored him as she tossed together her belongings, including a bucket borrowed from a neighborhood bar to ice her champagne. Shortly thereafter, the bar's patrons were startled as the door flew open and a furious little woman slammed an empty bucket across the floor and then wordlessly banged the door shut again.

"It was a sad thing," Donovan says. "Curiously enough, while *Riverside Drive* obviously was not a successful evening of theater, it was very good for Sylvia, and Miriam could have had the same kind of tremendous personal notices."

Professionally, Miriam was bankrupt. The following year she played the madam in *Fanny Hill,* directed by the originator of commercial skin flicks, Russ Meyer. The New York *Times* noted sadly, "Miss Hopkins, a ladylike actress, stands serenely amidst alien corn" while the *Hollywood Reporter* lamented, "Miriam Hopkins, so fine an actress in many first-class films, is woefully disgraced with inadequate material and ludicrous situations."

In July of that year she began work on *The Chase* with Marlon Brando and Robert Redford. Forecasting accurately what the critics would say, she confessed to columnist Hedda Hopper, "I was concerned about the emotional scenes, afraid I might get too hammy, so I asked Arthur Penn [the director] about it. He said to let go. So when I did a scene with Brando, who plays on a rather low key, and I came out with, 'You're a murderer!' I can assure you the audience will know I'm there." But as she had feared, many reviewers found her hammy.

After *The Chase* there was one more feature film, *Comeback,* with Gale Sondergaard and Minta Durfee Arbuckle. It mercifully never found a distributor. There were also guest appearances on television, but she found shooting schedules too arduous. For instance, while doing a segment of *The Outer Limits* series, she sent a messenger on the third day of filming to say she was ill and couldn't work. She had simply decided to set her own pace. When word got out about her tactics, producers were cautious about casting her.

Having sold her Sutton Place house, she spent the last years restlessly traveling back and forth between New York and Los Angeles. Her closest friends—columnist Becky Morehouse, stage manager Ben Strobach, importer Jim White, Hank and Lucille Potter, Donald and Zorca Oenslager—were in the East, as were her sister, Ruby, and her niece, Margot.

On the other hand, an apartment similar to the one she rented at the Shoreham in Los Angeles—an apartment she firmly believed haunted by former tenant Ronald Colman—would have cost at least $1,000 a month in New York. She also liked the Southern California climate, which made it possible for her to keep a year-round suntan. Flo Sundstrom had also settled there, and there were such old friends as Jean Negulesco, Kendall Milestone and Bernadine Fritz and such new ones as director Curtis Harrington and columnist Lee Graham.

Harrington, whose film *Games* Miriam admired, offered her a role in a picture he was preparing at Universal Studios. She read the script and said she'd love to do it. "But my price was set by *The Chase,*" she said. "I get five thousand dollars a week, and I have a limousine pick me up in the morning and take me home at night.* If you can't pay it, there's no use discussing it. We'll just be friends."

The project was abandoned, but their friendship continued. When the Delta Kappa Alpha fraternity at the University of Southern California held an evening honoring directors Mamoulian and Allan Dwan, Harrington invited Miriam and Bernadine Fritz to go. Miriam balked. She wanted her own escort. Harrington arranged for writer Charles Higham to escort her. When Higham mentioned he was writing a biography of Cecil B. De Mille, Miriam blurted out, "What on earth for?" Later in the evening, when David Chierichetti approached her to say that *he* was working on a biography of Mitchell Leisen, she responded, "Has the world gone mad?"

She shared none of the film buff's fascination with cinema history or trivia. "It was something she had been a part of, and it was not, in her opinion, worth discussing," Harrington said. Politics or writing or painting were worth analyzing—but movies? She could not only recite Ezra Pound's *Cantos* but also interpret them intelligently. She knew extensive portions of the works of e. e. cummings, T. S. Eliot, Emily Dickinson, the Irish Renaissance poets and many others—but the movies?

If she was not interested in recalling her old films or anyone else's, old lovers were an endless fascination. When with close friends, she

---

*Always an erratic driver, she lost her nerve behind the wheel as she grew older.

enjoyed reminiscing about the many men in her life, mostly concentrating on the pleasant moments and forgetting the bad ones. While she lived at the Shoreham, her lover of the moment suddenly disappeared without so much as a good-bye. She was shaken. "I feel as if I'd been put down the disposal with the cold water running," she confided to a friend. After that she had no further romances but kept on tap a supply of escorts to take her to parties, retaining her Southern belle attitude, deploring the idea of arriving at a gathering alone.

"I loved being at a party with her," Becky Morehouse says. "I only got to know her well after Ward died. She was the first person to call me, and she called regularly, inviting me out to see her. Finally I went. Even then she provided an electricity that's gone from my life now. She was just Miss Sparkle Plenty."

But eventually even parties lost their zest for her. She preferred to remain in her apartment at the Shoreham, where only the paintings, the hi-fi, a family candelabrum, many dresses and four hundred pairs of shoes belonged to her. Her first editions and furniture were stored in New York. About once a month Michael and his family came to see her. Only once, while recuperating from a knee injury, did she visit them. The experiment was not a success.

During much of her later life her existence was made more comfortable by two black manservants, who were friends as well as employees. In New York there was Perry. Whenever she arrived in Manhattan for any period of time, she would call him, and he would turn in his notice and come back to work for her. Theirs was a stormy but deeply felt relationship. Her unconventional way with him is illustrated by an incident that occurred in the 1960s. "Mama [Miriam's mother] was still alive then, and Miriam was having some of us in for Thanksgiving dinner," Flo Sundstrom recalls. "She arranged the tables so that Mama was sitting with three other people. And she said to me, 'Flo, I've invited Perry as a guest today. You don't mind if he sits with us, do you?' I said, 'Of course not,' because Perry was a friend. He'd been on the *Look Homeward, Angel* tour with us. But even so, Mama got incensed that Perry was going to eat with us. She was still a Southern belle, and finally Mims turned around and withered her with, 'Mother, this is Thanksgiving, and Perry has just as much right to be thankful as you do.'"

At the Shoreham in Los Angeles Perry was succeeded by Charles Whitfield. Miriam and Charles' was a stormier relationship than the one with Perry. "There was one party I'll never forget," Curtis Harrington recalls. "Something was wrong with the phonograph. She was fiddling with it and said, 'Charles, you broke this.' he looked at her and he said, 'I did not. You broke it.' she said, 'You broke it,' and he said, 'You broke it!' and here were all the astonished guests listening in on an outshouting contest. They were literally screaming at one another, and she turned on her heel and headed for her bedroom. Charles yelled after her, 'Are you going to leave your guests?' and she said, 'Yes!' and slammed the door. Now we all sort of made polite conversation for from three to five minutes, and suddenly she emerged from the bedroom as if nothing had happened."

On occasion, when Miriam provoked Charles beyond endurance, he would walk off the job and leave her to cope until one of her friends would intervene, persuading him to return since Miriam was totally unable to get along by herself. Then Miriam would apologize and promise to behave more reasonably. The game was repeated many times.

In the last years she retreated more and more to her bedroom with its blackout shades, where she would listen to yesterday's music—Mildred Bailey and Maurice Chevalier, especially—read omnivorously and drink champagne. Increasingly she slept through the day, staying up all night. When bored, she telephoned friends, no matter what time of the day or night, and chattered away for an hour or more. They facetiously dubbed her The Midnight Caller, although she often phoned them at 2, 3 or 4 A.M. But if anyone dared awaken her, she would fly into a rage.

Faithful friends dined with her in her bedroom and worried that she would suffer malnutrition if she continued drinking and refused to eat properly. She had lost her youthful appearance, was plagued by dental problems, developed a touch of emphysema and what she gallantly led everyone to believe was mild heart trouble. Yet the nitroglycerine capsules were always in her purse and on the bedside table.

In 1972, when the Museum of Modern Art in Manhattan prepared its sixty-year retrospective honoring Paramount Pictures, it was arranged through Becky Morehouse that Miriam and *The Story of Temple Drake* would open the series. All preparations were made for Miriam to arrive from Hollywood on a Sunday in July. Two press agents planned to cut short their weekends in order to accompany Becky to the airport to meet Miriam. Early on the appointed day Miriam called to say that she had fainted while packing and would not arrive until Monday. "I was panicky. I was afraid she wasn't going to show," Becky says. "I had to alert everyone to postpone for a day. Then, at the airport, our first glimpse of her was in a wheelchair. Everyone's heart sank."

On opening night, July 11, Miriam came through splendidly. she wore a stylish black dress and a huge pink satin stole that gave her something to fuss with. When she and her escort Jim White emerged from their car, Miriam looked every inch a star. At her request they were seated on the aisle two thirds of the way back so that she would merely stand but not be expected to get onstage or make a speech when the film ended.

After the lights dimmed, an unexpected short subject was shown. "It was Ginger Rogers with the chorus girls in bellhop costumes, doing three or four songs," White says. "Miriam asked in a loud stage whisper, 'Who's that?' I said, 'You know who that is,' and she insisted she didn't. About the third song she murmured, 'I guess they changed their minds.' Finally, *Temple Drake* started."

Afterward Miriam approached Becky Morehouse and suggested they find the ladies' room. "She was disappointed in the picture," Becky says. "She thought it didn't stand up very well. When we got in the ladies' room, there were lines of women at each cubicle, and she announced, 'I've suffered more than any of you. So let me in.' And they laughed and let her in."

At the gala she skillfully hid the fact that she was feeling ill. She met Andy Warhol, who knelt beside her with his video recorder while she talked and talked and talked. Donald Oenslager noted the pair and asked Jim White if he thought Miriam had any idea to whom she was speaking. "Not the foggiest," White replied. "She tuned out with Matisse." Miriam heard them and told them to shut up. "She loved Warhol," White said afterward. "She talked a blue streak, and she was crazy about anybody who was willing to listen to her three hours nonstop. Of course, if she'd seen him next day, she wouldn't have recognized him. You'd say, there's Harry Truman, and she'd say, 'Which one?' She never recognized anybody."

The publicity from the evening pleased Becky Morehouse. She clipped the photos and write-ups and took them to Miriam, who showed not the slightest interest. "I thought she has no vanity really," Becky says. "But later I concluded that's really the ultimate vanity. She knew she had a place. She knew that she had done worthwhile work, and then she forgot about it. It didn't interest her to talk about it or read about it or to dwell on it at all."

Shortly after the retrospective Miriam entered a hospital for treatment of her heart ailment. After three weeks she was released and rented a suite at the Alrae Hotel while her sister Ruby, Becky Morehouse and other friends searched for an apartment. "She still couldn't make up her mind whether to stay here or return to California," Becky says. "I was at the Alrae the night she finally called to give up her apartment at the Shoreham. I got so weary of the indecision. She was ill, and this particular night I said, "If you're going to get an apartment here, call tonight, or you'll have to pay another month's rent.' I sat there as she called, and that shook her up. She said afterward, 'I don't have a home anywhere now.'"

Throughout the summer and fall Miriam lived on at the Alrae, resisting her doctor's suggestion that she be hospitalized for further tests. Finally, she agreed to go. The evening before she was to do so Ruby called and was told Miriam had collapsed and had nurses in attendance around the clock. "But then Mims came on the phone. 'Dear, I haven't really collapsed, but the doctor is horrified at my going to the Medical Center in a cab. He examined my heart, and it seems to have slumped a little. He said I'd have to go in an ambulance. Well, I will *not*, definitely *not*, be seen on a stretcher. So he's shut off visitors and the phone, and in a week I'll be able to go in a civilized manner."

Four days later, at 5 A.M. on October 9, Ruby received a call from Michael informing her that Miriam had succumbed to a massive coronary.

There was a well-attended funeral service in New York.

There was a graveside service in Bainbridge, Georgia, where Miriam was buried on the family plot.

There was a small memorial service in Hollywood which fewer than fifty people attended.

The once luminous reputation had largely evaporated by the time of her death, although critic Andrew Sarris still considers *Design for Living* a "modern classic" and Howard Thompson's capsule TV review of it in the New York *Times* called the film "casually moored to Noel Coward's caviar, but grand sophisticated fun."

A few other admirers are as fervent as ever. Tennessee Williams.* wrote of her work, "Unfortunately these great stage performances do not survive except in the recollections of those whom they moved deeply. What we are left of her art is in her films. As in the case of Garbo, the screen star nearly always was of more importance than the material she worked with. But this fact will not seriously impair the liv-

---

*From an unpublished tribute to Miss Hopkins at the time of her death.

ing image of Miriam Hopkins on the screen any more than the genius of Garbo was obscured by the inadequacies of her vehicles.

"I know that Paramount Pictures must be aware of her value, the value of her unique talent and personality, and I trust that there will be continual rivals of her films . . . she has the quality of which a 'cult' could emerge comparable to the 'cults' of Garbo, Marlene Dietrich and Katharine Hepburn."

These enthusiasts aside, not only the majority of the public but also writers about film seem unaware of the esteem that this maverick, who challenged the system and was punished for it, once enjoyed as a screen actress. In *The Great Movie Stars* David Shipman cites William H. Rideout's *The American Cinema* (1937) as an "odd book," quoting Rideout's assessment: "On all counts, Miss Hopkins is easily the finest actress on the screen today." The days when Lubitsch and Mamoulian, Sam Goldwyn and Jack Warner vied for her services are all but forgotten. Who remembers that in 1932 columnist Cal York chose Miriam as the best bet for stardom, ranking her above Joan Blondell, Jean Harlow, Carole Lombard, Sylvia Sidney and Helen Hayes?

The late 1930s, when Miriam was staging her strongest scenes—on- and offscreen—are long past. Some of those scenes were laden with charm; some, violent. But whatever they were, through them Miriam managed both to defeat herself and to create the stuff of which legends are made. These stories about her hold the secret to how this mercurial creature managed to rise so high. They also contain the key to why she faded so swiftly.

On January 1, 1934, the future seemed infinitely brighter than the past had been, but as it happened everything that was to transpire in the future was an anticlimax. Big studios manufacturing mass entertainment had little patience with personal eccentricities or professional problem children—no matter how gifted. In the final analysis Miriam, for all her talent, intelligence and magnetism, was the victim of her individualism.

She composed her own epitaph when she observed, "If I had to do it over again, I'd do everything different."

RUTH ETTING

The Box-Office Bait

On New Year's Eve, 1933, Samuel Goldwyn's *Roman Scandals* sold out early. In addition to Eddie Cantor's popularity, Ruth Etting's name lured many customers into the Rivoli Theater.

In the late 1920s and early 1930s Ruth ranked as the Judy Garland or Barbra Streisand of her era.

Florenz Ziegfeld, Jr., who glorified Ruth in the *Follies,* rated her as "the greatest singer of songs" that he had managed in a forty-year career.

The recording company to whom she was under contract billed her as The Sweetheart of Columbia Records.

On radio she had established herself as America's preeminent torch singer. In listener polls she alternated with Kate Smith as the most popular female singer on the air.

She reigned as the acknowledged queen of musical short subjects.

Even as discriminating a showwoman as Mae West still vividly recalls the first time she saw Ruth in the *Follies.* "The curtains opened, and here was this girl. Not what you'd call a classic beauty—but unusual," Miss West says. "She had a sex quality that seemed to mesmerize the audience. And when she finished singing, they just kind of went crazy."

Producer Samuel Goldwyn had shrewdly planned, from the moment he signed her, to capitalize on Ruth's popularity in other fields to increase the box office potential of *Roman Scandals.*

Patrons of the film were sure to be disappointed to find that despite her big billing, Ruth sang only one song, "No More Love," and was on the screen for less time than in one of her popular musical short subjects. Even that single number offered little real opportunity since it was gimmicked with trick photography and one of Busby Berkeley's seminude phantasmagorias.

Nevertheless, *Billboard*'s reviewer acknowledged her importance when he summed up his notice: "All in all, exhibitors should not be afraid of this one. It will make money for you. The present radio programs of Cantor and Etting should mean something in small towns. . . ."

Unlike Ginger Rogers and Miriam Hopkins, Ruth was unconcerned about her professional future that December 31. She had long ago learned that success could not be equated with happiness. The important thing that night, as far as she was concerned, was that she had managed to return to her birthplace, David City, Nebraska, (population: 2,200) where she was spending New Year's Eve surrounded by loving relatives and friends. More significantly, she had contracted to have a white picket fence built around the lawn of the big old farmhouse which she owned and had entered into negotiations to have the building modernized and in readiness when she decided to retire.

Ruth was a popular singer in the real sense of the word—she had developed a delivery that appealed to all ages and levels of sophistication. The lilting, almost adolescent sound that had captivated early listeners was rapidly replaced by a plaintive, haunting quality which further enhanced her popularity.

Now, in Hollywood, she was attempting the difficult feat of extending her stardom to feature-length motion pictures.

On Broadway she had seldom handled more than a few lines of dialogue. But so powerful was the impact of her style as she confessed being guilty, begged her sweetheart to love her or leave her or bemoaned the degradation of being available to all comers at ten cents a dance that audiences, knowing little of her private life, tended to confuse the material she popularized with her personal biography.

Working in films presented new problems. To establish herself, she not only needed to be a consummate singing actress, but also to handle dialogue naturally, something she had never been trained to do. Nor was she in the first bloom of youth so that her natural effervescence would cause audiences to overlook awkwardly handled lines. In person her taffy-colored hair and boldly handsome features were as appealing as ever, but the uncompromising eye of the motion-picture camera exposed and magnified slight imperfections. Investment of time and money was required to produce a screen image that approximated her theatrical countenance.

The alternative was to give her big billing and minuscule parts. Since she was not under long-term contract to any studio, this was the practical, economically sane course. Consequently, her prospects were limited. Not for her the protection of only being photographed on her left, or good, side as Claudette Colbert was, or the care taken to ensure that no trace of the scar on Carole Lombard's face marred her screen presence. Ruth was "box-office bait," to be used and discarded.

In any case, Hollywood never understood her uniqueness. Long after she had retired, Metro-Goldwyn-Mayer made what purported to be her life story. They called it *Love Me or Leave Me.* It won a prize. But in the interest of melodrama the scriptwriters reduced Ruth to a clichéd, hard-drinking, lusty, amoral opportunist. The result was an effective formula drama that dismissed the most interesting aspects of her character. Like Sophia in Arnold Bennett's *The Old Wives' Tale,* Ruth left her provincial surroundings and had many worldly experiences. In Chicago she picked her way through the raffish world of show business at a time when it was as riddled with corruption as the city. She encountered kept women, mobsters, machine politicians on the take and tough chorus girls. She married Martin "Colonel Gimp" Snyder, a political flunky with strong underworld connections, who insisted that she live as austerely as a nun. Whether they were in Chicago, New York or Hollywood, her chief companions were fear and loneliness. Because of her embarrassment at Snyder's crude manners and dangerous temper Ruth chose to remain outside Hollywood's social life. For the same reason she remained free from the pressures and machinations of the big studio system. The result was that when she divorced Snyder and he shot the new man in her life, she was able to maintain her equilibrium in the face of a scandal that would have destroyed a less balanced individual. Even after a headline such as GIMP CHARGES EX AND NEW MATE PLOTTED TO KILL HIM, Ruth retained her dignity. Just as Arnold Bennett's Sophia had, she held tightly to the homespun verities of her childhood.

Ruth Etting was born in her parents' bedroom in David City on November 23, 1896.* When Ruth was five years old, her mother, Winifred, fell ill, and the two of them went to San Diego, hoping Winifred's family could nurse her back to health. Instead, her condition rapidly became worse and she died.

---

*For professional reasons she sometimes claimed 1901 and even 1905.

Alfred Etting, Ruth's father, took a leave of absence from his job as a bank teller and went to pick up his chubby, flaxen-haired daughter, bringing her to live with his parents temporarily.

Ruth quickly adjusted to life in a household made up of her grandparents and their unmarried daughter, Rose. "I went to bed by the evening train and got up by the morning one, twenty minutes after eight at night and twenty minutes to in the morning," she says. "Maybe that's why I've always been a day person. Even when I was appearing in nightclubs."

Early to bed, early to rise wasn't the only aspect of the Protestant work ethic that her Germanic grandparents instilled in her. The day after her arrival from California her grandfather bought her a toy bank containing a few pennies, preaching, "Any fool can make money, but it takes a wise person to keep it."

Her autocratic grandfather provided much-needed reassurance for a child feeling doubly abandoned by a dead mother and a happy-go-lucky father. Transfer of her affections was completed when Alfred Etting remarried and his new wife was unwilling to assume the duties of a stepmother. Although Ruth liked her father and loved both her grandmother and her aunt Rose, her first allegiance was to her grandfather.

George Etting, a handsome blond man, had arrived in David City by covered wagon. When the county offered him a deed to a large tract of land on condition that he erect a mill close to the Burlington Railroad tracks, he quickly accepted. The Etting Roller Mills prospered, and George assumed a prominent position in village affairs.

"I thought my grandfather hung the moon," Ruth said in her mid-seventies. In childhood she attempted to emulate him. In the winter they shot sparrows to keep them from dirtying the hay and hunted rabbits; in the summer they fished in the old Platte River.

Early in Ruth's life her grandfather stimulated her interest in show business by building the David City Opera House and by allowing traveling tent shows and circuses to pitch their tents on the lot behind his mills.

In spite of her interest in entertainment, Ruth did not participate in public performances during her youth. She hated school and, because of an inherited tendency to stutter, never acted in school plays or assembly programs. Her only public singing was smothered in the anonymity of the Congregational Church choir. "I sang in a high, squeaky soprano," she says. "It sounded terrible, but I didn't know I could sing in any other range."

Never a good student, during study periods she filled the margins of her textbooks with sketches while dreaming of becoming a newspaper illustrator. Her low grades precluded her attending the University of Nebraska after graduation, as was the family custom. After working briefly in an Omaha department store, Ruth left for Chicago to enroll in the Academy of Fine Arts. There, while living at the Young Women's Christian Association, she began studying costume design. Her first semester was uneventful, but during the second the manager of the Marigold Gardens nightclub asked the head of the academy to recommend an advanced student to sketch costumes which his wife could vividly describe but not render on paper. Ruth was sent to see him. After inspecting her work, the manager invited her to have dinner and watch the show, which might provide inspiration. The none-too-wholesome dancers looked like angels to the naïve David City girl, and when she was offered $25 a week to join the chorus, her answer was an enthusiastic yes. Shortly, the manager's wife brought Ruth to the attention of Mme. Maybelle [wife of Milton Weil, a songwriter and publisher], a Loop modiste, who hired her for an additional $25 weekly. Clearing $50 every seven days, Ruth had only one problem: she was too tired to attend classes. so she dropped out. Temporarily, the heady atmosphere of the Marigold made her oblivious to her grandfather's reaction. If only it were possible for her to arrange for him to attend the show and see her working with Sophie Tucker, Bill "Bojangles" Robinson and Isham Jones and His Orchestra, she was sure he could not fail to be impressed.

Then, in the winter of 1919, the killer flu epidemic caused the city to close all nightclubs, and Ruth supported herself by painting Christmas cards, while fretting about not having told her family that she had quit school. But soon the Marigold reopened, and among the new stars was a baritone named Bobby Roberts, who sang Ted Koehler's "Hats Off to the Polo Girl." To Ruth's surprise she found herself singing out full voice to Roberts' arrangements. Producer Ernie Young stopped rehearsal to inquire who was vocalizing so loudly. Ruth admitted it might be she and waited to be fired. "Well, keep it up! It gives the number some life," Young said, and when he staged the bows, he gave her a moment of recognition.

A month later Roberts called in ill. "You like the Polo number so well, sing it," Young commanded.

"The next thing I knew, it was like a scene from one of Warners' musicals. They dressed me up in Bobby's suit, put his top hat on my head and stuffed his shoes with tissue paper so I could keep them on. And there I was doing the number. It went over so well they let me keep it from then on.

"I was just a farm girl. So green the cows could eat me," Ruth says of that period. Still uneasy about having quit the academy without family consent and unprepared to deal with the problems arising from her unexpected success as an entertainer, she longed for her grandfather or anyone else to guide her.

One of the patrons of the club was prepared to do just that. Martin Moe (originally Moses) Snyder was obsessed with her sweet singing, wholesome personality and blond beauty. Snyder, a swarthy, powerful-looking man, walked so lamely on his left leg that associates had nicknamed him Colonel Gimp. Photographs taken at the time suggest a caricature combining the features of movie tough guy George Raft and television's Peter Falk.

Snyder flourished in the reflected glory of celebrities. Whether they were big-time politicians, entertainers or gangsters was immaterial to him. So relentlessly did he pursue them that newspaper people sometimes facetiously referred to him as the Mayor of Randolph Street. Now, after seeing Ruth at the Marigold, he dreamed of capturing a potential celebrity for himself. His cronies laughed when he talked of marrying her before they had even met. Unlikely? Snyder didn't think so.

Few facts could be verified about this strange man. That he had been born around Fourteenth and Solin streets, in the toughest part of Chicago's West Side, was easily documented. Snyder himself told of leaving school after the fifth or sixth grade and hawking newspapers on the streets in order to eat regulary. He had married young, fathered a child and was thought to be divorced or separated or widowed. He wasn't the kind of man that could be pressed for direct answers when he chose to be vague.

Even the explanation of how he acquired his limp came in several versions. The most common explanation was that he carried seventeen fragments of hot lead in his leg—put there by rivals of his gangster-friend Dion O'Banion.

The most elaborate story was that Snyder saw some Klansmen harassing an old Jewish man on a streetcar. When these bigots pulled the man's beard and threatened to set fire to it, Snyder knocked their heads together and tossed them out the trolley window. The conductor was said to have rewarded him by throwing him off the car and running over his leg.

The simplest and most likely version was that his mother accidentally dropped him while he was still a baby—an accident that might account for his eventual inability to trust anyone.

Snyder's underworld connections were equally complicated. Naturally, he always denied having any. Ruth, when asked whether he had been a gangster, replied, "No—anh-ah. He might have liked to have been, but I don't think he was quite good enough."

Yet, because he was a "protection man" in Chicago for such stars as Al Jolson, Jimmy Durante and Eddie Cantor at a time when penny-ante hoods regularly attempted to shake down entertainers playing the city, it stands to reason that Snyder had strong enough links to big-time mobsters to control the harassers.

His gangland associates also helped him carry out less than savory assignments from prominent politicians. He first worked in the Nineteenth Ward when he was fifteen or sixteen, then moved on to the notorious Twentieth Ward, operating as a floating voter, sometimes casting his ballot between seventy-five and one-hundred times in a single election. As he grew older, the assignments increased in difficulty.

On the side Snyder functioned as a circulation manager for the Chicago *Herald-American* and as a strikebreaker for Yellow and Checker Cab companies. During World War I he adopted the title of Colonel, making it possible for lawless doughboys to smuggle contraband into the country addressed to their friend, the "officer."

At the time he fell under Ruth's spell he carried business cards identifying him as a sanitary district official, a job regarded as a political plum, and he later claimed also to have been a secret "investigator for the district attorney."

"Show business was my ace in the hole," he told reporter John Blade in a 1975 interview in the Chicago *Tribune,* alluding to Ruth. "Knowing all the celebrities, being around them, doing favors for them. I knew Jolson, Durante, Lou Clayton. I worked for a song publisher, going around to houses like the Majestic and the Bijou, asking performers to sing our stage songs. That's how I met Ruth Etting."

Introduced to her by songwriter-publisher Rocco Vocco, Snyder aggressively moved in. And Ruth, unable to turn to her family for advice about her career, allowed him to make decisions and solve the quandries in which she found herself. Having someone to advise her was reassuring, but she became apprehensive as, increasingly, Snyder lurked in the wings at the club studying her every movement, mouthing the words of the songs she sang. Of those first weeks Snyder later said bitterly that she was "so dumb" she actually thought he *was* the mayor of Randolph Street. In what may have been the understatement of her life Ruth remarked she had never met anyone like him in David City, in fact, hadn't known such people existed.

Initially, her suitor curbed his violent temper, praised her work, protected her from "mashers" and tirelessly spread the word that "the little lady," as he called her, had stopped the show again that night.

Neither Snyder nor anyone else had to tell Marigold's producer Ernie Young that audiences responded to Ruth. In *The Passing Parade of 1921* Young gave her first-featured billing.

Closing at the Marigold Gardens, she moved to the Palais Royale and the Million-Dollar Rainbo Gardens. The Rainbo, a forerunner of theater-in-the-round, was circular in shape with a stage serving as the hub of the wheel. There Edward Beck produced a series of revues: *Rainbo Trail, In Rainbo Land* and *Rainbo Blossoms.* In the first of these Ruth began defining herself as a torch singer, delivering "Crying for You" and "Honolulu Blues."

Wherever she opened, Snyder was underfoot, having insinuated himself into her life so gradually that she was almost unaware at what point his praise began to be tempered with criticism and suggestions turned into commands.

On July 12, 1922, the obviously mismatched couple crossed the Illinois line to Crown Point, Indiana, and were wed. Attempting to explain her motivations, Ruth later claimed that she had married Snyder nine-tenths out of fear and one-tenth out of pity. In any case, the evening of the wedding saw the couple back in Chicago in time for her performance.

Granted a leave of absence, Ruth took her new husband to meet relatives in Nebraska. From there they went on to Washington, D.C., where her father was living. Acquaintances in Chicago were astonished at the unsuitable union. However, as Robert J. Landry—now managing editor of *Variety* but then covering the Chicago scene—observed: "I daresay there have been a fair number of similar cases in show business where an aggressive type has advanced talent, then made life miserable for that talent."

At the Rainbo Gardens one revue succeeded another; performers opened, played out their engagements and departed; but Ruth stayed on for what *Variety* reported as an unprecedented seven-month cabaret engagement in Chicago. When owner Mann and producer Beck billed her as "Chicago's Sweetheart," Snyder arranged for Mayor William E. Dever to give her the key to the city and had thousands of cards printed and distributed, asking:

HAVE YOU HEARD?

RUTH ETTING
Chicago's Sweetheart
at Mann's
Million Dollar Theatre

Clark at Lawrence

The record-breaking run finally ended, and Ruth moved on to a series of appearances at such once-famous nightclubs as the Terrace Gardens in the Morrison Hotel; the Montmartre Cafe; the Granada and the Green Mill. At the Mill a sad-eyed young singer with long, coal-black hair sang "Too Tired to Wash the Dishes." Helen Morgan wasn't sitting atop pianos in those days, but she had a stage mother who was almost as ambitious for her daughter as Snyder was for his wife. "Helen was a fabulous performer. Gorgeous to look at, she had an odd little quality in her voice," Ruth remembers. "I used to watch her act every night, and her mother, Lulu, was always there, keeping an eye on things. I never felt I got to know Helen well personally. I don't think anyone did. It was very sad. She was very bighearted and her own worst enemy."

Helen Morgan was obviously headed for stardom, but no one expected much from a blackface duo who were playing some of the same clubs. They called themselves Sam 'n' Henry and a decade later surprised those who had known them by becoming world-famous as Amos 'n' Andy.

Among Ruth's many engagements one stands out—Big Jim Colosimo's. It represented a tough grind from 7 P.M. to 7 A.M., seven days a week for no salary. "We worked strictly for tips. Colosimo's was an Italian place. No stage. No microphone. We were what they called table singers. I've always thought that's where crooning was born," Ruth says. "You went from table to table, sitting with each one, singing requests. There were about a dozen entertainers—everything from jazz singers to grand opera. A little guy named Louie—I never did know his last name—accompanied us on the piano. One of the twelve would raise a hand and call out a request. And this little guy would play it in our particular key. Anything from a popular hit to an aria. In order to be heard, you had to acquire a special voice quality, penetrating but intimate.

"The fine points of the game escaped me at first. We had a tin box

137

with a slot on it, sitting on top of the piano, and you dropped your tips in it. One night a little gray-haired man sitting by himself called me over and said, 'Sing "Melancholy Baby."' Those were days when they enjoyed crying in their beer. I sang it, and when he tipped me, he gave me two one-dollar bills opened up and pressed a folded twenty in my hand. 'Stick that in your shoe,' he whispered. I said, 'Oh, I couldn't do that. We have to put our money in the box.' He looked at me and said, 'You dumb kid. Why do you think Irving Foster and Benny Davis [composer of "Margie"] are always looking at the ceiling and putting their fingers in their collars?' Then he explained that when they pretended to loosen their collars, they were really sticking the big bills in there and carrying the small ones to the box later. They called them ceiling singers because they were always looking up like that. From then on I may not have been so honest, but I made a lot more money."

Big Jim Colosimo was a top Chicago boss, and rumor has it that he summoned Al Capone to the city. "Lots of gangsters came to the club," Ruth says. "They love being around show people. I'd sung many a song for Al Capone and seen him around Colosimo's often but never knew him as Capone. Everybody called him Al Brown. I heard all this talk about Capone, Capone, Capone, and the first time I saw his picture in the newspaper I said, 'That's not Capone. That's Scarface Al Brown!' You may not believe that, but I did my work, minded my own business and went home. I told you I was pretty green."

To understand how Ruth remained so naive, one must remember that Snyder had served as protection man for other entertainers and in many respects maintained a kind of surrogate father relationship with her. He refused to let her have her hair bobbed. Newspapers said he served as her "business manager and constant companion." Her cousins were quoted to the effect that he would scarcely allow Ruth to venture outside 4336 Kenmore without him. He shielded her from the seamier side.

In 1924 (just as Ginger Rogers was to do on a similar station in Dallas a couple of years later) Ruth promoted herself by appearing frequently as a guest on the *Herald-American*'s radio station, KYW. This resulted in bookings on a vaudeville circuit taking her to Omaha, Kansas City, St. Louis and Minneapolis. Because Snyder still held a position with the sanitary district, she was able to enjoy a brief respite from his constant surveillance. But she was so unaccustomed to being on her own that while appearing in Omaha at the Rialto, she shared an apartment with the violin player, his wife and their baby.

To Ruth's delight, she discovered her friend Blossom Seeley was headlining at the prestigious Palace in Omaha. The high-flying Blossom—who had already been a headliner in San Francisco during the 1906 earthquake, who first employed the down-on-one-knee stance Jolson made famous and who was generally acknowledged to be twenty years ahead of her time in singing and dancing styles—was appalled to learn Ruth was sharing an economy apartment. How could she hope to be a star if she didn't behave like one? Talent, Ruth said, remaining true to her grandfather's dictum that any fool could earn money, but that it took a smart person to hold onto it.*

Upon the close of the tour Ruth made a brief trip to New York to model a new line of shoes by Chicago designer William Goldstein in return for expenses—an opportunity to attend Broadway shows and collect free footwear.

Working again in Chicago, she played her regular stands, then opened at the College Inn, located in the Sherman Hotel, appearing with Abe Lyman and His Orchestra. She broadcast several times with the Lyman group from WLS studios, located atop the hotel, and was eventually given her own program.

Late in 1925 she attracted the attention of Columbia Records executives. Naturally, Snyder took credit for setting up the deal, but Ruth believed that Tom Rockwell heard her singing "What Can I Say After I Say I'm Sorry?" on the air and arranged a record audition, while Columbia Records officially credited director of recording Frank Walker with following up on the recommendation of Mme. Maybelle and songwriter-publisher Milton Weil. Walker immediately recognized Ruth as a "wax natural" whose instincts would surmount the mechanical limitations of the primitive microphones then in use.

For her initial release Columbia coupled "Let's Talk About My Sweetie" with "Nothing Else to Do." Pianist-songwriter Rube Bloom accompanied her on the piano and remained with her on a semiregular basis for the next three years. Her first recording with orchestral accompaniment was "Hello, Baby" with Art Kahn's Orchestra in 1926. Although she by then concentrated on torch songs in clubs, her 1926–27 Columbia records emphasized the upbeat, girlish quality in her voice.

She also began appearing at motion-picture theaters in Chicago at this time. Featured at McVicker's during Jazz Week, she moved to the Ambassador, where she was held over, and then opened on February

*In retirement Ruth lives comfortably on investments. Blossom was dependent on the generosity of friends for many years before her death.

26 at the Palace in the Loop. Al Jolson and ex-fighter Benny Leonard sent flowers. Snyder gathered a claque of municipal judges and politicians to add importance to the occasion. But as with so many of his ideas, the execution went awry. So much time was spent assembling the group outside the theater that Ruth's turn had been completed before the party marched in.

The following July she opened at the Oriental Theater with Paul Ash (who was later to introduce Ginger Rogers to New York), and *Variety* welcomed Ruth as "the real quality on the bill . . . the last word in attractiveness and possessing a voice that may be adapted to any type of song, Miss Etting stands as an artist capable of holding a place on any bill in any company."

Amid these triumphs Ruth's personal life was a shambles. Both embarrassed by and increasingly afraid of her husband, she saw no way out. "My sad story is that my first marriage wasn't a marriage at all—it was a mistake," is how she sums it up.

On February 18, 1927, Paul Whiteman arranged a covert tryout for Ruth at his club located at Forty-Eighth Street and Broadway in Manhattan. Neither daily newspapers nor *Variety* reviewed the brief stand, which was designed to test the compatibility of a temporary Etting-Whiteman collaboration. Nevertheless, Snyder urged everyone in Chicago from Mayor William E. Dever to Alderman Jacob M. Arvey to a covey of judges to telegraph their good wishes to "the little lady."

The audition turned out so satisfactorily that after playing a quick round of Balaban-Katz theaters in Chicago, Ruth and Snyder moved to New York permanently. "It was then or never. I was over thirty," Ruth says, "but I fooled New Yorkers for a long time. They thought I was a kid. I was little and slim and blond. Very few people knew I'd been working around Chicago for almost ten years. Even Ziegfeld didn't have any idea of my age."

Had that producer taken the advice of Irving Berlin, who was composing the score for the 1927 *Follies* and happened to hear an Etting recording of one of his numbers, Ziegfeld might have introduced Ruth to New York audiences. Instead, he waited until early June, when she and Whiteman were about to open at the Times Square Paramount, before summoning her to his office.

Fully aware of the cachet attached to Ziegfeld's management, Ruth was apprehensive as she walked into his sumptuous private office with its huge desk across which marched his collection of miniature elephants. He greeted her warmly and proceeded to talk about the show while she waited uneasily to audition. Finally, he asked her to stand up and walk around the room. "I walked. He looked at my ankles, and that was it. That was my audition. He wouldn't hire anyone—no matter how talented—with big ankles." Ruth smiles and adds, "Wouldn't you know that he had married one of the thickest pair in the business. Billie Burke. A lovely face, naturally wavy hair the color of a new copper penny, but she had thick ankles and wrists."

If Ziegfeld was not interested in hearing Ruth sing, Berlin was. In his office he was as friendly and encouraging as Ziegfeld, but his new discovery had hardly begun her audition when he clapped his hands over his ears and left the room. When she finished the number, he reappeared and asked her to do another song. Again he covered his ears and disappeared. When Ruth had finished, he returned to congratulate her. He had employed the hands-to-the-ears routine to test whether she could project his lyrics to the back of the balcony.

On June 8, Ruth finally signed to appear in the 1927 *Follies*, giving Ziegfeld a two-week escape clause. He was to pay her $400 a week—which his press agent escalated to $3,000, or twice what she had been earning in Chicago. "I realized it wasn't a matter of money. Having Mr. Ziegfeld's stamp on you was worth ten times what he was paying," she says. "He spoiled other producers for me after he died."

On June 11 she opened at the Paramount with Whiteman, singing "I Love You," "A Russian Lullaby" and "It All Depends on You" plus encores selected with an eye to the type of audience out front. Sime Silverman, founder of *Variety*, used Ruth's first official engagement in Manhattan as the occasion to welcome her to the city, review her professional achievements and assess her potential. "Ruth Etting waited quite a while before making New York professionally, but she accomplished two muchly desired results within two days last week after reaching Broadway," he wrote. "Thursday she signed a contract to open with Ziegfeld's new *Follies* and Saturday, on her New York premiere, made good at the Paramount. . . .

"Her quiet delivery leaves a likable impression right away. An extremely pleasant single for the picture houses, while for the *Follies* Flo Ziegfeld and Stan Sharpe [Ziegfeld's assistant] need not worry if the right songs are furnished this girl," he concluded.

In the twenty-first edition of the *Follies* the cast included Eddie Cantor, Claire Luce, Irene Delroy (from whom Ginger Rogers was to steal *Top Speed*), the Brox Sisters, Cliff "Ukulele Ike" Edwards and Dan

Healy. Since Cantor was the star, he naturally wanted the songs that seemed potential hits, leaving to Ruth and the others in the cast the less accessible numbers.

On opening night Cantor wired Ruth, "Whatever I wish for myself may you also receive"—which to a great extent turned out to be the case. *Follies* audiences responded to her essential elegance and dignity, even though for her first entrance she sported a black wig and did a takeoff on Fannie Brice singing "Rose of Washington Square" and in her second wore what the designer described as "a frock of white satin, with hand-painted dice adorning the princess bodice . . . a fichu of white net . . . [suggesting] Aunt Dinah's kerchief . . . [and] a white hairband set off in front with a red bow that suggests a bandanna drape." For all its garish theatricality, the gown could not diminish Ruth's womanly grace. Audiences responded to her before she emitted the first note of Berlin's intricate "Shaking the Blues Away," described as "an up North version of a down South spiritual." And as the number developed, the Jazzbo girls jazzed, the Albertina Rasch dancers pirouetted and the seminude Banjo ingenues postured and posed, but none of them could wrest attention from Ruth as she projected the song's broken rhythms. Audiences invariably were blended into a volatile, rhythmic mass at the finish of the ten-minute production number.

Ruth's ovation was so great that upon every subsequent appearance applause greeted her. Although the show was built around Cantor as the solo star, Walter Winchell, Percy Hammond and most other first-string critics singled Ruth out for special praise. *Variety* predicted that she had in this initial appearance established herself as a *Follies* regular of the future. Many of her notices were enthusiastic, but Whitney Bolton of the *Morning Telegraph* was obviously seized by Etting-mania, writing that she was "out of place in the *Follies* . . . she ought to be in a hospital . . . anyone with a voice like that . . . could sing paralytics into life . . . and heal wounds with her emotional croons . . . she should sing in the slums . . . and spread sunshine . . . where the elevated structure casts heavy shadows on human misery . . . there's ultra violet rays in them there notes . . . she makes most 'blues' singers sound like doxologists . . . ."

In response to the enthusiasm she aroused, Ziegfeld drew up a run-of-the-play contract, increasing Ruth's salary from $400 to $600 a week, telling her, "I'll glorify you, and you'll glorify the American song." It was the last written agreement they were ever to sign. Thereafter terms were agreed upon verbally and sealed with a handshake. "With Mr. Ziegfeld you didn't need anything spelled out on paper,"

142

Ruth says. "You knew all he wanted for his stars was the best. When he left the scene, I never wanted to do another Broadway show. The glamor was gone."

The higher Ruth climbed in public esteem, the more retiring she became offstage. Upon arrival in New York the Snyders had rented a suite at the Piccadilly, on Forty-fifth Street, west of Broadway. The hotel was then a favorite of entertainers because of its proximity to vaudeville and legitimate theaters. But even after Ruth's success the Snyders stayed on since she had neither the time nor the inclination to furnish and oversee a household. She was happy to have maids tend to the cleaning, but she was not accustomed to and did not want anyone fussing over her. "I've never felt comfortable with servants," she has said. "I like to do things for myself. Theater maids liked working for me because I was easy. I've walked out of my dressing room and seen Helen Morgan's maid down on her hands and knees putting Helen's stocking on her. I would no more have thought of letting anyone do that than I would fly. I wasn't brought up that way. It wasn't my style. I was taught to do for myself."

By residing in a small suite, Ruth also avoided entertaining at home. In Chicago, although her spouse had been smitten by show business, his job with the city had kept him occupied during the day. In New York all of his unruly energy and ego were concentrated on Ruth.

In order to justify his existence and the fact that her earnings paid the bills, he insisted upon taking a more active role in her management—even though she had an agent. The result was that he humiliated her with his efforts. In those days threats and promotional gimmicks were useless. If, as a performer, she could not make herself heard in large theaters or cope with unreliable recording equipment, all of Snyder's demands for "the little lady" were useless.

"It was ridiculous," she once said. "In those days, you either had it, or you didn't. No matter who threatened, if audiences couldn't hear you, you were dead. You didn't work."

In order to divert Snyder's energies, it was arranged for him to manage Abe Lyman's Orchestra. At Lyman's Long Island opening news accounts described Ruth as visibly cringing as her ebullient spouse leaped up after each number, applauding and shouting, "I like it, I like it! Hey! Hey!"

But soon the agreement was canceled, and Snyder again concentrated on his wife's career, pushing, wheedling, demanding, cajoling, threatening—helping her form his point of view, creating unnecessary confusion, according to others. Socially, it was worse. Robert Landry recalls encountering Snyder on several occasions at Sime Silverman's apartment. "He was loud and uncouth, and she was obviously afraid of him," Landry contends. Whatever agonies she may have suffered because of her husband's crudity, Ruth had long ago learned to shrug them off as past and forgotten. In the late twenties and early thirties however, the Snyders' social life was confined to performers—Gracie Allen and George Burns, Blossom Seeley and Benny Fields, Jack and Mary Benny, Ted and Ada Lewis, Mr. and Mrs. Jesse Crawford—who were accustomed to his gaucheries and found them amusing.

There were, of course, a few new friends. Cantor was fond of Ruth and had known enough men of Snyder's stripe during his own poverty-stricken youth to accept the Gimp. But the closest and warmest of Ruth's new acquaintances were June and Walter Winchell. After his laudatory opening-night review the critic-columnist went on to call her "Queen of All Torch Warblers." They saw one another frequently, and when the Winchells wanted to go on the town, they often called Ruth, who would hurriedly remove her stage makeup after the curtain fell and rush to their house to baby-sit. Later, when Ruth became caught in scandal, the Winchells were among the first to rally to her defense.

Snyder quickly met everyone, whether they wanted to meet him or not. Midday generally found him at Lindy's, where he'd clump up and down the aisles, stopping at tables to buttonhole people who might be useful and giving them a boisterous account of his "sweet singer's" latest triumphs. In the evening, if as he increasingly was, he happened to be barred backstage, he would while away time gambling, running up small losses, before going to pick up Ruth. Occasionally after the *Follies* both would come to Lindy's. "Everyone liked her," a waiter said. "She was sweet and retiring. He was ready to fight about anything—even the weather. A nuisance."

When Ruth's schedule permitted it, she liked to go to the beach or to attend a play or a movie. She almost never entered a nightclub, preferring to return to the Piccadilly for a glass of milk before retiring. Much of her time was spent in their suite, sewing, painting or reading voraciously both fiction and nonfiction.

She had by this time become the best-selling popular singer on the Columbia label, recording mostly torch songs. Her contract called for the release of a single disc containing two numbers each month. An average sale of 40,000 per release may seem minuscule now, but in the late 1920s few artists equaled it. Occasionally, as with her revival of

"My Man," which sold 75,000 in the first six weeks, her hits continued to sell for two years.

To reach and maintain her position, Ruth devoted a good deal of time to choosing songs. That her taste was catholic can be seen by glancing at her discography (see p. 327).

"Every song must be studied separately to find a way to make the audience hear, see and feel the story it tells," Ruth once explained. Her standard approach was to listen to a pianist play the melody of a song four or five times to see whether any of it remained with her. When she had satisfied herself on that count, she would take the lyrics and learn them without regard for the melody. When both became familiar, she would fit them together, attempting to add a dimension to heighten the songwriter's intentions.

The result was that unlike many other recording stars, she was fully prepared when she arrived for a session. And she quickly learned that if she held the same volume throughout, only a couple of takes were required. "I had a big voice. I mean, you could hear me for blocks," she says. "But when I recorded or sang on the radio, they didn't have to fool with the dials. Singers don't have to worry about that now. To me Sinatra was king, but he'd be singing so softly you could hardly hear him, and then he'd bellow out. In my day we couldn't do that. I learned to hold my volume steady. That's why Joe Venuti, the jazz violinist, and some of the other boys liked to work with me. I was a quick recorder, and they could use the rest of my time after I finished."

When the 1927 *Follies* closed, Ruth had solid proof of what strides she had been making. Signed to play the Oriental in Chicago, she was happy to find her salary had leaped to $8,000 per week, and she demonstrated her worth by breaking the previous house record by $100.

Her West Coast contract with Pantages was even more remunerative. Scheduled for San Francisco, San Diego and Los Angeles, she was guaranteed $1,000 a week, plus 30 percent of the gross over $14,000 and 50 percent over $19,000. In San Francisco critics vied with one another for superlatives. A reviewer signing himself M. W. began rather conservatively in the opening sentences but then warmed to the task, writing, "Ruth Etting is the headliner of the vaudeville program. She holds her audience breathless with her singing of a no more important song than 'Away Down South in Heaven.' Her singing of 'Sunshine' is enough to give one emotional sunburn. It reaches the corners of one's heart." But a nameless scribe in San Diego easily triumphed in the tri-city hyperbole sweepstakes: "Has she got IT?" he asked. "Well, dearie, she positively exudes IT. She makes you think of orchards in the moonlight and other things that leave you absolutely breathless. I read that Ziegfeld called her exotic when she was in the *Follies*. She was better than that. She's gorgeous. She's the kind of girl who could make a $15-a-week clerk buy orchids. . . ." By comparison, everything written by critics in Los Angeles, the home of hyperbole, was dangerously anemic. But in all three cities Ruth stopped the show, had to beg off with a curtain speech and broke box-office records.

After vacationing in California, she signed to play the role for which Ginger Rogers had been angling in Ziegfeld's *Whoopee*. Adapted from Owen Davis' *The Nervous Wreck* by William Anthony McGuire, who also directed, *Whoopee* had music by Walter Donaldson and lyrics by Gus Kahn.

Besides Eddie Cantor and Ruth, the cast included Ethel Shutta, Gladys Glad and Albert Hackett, who had appeared in the straight version. Noticing that Ruth, who was handling dialogue for the first time, was having difficulty with her few lines, Hackett undertook to assist her with the scene they had together. "Ruth was wonderful to work with. She had no side at all. But she'd speak her lines rather flatly.

"Colonel Gimp was very much in evidence, but I didn't think anything about that. So was my wife. It was quite evident that Ruth and I were rehearsing.

"About the third day someone said to me, 'Come here.' I went over, and this fellow said, 'You know, the Gimp, he carries a knife.' I said, 'Oh?' And the fellow said, 'He don't like you talking to the little lady.' That was all. But I began to be aware that he was keeping both Ruth and me under surveillance.

"McGuire never called the scene for rehearsal. I don't know whether they cut it because I played sort of a heavy and they decided it would start the song badly or if the Gimp had McGuire cut it. Anyway, Ruth just came out and sang the song and always came off to a very big hand." Hackett and his wife, Frances Goodrich, who became successful as screenwriters and dramatists, were highly amused since his intentions were strictly professional.

Others, including Ziegfeld, grew impatient with the Colonel's meddling, paranoia and threats. In his anxiety to protect Ruth he robbed her of a chance for growth. It was easier for a director to restrict her to singing and dancing than risk Synder's wrath by attempting to teach her to deliver lines. Since she was a consummate artist in conveying emotion through popular songs, she probably was not a "lousy actress," as she always described herself, but simply untrained and inexperienced in the mechanics of projecting a character's feelings without the help of music. In any case, her lines were kept to a minimum.

On December 24, 1928, at the New York premiere of *Whoopee,* Ruth demonstrated once again that she was a critics' favorite. So glowing were her notices that after a few weeks Ziegfeld decided to augment her Donaldson-Kahn numbers, "Love Me or Leave Me," "I'm Bringing a Red, Red Rose" and "Gypsy Joe," with Cliff Friend and Irving Caesar's "My Blackbirds Are Bluebirds Now."

Before they had left for the out-of-town tryout, Ziegfeld had granted permission for Ruth to go to Paramount's Astoria studios one morning to film two five-minute short subjects. The initial one-reeler consisted of "Roses of Yesterday" and "Because My Baby Don't Mean Maybe"; the second of "My Mother's Eyes" and "That's Him Now." They were shot almost entirely in close-ups and were among the first musical shorts ever produced. Audience reception was so enthusiastic that Warner's Vitaphone immediately hired her to make an untitled one-reeler, supported by the popular piano duo Phil Ohman and Victor Arden. This production featured trick photography. For instance, after Ruth sang her first number, she faded slowly from the screen while the pianists performed. Then, for the finale, by use of double printing, she was shown standing by each pianist with one image of herself watching the other perform. This novelty proved so successful that the same cast repeated the technique in a sequel titled *Glorifying the American Song.**

Over the next few years she would earn between $5,000 and $15,000 per short.

The third *Vitaphone Variety* represented still another departure—a mini musical comedy in which she played a song plugger who, according to the review in *Billboard,* "falls madly in love with a handsome lad, who constantly sidesteps the date for wedding bells to ring out. Her happiness goes 'blooey' when a burlesque showgirl breaks the news that the guy is her hubby. The way this girl spiels the Broadway lingo is great stuff.

"You're sure to like the way Miss Etting sings, 'Where Is the Man I Love?' and 'From the Bottom of My Heart.' "

The handsome lad and the burlesque girl who didn't rate identification were Humphrey Bogart and Joan Blondell. "They passed out

---

*Leonard Maltin in *Film Fan Monthly* questions whether there were two or one of these Ohman-Arden films, but since the first is listed as Vitaphone 886 and the second as Vitaphone 894, there were undoubtedly two.

scenes, rehearsed them and slapped them through. If you were a natural with dialogue like Joan Blondell, you breezed through it. I wasn't,'' Ruth says. "Humphrey Bogart could see I had trouble with lines. And the poor guy spent every spare minute trying to get me to deliver them naturally. He was such a handsome kid and so nice. And I was hopeless.

"Somebody should have insisted I go to acting school or get a coach. But they just shoved me in front of the camera and yelled, 'Say it!' The songs were all they cared about."

Asked by a reporter how she felt when she first saw herself on the screen, Ruth replied, "I shuddered." Her response never changed. She was nonplussed at the casual way everything except the microphone and camera were treated. "Shorts were made to fill out the program along with a feature, a cartoon and a newsreel. Sometimes there was a simple plot, sometimes I just sang. The plot had to be simple to make room for at least two songs. And the emphasis was technical— white didn't photograph. Pink, beige and tan were best. Even lipstick and eyeshadow were brown."

Ruth starred in at least thirteen additional *Vitaphone Varieties* or *Broadway Brevities* between 1931 and 1933 and in fourteen shorts for RKO between 1933 and 1936. In a couple of others she was seen briefly or her voice was heard. Her total output, as far as can be determined from sketchy records, was thirty-five one- and two-reel featurettes. In the early days of television a few showed up, but both Ruth and collectors believe most are lost.

Whoopee, which had closed after a run of 379 performances, began a national tour with Cantor, Ruth and most of the Broadway principals. "I liked Eddie, He was a lot of fun," Ruth remarked later, and when a reporter said that Cantor obviously liked her, too, she countered, "Well, someone had to go on while he changed costumes—and I didn't tell jokes, only sang, so I wasn't direct competition. We got to our first stand. The theater had those big doors open to move in scenery, and Eddie got the sniffles. That was that. He was a real hypochondriac. The rest of us worked with double pneumonia. I had my tonsils burned out one Sunday and went on the next evening. But Eddie believed 'the show must go on' was just a lot of nonsense."

As a result, a dispute developed between Cantor and Ziegfeld, who was in financial difficulty, and the tour was canceled. This freed Ruth to appear in one of those productions that promise on paper to be a surefire success—Ruth Selwyn's *Nine-Fifteen Revue.* Songs were by

Rudolf Friml, Victor Herbert, Harold Arlen, Cole Porter, Rodgers and Hart, Vincent Youmans, George and Ira Gershwin, Kay Swift and Paul James. The sketches were by Anita Loos and John Emerson, Leslie Howard, William Anthony McGuire, Eddie Cantor, Irving Caesar, Rube Goldberg, Ring Lardner, Paul Gerard Smith and Robert Riskin. Choreography was by Busby Berkeley.

Ruth Etting was understanding about repeated delays in going into rehearsal, but unhappy at being allotted, besides a number of songs, only two sketches, *The Plumber* by Cantor and *Meet the Wife* by Smith. She was also perturbed that Harry Richman withdrew at the last moment and she found herself singing with a couple of girls. All was confusion as new sketches and songs replaced the original ones. Still, the production received dancing-in-the-streets, hats-in-the-air receptions in New Haven and Boston, and Ruth was incontestably the star of the show. George Gershwin called her handling of Arlen and Koehler's "Get Happy" the most exciting finale he had ever heard in a theater. She stopped the show with Kay Swift and Paul James' "Up Among the Chimney Pots." But somewhere between Boston and New York the magic vanished.

Not a single memorable moment, said the New York *Times*. The engagement lasted less than a week. On closing night Ziegfeld called from Boston, where he was trying out *Simple Simon*, starring Ed Wynn. He begged Ruth to replace Lee Morse, who was playing Sal. Morse had shown up drunk and ruined a great new number Rodgers and Hart had written for her.

Recollections vary on what happened next. Richard Rodgers believes Ruth took over after the production had returned to New York, performed the song exactly as written for Miss Morse but never sang it to an audience before opening night.

Ruth is certain she went to Boston and found the Wynn vehicle in disarray, but it may have been on closing night that she saw the show. As Sal, she realized, she had two wonderful songs, "I Still Believe" and "Ten Cents a Dance." The latter presented problems. "I wasn't worried about getting up in the two sides of dialogue—which was all Sal had—but the girl they'd originally hired had a full three-octave range. On my best day I never had much more than an octave and a half. There was no way I could sing that song. So Richard Rodgers, Larry Hart and I stayed up all night cutting down the range to fit my voice. Maybe that's how the story started that the song was written for me. It wasn't written for me. It was *re*written for me."

At *Simple Simon*'s opening on February 18 Ruth faced the New

York critics for the second time within a week. In the slapdash approach then fashionable in musicals Ruth's lament as a taxi dancer was inexplicably introduced by having Wynn pedal on stage with a combination tricycle and grand piano he had used in vaudeville. Ruth, who was perched atop the piano, inquired whether he could play in A-flat. Wynn replied that he could play in any flat to which he had the key. Such a facetious, if not foolish, introduction to the lachrymose wail of a dime-a-dance girl was overlooked by audiences and critics. But not Ruth's feat of stepping into the show on short notice. In the *Daily News* Burns Mantle announced she was more affecting than ever before. In the *Mirror* Winchell cited her performance as added proof that "Miss Etting is alone in her field, far outdistancing any of her competitors." And Brooks Atkinson commented in the *Times* that she had been "rushed out of the limbo of the *Nine-Fifteen Revue*" and that "although she appeared under the sketchiest preparation, she was letter-perfect and she contributed perceptibly to the performance that needs color and personality."

Among the more than one hundred telegrams was one from Ed Wynn ("Thumbs up for a personal success") and an especially meaningful one from Billie Burke Ziegfeld ("It's great news to know you are there tonight, gorgeous—success to you"). There were flowers from Rodgers and Hart ("Good luck to our newest star, Dick and Larry") and from Ziegfeld ("Hand it too[sic] them, kid"), as well as wires from Jolson, Cantor and her husband.

It should have added up to a sense of fulfillment, but even as bright-faced well-wishers crowded her dressing room, Ruth could hear Snyder hippety-hopping about, buttonholing the biggest celebrities, bragging to them how he and the "little lady" got Ziggy off the hot spot. Without them there would have been no show. Even the satisfaction of a job well done was lessened by Snyder's showboating.

With the opening and the reviews out of the way, Ziegfeld dropped "I Still Believe in You" and interpolated Fred Fisher and Billy Rose's "Happy Days and Lonely Nights," plus Ruth's *Whoopee* showstopper "Love Me or Leave Me." He also decided to scrap the mobile piano and let Ruth sing "Ten Cents a Dance" standing at the proscenium arch. "Ed Wynn was a sweet person and a lovely artist, but he had the same habit as Cantor," Ruth told a friend. "The minute I sang my last note he'd walk out to kill the applause. Sometimes he'd have to exit while I did an encore. But a lot of times he killed it. That's a star for you. That's why they became stars and stayed up there. Show business doesn't reward shyness."

150

When hot June weather arrived, *Simple Simon,* like most legitimate productions in those days, closed for the summer. So the last week of June Ruth opened at the Palace, headlining a vaudeville bill that included Lou Holtz, Bill "Bojangles" Robinson and what were advertised as "Hundred Percent American Variety Performers"—among them, however, Pepito, the Spanish clown.

Business proved so good that Ruth and Holtz were held over for a second week, teaming for a travesty, "True Blue Lou—Holtz," plus fresh songs for Ruth—all new except for the obligatory "Ten Cents a Dance."

Upon closing, the Snyders headed for David City to vacation with her aunt Rose and uncle Alex.* She was now famous enough to rate an interview in the Butler County *Press* and to surprise the reporter by remaining "unassuming, cordial, unaffected . . . unchanged by her marked success." In the Omaha *Bee* a photograph showed Ruth enthusiastically lending a hand with repairs on her farm and predicting that it wouldn't be long before she'd be forsaking crowded cities to retire to Nebraska.

After the vacation there was a picture-house tour of Cincinnati's Albee, Chicago's Palace, Buffalo's Shea and Brooklyn's Fox. She performed a medley of her hits, begging off with a curtain speech in which she introduced *two* accompanists, Victor Breides and Phil Schwartz, describing them as her only extravagance.

Wherever she went, theater managers and reporters were agreeably surprised to find that fame had wrought so little change. In Chicago Rob Reel wrote, "One notes that while stardom has perfected her work and increased her importance tremendously, it apparently has made no difference in her private life. She seems the same sincere girl of simple habits that she always was. There are no coteries of 'yes' people surrounding her . . . not even a maid . . . only an adoring husband. . . ."

It was while Ruth was doing four and five shows a day at Brooklyn's Fox that Ziegfeld requested a mind-boggling favor. The following night, he said, he was opening Vincent Youmans' *Smiles* with a cast that included Marilyn Miller, Fred and Adele Astaire, Eddie Foy, Jr., Larry Adler, Virginia Bruce and Bob Hope. "The finale's dying," he confessed. What he proposed was that Ruth, unbilled and unexpected, appear to sing this final number, "Syncopated Wedding."

Out of loyalty Ruth agreed and performed the song without any re-

*Her grandfather had died in 1923; her grandmother and her father, in 1926.

hearsal at the premiere on November 18, 1930. "It didn't make any difference how well or badly I did it," she observes. "The audience was so surprised to see me they applauded halfway through. Nobody knew whether it was good or bad."

On another occasion a song failed to get across. Ziegfeld asked Ruth to go to Boston to sing the number at a single performance. "If the audience doesn't respond, I'll know it's the song, not the girl," he explained. Ruth hesitated out of deference to the other performer's feelings, but finally she sang it and exited to an ovation.

Why would she perform such favors?

"I admired Mr. Ziegfeld and was grateful to him. It was wonderful to be in shows where everything was the best he could buy. That was his secret: to get the best—Joseph Urban to design that wonderful scenery and John Harkrider for those lovely costumes; that was Ziegfeld's method.

"He had no sense of humor. I've seen him sitting out front while Cantor would be doing something that had us in hysterics. Mr. Ziegfeld wouldn't crack a smile. Then, when he realized we were laughing, he'd laugh too. He rejected some wonderful songs and made us sing some stinkers. But what he didn't know about little things he made up for in showmanship. You had to respect that. So when he asked me to do these favors, I was glad to. I wanted to repay him for what he'd given me."

In recognition of Ruth's loyalty Ziegfeld presented her with a signed photograph of himself:

> To Ruth,
>> My Standby,
>>> Love,
>>>> Ziegfeld.

By the early thirties a kind of Etting mania had spread to vast segments of the population, including a *Screenland* columnist, who signed herself "Miss Vee Dee," and "Pops," the record reviewer for *The New Yorker.*

On a commercial level Snyder promoted Ruth Etting blouses, tams, hosiery and ice-cream sundaes. The 1931 Christmas show at the Roxy, traditionally a spectacle, dispensed with trimming and depended on Ruth, the Mills Brothers, ballerina Patricia Bowman and the corps de ballet. Furthermore, the bill proved to be so salable it played a second week.

In early 1930 a radio salesman accosted Ruth on the street and identified himself as the author of some two hundred passionate but anonymous love letters she had received. Since some of them carried veiled threats, Ruth called the police. Upon being booked at the station house, the salesman produced forty newspaper clippings about Ruth and claimed she was his "legitimate sweetheart." Asked how he had reached this conclusion, he explained that they had met in the movies. "I've seen every one she's made," he said. He was released into the custody of relatives, but in June, 1931, he was again arrested for writing several more letters in which he discussed taking Ruth to eternity with him.

In 1931 eighty-seven mothers informed her that they had named their daughters in her honor.

By 1932 she was so famous that a letter from Blair, Nebraska, addressed: "Ruth Etting, Studio, New York, New York," promptly reached her.

Walter Winchell, who mentioned her at least once weekly, commented:

> The tales I hear about myself. . . . Now the newest legend—that I boost Ruth Etting's phonograph platters and her stage activities because she is my sweetheart—heheheh—that's what I get for saying something nice about somebody. . . . You mustn't throw word bouquets at people. . . . If you hammer them, you're jealous of their success, but when you boost 'em—ah-hah! Particularly if the recipient of the posies is femme. . . . What was that grand crack by that philosopher. . . . Oh, yes—jealous ears hear double.

In 1932 "Pops' " infatuation with Ruth's singing was stronger than ever:

> Ruth Etting gives another of her lessons to other singers with "Kiss Me Goodnight" and "When We're Alone" (Columbia 2630-D). Miss Etting always knows what to do about a song. She can embroider it when the tune needs trimmings, and she can put it over by sheer simplicity. This record is notable for her effortless delivery and understatement.

In 1928 he had alerted readers:

> A curious version of "Deep Night" is available by Ruth Etting, who was heralded hereabouts some three years ago (nothing like bragging

about a discovery) and who still is queen of her own style. The accompaniment is notable for rhythmic variety, and the temptation to drag is resisted. "Maybe—Who Knows?" which graces the other side, is a torch aria of the usual sort, exceptionally well done.

In 1930, faced with a choice of three leading singers' versions of "Body and Soul," he wrote:

Helen Morgan, Ruth Etting, Libby Holman, which of these discs will spin on your turntable depends on your predilections. If you happen to be a worshipper of Miss Morgan, Miss Etting or Miss Holman, nothing that I can tell you will be of much service—but, if I had to buy a pressing of this *chanson triste*, I should invest in Miss Etting's edition. The others are good, too, but the Etting presentation is coupled with a mercurial setting-forth of "If I Could Be With You," which eclipses the various "Something to Remember You By" intonations that are mated with "Body and Soul" on the competing discs.

Later in 1930 he apologized:

"I'm Yours" and "Laughing at Life" are treated with charm and imagination by Ruth Etting (Columbia 2318). I don't like any more than you this business of singling out records by Miss Etting and the Revelers to the exclusion of others, but their competitors don't seem to be able to keep up with them.

In another review in 1936:

When Ruth Etting started making records, her variations on any given melody were a novelty. They still are, because Miss Etting can depart momentarily from the tune without losing track of it. For a demonstration, her Decca-1107, which is a charming doubling of "May I Have the Next Romance With You" and "Goodnight, My Love."

With this kind of adulation being heaped upon Ruth, Snyder only became more demanding and irascible in his relations with everyone, including Ziegfeld. If it was Ruth's style to count her blessings, send notes of appreciation and do favors, it was Snyder's to suspect everyone of trying to take advantage of them. He snarled, slapped, punched or otherwise threw his weight around.

Snyder became most vindictive when Ziegfeld approached Ruth

with a new offer. Debt-ridden and beleaguered, the producer was attempting to raise money to mount the 1931 edition of the *Follies*, and Snyder's initial opposition and subsequent tirades made life no easier. Even with interpretive performers of the caliber of Helen Morgan, Harry Richman, Jack Pearl and Ruth or such creative contributors as Dimitri Tiomkin, Walter Donaldson, Gene Buck, Mack Gordon, Harry Revel and Mark Hellinger, money was hard to come by.

As the Depression deepened, more and more people felt that in lean, hungry 1931 the lavish revue was too slow-moving. Harry Richman, in spite of long service in George White's *Scandals*, was an unsatisfactory substitute for a Will Rogers, a W. C. Fields or a Cantor. And although Helen Morgan and Ruth were in good form, most of their numbers weren't. Out of town Helen Morgan sang Noel Coward's "Half-Caste Woman," which was ill-suited to her style and was jettisoned. "Love Is All I Live For" was slightly more satisfactory, but only slightly. Her best contribution was a duet with Harry Richman, called "I'm with You." Jack Pearl was acceptable in sketches and revived an old "Rip Van Winkle" song.

Ruth also had problems. "Here We Are in Love," which she performed with Richman, drew yawns and was discarded. In Revel and Gordon's "Cigarettes, Cigars" she showed her shapely legs for the first time. The song, an obvious attempt to repeat the much-admired "Ten Cents a Dance," was enthusiastically received during the tryout but scorned by New York critics, who were derisive about the rhyming.

The single legitimate showstopper in the production was the revival of "Shine On, Harvest Moon." Written and popularized by husband-and-wife team Nora Bayes and Jack Norworth in the *Follies* of 1911, it had always been in their repertory until their divorce—after which it had been forgotten until Ruth made it a hit all over again.

"The chemistry of the show was never right," Ruth told a reporter years later. "The scenery and costumes were beautiful, and what a gorgeous group of girls! But the principals didn't complement one another. 'Here We Are in Love' was a pretty thing, but audiences didn't accept me with Harry. Now Harry and Helen did a number that went over big, and Jack Pearl and I did 'The Picture Bride,' a dialect novelty. In it we'd exchanged other people's pictures through a lonely-hearts club. He wore yellow button shoes, and I had blond curls and a kerchief over my head. We sat in a buggy on a little humped-back trunk, and the audience really liked it.

"Helen was a gorgeous thing. I would spend hours at makeup, trying to get beautiful. Helen would rush in, dab on a little makeup, run her fingers through her hair, maybe cut off a lock or two and walk out looking like a million.

"Sometimes when she'd had too much to drink, they'd drape a table with gold cloth and place her behind it. She couldn't stand up, but she could give a perfect performance. Her best number was 'Here Lies Love'—which they killed for her. She sang it at the proscenium arch, holding some love letters, and when she hit the last note, they blacked out. A blackout is for a joke. If they'd used a pin spot that gradually faded, the number would have gone over big. I know. I used it in cafés later. But I would never have dreamed of telling Mr. Ziegfeld how to stage a number."

Snyder scoffed at Ruth's humility and became more obnoxious than ever. He threw a tantrum learning that Ruth and Miss Morgan shared equal billing. He griped about Ruth's songs and badgered Ziegfeld to give her sketches. He announced no one was shoving the "little lady" around and threatened to pull her out of the show. Ziegfeld, nerves frazzled by financial and production problems, ordered Snyder banned from the theater. "I can't stand this heckling another minute," he said. Thereafter Snyder clumped up and down the alley outside the stage door, muttering imprecations against the great glorifier. Stopping anyone who would listen, he threatened, "If anybody pushes us around, I'll take care of him. We don't need no Ziegfeld. One more lousy crack, and I'll pull the little lady out of the show. See how long he runs without her."

Ruth, humiliated by what was taking place, apologized to Ziegfeld. When asked why, since her marriage was obviously unhappy, she didn't divorce Snyder, she replied, "I can't. He'd kill me."

There were numerous incidents to support Ruth's fear. Attendants at a radio station told how Snyder sat in the control booth one evening, apparently transported by his wife's plaintive lament—dangling a gun on his finger.

Others recalled a comedy duo who lusted after Ruth, offending her husband. He waylaid them in an alley after a matinee. When they appeared for the next performance, their eyes were blackened, their noses swollen and their lips so puffed that the audience even laughed at some straight lines. Their success was so marked that one of them permanently adopted the battered-face makeup.

Ruth kept her own counsel about her marital life except to a few loyal friends of whose taciturnity she was certain. But other people heard and saw incidents. A newsman who had interviewed Ruth found himself confronted by her angry spouse, who accused him of misquoting her. The reporter insisted on the accuracy of his story and finally suggested they consult Ruth. When she backed the newsman, Snyder slapped her.

Residents at the Piccadilly said that when Ruth displeased Snyder, he would slap her around and then make up for his boorishness by giving her expensive presents—which they assumed were paid for with her earnings.

The *Follies* girls marveled that she hadn't left Snyder long ago. One moment he would be calling her Angel, Pookey or Momma; a few minutes later he would punch her around. Katherine Renquist, a chorine, said that Snyder tagged after Ruth so persistently that the girls dubbed him the Watchdog.

The 1931 *Follies* opened on July 1 and closed on November 21. Although *Women's Wear Daily*'s critic Kelcey Allen, who had seen every edition, considered this the best, few agreed. Most concurred that Helen Morgan had been given short shrift in musical numbers and that Harry Richman's racy personality cheapened the show. Jack Pearl received his share of praise, but Ruth and Hal LeRoy, a young dancer with the face of a bumpkin and the feet of Mercury, fared best.

Ruth never missed a performance until November 10, shortly before the show was to go on the road. It was first announced that she was suffering from bronchitis, later emended to bronchial pneumonia. Newspapers reported she was off to Hot Springs to recuperate.

When Broadway's "in" crowd learned this, they assumed that Snyder had pulled her out of the company to even the score with the financially and physically ailing Ziegfeld. Especially since six weeks later she was breaking records headlining the Roxy's Christmas show, playing to 186,000 people in a single week.

Prior to the opening and during the run of the 1931 *Follies* Ruth made frequent appearances on the thriving new medium, radio. She was so often a guest of Vagabond Lover Rudy Vallee (who had had a crush on her back in Chicago) that she became an irregular regular on his *Fleischmann's Hour.* She worked with Eddie Cantor and Rubinoff and numerous other radio stars so successfully that on May 1, NBC attempted to sign her to a five-part contract: radio, records, RKO vaudeville, short subjects and full-length features.

Instead, she joined Chesterfield's *Music That Satisfies,* which was aired over WABC of the CBS network. She, the Boswell Sisters and Alex Grey each had two nights a week. All were accompanied by Nathaniel Shilkret's Orchestra. Since the others had previously been reviewed on this program, *Variety*'s man concentrated on Ruth's fifteen-minute segment. Reporting that she had been anticipating moving to Hollywood for film work, the reviewer said that Chesterfield had been forced to give her a bonus to sign a thirteen-week contract. On the basis of her performance he was of the opinion that no matter what the tobacco company had to pay, the money had been well spent.

The cigarette manufacturers obviously agreed. For in August Ruth signed a new contract, this time sharing the schedule with the Boswells and Arthur Tracy, the Street Singer. In December of that year the sponsor again revamped the lineup so that Ruth, Bing Crosby and the comedy team of Tom Howard and George Shelton headlined, with Lenny Hayton's Orchestra replacing Shilkret's. In early negotiations Fannie Brice, who represented the pinnacle of Ziegfeld stardom to Ruth, let it be known through her agent that she was willing to cut her $1,500 to $750 per week to demonstrate her radio potential. But Chesterfield consulted Crosley Reports (an early audience-rating service) and surprised Ruth by renewing her at twice the salary asked by Miss Brice.

As Ruth's popularity blossomed, Snyder took this new medium most seriously of all. He understood radio's commercialism perfectly and did something about it. Around the studios or on Broadway he'd march along, approaching smokers and demanding, "Are you loyal?" If the unlucky object of his attention happened to be smoking a Camel or a Lucky Strike, Snyder would snatch it from the offender's lips and offer a package of Chesterfields, with the "compliments of the little lady."

So outrageous did his conduct become that at one point columnist Louis Sobol ran an item asking whether Ruth and Norma Terris' husbands, whose only interest in life was seeing that their wives received every break, didn't close more doors than they opened. Concluded Sobol, "Broadway sometimes wonders whether those two devoted husbands don't interfere a little too much."

Snyder had no such doubts. He fully intended that he and Ruth would rise twice as high as they had already climbed. No longer content to sit in the control booth dangling a pistol, he now began to intrude upon the rehearsal area. He even drew a chalk circle into which musicians were forbidden to enter when Ruth was singing, lest their accompaniment detract from her effectiveness. When one intrepid fellow ignored instructions, Snyder felled him with a cane. Everyone became a potential enemy trying to steal or destroy his prized possession.

And what a prize she'd turned out to be! Readers of *Radio Guide* voted her second place in the publication's "IT" contest of 1932, placing her second to the glamorous half of the "Myrt and Marge" comedy team. In selecting his ideal radio program for that year, Ring Lardner wanted to hear "Ruth Etting, Queen of the Torchers, singing, perhaps, Irving Berlin's old 'Remember.'" The radio editor of the *World-Telegram*, Jimmy Cannon, later a noted sports columnist, marveled in his radio comments that CBS should devote so much energy to promoting Kate Smith as "Radio's Number One Songbird" when Ruth, with only guest shots and a new program, was already close on Miss Smith's heels. "I think I can explain Miss Etting's popularity," the obviously partisan Cannon wrote. "She sings the blues with a laugh in her throat; she is a very handsome lady; and she wears her bonnet of laurel wreaths with calm pride." By the time the votes in the next *World-Telegram* poll were tallied Ruth's harvest moon was shining on more listeners than Miss Smith was getting her moon over the mountain to. In February, 1933, a poll of 127 U.S. and Canadian radio reviewers overwhelmingly named Ruth as the leading singer of popular songs; in March the New York *Times* ran a layout featuring Leopold Stokowski, the Boswell Sisters, Guy Lombardo and Ruth under the title ALWAYS ON TOP; and then, suddenly, on April 15, Chesterfield, in search of novelty, canceled its sponsorship of *Music That Satisfies.* Ruth, Bing Crosby and Jane Froman were the rotating stars.

Numerous offers came Ruth's way. The producer of radio's *Captain Andy's Maxwell House Showboat* proposed adding her to the cast. Negotiations on billing, salary and other considerations proceeded without a hitch. Contracts were to be drawn. "By the way, there'll be no need for you to come to rehearsals," the producer remarked to Snyder, who replied he'd be on hand as usual. "In that case the deal's off," the producer said, and nothing agent Joe Glazier did could revive it.

Ruth told Jimmy Cannon, when he interviewed her about the Chesterfield cancellation and her lack of commitments, that she felt relieved. "I'm so tired I want to get on a boat and relax," she said. "I'm going to sail through the Canal and then go through the Canadian Rockies. I've always wanted to travel, but I've been too busy."

Snyder did not oppose water travel, but he shared none of his wife's enthusiasm for vacationing in the Rockies. However, if he was unsympathetic to mountain hikes, Edith—his sixteen-year-old daughter from his first marriage who had recently come to live with the Snyders—was ecstatic at the prospect.

Ruth had partially supported the girl since marrying Snyder, and there had been instant empathy between the strongly maternal star and the woebegone child of the slums whose "dese-dem-doze" diction Ruth had taken steps to correct before enrolling her in the famous Cumnock school in California, along with Flo and Billie Ziegfeld's daughter, Patricia.

In 1932 Edith had come to live with her father and stepmother, and a camaraderie had grown between the two women. An attractive dark-haired adolescent, Edith was frightened of her unpredictable father, who careened from tearful sentimentality to peace-shattering violence in the flick of an eyelash. Basically diffident and vulnerable, Edith found much-needed reassurance in Ruth's easygoing ways and gently loving acceptance of her.

The three of them set out on the trip through the Canal, but the vacation in the Rockies failed to materialize because Samuel Goldwyn approached Ruth to appear in *Roman Scandals* with Eddie Cantor.

HOLLYWOOD!

The big studio system's various arms began to churn, seemingly setting out to achieve one goal while aiming at another. Shrewd psychologist that he was, Samuel Goldwyn hypnotized Ruth into believing that a filmmaker would employ a personalized approach in handling her career, despite the fact that she was already thirty-two years old.*

It was a ploy he had used before and one he was to utilize again a few years later with Miriam Hopkins. Agents, Broadway producers, directors—none of them had understood how to present Ruth, according to Goldwyn. Eventually, when the audience saw her through his eyes, she would become as popular on the screen as she was on radio.

Having read the script of *Roman Scandals*, Ruth pointed out that her role hardly existed. This was not a Broadway musical, Goldwyn countered. Forget the script. She was in Hollywood. Scripts were written to be rewritten. Would he be wasting his time going to all this trouble for a glorified extra—even a Goldwyn extra? Would he insult the greatest singing star ever managed by his old idol Flo Ziegfeld by offering her a bit role? The part would be built up. He had alerted the press to his plans for expanding it. He showed her the newspaper clips. There it was in black and white.

She was worried about her ability to handle dialogue? Goldwyn Stu-

*Actually, thirty-seven.

dios had dialogue directors and acting coaches, as well as the time and determination to ensure an expert performance. She would play Olga, a slave maiden—or maybe a captive princess—opposite Eddie. The part would not just be a part. The writers would design it to fit her personality like a glove. Eleven months and $100,000 would be spent filming. What was more, he had only to give the word, and Al Dubin and Harry Warren would write at least two surefire torch songs. And those songs, like the script, would be tailored for Ruth Etting. With Ziegfeld a handshake had always been sufficient, but this time there was a formal contract, calling for payment of $10,000 a week. Ruth signed.

As Goldwyn had promised, director Frank Tuttle and the brace of writers originally enlarged the part of Olga, and Al Dubin and Harry Warren wrote two new songs for the picture, but as Cantor inserted jokes and sight gags—some of the period, others anachronistically modern—her role shrank again.

True, she was cast opposite Eddie. Eddie Arnold, the character actor who played the emperor—not Eddie Cantor, the star.

True, too, she received $10,000 a week—but there was no guarantee for any number of weeks. As it turned out, her scenes could easily be shot in a week. The wonderful new Dubin-Warren songs created to complement "No More Love" ended on the cutting-room floor. Years later even Ruth couldn't recall the titles.

It soon became evident that her value to Goldwyn Studios lay not in her on-set and on-screen contributions but in posing for stills that would milk every last inch of news space, in exploiting the stellar position she had achieved in other fields and in using her name for its marquee value.

Long after she had realized that she was little more than box-office insurance, Goldwyn flacks were conning reporters into writing glowing predictions about her Hollywood future, such as this one by W. E. Oliver in the *Herald Express*:

A girl you'll see on the Chinese Screen November 27th, when the new Eddie Cantor film opens, has been setting the world's air-lanes and Broadway revues pulsating for these years as a singing star, but to Hollywood, where astral personalities must rise out of the movie box-office, she is less well known.

As yet not one of the shining galaxy, but unless your seer is astray, more than likely to be. It's Ruth Etting, I mean, whose lowdown vocal chords have marked her as a female Bing Crosby.

In *Roman Scandals* she plays an emperor's toy who is sold in slavery when he gets a new yen. One of the musical interludes in the picture is Miss Etting's blue lament "No More Love," done against a living frieze of scanty-togged girls.

In California the Snyders lived in a suite at the Hermoyne Apartment Hotel, located on Rossmore—directly across from the Ravenswood, where Mae West had taken the penthouse—only a short drive to the Goldwyn Studios. Ruth liked California at once. She loved the early-to-bed, early-to-rise regimentation that the studio shooting schedules imposed. She enjoyed the sun, the beaches, and the opportunity for sports. Since Ziegfeld's death Broadway no longer interested her, and with network radio a reality, she saw no reason to return to New York when she could be enjoying the more congenial outdoor life on the West Coast. As for work, she intended to divide her time between broadcasting and film assignments.

She started searching for a house. Still influenced by her grandfather's advice on thrift, she accepted every job offer in order not to live on capital or take a large bank loan to pay for her new home.

On September 10, 1933, she began starring in a weekly radio series for Chase and Sanborn coffee. Since Cantor, the usual headliner, was busy filming *Roman Scandals*, Jimmy Durante—still unknown to radio audiences—filled in for him.

Concurrently, Ruth also appeared in another feature-length film, which was not released until 1934. It was Wheeler and Woolsey's *Hips, Hips Hooray*, advertised as "a musical girly-go-round." Once again Ruth had only a line or two of dialogue. This time she played herself and sang Bert Kalmar and Harry Ruby's "Keep Romance Alive." When the picture opened in New York on February 23, 1934, Marguerite Tazelaar of the *Herald Tribune* wrote, "It would be impossible to convey the plot because there isn't any. . . ." Then, after dismissing the antics of Wheeler and Woolsey, she complained, "Just why Ruth Etting was given her insignificant part in the story is another of those enigmas frequently confronting the picture-goer. Dorothy Lee was engaged to do the bulk of the singing while Miss Etting's brief appearances are pretty much limited to static silence. . . ." *Variety* found only two good things to say about the disastrous conglomeration: "Ruth Etting is on briefly for one song, but it means that at least one number is well-handled. Also the Etting name gives added heft to the billing."

In *Gift of Gab*, Ruth's final full-length film, shot and released in 1934,

162

Universal Pictures set out to satirize radio while capitalizing on the rival medium's stars, including Ethel Waters, Phil Baker, Gene Austin, Alexander Woollcott, Victor Moore and Ruth, in a picture trumpeted in promotion as a "30 Star Sensation." The *Times'* stunned observation was: "It constitutes a minor miracle that the sum of so much talent should be such meagre entertainment." The *Herald Tribune*'s Richard Watts observed that satirizing radio was clearly impossible since "no means have been yet devised to mock the form of expression that is its own mockery." He went on, "Miss Etting and Miss Waters are reasonably successful in their valiant efforts, despite unimpressive songs, but such inexperienced comedians as Messrs, Baker and Woollcott are less happy."

By common agreement Hollywood executives who earned thousands a week weren't going to be told how to run a business that grossed millions by newsmen who earned hundreds. The thinking reduced itself to the cliché "If you're so smart, why aren't you rich?"

Also, in Ruth's case age was a factor. Nor were her simplicity and salt-of-the-earth personality impressive to moguls and their acolytes. They were more accustomed to Miriam Hopkins' conspicuous consumerism inherent in her "What's the point of being a movie star if there's no champagne?" or in the flashy careerism of Ginger Rogers. By not playing the social game, Ruth closed valuable career opportunities. In the film business friendship casting and nepotism were rampant.

"I had the handicap of never knowing what my husband was going to do," she once explained. "It was easier not to mingle with picture people. So I either saw nonprofessionals or New Yorkers, who knew how to take Snyder. They got a lot of laughs out of him. He could be very funny. Only you never knew when he'd turn on that violent temper. He was a lot like Mike Todd in that respect. He wasn't a drinker, but a couple of times at parties he had champagne and behaved like an angel. If I could have kept him drunk all the time, it wouldn't have been so bad.

"That's why I didn't enjoy show business. Had I been married to Myrl, who was a musician, we'd have had something in common—like Lena Horne and Lennie Hayton or Judy Garland and David Rose. We'd have had the same feeling for music, and I'd have enjoyed my life. As it was, I was like a puppet. Moe was interested, but he didn't know. He just didn't know.

"He made people uncomfortable. We met Joan Crawford, an awfully nice girl. She was the prettiest thing and one of my favorites. Well, at Christmas in 1933 she sent that wire that's in my scrapbook: 'Merry Christmas to you and Edith.' You see, people weren't comfortable with him around.''

After spending the holidays in David City, Ruth plunged into a six-week theater tour at the beginning of 1934. Before it was completed, she received a call to hurry West for a big role in *Strictly Dynamite*, with Lupe Velez, Jimmy Durante, Norman Foster and William Gargan. Upon arrival she discovered that in the rewriting, her part had been eliminated.

Instead, RKO put her to work in shorts. In one of the skits she was called upon to weep, but nothing—including glycerine fakes—produced satisfactory tears. Finally, the scene was shot without them.

Shortly afterward, she visited the set of *The Little Minister*. "Katharine Hepburn was standing with some stage hands laughing uproariously at something when they called her for a scene," Ruth recounts with a note of awe in her voice. "The shot called for her to make an entrance from behind a tree. She was still laughing when she went behind that tree, and when she reappeared, she was the picture of dejection, with tears welling up in her eyes and rolling down her cheeks. I thought, Well, by God, there's an actress! I could never do that. As I say, some naturally have it, and some don't. I didn't.''

Meanwhile, with earnings from the shorts, *Gift of Gab* and a thirteen-week contract for broadcasting for Oldsmobile, Ruth bought a rambling white brick bungalow in Beverly Hills. Not the least of its appeal was the location on a dead-end street where there would be little traffic to interfere with bicycle riding and roller skating, which Edith and Ruth enjoyed. An adjoining vacant lot made an ideal location for a swimming pool. Then the grounds were walled for privacy. "It was a cute little place with plenty of room for a summerhouse and a beautiful fish pond," Ruth remembered. "I had a lot of exotic fish, but I kept finding my Japanese fantails missing.

"One morning I went out, around four in the morning, and sat on the patio. Sure enough, about daybreak here came this little bird after my fantails. You know how a bird runs and then freezes. I shot, and this one ran into the bushes. I thought I'd missed him, but when he didn't come out, I went over, and there he was.

"I had a bird book, and he was a rare least bittern. So I called the man who'd built the pool, and he came over and took the bird to UCLA, where they stuffed him for their collection. The builder told me when they got ready to stuff the bird, they found I'd shot him right through the heart. All those sessions with my grandfather paid off. But ordinarily I never shot living things—just skeets and targets."

However fitfully Ruth's film career sputtered by way of RKO shorts, she recorded for both Columbia and American Record Corporation labels, and her radio popularity remained high. In 1934 the *World-Telegram* survey of radio editors placed her in the top slot, followed by Kate Smith, Gertrude Niesen, Mildred Bailey, Jane Froman, Ethel Waters, and Jessica Dragonette; while in the *Daily News* poll she and Miss Smith reversed positions. In 1935 Ruth won the *World-Telegram* listeners' poll—leading in teenage, college student and adult divisions. During that year she starred on Kellogg's *College Prom* with Red Nichols' Orchestra over NBC but found all material rewards meaningless because of her marital situation. "Radio is nervous work," she told one reporter. "After all, there's not much gratification singing to a microphone." To please her, NBC provided a studio audience.

During this period NBC press agent Lewis Lane wrote a Candid Cameragraph which still evokes a vivid portrait of Ruth's broadcasts:

> Ruth Etting, . . . radio's number one blues singer, . . . unobtrusive, modest, mild-mannered, . . . takes to the microphone without any fuss, . . . rests both hands lightly on hips as she tries to sing, . . . flips right hand gracefully to give conductor Red Nichols the tempo, . . . sways imperceptibly . . . . "First 16 bars are sweet and flowing," she explains after a chorus . . . . "Sounded a little bit corny," she adds . . . resumes singing . . . looks at music on rack, standing directly beyond microphone . . . song over, asks control room engineers through microphone, "How was it?" . . . no answer . . . tries again, says, "So what?" . . . wears hat when program goes on the air . . . sings with back to the audience . . . between numbers sits curled up against grand piano . . . still with back to audience . . . crosses legs . . . fumbles with handbag . . . sits back, looks at orchestra interestedly . . . smiles at tricky finale . . . applauds . . . gets an extended flurry of applause herself as she stands up at the conclusion of the program, bows modestly . . . and again . . . drapes her fur coat over her shoulders . . . makes for the studio door . . . signs autographs on the way out.

In mid-July, with her radio season completed, Ruth and Snyder made a quick trip to David City for "Ruth Etting Day." Back in California, she completed four shorts for RKO, and then, in December, 1935, her husband may have made one of his greatest miscalculations: he allowed Ruth to take his daughter to Hawaii, as a delayed celebration of Edith's graduation from Cumnock School, while he visited Chicago. Ruth and Edith toured the Islands, and Ruth obliged photographers by playing catch on the beach with pitcher Charlie Root of the Chicago Cubs. This brief taste of freedom changed her attitude, making a return to Snyder's regimentation much more difficult.

Since the Colonel's bad temper and threats had closed so many doors in Hollywood and Ruth refused to consider Broadway, she toured RKO picture houses. On February 24, while she was appearing in Boston, the theater was robbed. Front-page stories described the $12,800 heist as a "record sum" for theater robberies in that city and attributed its size to "the throngs attracted by the popular singing star." The newspaper articles brought no Hollywood offers, but they did attract the attention of Woolworth heir Jimmy Donahue. Donahue, an aspirant to the late Florenz Zeigfeld's mantle, was co-producing a London revue, *Transatlantic Rhythm*, with Felix Ferry, a Hungarian ex-racing driver with managerial ambitions.

Donahue contacted Ruth and persuaded her to head a cast that already included Lupe Velez, Lou Holtz and the talented black singing-and-dancing team Buck and Bubbles. With Irving Caesar to write sketches and lyrics; Raymond Henderson, the music; and Marcel Vertes to create costumes and scenery, there was good reason to be optimistic. Anyway, as Ruth said, she had never seen London.

Once there, Rex, "The King of Records," engaged her to record three discs, and Regal, another. When England's reigning musical comedy star Jessie Matthews was unable to broadcast because of illness, Ruth stepped in, bringing herself to the attention of members of the BBC audience who were potential patrons for the revue.

But *Transatlantic Rhythm* was a bust. Nobody liked the songs or sketches. Vertes' scenery had to be cut down to fit the Manchester Opera House stage. Dress rehearsal turned into an endurance grind. By midnight only five numbers had been performed. The orchestra threatened to strike, having rehearsed all day. Even the volatile Lupe Velez was too disheartened to stage one of her famous tantrums and turned her attention to mothering the exhausted Ruth.

"I've never known anyone who was sweeter to me," Ruth says. As the dress rehearsal dragged on, Lupe sent out for silver trays, a heat lamp and two thick steaks. When the tray was red-hot, she dropped a steak on it, let the meat sear, then turned it over, let it sear again and then she and Ruth had a snack to keep their strength up.

When Ruth saw one of her gowns, a maribou-trimmed nightmare with a flounced skirt, she was distressed and Snyder threw such a noisy scene about it that rehearsals were halted until he could be ejected.

After six hours Ruth's iron throat—the one that had allowed her to go on for Ziegfeld the day after a tonsillectomy—began to bother her. She left the theater to take to her bed, and when Lupe collapsed, the dress rehearsal was temporarily called off. The show was postponed but finally opened on September 12, 1936.

Additional problems arose. Two nights after the premiere, as stage manager Edward Clark Lilley left the theater, Snyder leaped out of the shadows, fists and feet flying in the best Chicago street fighter tradition and trounced his unsuspecting victim. Ruth rushed out to stop the attack. The management complained to authorities, and Snyder's passport was picked up. He insisted that if he was deported, he would take Ruth out of the show. Lilley intervened in his behalf, saying that however mistaken Mr. Snyder's actions might have been, he had been protecting his wife's interests. Charges were dropped. But that incident convinced Ruth that she must divorce Snyder—no matter what the consequences.

Prior to the West End premiere Ruth presented her salary check at the bank and found there were insufficient funds to cover it. After two additional attempts she left rehearsals to go boating on the Thames and visit Windsor Castle. Word spread that she had left the cast. "I've never considered such a thing," she told reporters. "It isn't the audiences' fault that I haven't been paid. Audiences have given me a wonderful reception, and I'm not going to let them down. They've been wonderful to us all, but I will leave after we open, unless we're paid immediately."

Felix Ferry explained in the press that the production, budgeted at $80,000, had ballooned to $140,000 by the time it reached the Adelphi. Nevertheless, he contended that he and Donahue were optimistic about the show's future, pointing out that with excellent reviews they anticipated a gross of 5,200 pounds ($26,000) per week with operating expenses of only 3,800 pounds ($19,000)."

When, subsequent to the premiere, the checks were still not honored, Ruth quit the show. In a somewhat garbled account in the *Daily Sketch* a person with the by-line "A Woman Reporter" quoted Ruth as saying, "I'm going back to my farm in Beverly Hills, but I'll always remember Windsor Castle—and someday I'm coming back."

Months earlier Ruth had allowed a friend to persuade her to have her horoscope cast. She considered it a lark and afterward decided the astrologer not only lacked skill but had also never read the amusement pages. "She told me that I was to have a marriage made in heaven—

and I thought of Moe and wondered how much farther in the opposite direction I could get. She said I'd go to Europe to do a show. Because of Moe's troublemaking I could hardly get a job here, let alone abroad. And she warned if I went before July 1, I wouldn't get paid. That seemed impossible. Actors' salaries are taken out of Equity bonds if the money runs out. But it turned out that she was very close on every count. I don't know why I never had any more horoscopes done. Except I'm a fatalist, honey: whatever will be, will be."

The stars impel but never compel, as we are told over and over, but there were an increasing number of clues that Ruth had outgrown the need for a father figure. Whether she was ready to stand alone now or not, it was easier to dream about freedom than to gain it.

She sailed from England on the *Normandie* in mid-September along with a glittering passenger list, including Jimmy Donahue. Donahue confided that he had held his losses on *Transatlantic Rhythm* to $50,000, which he considered cheap in view of the experience he had gained. Ruth wasn't about to underwrite a Woolworth heir's education and reminded him that he owed her $2,575. "But that's all right," she remembers telling him. "I'll get more than that in publicity." Donahue wanted to know how. "Well, naturally some of the first people I'll see will be Walter and June Winchell. And when Walter asks how things went, I'll tell him you backed the show and I didn't get paid." Donahue was alarmed, protesting that she wouldn't do that. "Why not?" Ruth asked. "It's the truth." The upshot of their exchange was that Donahue wrote out his personal check, paying her in full, and when the ship docked, the smiling producer and the happy singer were photographed arm and arm, with Ruth whispering, so the caption stated, "something amusing in the Woolworth heir's ear."

The year 1937 was a time of endings. Except for four recordings for Decca, including the haunting "There's a Lull in My Life," Ruth made no attempt to work. Then, sometime between August 15 and 20, Snyder humiliated her by lashing her across the legs with his cane in front of guests.

When they were alone, despite fears of disfigurement or death, she told her husband that she was dissatisfied with her life. She said she wanted to retire, to live alone and to obtain a divorce. That was all Ruth would tell reporters at the time, and thirty-nine years later she still kept her silence. But according to Snyder's later testimony, when he asked whether there was another man, she assured him that there wasn't. He believed that she only wanted to relax and take Edith on a trip around the world, and he reluctantly agreed, confident that she'd eventually return to him.

News that Ruth had won an uncontested divorce in Chicago on November 30, 1937, charging desertion and cruelty, stunned show business circles. In a prearranged property settlement she gave Snyder approximately $125,000 (deducting $50,000 that she had paid to cover his gambling debts and to buy a home for his mother), plus half interest in their Beverly Hills home. Once the divorce was granted, Ruth did not go to David City, as her ex-husband had expected, but boarded the Santa Fe for Los Angeles, where Edith was.

Before retiring, Ruth had been regarded as the world's greatest torch singer. After the divorce Snyder was said to carry the brightest torch on Broadway. The cold-eyed ex-protection man, who had gloried in his reputation as "one of the toughest apples in the toughest apple orchard in the world," masochistically flaunted his agony.

One moment he would sit brooding over his drink at Lindy's, the next he would be galumphing up and down the aisles, waving a letter purportedly from the "little lady." She was angling for a reconciliation. She had to come back. What was she without him? A nothing. But he was going to teach her a lesson, make her beg.

Then he'd clump back to his table and gulp down his drink, engulfed in fierce loneliness. Through it all he never understood that such exhibitionism was part of what had driven her from him.

Never a natty dresser, he went to a tailor, ordered half a dozen new suits and then headed for Lindy's to boast, "Wait'll Ruthie gloms this umbrella pusher now! She'll be back"—as if the problem between them had been sartorial. Or he bought a gold-and-platinum bracelet which he ordered the jeweler to engrave "To Mommy—For the best years of my life."

When his letters went unanswered and he at last dimly perceived that she was gone for good, he bored listeners with endless confessions that it had all been his fault. He speculated that possibly there was a new man in her life. If there was, he wished her all the luck in the world. But he always quickly rejected the possibility. He had never allowed her out of his or Edith's sight long enough to meet anyone. Still, the mere mention of a possible rival drove him into a frenzy. He would smash his fist against a lamppost, a brick wall—anything. Then he'd thrust the bloodied fist before his companions' eyes and melodramatically announce that that was how his heart felt.

As weeks passed, Snyder, who had been out to take the world for a sucker, begged to be taken. The thousands of dollars that Ruth had settled on him were tossed away on booze, broads and bets. The kind of liquor was unimportant. He had no taste for booze—only for its effect. Whether the women were gold diggers or real professionals was unimportant if they temporarily exorcised his obsession. He laid heavy money at impossible odds on horses that never had a chance, unconsciously giving evidence that gamblers seek absolution by setting themselves up to lose.

Forever in and out of Lindy's, he'd glower at the world with hooded eyes and cynically boast that he was going to run through his settlement and then "pop" himself in "the topper" or maybe just walk into the water until his hat floated.

After a couple of months of torching he heard that Ruth had been seen at the fights with a man. He disputed the report but upon checking learned that it was true. Then a West Coast gossip broadcaster predicted wedding bells for Ruth and Myrl Alderman, a music arranger. Myrl Alderman! Snyder was stunned. Alderman, the Iceman, as he'd called him, was the accompanist he had hired for Ruth in 1935. She hadn't seen him since. How could it be?

He got drunk and telephoned her. Aware of the gossip's broadcast, Ruth suspected who was calling and at first let the phone ring but finally answered. He accused her of seeing Alderman, and she asked why she shouldn't since she was divorced. He accused her of holding out on him in the settlement and demanded half of her family inheritance. She refused. He begged her to come back, and when Ruth refused again, his mood turned uglier. He reminded her that she'd once said she'd rather be dead than to live with him and told her she was going to get her wish. He was hopping a plane to come out to kill her.

Ruth and a cousin, who had listened to the conversation on an extension, went to District Attorney Buron Fitts. Fitts assigned an around-the-clock police guard and alerted District Attorney Thomas E. Dewey of New York to the threat. Dewey gazed into his clouded crystal ball and told reporters that he never commented on publicity stunts. Later, after an "investigation" that consisted of asking Snyder whether he had made the call (but neglected to check the telephone toll charges for Snyder's Piccadilly suite), Dewey and his chief investigator dismissed the incident.

Shortly afterward there was another call between Ruth and her ex-husband, which she transcribed in shorthand and which was subsequently read into the court record.

SNYDER: You know, my angel, I wouldn't hurt a hair on your head. I'd kill for you.

RUTH: Well, it was no little thing to have heard you were going to kill me. I'm afraid to see and talk to you. I've always been afraid of you.

SNYDER: You get your lawyer to go to Buron Fitts and say that the complaint that you made was all a misunderstanding.

RUTH: I don't know. I'm afraid of you, and I don't want you to come to California. What do you want? More money?

SNYDER: Mommie, you have me crying.

RUTH: Oh, snap out of it.

SNYDER: You took a lot of money out for my gambling. Wasn't that cold-blooded? You don't want me in California.

RUTH: No, I don't want you in California, but I won't stop you.

SNYDER: All I want is to go into the show business, but now on account of your complaint I can't do that because of Buron Fitts, who wants his picture in the paper.

RUTH: I'll fix that.

Ruth and Harry Myrl Alderman had fallen deeply in love. Now, with Snyder threatening to come to California, Ruth and Edith felt it imperative to find a refuge where they would be safe from intimidation. They decided that Myrl's modest, relatively secluded seven-room house at 3090 Lake Hollywood Drive would be a safe place. Myrl, handsome, polished, easygoing and sensitive to the needs and anxieties of others, would provide much-needed reassurance as well as physical protection not only for Ruth but also for Edith, who was hysterical at the prospect of her father's arrival.

Once settled, in spite of the knowledge that Snyder had arrived, Ruth felt secure and content. When she mentioned a peace bond, her lawyer reminded her that barking dogs seldom bite. She thought he was probably correct. Her greatest regret was that she had waited so long to make the break. Later she said she couldn't help thinking what a difference it would have made if Alderman had been with her when she was pursuing her career. Hers was an untrained, instinctive talent, while Alderman's abilities had been enhanced by formal training. "I was a lowbrow," she admits. "He might have encouraged me to experiment and to broaden my interests. Because Myrl liked all kinds of entertainment."

On October 15, 1938, Ruth was thinking about resuming her career as she prepared vegetables and pork chops for dinner. Glancing out the window, she saw Alderman's car pull up. A moment later, she was panic-stricken to see her ex-husband emerge from the car, gun in hand.

In recounting the incident, Ruth, Edith and Alderman agreed upon what had transpired, while Snyder's version differed substantially. He claimed that he had gone to NBC studios at 7 P.M., located Alderman and explained he needed to discuss some business details with Ruth which would avoid a nasty court fight and that Alderman had agreed to take him to her.

Alderman's version was more colorful. He said that when he'd stepped into the NBC parking lot, Snyder had suddenly appeared from between some cars, demanding his ex-wife's phone number. When Alderman said he'd call to see whether Ruth was willing to let Snyder have her number, Snyder had jammed a pistol in his ribs, saying, "Make a move, and it'll be your last."

Ruth, Edith and Alderman claimed that once in the house, Snyder herded them into the music room at gunpoint. According to Edith, when her father snarled, "This is going to be the end of all of you," she told him, "If you're going to shoot, shoot," to which he replied, "You're going to sit down and shut up." She saw he meant it and sat.

Snyder, on the contrary, portrayed himself as calmly inquiring whether Ruth and the Iceman were married. Ruth denied it, and when Snyder said that meant they were just living together and Edith knew it, Ruth told him it was none of his business. Alderman, Snyder claimed, pulled a gun as the lights flickered, and in response he drew a pistol he always carried to protect the large sums in his wallet* and shot twice—the first bullet going above Alderman's head, the second hitting him. According to Snyder, as Alderman fell, he cried, "Honey, get that son of a bitch. . . ." and Ruth rushed to a bedroom for a gun. As Ruth and Snyder struggled, Snyder claimed, he grabbed Ruth's hand, and the gun went off.

Edith said she first rushed to Alderman's side to aid him. Hearing a shot in the bedroom, she ran in there and grabbed her father, pulling him away from Ruth and begging, "Please, don't kill Ruthie. You've already killed Myrl. She's been kinder to me than anyone, and she's all I've got."

Ruth slipped out of the room. Snyder started to pursue her, but Edith blocked him. He knocked her to the floor and went after Ruth. As Edith fell, she found Ruth's pistol† on the floor. Grabbing it, she ran after her father, shooting at him and missing. When he ran outside,

---

*His billfold contained $200 when he was arrested.

†A gift from Al Jolson several years earlier.

172

Ruth and Edith immediately bolted the door and called the police to report the shooting and ask for an ambulance.

Snyder went next door and told the neighbors to summon the law.

Examination by paramedics disclosed that the bullet had penetrated Alderman's abdominal wall on the left side below his rib cage but had missed vital organs. He was taken to Hollywood Receiving Hospital for emergency treatment, then transferred to St. Vincent's. Ruth and Edith spelled each other at his bedside during his rapid recovery.

The police picked up Snyder, who was awaiting them on a street corner, and took him to the station. After booking he called lawyer Jerry Giesler to represent him.

In an exclusive interview in the New York *Daily News* October 17 Snyder appeared to the reporter to be unconcerned that the man he had shot two days earlier was recovering. He also insisted that the shooting was the result of a plot devised by Ruth to provoke Alderman into killing him. "She would have liked that," he told the *News* reporter. "My God, how mean a woman can get when she wants to! No man could be that mean. Why, to think how I worshiped that woman, and now she would like to see me dead!

"I couldn't believe it if anybody told me, but now the picture is getting clearer. I'm the old Colonel I used to be. The brain is clicking again, and I'm seeing things clear once more." Later in the story the uncredited reporter wrote "Snyder seemed irrational on other parts. Previous to his tirade, in which he virtually accused his wife of trying to put him on the spot, he told detectives that he did not think Ruth would prosecute him.

"There were reports, seemingly well authenticated, that this was so. This peculiar announcement was made at the District Attorney's office: 'Even if Miss Etting does not prosecute Snyder, he may still face a felony charge.''

Giesler arranged for Snyder's release on $10,000 bail, and Ruth engaged a room adjoining Alderman's at St. Vincent's, requesting police protection. Then the Municipal Court charges of shooting Alderman were dismissed upon a motion by the district attorney's office, which proposed to bring Snyder to trial under grand jury indictments charging him with (1) attempting to murder Alderman, (2) attempting to murder Ruth, (3) attempting to murder Edith, (4) kidnapping Alderman and forcing him to drive to 3090 Lake Hollywood Drive, (5) kidnapping Alderman, Ruth and Edith by forcing them to move from one room of the house to another, (6) obliterating the serial numbers on a gun he carried. Bail was set at $50,000, which Snyder was unable to raise, and he returned to jail.

By December 12, 1938, when the trial opened, Ruth was being harassed by a $150,000 alienation-of-affections suit brought by Alderman's second wife. During Snyder's trial she was subjected to a cross-examination in which lawyer Giesler was "as searching with her as I have ever been with any woman" as he later boasted. Looking back, Ruth once observed, "A trial is something I would never wish on anyone. It breaks your heart. Snyder was the defendant, but Giesler tried Myrl and me."

In the midst of the proceedings Ruth and Alderman chartered a plane and flew to Las Vegas, where they roused the county clerk at 7:30 A.M. to obtain a marriage license. With Edith and Ruth's attorney as witnesses and the hastily summoned Reverend C.H. Sloan officiating, they were married.

After the ceremony a smiling Alderman told newsmen, "I love her dearly," and Ruth hesitantly added, "We've been in love a long time. We were only waiting for Mrs. Alderman's divorce to become final so that we could be married."

When Snyder heard the news, he dismissed it as a bum joke, then added, "I guess it's all over now. Anyway, I wish 'em all the best. Just say the Colonel wishes the little lady and the Iceman all the luck in the world."

Before the case went to the jury, late on December 20, the DA moved to dismiss the charge that Snyder had kidnapped Alderman, Ruth and Edith by moving them from the kitchen to the music room. The jury, consisting of six men and six women, deliberated for two days, during which Ruth, Edith and Alderman maintained low profiles, attempting to salvage whatever dignity was possible under the circumstances. Not so "the Colonel," as the press called him. He sobbed as the case was handed to the jury, then recovered to indulge in a variety of exhibitionistic devices. He symbolically severed his last tie to his ex-wife by removing a gold watch inscribed "To Moe from Ruth." Spitting on it, he handed it to his friend Phil Kessler, saying, "You know what you can do with it." (A reporter who had caught the routine previously commented that if Kessler did what he had done before, he would return it to Snyder.)

When a verdict was reached on December 23, the jury found Snyder innocent of two charges, deadlocked on the charge that he had kidnapped Alderman and found him guilty of attempting to murder Alderman. The conviction carried a one- to twenty-year sentence. Upon hearing the verdict, Snyder leaped up, hugged Giesler and kissed him on the forehead.

Informed of the verdict, Ruth responded that she had always placed her faith in the jury system and felt justice had been done.

Alma Alderman, who was eventually to lose the $150,000 alienation-of-affections suit she had filed against Ruth, told reporters, "If I'd been sitting on the jury, I'd have given Mr. Snyder a vote of thanks."

Snyder wished "Miss Etting" a Merry Christmas and predicted that in the end she would be the sorriest of all.

Subsequently Gielser appealed the verdict and succeeded in getting a new trial. This second trial was abandoned on a motion by the district attorney when Ruth and Myrl declined to testify. Edith, while living at the St. Clair Hotel in Chicago, had succumbed on August 4, 1939, to heart failure, caused by an early bout with rheumatic fever. Without the Aldermans no eyewitnesses to the alleged shooting were available to the prosecution. Snyder, who had been unable to make bail, served only the year that elapsed while he awaited decision on the appeal.

At the end of the first trial money-minded entrepreneurs, hoping to capitalize on Ruth and Myrl's notoriety, had pressed them to appear together, but Myrl rejected all offers saying, "We'd just be freaks. They only want us because we've been in a scandal."

Ruth agreed. Given hindsight, she says, "What we probably should have done was to have gone to work. People would soon have forgotten the trouble. As June Winchell wired me when all the bad publicity broke: 'Remember, today's headlines are tomorrow's toilet paper.'"

Instead, the Aldermans made trips to Canada, Argentina and Brazil before booking passage for England on the *Normandie,* arriving at Southampton on July 25, 1939. In London Alderman settled down to work on a musical comedy, and when music hall bookers discovered that Ruth was in England, they persuaded her to sign for a tour of the provinces which was to end with a London engagement. But as the headlines became more ominous daily, the Aldermans flipped a coin to decide whether to stay abroad or come home. The coin sent them back. They booked a cabin on the *American Banker,* which had installed bunk beds and increased its normal load of 75 passengers to 108 persons and Gene Autry's horse.

Back in the United States, Ruth and Myrl kept their whereabouts unknown to avoid problems with Alma Alderman and Snyder. Three months after Pearl Harbor Alderman was inducted into the Air Corps. Ruth followed him from camp to camp until he was shipped overseas, then settled near his family in Colorado Springs.

Alderman spent three years as a verbal courier of sensitive information. Finally, the undercarriage was blown off the plane in which he was riding, and the pilot brought it in for a belly landing. Leaping out, Alderman and the pilot barely made it to a ditch before a 500-pound bomb exploded, close enough to cause bleeding from ears, eyes and noses and to put them in shock. After treatment at three medical facilities they received discharges.

Alderman returned to Colorado Springs in 1946, a severely shaken man. Army psychiatrists soon decided that music was the best palliative, and the Aldermans moved to Hollywood, where Myrl began doing musical arrangements. In January, 1947, Rudy Vallee booked Ruth as a guest on his radio program. Newsmen turned out feature stories and columns, dwelling on the past and speculating on the resumption of her career. Their attitudes were summed up by Robert Sylvester of the New York *Daily News* who ended his piece: "If she has anything left, she'll give modern crooners something to think about."

Never one to be left out, Snyder told a Chicago reporter, "If she's half as good as she used to be, she'll be better than ninety percent of these canaries today."

Her initial booking drew four hundred fan letters and two additional appearances on the Vallee show. More important to Ruth, the professional activity proved effective therapy for her husband. After the second radio broadcast Monte Proser booked her to headline at the Copacabana for three weeks, at $4,000 a week. The Copa at the time shared honors with the Latin Quarter as Manhattan's biggest, most lavish nightclubs.

Ruth hesitated because the proffered booking fell during Lent, the leanest business period of the year, and she was perturbed at the prospect of working to a sea of white tablecloths. She need not have worried. Newsmen, who had always liked her, played up her comeback, emphasizing her enormous popularity and mysterious personal life, and when she finally opened, reviews were enthusiastic. Abel Green, the editor of *Variety*, wrote that during Holy Week business was "No panic, but with nighteries folding like Peace Conferences, she's plenty okay for the biz." Quoting extensively from his predecessor and personal idol Sime Silverman's review of Ruth's debut, Green wrote: "A lot of it [Sime's review] still holds. She still has class, personality and talent. Her blonde good-looks are now generously grey but her figure is still svelte and her song selling effective, if betimes now she wisely skirts top notes. But she makes an orchidaceous appearance and chirps what might be an autobiographical song cavalcade. . . ."

During the Copa engagement executives of MGM's radio station WHN invited Ruth and Myrl to do a husband-and-wife radio show five days a week. The Aldermans agreed, stipulating that the emphasis be on music, with a minimum of chatter, and on May 19 *Time* ran a story reporting: "To modern bobby-soxers, her name means next to nothing. But it is sweetly nostalgic news to folks in their forties that a trim, silver-haired, fiftyish, blues-singer next week begins a new radio show—her first in 12 years." *Time* noted that Ruth was still "an item," as she'd proved in her Copa comeback, and recalled that in the Scott Fitzgerald era a stack of her records had been standard fraternity house equipment, while Yale undergraduates had mobbed her and wrecked an establishment where she was signing autographs. Ziegfeld, recordings and radio had made her *the* top singer for ten years prior to her retirement—and now she was back.

For a year Ruth and Myrl broadcast from WHN's studios atop Loew's State Theater, but television was emerging, and when her contract expired, they returned to Colorado Springs, where Myrl was engaged to provide an orchestra for dancing in the new Fun Room of the Antlers Hotel. When one of the owners inquired whether Ruth would consider opening the room for them, Alderman suggested they ask her. "We had just come from New York, and I had plenty of clothes and arrangements, so I thought why not? People here had never seen me work," Ruth explains. It was her final professional engagement and a triumph. Commenting on her retirement, she once said, "I think there's nothing more pathetic than a performer who doesn't know when to quit. Take Sophie Tucker. I knew Sophie at her height. She was marvelous. Boy, when she gave out a song—talk about Kate Smith or Ethel Merman—you could hear Sophie six blocks away. A wonderful, big, beautiful voice. Then she lost the high notes, and she began talking a song. Then she got to the stage where her material had to be risqué to get across. That was one of the first things I learned in show business. Any time an actor has to resort to blue material his talent's gone. That's what Sophie did. And after that she waved the flag. It was embarrassing because I'd known her when she was a great entertainer. It's a pitiful thing to see someone come out and try to work when they can't cut it anymore. And some of those hams are still taking bows. Not me, I knew when I was through."

Upon the close of Alderman's stand at the Fun Room he secured a booking to open Club 66 in Fort Lauderdale, Florida. Both Aldermans liked the climate, and with many new nightclubs making gigs plentiful for musicians, they bought a small house and settled down for the next six years. At last out of the public eye, Ruth was free to please only herself for the first time in her life. Even gossip columnist Dorothy Kilgallen's erroneous "Isn't It Sad" item to the effect that Ruth Etting, who once earned $200,000 yearly, was living in a broken-down trailer park in Florida didn't bother her. Ruth was oblivious to the press by now, having survived so many distorted newspaper stories, but Winchell rushed to her defense, swearing that before her retirement he had seen a $250,000 trust fund she had established for herself and admonishing Miss Kilgallen to get her facts straight.

In 1954 two events occurred to change Ruth's life. MGM acquired rights from Ruth, Myrl and Martin Snyder to make a film version of their tangled relationships. *Love Me or Leave Me,* mixing fact and fancy and formula picture-making, showed Ruth rising from the dime-a-dance background which she had created so brilliantly in Rodgers and Hart's song, turned her from a teetotaler into a lush and implied she had been a sexy tramp instead of an overprotected prisoner of love.*

Snyder's characteristics were heightened for theatrical effect,† and he was carelessly given a lame right instead of left leg. The time span was compressed radically; instead of meeting Myrl in 1935, when her career was almost finished, he was her accompanist-tutor-suitor in the 1920s. Yet the portrayals by James Cagney, Doris Day and Cameron Mitchell of Synder, Ruth and Alderman were so vivid and the gritty subject matter so much more pertinent than the perennial will-they-or-won't-they get the show on or be reunited that accuracy—or lack of it—bothered only those personally involved.

The second change occurred when the Aldermans sold their Florida home and bought one in Las Vegas, where the growing number of hotels with their emphasis on entertainment provided employment opportunities for Alderman.

After the release of *Love Me or Leave Me* in 1955 Ruth was offered a five-figure salary to come out of retirement. "No way," she told the bookers. "I'm never going to go out there to have people in the audi-

---

*Doris Day, who never knew Ruth, claims in her autobiography that Ruth clawed her way to the top and was a kept woman. Ruth laughed and said, "I never was that lucky." Urged by friends to sue, she recalled that June and Walter Winchell had always said litigation only brought the gossip to the attention of those who hadn't seen it the first time.

†For instance, in the film he calls Ruth "Ettling" to needle her—which in truth had been Earl Carroll's habit.

178

ence say, 'Gee, I remember her when she was really something.'"

As completely as possible, she settled into the happy anonymity of being Mrs. Alderman. The extent to which she succeeded can be illustrated with a story told by Jack Langdon, executive secretary to George Burns. Langdon, an Etting admirer, escorted Gracie Allen, who had retired, to a post-premiere party following the opening of Burns and Carol Channing at the Dunes in Las Vegas. In the course of the evening he was introduced to numerous headliners, past and present, and was especially fascinated by Blossom Seeley and a vital but unassuming silver-haired woman, who, it seemed to him, must be a local nonprofessional. Afterward he mentioned to Gracie how much he had enjoyed Blossom. "Mrs. Alderman is very interesting, too," he said. "Just what's her connection with show business?" He was astonished to hear that he had spent half an hour talking with the legendary Ruth Etting, who had never once referred to her eventful past. Upon hearing the story, Ruth shrugged and said, "I told you, I'm no ham."

While living in Las Vegas, both Ruth and Alderman became ill. In 1967 she was successfully operated on for cancer and a few years later underwent open-heart surgery to have a blocked aorta replaced by a Dacron one. In early 1975 she had abdominal surgery. She shrugs. "If it's your time, it's your time. Anyway, what difference does it make whether you die from tuberculosis or a heart attack? It's not that I'm particularly brave. I just have a God-given easygoing nature."

After eight years in Las Vegas the Aldermans moved back to the big, beautiful home they had built on the outskirts of Colorado Springs. Myrl died of a liver ailment on November 16, 1966. Ruth sold their home (which has since been turned into a restaurant) and moved into a new apartment building, where several relatives by marriage live. When the fancy strikes her, she simply locks the door and visits her stepson, John Alderman, a vice-president of Warner-Lambert, Inc., his wife, Violet, and their three children in New Jersey, goes to Florida, or, occasionally, to the West Coast to see old friends.

In 1971 producer Stan Sideman staged a "search" for Ruth Etting to fill a spot in a nostalgic revue, *The Big Show of 1928,* but it was all a publicity gimmick since she had already turned him down. "Nick Lucas and Gene Austin never lost their high notes; my voice dropped," she explains. "Nick sings as well as he ever did. I wouldn't attempt to sing professionally or for charity. Any charity work I do—such as visiting hospitals or prisons or driving shut-ins around—is much more helpful than any singing I could do. Anyway, birds sing for free."

Nor does she often grant interviews. "Why should I?" she asks modestly. "I don't work anymore. I've reached an age where I can say anything I want and it can't help or hurt me. But hardly anyone remembers me, and it just takes up my time and doesn't really mean anything."

Yet it meant a great deal to Ruth when on June 12, 1973, she returned to David City, Nebraska, for the first time in many years to attend the High School Alumni Association reunion and to participate in the Centennial Pageant, in which she saw herself portrayed by another David City girl as a part of the community's history.

Then, in November of the same year, Biograph Records released an album titled *Hello, Baby*, compiled from her early recordings. Of it music critic John S. Wilson of the New York *Times* wrote:

> "It [*Hello, Baby*] serves not only to rescue Ruth Etting from the oblivion of being a character in a Doris Day movie, but also as a reminder that not all pop singers of the twenties were the ridiculous camp characters that have recently been portrayed.
>
> Ruth Etting was certainly a product of the period, but within that context she had a style that sounds just as valid today as it did then—an easy, relaxed, floating delivery filled with attractive phrases that were stretched, raised and sometimes adventurously bent. She developed her songs with imaginative turns, twists and changes of tempo. . . .

Just as she eventually developed her life. Retaining her basic personality, she has changed with the times. When she attends a party, people—young and old—who have no idea who she once was are drawn to her. She exudes the serenity of one who has seen, experienced, understood and forgiven almost everything.

Of all the golden girls of 1933–34 Ruth is least wedded to the professional image projected in her day. Possibly because she never became entangled in the big studio complex, she escaped the dehumanizing battles for important roles, the stresses of options being exercised or dropped, the promotional foofaraw associated with stardom and the eventual adoption as necessity of the pretentious life-style originally developed to titillate the public. She never became enmeshed in striving to attain the unattainable, an attempt that drove many contemporaries into bitterness, alcohol, hard drugs, nymphomania, suicide or obsessive pursuit of eternal youth. Never having been led to expect paradise on earth when her career ended, Ruth was able to adjust to reality most successfully of all.

Ginger's greatest acclaim as a dramatic actress came in *Kitty Foyle* (with James Craig, left, and Dennis Morgan). For her work she won an Oscar in 1940. *(Robert W. Friess)*

Mommy tries to look younger, Ginger older, in a publicity photo for *The Major and the Minor.* Lela guided Ginger's career for over 50 years. Says Lela, "In show business, two heads are better than one."

Flying Down to Rio in late 1933 represented an auspicious debut for the Astaire-Rogers team. *(Robert W. Friess)*

Handsome Lew Ayres was the second of Ginger's five husbands. Although all marriages ended in divorce, she regrets none of them—may wed again.

Ginger was at her chichiest in such films as *Roberta*. Analyzing the reasons for the success of Astaire-Rogers, Katharine Hepburn reputedly observed: "She gives him sex, and he gives her class." *(Robert W. Friess)*

Blond in *Follow the Fleet*, brunette in *Roxie Hart* (with George Montgomery), Ginger has had almost as many images as ex-husbands. In *Sitting Pretty*, 1933, she played a fan dancer. Today, she says, "It's not my place to find fault, but you'd never get me undressing in front of a camera. I'd scream or die before that." *(Robert W. Friess)*

Miriam Hopkins was a complicated mixture of thistledown and steel wool. She had wit, warmth, and charm, but a chance remark could turn her into a foot-stamping, ashtray-throwing virago—which caused a fan magazine writer to describe her as "the town's most ferocious tigress." *(Richard Lamparski)*

Miriam relaxed at her beach house with adopted son, Michael.

In Ernst Lubitsch's *Trouble in Paradise*, Miriam and Herbert Marshall played fanciful crooks out to bilk rich Kay Francis.

Above: Miriam, Fredric March, and Gary Cooper appeared in *Design for Living* in late 1933. *(Museum of Modern Art/Film Stills Archive)* Right: She feuded with Bette Davis in *The Old Maid* in 1939, although things seem relatively calm in this candid shot. *(Lee Graham)* Below: Recalling her beginning in films with *Fast and Loose*, with Carole Lombard, left, and Charles Starret, center, "If I had it to do over again, I'd do everything different." *(Lee Graham)*

In 1933, Ruth Etting, Broadway star, Sweetheart of Columbia Records, and premiere torch singer on radio, received big billing but little to do in Samuel Goldwyn's *Roman Scandals*. *(Ruth Etting Alderman)*

At right, baby Ruth poses for a photographer in her hometown; David City, Nebraska. *(Ruth Etting Alderman)*

At the Marigold Gardens in Chicago in 1917, Ruth Etting poses in a costume she designed for the chorus girls. *(Ruth Etting Alderman)*

Ziegfeld glorified her in several shows, in which she introduced such great hits as "Love Me or Leave Me" and "Ten Cents a Dance." *(Ruth Etting Alderman)*

She reigned as the acknowledged queen of musical short subjects. Made in a couple of days, they are only a blur to her today. She thinks the photo may have come from either *Old Lace* or *The Modern Cinderella.* *(Ruth Etting Alderman)*

Ruth and Jimmy Durante appeared regularly on radio's *Chase and Sanborn Hour* in 933. Will Rogers, center, was a guest star. *(Ruth Etting Alderman)*

Columnist Walter Winchell, right, was a vociferous Etting booster. Here Ruth attempted to patch up a publicity inspired "feud" between Winchell and band leader Ben Bernie. *(Ruth Etting Alderman)*

th and Myrl Alderman married hile Ruth's ex-husband was on trial for allegedly trying to murder Alderman. "The years with Myrl—those were the important ones," says Ruth. *(Ruth Etting Alderman)*

Ruth tried a comeback in 1947. She appeared at New York's Copacabana and had a radio show. After Arthur Godfrey interviewed her, he sent her this photo, signed "For Ruthie—lovelier than ever! Arthur Godfrey." *(Ruth Etting Alderman)*

Kay Francis was the perfect Art Deco Beauty. Artist James Montgomery Flagg admired the "gauze eye-lashes" of Dietrich, the "scowl" of Katharine Hepburn, and the "incomparable sneer" of Mae West, but his favorite actress was decorative Kay Francis. (R. C. Perry)

Kay and Lilyan Tashman appeared in *Girls About Town*, a comedy about two "models."

One-Way Passage starred Kay and William Powell. It remains unique, because of the humor and style utilized in telling this penny-dreadful tale. *(Richard Lamparski)*

Her role in *The House on 56th Street* provided Kay with sixteen eye-catching gowns—as well as some unflattering coiffures.

Carole Lombard gave Kay a chance to redeem herself in *In Name Only*.

Loretta appeared with sisters Polly Ann Young, Sally Blane, and Georgianna Young in *The Story of Alexander Graham Bell. (James C. Madden)*

Loretta married twice. The first, Grant Withers; the second, Thomas H. Lewis, right. *(James C. Madden)*

Loretta was so young her legs required symmetricals when she played Lon Chaney's leading lady in *Laugh, Clown, Laugh. (James C. Madden)*

As 1933 ended, *A Man's Castle* provided Loretta's career with a great boost. She and leading man Spencer Tracy were deeply in love. *(James C Madden)*

Rumor had it that she and Clark Gable were romantically involved during filming of *Call of the Wild*, but critics complained their love scenes lacked conviction. *(James C. Madden)*

Zoo in Budapest, 1933, with Gene Raymond, did much to earn critical acceptance and establish Loretta as a real actress. *(James C. Madden)*

Twentieth Century-Fox frequently teamed Loretta and Tyrone Power as here, in *Second Honeymoon.* *(James C. Madden)*

Although Loretta left Twentieth to find more challenging roles, many of those she played, including the ones in *China,* opposite Alan Ladd, and in *The Stranger,* with Orson Welles, proved no more ambitious. *(James C. Madden)*

Pert, diminutive Irene Bentley was prettier than many girls who eventually became stars, but Irene dropped out. *Smoky,* with Victory Jory, which opened in New York as '33 turned into '34, was one of her three films. Says Jory: "The picture made a fortune, but in all fairness, you'd have to say the horse was the star." *(Motion Picture Academy of Arts and Sciences)*

KAY FRANCIS

The Sellout

Kay Francis' crown as Warner Brothers' queen of fantasy was slightly askew by New Year's Eve, 1933. But few fans could have guessed as much during her December visit to Manhattan.

Attending Miriam Hopkins' *Jezebel* on December 19, La Francis, resplendent in her emerald earrings, bracelet and necklace, regally waved aside proffered playbills as she declined to sign a single autograph.

A week later, at the disastrous production of *The Lake*, starring Katharine Hepburn, Kay sailed forth from Paul "Piggy" Warburg's limo and into the lobby of the theater, her velvety eyes focused at least six inches above the tallest commoner.

On December 29 and 30, wearing Bernie Newman and Orry-Kelly gowns, she moved in unapproachable beauty, dispensing only an occasional smile or small nod. She claimed that dime-store clerks and seamstresses weren't expected to work on vacation. So why should actresses?

Nor did her reserve evoke any resentment from admirers. For Kay to tarry or acknowledge their existence would have been as inappropriate as if Queen Mary had suddenly hopped out of her carriage and begun kissing her subjects. Kay was expected to be aloof, just as Janet Gaynor was always girlishly shy; Jean Arthur, endearingly eccentric; and Mae West, humorously sexy. Kay represented someone for women to envy or admire—but to emulate? Never. For men, she embodied the impossible dream.

She noted in her diary on December 31: "Bee's lunch for

gang. . . . Tennis later. . . . Then to Jo Forrestal's for dinner and on to Winthrop Aldrich's party at the club. Swell fun!''

Bee was Beatrice Ames Stewart, a Santa Barbara society girl who had married writer-wit Donald Ogden Stewart. The guest lists of Bee Stewart, Jo Forrestal and Winthrop Aldrich are long gone, but they were composed of a sprinkling of Old Society, Café Society, playboys, artists, playgirls, writers, songwriters and assorted bohemians. These were the lucky ones, who at the height of the Great Depression were still clinging to the merry-go-round that had rudely dislodged so many riders in 1929.

Who in 1933 could have guessed that this seemingly invincible goddess known as Kay Francis would be undone by putting her fate into the hands of the studios—by leaving the decisions up to them as long as they paid her handsomely? That she would be plagued by illness, become addicted to pills and liquor and end her days in bitter seclusion?

Kay was a personality who always evoked strong responses. Years after she was washed up in Hollywood, she laughed about climbing into a taxi to be told by the driver that he hated her. "Nothing personal," he added. "But when I wanted to see Tom Mix, Ma'd drag me to see you 'n' George Brent."

Upon hearing the story, an acquaintance volunteered that her father used to snort, "*You,* what do you know! You like Kay Francis and Herbert Marshall pictures."

Yet in the 1930s, when James Montgomery Flagg caricatured Hollywood screen queens Joan Crawford, Claudette Colbert, Mae West, Constance Bennett, Katharine Hepburn, Marlene Dietrich and Kay for *Vanity Fair,* the magazine's readers learned that while Flagg admired the "gauze eyelashes" of Dietrich, "the scowl" of Hepburn and the "incomparable sneer" of Mae West, his greatest ardor was reserved for his favorite actress Kay Francis, who, the caption writer noted, "appears in every Warner Brothers film and every third film made by other motion picture companies—which keeps Mr. Flagg in a state of contentment."

The elegant Kay's popularity with Flagg and other sophisticated New Yorkers is understandable, but her appeal to Mid-America is more difficult to explain.

A determined faultfinder could reduce Kay to an anthology of defects. In the early sound era, when experienced stage actresses were in demand, Kay's formal dramatic training was nil. Her practical experience was limited to one season of stock and a few minor roles on

Broadway. She had a lisp that interfered with her pronouncing *r's.* She stood five feet seven inches—considered too tall for films. Her handsome head was too small in proportion to the big-boned, wide-shouldered frame which balanced precariously on her inadequate (size 4) feet.

Fortunately for her, audiences found the combination beguiling. Given her raven hair, ivory skin, luminous eyes and a piquant mouth that spread into a dazzling smile, only the most misanthropic picture goer would carp about her imperfections.

Kay represented the epitome of chic and cheek. No list of best-dressed women, most intelligent stars or hardest-working actresses seemed complete without her. Kay offhandedly brushed all this aside. "I may or may not be intelligent, but I'm too shrewd to take those lists seriously," she said. And when reporters asked her to comment on being "the best-dressed woman on the screen," she snapped, "I'm not well-dressed, I'm overdressed." As for being a clotheshorse in a class with Norma Shearer or Lil Tashman, Kay emitted a characteristic guffaw and suggested "old workhorse" as a more apt description.

All these warring elements can be resolved by recognizing that behind the façade of Kay Francis lurked an impoverished but ambitious girl, born Katherine Gibbs. Katie Gibbs had been determined to get on in the world and so, having taken stock of her assets, created Kay Francis. Yet Katie couldn't resist deriding these synthetic lists, even though she recognized their commercial value.

She was quick to learn. She possessed an observant eye and an analytic mind. She rapidly figured out the rules of the Hollywood game. Reduced to its simplest terms: everyone, even those of the highest echelon, is on the make. For instance, her insight saved professional gloom chaser Elsa Maxwell from disaster when Elsa was staging her first West Coast gala. The gathering included only the most famous stars, directors, writers, producers and studio executives. The setting was beautiful and the party boring. Kay assessed the situation, took Elsa aside and urged her to call Hymie Fink, the fan magazine photographer, at once. Elsa protested that her guests would resent such an intrusion on their privacy. "Elsa, this is Hollywood—not New York or Paris. Try them," Kay insisted. "They're here because they want to see themselves in photos captioned 'Among Those Present.'" Elsa reluctantly summoned Fink, and the party turned into a roaring success.

No matter how many such parties and premieres Kay attended for business reasons, her real social life centered on the man of the moment and his friends, plus Carole Lombard and William Powell, the

Herbert Marshalls, the Lewis Milestones and Miriam Hopkins. But if people can be divided between those who entertain and those who are entertained because they are entertaining, Kay belonged to the latter group. She repaid her social obligations with a huge party every other year. Probably the most memorable of these was a fancy-dress ball. "It was one of the best parties I ever attended in Hollywood," writer George Oppenheimer says. "She rented a stylish restaurant and converted the entrance into the prow of a ship. You went up the gangplank and slid down into the ballroom. There, there were big photographic blowups like those in front of theaters. I remember distinctly Ken MacKenna had scored a big hit on Broadway in *Merrily We Roll Along*, and Kay, who had divorced him not long before, had a huge sign: MERRILY WE ROLL ALONG WITHOUT KENNETH MACKENNA.

But no matter how well Kay understood Hollywood or how long she stayed, she always behaved as if she were there on a work visa. Her innate good taste protected her from the sometimes unintentionally comic excesses of a Clara Bow, a Jean Harlow or a Joan Crawford, who, it is said, humorlessly took lessons to develop a sense of humor.

For so beautiful a woman she had surprisingly little vanity. She wasted no time gazing into mirrors. She hated shopping. If she was not on view professionally, her clothes were functional. She considered having her hair done a bore. Later she resorted to a wig. When someone told her that in medieval times, in the interest of sanitation and convenience, prostitutes shaved themselves and resorted to pubic wigs or "merkins" for business, the idea appealed to Kay's bawdy sense of humor, and she christened her wig "Miss Merkin."

Perhaps her lusty humor, lack of vanity, low voice, boyish hairdo and tailored suits—plus the inevitable rumors that surround celebrities—gave rise to the widely held but false assumption that she was bisexual, if not lesbian. But both her private diaries (agonizing over Dwight, Allan, McKay, Billy, John, Ken, Del, Don and later Hap, Joel and Dennis—to mention only a few of her romantic attachments) as well as assurances of her friends lay this rumor to rest. "Oh, there may have been some occasion when she was very, very drunk," says a friend. "But that wasn't where her head was—as they say these days. There was never the slightest doubt that she was man-oriented, and don't let anyone persuade you otherwise."

Kay could never adjust to the assumption that stars were not entitled to privacy. But after a few episodes the studio protected her by sending along superb traveling companions to handle crises. On one occasion Andy Lawler, a man of many functions in Hollywood, was paid

$10,000 to accompany her to Europe to keep her out of trouble at any cost. Lawler succeeded admirably until they reached London. Exhausted, he retired early while Kay proceeded to get roaring drunk. He was aroused a few hours later by a wild disturbance. Still groggy, he rushed to his bedroom door in time to see Kay, obstreperous and totally nude, standing in the center of the drawing room, proclaiming, "I'm not a star. I'm a *woman*, and I want to get fucked!" Asked how he handled the crisis, Lawler replied, "I earned my ten thousand dollars."

On other occasions Kay landed in the headlines. When an enterprising photographer and reporter surprised her doing an ecstatic tap dance as her current lover's plane descended at Newark Airport, she shattered her ladylike image by attacking them. For the most part, though, she managed to keep out of the newspapers and behaved as if she had sold her body to the movies and the studios were free to do with it as they liked.

Had she not taken stock of her assets, considered becoming a model or a Ziegfeld girl and decided she could earn more as an actress? The idea had been to exploit her youth, beauty and personality.

The result was that by the end of 1933 Kay had completed twenty nine features in which she paraded in eye-catching fashions against lavish settings in stories that were awash with sentimentality and pseudo-sophistication. Where Ruth Chatterton, Genevieve Tobin and Barbara Stanwyck read and feared to tread, Kay rushed in, playing roles they rejected. Whether her decisions were angelic or foolish, initially she was rewarded for her cooperation by Warner's so that by the end of 1933 she had attained such a position in the "Woman's picture" genre that the name KAY FRANCIS dwarfed the title of her current release, *The House on 56th Street*.

What did the moguls count on to sell her pictures? Not the leading man, the supporting cast or the director. They depended on Kay's name, "thirty six gorgeous gowns" and true-confession-type stories.

In return for her cooperation Kay asked only one thing of the studios: money, plenty of it. "Money? Is that all she cares about Hollywood?" Elsa Maxwell asked in one of the articles she wrote about Kay. "It is. All," Miss Maxwell continued. "Were she to stop making it, she would be aboard the Eastbound train the day after."

"Money is handy stuff to have," Kay told Lois Long, a remark repeated to many people. Whatever happened, she never had to revise her priorities. She was shrewd in accumulating capital and parsimonious when it came to parting with it. Nor was she shy about letting her views be known. During a poker game Elsa Maxwell suggested raising the stakes. Several players reluctantly agreed. Since Elsa earned spending money by gambling and writing about stars, she was, they felt, no one to offend. Kay disagreed. She said if the stakes were raised, she'd quit. "I work hard for my money, and I'd hate losing it, just as I'd hate taking yours," she told Elsa. The other players predicted dire consequences, but when Elsa subsequently wrote about the incident, she used it as an illustration of Kay's frank and forthright manner.

Chances are Elsa was fortunate. For Kay was a cutthroat player who often won large sums. This became so well known in Hollywood that once, when she was bemoaning the cost of maintaining her mother, Connie Bennett tired of the routine and said, "Oh, come off it, Hetty. We all know you support your mother on your poker winnings."

Years later Dennis Allen, an actor-director and Kay's lover, recalled, "She was very funny about money. She often laughed about Hollywood friends calling her Hetty Green* because she was so slow to part with a buck. I don't mean she was stingy. She could be incredibly generous, but she did pinch pennies."

Kay would raise hell over an excessive tip. Yet she spontaneously sent $5,000 to the high-living Ruth Chatterton, who had run through her earnings. Or, upon learning that a friend's summer theater was going broke, she volunteered to appear for him and secretly return her salary.

Kay's mania for money can be understood by recognizing that she was an insecure woman who equated money with happiness. Her insecurity could partly be attributed to a persistent rumor that her mother came from Trinidad and was the daughter of a black mother and a white father. It was Kay's Achilles' heel in a harshly racist society.

On the other hand, the stories of a "social family" who sent her to the most exclusive private schools are fabrications. Nor did her mother found the Katharine Gibbs Secretarial School which Kay attended.

Kay contributed to the obfuscation of her early life, claiming to have been born anywhere between 1899 and 1910. But in a genealogical letter to Kay her elderly mother, Katherine Clinton Franks Gibbs, made no mention of Trinidad and informed her daughter that the Clintons had arrived in Ipswich, Bay of Cod, Massachusetts, in 1665, making Kay a ninth-generation American. Katherine Clinton Franks dropped the surname when she became an actress in a musical produced by Au-

*Hetty Green (1867–1916), known as the Witch of Wall Street, lived a niggardly existence while by shrewd investments and stock manipulation she probably became the richest woman in America.

gustin Daly in 1898. Soon she was playing Jessica in Ada Rehan's company of *The Merchant of Venice,* and her career seems to have flourished until, on December 7, 1903, she married Joseph Sprague Gibbs and retired. Gibbs, a hotel manager who moved frequently was working in Oklahoma City on July 13, 1905, when Kay was born. Her slightly tipsy father celebrated the event by riding his horse through the hotel lobby and up the big staircase leading to the room where his wife lay with their newborn daughter, Katherine Edwina.*

Shortly, Gibbs moved his family to Denver, then to Santa Barbara and Los Angeles. He drank excessively, and his wife reportedly nipped a bit, and each seems to have found the other intolerable in his or her cups. When Kay was three or four, her mother took her east and returned to the stage. In public Kay always said Joseph Gibbs had died early, although in diaries as late as 1923 she noted:

March 12: Mother here in afternoon.
March 13: Dad here after dinner.

In any case, Gibbs was an absent father, and Kay could never forgive him. In her mid-forties she told friends that she didn't know where he was and didn't care. "Either because she was taught or decided on her own, Kay never had a good word for him," a friend recalls.

Kay spent much of her childhood touring with her mother, moving from one broken-down rooming house to another. She never forgot those barnstorming years when they were so desperately poor that they frequently filled up on salty popcorn and drank water to save the cost of dinner. Her early education was catch-as-catch-can, provided by her mother and other troupers. Kay intimated that some of the males in the troupe tried to educate her in other ways, too.

As an adult, Kay would sometimes speak of those early experiences to close friends. Out of respect for her sense of privacy none will divulge specifics, but all agree that her childhood was sordid. "That was a pretty dreadful time of life for Kay," Mrs. Dwight (Stephens) Wiman said. "I know her mother had an awful lot of odd jobs. Some of the things Kay told me I wouldn't repeat. They were horrible. It was all very third-rate."

The result was that Kay preferred to forget her father and held an ambivalent attitude toward her mother. In later years she was dutiful in material ways while she all but banished Mrs. Gibbs from her life. The

*For her uncle Edwin.

mother was never allowed to visit the set of any of her daughter's films. She was welcomed at Kay's home only upon invitation. Few of Kay's friends, except Ruth Chatterton, whose mother lived next door to Mrs. Gibbs, ever met her.

Beatrice Stewart, Dorothy di Frasso, Jessica Barthelmess and Kay were part of a group that often played backgammon. One afternoon, when Kay had said she didn't think she could make the game, Mrs. Stewart impulsively directed her chauffeur to drive by Kay's home. "I thought perhaps she'd change her mind. So I rang her doorbell, and this perfectly beautiful little woman—snow-white hair, charming—answered. I said, 'Oh, I'm sorry. I'm Beatrice Stewart. I wonder if I could see Miss Francis.' And she said, 'Of course, I'm Kay's mother.' Oh, I gave Katie an awful dressing down after that. Why wouldn't she let us meet this charming woman?"

In her Hollywood biographies Kay claimed to have spent her childhood at the Holy Angels Convent in Fort Lee, New Jersey; Notre Dame in Roxbury, Massachusetts; and Holy Child of Jesus in Manhattan. No record of Kay's having attended any of the three exists. Mrs. Gibbs did, however, scrape together money for fourteen-year-old Kay to attend Miss Fuller's in Ossining, New York, where Kay's lack of conventional education proved her undoing. Her mother bitterly alluded to this fact in one of the few interviews she was ever allowed to give about her famous daughter. "Now you tell me: what did it matter that she failed geometry?" she demanded. "I've always thought it ridiculous for an attractive woman to study such things as Latin and Greek. I wanted her to do well in piano. But what possible use would geometry be? She was like her father. He had this great personality. He was a clear thinker and possessed excellent judgment. Kay has that, too. And you must remember, Kay has the greatest gift in the world for an actor—personality. That's a star's most valuable asset."

Kay herself once said that at Miss Fuller's it was "Katie-did" when she was good and "Katie-didn't" when she performed poorly. "Mostly it was Katie-didn't," she acknowledged.

For her junior year she transferred to the Cathedral School of St. Mary in Garden City, Long Island, where she remained from September, 1920, to May, 1921, earning 77 in conduct and 80s in everything else except for a 98 in spelling and another failing mark in geometry.

She made her first stage appearance at Cathedral. The script, *You Never Can Tell*, was written by a classmate, Katty Stewart. "Katty played the female lead because she was the author, and I played the leading male role because I was the tallest girl in the class," Kay later recalled.

Instead of returning to Cathedral for her senior year in the fall of 1921 Kay enrolled for a short course at the Katharine Gibbs Secretarial School. She did so at her mother's insistence that she prepare herself to earn a living. Kay decided shorthand and typing would provide the necessary skills.

Upon graduation, Kay went to work at thirty dollars a week for two businessmen for a short time. In the next two years she moved from job to job frequently, working as a publicist and promotion woman, a real-estate salesperson and a model. Her most important position was as an assistant to Juliana Cutting, a woman of good family who earned her living booking coming-out parties for debutantes. Since her duties included arranging invitations to desirable college boys, Kay made useful social contacts. She became engaged to Allan Ryan, Jr., of the Thomas Fortune Ryan family. The engagement was broken, but the friendship continued through his first marriage, and she and Ryan precipitated a small scandal when he escorted her to the Cotton Club the night before his second wedding.

Rumor had it that she been social secretary to Mrs. W.K. Vanderbilt and Mrs. Dwight Morrow. But Kay later said she was only secretary to their financial secretaries. She also worked as a model in the 1920s, posing for her future father-in-law, Leo Mielziner, and Charles Baskerville, who illustrated and wrote cabaret news under the pseudonym Top Hat during the first six months of *The New Yorker*'s existence.

Then, on January 4, 1922, she wrote in her diary, "Met Dwight Francis through Lyn. Tea date expected?"

Every other day thereafter Dwight visited her at the office, took her tea dancing, to dinner, to the theater or nightclubbing. James Dwight Francis, whose surname Kay always retained, was the handsome, wellborn son of a Pittsfield, Massachusetts, family. He attended Phillips-Exeter Academy and in 1915 entered Harvard. But his interest was not so much in educating himself as living it up, and he left in 1919 without a degree.

By the time he came into Kay's life he was drinking well beyond his financial means, but his background and charm blinded her to the dangerous implications of his frequently lurching gait. Unlike some of her later romantic alliances, the early stages of this one seemed placid. The brief entries in the diary are suffused in a sentimental glow. On October 27 she recorded their engagement, and on November 3, it was up to

189

Pittsfield to meet the family, who approved. On November 17 she noted, "GOT MY RING!"; December 5: "Dwight and I to be married St. Thomas 12:30 Wednesday"; and for the final entry in 1922 the bride wrote, "My most wonderful year!"

Handsome and entertaining though he might have been, Dwight Francis had some surprises in store for his bride. While notably short on funds, he refused to give up the Racquet, Squadron A or any of his other clubs, and it was clear that Kay was going to have to contribute substantially to their household expenses. An ensuing pregnancy was terminated, but it so disturbed Francis, she later confided to Charles Baskerville, that it led to "advanced sexual practices" that damaged her emotionally. After a year in the city the young couple retreated to Pittsfield, but things went badly. When Francis' manhandling grew too severe, Kay regretfully decided to divorce him.

"I'd been aware of Katie Gibbs before her marriage but actually met her in Paris in 1924," says Beatrice Ames Stewart. "I was living there with my parents, and she was at the Vendôme with a Miss Francis. Katie was getting a divorce but at the family's request kept their name. They loved her so and realized how much in love she was with that poor, dreary, sodden offspring of theirs. She felt badly about leaving him, but she couldn't stand the beatings. So his aunt took her to Paris, and the family paid for the divorce. He was her real love. Oh, I could tell you about Katie, but I wouldn't. She wouldn't like it. I will say I don't think she ever stopped loving him."

David Lewis, who produced one of Kay's last films at Warner's, concurs. "She married several times and had many lovers but she never really recovered from that first marriage. The affection was still there."

Whether or not she recovered, upon returning to New York, Kay took an apartment with Virginia Farjeon, a Cathedral classmate, and through her met the nineteen-year-old scion of a Boston family whose grandfather had been governor of Massachusetts. The attraction was immediate and mutual. About that time she met Lois Long, who was then working on *Vogue.*

"I was introduced to Kay at a Beaux Arts ball after her first divorce," Lois Long recalled in 1974. "She was nineteen, just back from Paris, and she met Bill Gaston, a very good-looking bastard. She had a wild affair with him, thought she was pregnant and married him. They were keeping it a secret from his family until the baby came. *And*—two days after the marriage she got the curse." Miss Long laughed. "Oh, boy! Then he wanted a divorce. Eventually he married Rosamond Pinchot—and that ended with her suicide.''

The next summer Lois, Kay and Charles Baskerville went to Paris. ''She was an extraordinary person. That summer she had no wardrobe, and neither of us had much money,'' Baskerville says. ''But she took a paisley—gray, black and white—Persian shawl and had it made into an evening wrap. Whenever we were going to any swell place, she would put the paisley wrap over her gown, and she was a knockout. She carried herself beautifully; her hair was cut as short as mine, and she wore no jewelry, only lipstick. No eyeshadow or anything; she didn't need it. People were stampeded by this creature. They thought she was an Indian. I don't mean an American Indian. They thought she was a maharani on the loose or something like that.''

Kay made an equally strong impression on Miss Long, who herself was regarded as the quintessential fashionable Manhattanite. ''Kay was five feet nine* inches tall, had tiny feet—I think she wore size three or four. I know I was able to get her sample shoes—whatever the size was then. She loved shoes. And her head was twenty and a half. She was terrific-looking. Before we left Paris, she managed to get a beige Patou outfit and hat, a black Patou outfit and a hat and a black lace evening dress—and that's what she wore for two years. And always looked stunning.''

Kay and Lois rented a flat at 140 East Thirty-ninth Street upon their return. Lois' memories of that period remained vivid to the end of her life. ''We had a tiny apartment with no kitchen and a bedroom so small you had to crawl over the end of one bed to get to the one near the wall. But we had three telephones, and they were always ringing.''

A clique developed—three women and eight or nine men. Although no dates were made, around 5 P.M. the group would gather at some apartment—generally at 140 East Thirty-ninth or Bill Lebrow's, a playboy who owned a plantation on the eastern shore of Maryland. After a few drinks they would go their separate ways and meet again around midnight at a popular watering spot, Tony's, to drink sidecars. ''Then we'd split up, and finally some of us would meet again at the Owl Club on West Forty-fifth Street,'' Lois recalled. ''It was Negro entertainment, a low-down place where the girls scooped up dollar bills in unmentionable ways. One night Kay and I were there with a couple of gently reared fellows when the place was held up. Fortunately, one of these gently reared fellows wasn't so gently reared that he didn't get

*Like her birthdate, her height is never the same.

the table top between us and the gunmen before the bullets started flying, or I might not be telling you this now.

"We all drank heavily. It was a wild generation. Katherine—or Kay—always had a tumbler of gin for breakfast. We got it for twelve dollars a case from Frankie Costello, who was our bootlegger. She wasn't too knowledgeable about alcohol. I remember her saying once, 'I'm so sick of champagne and brandy. Isn't there any light alcohol I could drink?' Some clown asked if she'd ever heard of Pernod? So she started carrying a flask of it because clubs didn't seem to stock it.

"We were really quite innocent. I wasn't sleeping with any of the gang. I was too busy dancing all night. Kay did some—maybe with all of them. Anyway, a couple of them confided she was a big disappointment in the hay.

"When I was first living with her, even though I couldn't call anyone before eleven thirty, Crownie (Frank Crownshield, first of *Vanity Fair*, then *Vogue*) insisted I had to be on the job at nine or they'd penalize me by taking some of that magnificent thirty five dollars a week I was earning. Kay'd get home at six in the morning, and there was no way you would win. If I took the rear bed, I disturbed her when I crawled over her to go to work. If I took the front one, she woke me when she arrived home at dawn."

The situation eased after Kay confided to her friend Dwight Deere Wiman, already a fledgling theatrical producer, that she wanted a stage career. Wiman suggested speech therapy, and she managed to overcome the hesitation and to modify her lisp somewhat.

That fall Charles Baskerville introduced her to Edgar Selwyn, and Selwyn hired her to understudy Katherine Cornell in *The Green Hat*. "Luckily she never went on," Baskerville says. "She couldn't act for sour apples, but she was physically a similar type to Cornell."

She made her Broadway debut that same year as the Player Queen in the first modern-dress *Hamlet* ever presented in the United States. The controversial Selwyn production, which opened on November 9, starring Basil Sidney, ran at the Booth for sixty-eight performances. Kay, who then used her real name, Katherine, went unmentioned in reviews. Asked later how an inexperienced girl had managed to land a part in such estimable company, she quipped, "By lying a lot—to the right people."

Director James Light thought she had star potential and arranged an audition with Stuart Walker, who in 1926 ran his Portmanteau Theater companies in Indianapolis, Dayton and Cincinnati. Kay read for Walker, who added her to a group of players that included Peggy Wood, Elizabeth Patterson and McKay Morris.

In May Kay opened in Indianapolis, and during her five months with Walker she played bits, walk-ons or second leads in such stock favorites as *Candida, Polly Preferred* and *Puppy Love.* Years later she told a reporter, "My real training in acting came with Stuart Walker. Sometimes, while I was playing in Cincinnati, I'd get up early to take a train to Dayton, rehearse the next week's bill and get back to Cincinnati in time to appear that night. My parts were heavies, but I always wanted sentiment. Once, when I was begging for a weepy part, Stuart Walker actually shook me. 'I'll shake some sense into you,' he said. 'If you learn to play heavies well, leads will come easy to you.' I later found that this was true."

The summer was no undiluted joy. Kay and McKay Morris, a handsome, gifted actor, fell in love. "The whole episode was something," Lois Long remembered. "Somehow or other she broke her collarbone, and when she came back, she was in a plaster cast to here. We'd given up the Thirty-ninth Street place, and she went to live with McKay at the Hotel Marlton on Eighth Street. She was madly in love with him. Neither one had a job, and she had no money. He was a great actor and very handsome but impotent, which didn't really seem to make a great deal of difference to her. I don't think sex meant that much to her, I really don't. Anyway, she behaved so well and was so broke that Bill Lebrow and I got eight of the gang to put in one hundred dollars, and then Bill bought a cashier's check for one thousand dollars and sent it to her anonymously. She had no idea where it came from, and it took her ages to find out." (A few years later, finding herself temporarily penniless, Lois wired Kay for a loan. When she didn't receive any answer, she went to the bank to make other arrangements and found $1,000 deposited in her account.)

Miserable about her finances and lack of prospects, Kay frequently recorded in her diary: "shared a quart of gin," "got quietly drunk," "cockeyed drunk" or "smashed" during her wanderings—to such places as Club Avalon, Texas Guinan's, Cerutti's, Tony's and The Owl. But precarious as her financial condition was, she traveled in a set where not dressing for dinner was rare enough to be recorded in her diary.

Finally, things began to look up. Producer Al H. Woods was presenting an underworld drama starring young Sylvia Sidney and Chester Morris. Kay read for the part of Marjorie Grey and got the job. *Crime* opened on February 22, 1927, for a run of 133 performances at the Eltinge Theater. The critics ignored Katherine Francis, but audiences were enchanted by the beautiful dark-haired girl in a gold dress, and to the end of Kay's life Sylvia Sidney maintained that Kay had stolen the play from her.

Although Kay dismissed herself as a personality in the business for the money rather than out of dedication, there is evidence that she had not yet acquired a totally venal attitude at this point. Charles A. Lindbergh upon his return from his solo flight to Paris, was made miserable by his spectacular welcome as a hero and hid away with Bill Maloney, a member of Kay and Lois' gang. In his Sixty-seventh Street and Madison Avenue penthouse Maloney, who loved gadgets, had a secret passageway leading to a secluded bedroom on the floor below. He offered it to Lindbergh, who, in gratitude, agreed to meet a group of Maloney's friends. Among them was Kay, who mystified everyone by asking such questions as: "Tell me, were you scared?" or "What makes a man become an aviator?" or "Are fliers unique in any way?" Lindbergh, who obviously suspected her motives, politely evaded the banal questions. Friends remained puzzled at her gaucherie until Rachel Crothers' *Venus* opened at the Masque Theater on December 26. *Venus'* premise was that a pill had been developed that made men experience feminine desires and women masculine drives. After taking one, the character Kay played was seized by an urge to become an aviator.

She next appeared in Ring Lardner's *Elmer the Great,* a satirical comedy about baseball, which George M. Cohan produced at the Lyceum Theater. Cohan's broad revisions failed to meld with Lardner's acerbic view, and the show lasted only forty performances. The engagement might have meant little to Kay had Walter Huston not received an offer from Jesse L. Lasky to play the newspaper editor in the film version of Ward Morehouse's *Gentlemen of the Press.* Huston, who had worked in all forms of show business from tent repertoire to vaudeville, was eager to do a film which would be shot both with and without sound. Betty Lawford, producer Monta Bell's girl and later his wife, was playing the heroine, but in the rush to get the picture before the cameras no one had been cast as the female menace.

Bell, director Millard Webb, writers Bartlett Cormack and Ward Morehouse and dialogue director John Meehan looked over Paramount's contract list and were dissatisfied. "So we all immediately went to Tony's and there, in the haze of that famous backroom . . . we found Kay Francis," Morehouse wrote in *Forty-Five Minutes Past Eight.* "She was resting comfortably behind a Tom Collins. She was tall, dark and interesting-looking but had made far more appearances in Tony's than she had on the Broadway stage. She looked the part of Myra, all right. But the day of just looking it was gone forever. Could she act, and how was her voice? She was hustled over to Astoria. In the first test her voice came through strong and clear and vibrant. Her career began that very day."

Kay claimed that she had expected to look like an angel in the test but got the shock of her life. "My face was shiny, and I looked more like the devil," she commented. She disappeared for several days and, when she turned up at Tony's, was surprised to be offered a contract.

The new technology had two profound effects on Kay's life. Because the sound version was widely released, the silent school of vamps who physically pursued their victims became obsolete. Primitive microphones required vamps to remain stationary while working their wiles through glamorous appearances, arched eyebrows and transfixing gazes. For an inexperienced actress the limitations imposed by the mikes were a godsend. The New York *Times* might accuse Katherine Francis of overacting, but fan magazine writers heralded her as the "foremost exponent of vamping technique, 1929 model."

The second effect that sound worked on her life was that since she was a neophyte actress, she needed an unusual amount of time with dialogue director John Meehan,* who not so coincidentally became, briefly, her third husband. So briefly that many close friends never realized she had married him.

During filming, Paramount executives liked what they saw in the dailies. So in spite of the fact that *Gentlemen of the Press* was not yet finished, Kay began rehearsing to film *The Cocoanuts* with the Marx Brothers. After rehearsals she went to see some dailies on *Gentlemen of the Press*. Director Millard Webb, Meehan and Kay agreed that she could improve some of her work, and on February 19 she spent a full day doing retakes on GOTP. That accomplished, she returned to *The Cocoanuts*.

Paramount almost at once decided that this vivid, aristocratic-looking girl stood a good chance of becoming a popular star. She was signed at $500 a week.

The studio brass was hardly surprised that the prestigious critics ignored her when *Gentlemen of the Press* and *The Cocoanuts* were released. They had placed her with the Marx Brothers immediately after

---

*Diary entry, January 28, 1929: "Working all day hard—Betty Lawford, John Meehan and I. Back to the studio until 3:15 A.M. Some day!"

the first film, in hopes of bringing her to the attention of two widely divergent groups of filmgoers in the shortest possible period of time. The reasoning was that since she possessed no such stage reputation as Miriam Hopkins, Sylvia Sidney or Claudette Colbert, no harm could be done. Far from denigrating her importance by casting her as the shady lady who attempts to steal Margaret Dumont's jewels in a knockabout farce where subtlety would be lost, the studio provided Kay the opportunity to learn camera technique while being paid for it. (Later, a sardonic Joe Mankiewicz remarked that never again was she so good.)

The studio press department took an upbeat view of mike limitations and persuaded fan writers such as Leonard Hall that Kay was creating a new kind of vamp. "This modern, up-to-date man-killer of the screen must be a far smoother and more seductive article," Hall assured *Photoplay* readers. "A come-hither look and a provocative rolling of the eyes and hips must do the work the half-nelson and stranglehold performed in the dear old days." Then, warming up to his subject, Hall, breathing hard, proclaimed, "Others will come, do their dirty deeds, and pass, but as the pioneer of the clan, Miss Francis will occupy a sizable place in the yet unwritten history of the talkies."

Late that spring she arrived in Hollywood, where she was thrown into one production after another so that three more films in which she acted were released before the end of 1929. She worked six and sometimes seven days a week. In *Dangerous Curves*, a circus picture starring Clara Bow, outdoor scenes were shot between 4:30 P.M. and 6:30 A.M. Kindhearted, hoydenish Clara helped the dignified-looking newcomer by suggesting that the studio change Katherine, as the actress had been billed, to Kay, which would fit marquees better. And in their first scene together Clara counseled: "Now, Kay, I'm the star, so naturally they train the camera on me. But if you cheat a little, you'll get in it just right, too. You've got to keep that face in the camera, darling, That's what it's all about."

The Illusion, with Buddy Rogers and Nancy Carroll, and *The Marriage Playground*, starring Fredric March and Mary Brian, followed quickly. And 1930 opened auspiciously with *Behind The Make-Up*, in which Kay was singled out for favorable mention by the New York *Times*. It also marked her first teaming with William Powell, resulting in her being cast opposite him in *Street of Chance*. Powell played a compulsive gambler who repeatedly promises to quit but always finds a reason to try to beat the odds. As his wife, Kay had to project a mixture of passion, frustration, compassion and, finally, courage to face his probable murder. For the first time she was seen portraying a sympathetic and complex character. It marked another step in the buildup the studio had planned.

After making *Paramount on Parade*, an all-star extravaganza, she was lent to Warner's-First National for *A Notorious Affair*, a Billie Dove vehicle. In it Kay played a nymphomaniac countess effectively enough to cause the *Times'* man to write that she "puts Miss Dove somewhat in the shade," which may have encouraged Warner's to steal her from Paramount when her contract was about to expire.

She again teamed with William Powell in *For the Defense*. The San Francisco *Chronicle* described her as "beauteous to look at and an actress of no small ability." Opposite another popular male star, Ronald Colman, in Samuel Goldwyn's *Raffles*, she drew mixed reviews. Whether she had played too broadly or demonstrated a flair for comedy was the center of the controversy. Judging by the increase in fan mail, audiences liked what she had done.

A relatively minor role in *Let's Go Native* which misguidedly tried to combine the talents of Jeanette MacDonald and Jack Oakie, fell in with the studio policy of keeping Kay's name before the public. From Kay's viewpoint there was a dividend. The director, a newcomer named Leo McCarey, helped her develop her characterization beyond the script. She profited even more in *The Virtuous Sin*, co-directed by Louis Gasnier and George Cukor. Cukor had originally been brought to Hollywood from the stage to work as a dialogue director, and in this, his first film, he encouraged Kay to reach beyond her capabilities and create a real character. *

Her final release of the year was on loan-out to MGM for *Passion Flower*, directed by William C. De Mille. By then Kay had begun to muster new self-assurance. The microphone no longer frightened her, causing psychosomatic colds as it had in her earliest days, and she told a reporter that she had now become accustomed to observing camera lines by instinct and found them nothing to worry about.

Kay's Hollywood life-style qualifies her as the film colony's first dropout. From the beginning she exhibited an unusual amount of confidence in going her own way. Let others buy palatial estates, employ proper staffs and squander their earnings on yachts and pretentious automobiles. Kay's first two homes were unexceptional six- and seven-

---

*In *On Cukor* Gavin Lambert reports being told by the director, "Happily, some prints of movies have been lost and this was before the days of the archives, and I'd be in great shock if they rescued this one. I remember that I enjoyed working with Kay Francis and Walter Huston, though."

room bungalows located within a block of each other on De Longpre Avenue. And when she signed a two-year contract with Warner's, she leased ex-cowboy star William S. Hart's former residence for twenty-four months. "Why Bel-Air or Brentwood?" she asked. "If these houses were good enough for the old silent stars, they're good enough for me."

She drove a Ford, not a Rolls, and when someone commented on it, Kay snapped that the point of a car was to get you there. "If I wanted a show window for myself, I'd hire one. But I certainly wouldn't have it on wheels." Clothes and jewels were an investment to a practical, penny-pinching actress—houses and cars weren't.

She arrived in Hollywood with a black woman, Ida, who doubled as her secretary and maid. "She's a lady's lady if there ever was one," Kay said in those pre-black-pride days "It's always 'our' career, and she shares every phase of it." Later, after Kay moved into the Hart house, she hired a cook and a gardener. The latter drove when she required a chauffeur. Even then she had neither a swimming pool nor a formal garden but only a pretty lawn to be cared for. She summed it all up by observing, "I'm like a cat. I like to be comfortable, and I'm not comfortable when I'm on display."

Kay's appearance bespoke such elegance that she made this noncon-formity seem interesting and chic. "In many ways she was a lonely lady," Ouida Rathbone said. "People were afraid to approach her." Fan magazine writer Ted Magee observed the same thing: "I watched her many times on the set . . . knitting endlessly between shots, apart from the bustle of life around her. . . . When someone stepped up to talk, she would smile brightly and find some inconsequential thing to say. . . . but she seemed to withhold herself."

"Kay was an original," an ex-publicity man says. "She wasn't like some of the great beauties who never smiled because they might develop lines. She wasn't vain. She was warm and funny about herself if she trusted you. But that was on a personal level. She just didn't want to bother with publicity."

She described posing for publicity stills as agony and simply endured this ritual required of everyone—including Garbo, who once posed for cheesecake. Kay also put obstacles in the way of columnists and fan writers, even though she demanded approval of everything written about her. She volunteered nothing. Elsa Maxwell, who had met Kay during Kay's employment as Juliana Cutting's aide, mixed up—or at least pretended to—Kay's sequence of husbands. And even Billy Gaston's wife, Rosamond, protected Kay as best she could when asked by a reporter if she had taken Gaston from the star. "The point is that we both loved Billy, but at different times," Mrs. Gaston said. "Most certainly I did not steal him away from Kay. . . . When and where she was married to my husband and why they were divorced is none of my affair."

Like it or not, Kay could no longer move behind a veil of secrecy. When, in the early winter of 1930, she found herself in love with Kenneth MacKenna,* who was playing her husband in *The Virtuous Sin*, they did their best to keep the romance secret. Kay scoffed at their rumored engagement.

MacKenna, who had been in the business longer than Kay, neither confirmed nor denied the reports. Although handsome enough to have become a big star, he failed to project some necessary ingredient. Luckily, his talent and intellect made it possible for him eventually to become a director, story editor and producer.

When he and Kay decided to marry, she had become wary enough, because of her previous marital failures, to have her lawyer draw up a contract nullifying California community property laws—a practical, if unromantic, step. Since she had accumulated considerable capital and was earning more than her fiancé, it was clear whom she was protecting.

"She was always, always frightened someone would marry or get friendly with her to get something out of her—which I can guarantee nobody ever did," says a friend of later years. "And you don't have to be Freud to guess that that attitude extended to her emotional approach, too."

Despite her pragmatism, Kay believed that the marriage would be a happy one when she became a bride for the fourth time on January 17, 1931, at Avalon on Catalina Island.

The film industry was in turmoil. Buffeted by the Depression, executives suddenly realized they were spending two dollars for every one earned and banks might soon take over. In the midst of the ensuing panic Warner's gambled by staging its Great Talent Raid. Having previously lured Edward G. Robinson away from Paramount, it signed Pathé's Connie Bennett for two films at a well-publicized $30,000 a week. Angered at Paramount's invasion of Philadelphia (an almost all-Warner town) with its own theater, Warner's began negotiations with

*His real name was Leo Mielziner, and he was the son of the painter for whom Kay had modeled in the 1920's.

Paramount contractees Ruth Chatterton, William Powell, George Bancroft and Kay.

Industry spokesmen deplored this violation of a gentleman's agreement not to raid other studios' contract lists. Will Hays was called upon to impose sanctions but was powerless.

At Paramount, Kay's defection was particularly resented. She had been developed from an unknown into a featured player and was on her way to stardom. No longer concerned with protecting her name or image, Paramount vindictively assigned her to a maid's role, but Kay checked the move by producing a medical certificate stating that she was too ill to work. So the studio concentrated on getting as much return on its investment as possible before her contract expired. Nine films were released before her initial Warner Picture. There was the melodramatic *Scandal Sheet* of which *Variety* said one saving grace "is the presence of Kay Francis and [Clive] Brook, Miss Francis because of her strong playing of an impossible role . . . ," followed by *Ladies Man*, with William Powell as a suave gigolo and Kay as his true love and then *The Vice Squad*, in which she had to be in love with military attaché Paul Lukas. In RKO's *Transgression* Kay appeared as the errant wife who scurries home in time to save her marriage after her lover is murdered. MGM's *Guilty Hands* was a courtroom drama with an improbable denouement that finds accused murderess Frances cleared and prosecuting attorney Lionel Barrymore exposed as possessing "guilty hands." She received billing over the rising Miriam Hopkins in *24 Hours*, just another melodrama. But *Girls About Town*, then not regarded as anything special, turned out to be her best film yet. Under George Cukor's subtle handling Kay and Lilyan Tashman, as two gold diggers, managed to convey implications strictly prohibited by the censors and to deliver charming light comedy performances. This film reinforces the feeling that Kay's real forte was light comedy.

Her final films under the Paramount contract were *The False Madonna* (she impersonated a dead woman) and *Strangers in Love*, a comedy with Fredric March, directed by Lothar Mendes, who had performed the same task on Kay's first three Hollywood pictures.

Despite the ramshackle carpentry of most of her movies, 1931 turned out to be a happy year for Kay. Her marriage was working well. She and MacKenna shared interests in the theater, books and tennis. Kay curtailed her hectic social life and, under MacKenna's tutelage, took up sailing. If not the passionate affair her earlier marriages had been, the relationship was fulfilling. Luckily, one problem that had worried her failed to develop. Since Mackenna had decided to branch out into directing, comparison of career progress was less likely.

In Kay's case, her notices were far better than she had ever dared hope. Her throaty voice, charming mannerisms (including her struggles with *r*'s and *l*'s) and elegant appearance gave her strong appeal. Trade papers and fan writers remained solidly behind her, and even the New York *Times*' men, who maintained a rather pecksniff attitude toward films, gave her respectful attention. Miriam Hopkins had far overshadowed Kay in the legitimate theater, but in *24 Hours*, *Variety*'s critic wrote, "Her part doesn't give Miss Francis much of an acting opportunity, but the very vividness of her style makes her a positive individuality. The fireworks are allotted to Miriam Hopkins, but she doesn't quite realize the vigor of the Rosie Regan role. . . ."

Small wonder then that Kay should begin to show uncharacteristic ambition, telling interviewers, "Now I've decided I really like pictures, I want to graduate, eventually, from these siren things and play sophisticated leads—the Katharine Cornell type part."

With that thought in mind, she had turned down the $15,000 bonus and an increase in salary on a fifty-two-week-a-year basis at Paramount, even though by losing the bonus and going to Warner's on a forty-week-per-annum deal, she temporarily cleared less money per week. Leaving Paramount, she took along only the numeral 66 from her dressing-room door, because Miriam Hopkins assured her that 66 added up to 12, which, Miriam said, was Kay's lucky number.

Lucky or not, Kay was going to need all the help she could get. Warner's promised she would soon be elevated to solo stardom and groomed as the "quality star" successor to Ruth Chatterton. While Kay held no illusions as to their comparative natural gifts, she saw no reason why this should pose any problem in a "business-art." A quality star need not be the best actress on the lot, she need only exude an aura of glamor and distinction—and Kay felt up to that.

She quickly learned that the atmosphere at Warner's was as hectic and impersonal as at Paramount. The Factory, Warner's stars sometimes sardonically called it. Popular players like Joan Blondell occasionally found themselves working in three productions simultaneously. Frequent meetings were held at which studio writers suggested ideas for features based on personal experience, gossip or news stories and received assignments to develop those accepted for a particular star. Later, progress was checked and a project pursued further or killed. These conditions created an environment in which so much was happening that even most of the overworked stars were buoyed up by the excitement.

Kay was no exception, but from the first she remained slightly aloof. Starlets called her Miss Francis, never Kay. Olivia De Havilland, who arrived on the lot somewhat later, recalled that ingenues were afraid to speak to Kay in the central makeup room because she seemed old and remote. "One day," Miss De Havilland said, "we were all around in various stages of undress when she came in with her lover. We were scandalized and embarrassed. Because we thought that she was so much older than he was. Well, he recently visited me in Paris and cleared that up. She was six months older."

For all their promises, publicity and coddling, Warner's gave Kay neither script nor director approval. Luckily, when *Man Wanted*, her first release under her new contract, opened, the verdict was that director William Dieterle and the players had invested this turnabout triangle of an ambitious wife, lazy husband and sexy male secretary with the elements of an entertaining trifle. Kay endowed the role with qualities the writers had neglected to provide, and Richard Nason of the New York *Times* turned out a virtual love letter. "Kay Francis," he wrote, "radiates so much charm throughout *Man Wanted* at Warner's Strand this week that the familiar theme somehow does not matter. . . ."

She was not so lucky with *Street of Women*, which turned out to be a boring, static movie made from a boring, static script.

Her third and fourth films teamed Kay with William Powell. In *Jewel Robbery* there were a few quibbles about her performance, but *One-Way Passage* turned out to be a memorable achievement. As passengers on a ship bound from Hong Kong to San Francisco, Kay and Powell fell deeply, and instantly, in love. She was doomed by heart disease, and he was a murderer headed for San Quentin. Each withheld the unhappy truth as they lost themselves in one last enthralling romance. At a stop in Honolulu, with his captor distracted by a fake countess, Powell sacrificed his last opportunity to escape by carrying his unconscious sweetheart back to the ship after she suffered a heart seizure. She, meanwhile, learned his true identity but pretended ignorance. At parting, they planned a rendezvous in Agua Caliente on New Year's Eve—a meeting each knew could never be. The bittersweet ending found the murderer jauntily waving good-bye to his dying inamorata—while his coat hid the handcuff locking him to his captor.

Several treatments emphasizing the story's sentimentality had been rejected before director Tay Garnett suggested the sad tale be burnished by a light comedy patina. The finished picture became one of Kay's favorites. Forty-five years later—viewed within the conventions of the period—it remains an entertaining movie, retaining both its humor and emotional power.

How chancy any success is may be illustrated by this film. Aline MacMahon, the gifted actress who played the fake countess, recalls the unpromising circumstances under which it was made. "Warners engaged a broken-down iron boat for location shooting and sent the cast offshore, allowing us some fantastic sum like thirty seven cents a day for food," she says. "It was an uncomfortable assignment, and we were all pretty miserable. It was boiling hot. The food was terrible. The kids got drunk, and Tay Garnett took this occasion to be difficult. So the assistants were doing what work there was done—which wasn't much. Finally, the studio lost patience and brought us back to the lot to finish it. Through it all Miss Francis behaved with great dignity and did her work without complaint."

Comparing the compensation she received with Kay's, Miss Mac-Mahon is inclined to be philosophical: "After you say talent, then you have to ask, What does the audience want? The audiences wanted what Miss Francis had. After all, Kay Francis was in a special class. She was very elegant, and she had taste and special clothes, and she fulfilled a need audiences felt." It is the homage paid by a brilliant actress to a personality star.

Orry-Kelly, assigned to design Kay's clothes for *One-Way Passage*, revised his opinion of her several times before concluding that she was one of the most generous, down-to-earth stars he ever had worked with. Their eventual relationship, he felt, was summed up in an incident which happened later, at a time when Kay's career was faltering and he was drinking heavily. A great deal of confusion occurred during one fitting, climaxing when she tried on a hat he had designed which was at least two sizes too large and sank to her eyebrows. It was the last straw. "What's the matter with you? Are you drunk?" she demanded. And the hung-over Kelly snapped, "No! Your head's shrunk two sizes since your last couple of flops!" which caused Kay to burst out laughing and embrace him.

"In the beginning, she was very reserved but well mannered and knew exactly what she wanted," he said. "I designed simple unadorned evening gowns in velvet, chiffon and crepes for *One-Way Passage*. And I introduced what was the forerunner of the shirtmaker dress for evening. . . . At first, only those with sensitive taste were impressed. Luckily, Kay was the essence of good taste."

Kelly's approach was to simplify, and Kay agreed. Unlike many stars, she had developed a philosophy of fashion in relation to the characters she portrayed. She felt designers often tipped their hands by dressing types similarly. Explaining this later, Kay told agent Robert Mayberry, "Kelly and I decided to change that. If I were playing a woman good and true, we used tailored, sophisticated clothes ordinarily reserved for the femme fatale. But when I played the heavy, I had them design my clothes with lots of frills. Very fluffy and feminine and sweet. Very girlish. I think it makes more sense to reverse it," she said. "To dress counter to the character. Because whether audiences realize it or not, they get clues about who will end up with whom from the clothes."

When Kay's first twelve-week vacation rolled around, she abandoned plans for a European trip and instead returned to Paramount to make *Trouble in Paradise*, in which she, Miriam Hopkins and Herbert Marshall benefited from Lubitsch's unorthodox approach to outrageous characters and situations. It is on all counts her best film. Yet she never worked with Lubitsch or at Paramount again. Having been billed over Miriam Hopkins in *24 Hours*, she sulked at finding Miriam above her in this one.

Kay also made two other films during her vacation: *Cynara* for Samuel Goldwyn and *Storm at Daybreak* for MGM. In *Cynara*, under King Vidor's direction, she and Ronald Colman received excellent notices. Playing a wife whose marriage is ruined when her husband's name is publicly connected to his mistress' suicide, Kay was later asked if modern wives would similarly overreact. "Not sophisticated wives," she said. "But they are a minority. There are thousands of women all over the country who could never bring themselves to live with their husbands again after finding out an infidelity." Then, perhaps revealing more than she had intended, she continued, "As in Pittsfield, Massachusetts, where I once lived. Women in that town, and it's typical of other towns, would have felt the blow to their pride too severely to make up after a public scandal such as followed the husband's affair in *Cynara*.

"I think that's true of so many divorces. It's pride that goads women on to an unforgiving attitude. They simply can't believe it, and they can't walk out of the house and know the neighbors are whispering."

Sophisticated or not, Kay apparently never got over the collapse of her first marriage. Nor was she able to forgive infidelity in later relationships. Discussing Kay, Lois Long said, "The thing about it was that she had this exotic exterior, and people who were attracted to that were always disappointed because she was a regular guy. What one of our gang said later was that she should have married, had lots of children, run the Women's Club and everything else in some small city. But the kind of men who would marry a gal who would do that were frightened by her exterior. She always said, 'I'm not an actress, I'm a personality.' But she would have fared better if she could have been just a wife.''

When the best-film lists were published, *Trouble in Paradise* was among the top ten, and *One-Way Passage* and *Cynara* appeared in the top fifty chosen by the New York *Times'* critic and *Photoplay's* readers.

The happy first two months of 1933 were spent with MacKenna in New York, where she posed for a Steichen portrait for *Vogue* and submitted to other prestige publicity. They saw old friends and new plays. Mostly they killed time until Jessica Barthelmess finished decorating their recently acquired house at 1010 Benedict Canyon.

In Hollywood all studios were unsettled. At Warners, losses in the first thirteen weeks of 1933 were reduced to $1,579,000.*

Still, studio executives showed evidence of regretting their huge investments in Chatterton and Powell while their attitude toward Kay wavered. *The Keyhole,* with her frequent screen lover George Brent, and *Mary Stevens, M.D.,* with Lyle Talbot, were economically made assembly-line products turned out to meet a quota, pictures of the type most Warner stars were expected to make. But hints of ambivalence toward Kay occasionally surfaced, as in Edward G. Robinson's *I Loved a Woman,* where she played a run-of-the-mill leading woman— or, as the *Times* said, was "part of the supporting cast."† Was that any way to treat a woman supposedly being groomed as a prestige star? Kay thought not. But billing was not the main problem, as her diary makes clear. Having promised her star treatment, Warner's offered her

---

*To achieve this reduction in losses, everyone under contract was asked to take a 25-percent cut in salary. Aline MacMahon remembers all agreed except a sweet-faced little Irish girl named Ruby Keeler. "That night I went to the Brown Derby, and waiters were carrying large bowls of caviar behind a screen," Miss MacMahon says. "And behind the screen were the Warner families celebrating with caviar. It was a great break for them."

†Kay played an opera singer, Rose Dirman, who also was the voice for Marion Davies and Miriam Hopkins, supplied the voice for Kay, according to musical film historian Miles Kreuger.

a succession of potboilers. She read each newly proposed script with increasing dismay. In time she quietly submitted, hoping only that filming wouldn't take too long. The diary has many entries similar to: "Big party. Finished damned picture. Very cockeyed. Ken carried me out." Or: "Finished *Mandalay*! I AM WOW!" While she was working, the notations were invariably downbeat: "Bed early, nearly dead." "Home at 8:30. Dinner on tray in bed. DEAD!" "Dinner Marshalls, 7:15. Me working. Too tired to go." "Exhausted. Ill. How long can this go on?" Only occasionally would she report rebelling: "Big fight with Hal Wallis [First National and Warner production head] re *Red Meat*." Rarer still were notations about social engagements during filming. "Stewart's 'Movie Ball.' So drunk! As Naldi." (She was referring to silent screen vamp Nita Naldi, who, when she grew old and fat, customarily described herself as "Dracula in Drag.") Where originally there had been flaring hope and aspiration, she now merely attempted to make the most of whatever was offered, earning her salary and saving it.

Her final release of the year was *The House on 56th Street*. The script had been tailored for and rejected by Ruth Chatterton. Kay had accepted it without a murmur. She portrayed a former Florodora girl, who has broken off with her lover to marry wealthy young Monte Von Tyle. Von Tyle gives her the Fifty-sixth Street house as a wedding gift, intending that it be hers forever. Life is great, life is grand for Kay until she is called to the side of her ex-lover who is ill. When he threatens to shoot himself, she struggles to stop him, and he is killed. She is convicted of manslaughter and sentenced to twenty years. By the time she is released her husband is dead and her daughter has forgotten her. In keeping with the flavor of the picture, she returns to her former home, now a speakeasy, as a blackjack dealer and assumes blame for a shooting there to save her daughter from the fate that ruined her own life.

The film was contrived and sentimental. Yet, *Billboard* said that at last Kay had been given a story that fitted her perfectly and that she had made the most of it. And Mourdant Hall of the *Times* rated it "quite an original and intriguing pictorial drama."

But Kay was too shrewd not to recognize it for what it was. "If it does better than my other films, it's because I parade thirty-six costumes instead of sixteen. I wear the best of everything from the Gay Nineties to post-World-War One," she observed cynically.

During the making of her films, she arose at 5:45 or 6 A.M., depending on how complicated her makeup was. By 9 A.M. she was at the stu-

206

dio (where she customarily had a ham sandwich, a pickle and ice cream for breakfast*) in costume and makeup, and she worked on the set, with a short luncheon break, until 6:30 P.M. She then conferred on scenes for the following day and looked at dailies, arriving home at 7:30 or 8 P.M. After a quick shower the MacKennas were served dinner on trays. Then, in order to look fresh the next day, she retired at 10:30. That regimen had to be followed for no less than six weeks to complete a picture.

Her salary was in the four-figure bracket weekly. But could any secretary, saleslady or trucking executive match that working schedule? Kay made no pretense of being an artist in the sense that Garbo, Katharine Hepburn or Ruth Chatterton was, but she gave ground to no one in merchandising glamor and manipulating the emotions of moviegoers.

Still, when it was time for her to leave for New York to stimulate interest in *The House on 56th Street*, she was overjoyed to leave Hollywood. Before leaving, she and MacKenna attended Eddie Cantor and Ruth Etting's *Roman Scandals*. Afterward, at producer Sam Goldwyn's, they appeared completely happy, and friends were bewildered to read in their newspapers on December 20 that the two were "amicably separating."

That there was a hidden vein of hostility on Kay's part can be seen by her December 30 entry in her diary: "5:30 cocktails with 'Mr. MacKenna,'" as she now referred to him. There were too many drinks, and Kay turned quarrelsome. As often happened in her personal relationships, the charming, cultured Kay Francis was transformed by alcohol into frightened, ferocious little Katie Gibbs, going for the jugular vein. Knowing that MacKenna was uncomfortable about having changed his name, she struck where it hurt by calling him a turncoat Jew. MacKenna, always the gentleman, ignored her drunken outburst and walked out on her.

Later Kay would regret her cruelty, but when she was drunk, homosexual friends became "fags" and "dykes" and a black, a "nigger." Sober, she could regretfully record in her diary: "I guess I'm a pretty stupid, unattractive person," but in her cups there was no holding her.

That night, after the contretemps with MacKenna, she met her escort George Hawkins (in spite of Warner's announcement that she had

---

*Although this sounds like publicity, David Lewis, who produced *Secrets of an Actress*, swears that this is what she ate every morning.

left town to avoid publicity), put on a happy face and attended *The Dark Tower*, looking every inch a genteel, civilized lady.

The domestic situation quickly resolved itself. On February 21st, her diary reads: "In court!" There a subdued Katherine Mielziner testified that Leo Mielziner "nagged and harassed her . . . ridiculed her selection of home, manner of dressing and even her acting did not suit him. [He] assumed an air of superiority and made slighting remarks in the presence of friends." MacKenna maintained a gallant silence. The divorce was granted, and Kay had decided never to marry again.

Her career could not be managed so easily. Film people knew that two of her upcoming releases, *Mandalay* and *Doctor Monica*, had been written for and refused by Ruth Chatterton. Genevieve Tobin had turned down Kay's role in *Wonder Bar* and Barbara Stanwyck, Kay's part in *British Agent*.

Mandalay contained the famous scene where, as hostess of a dive in Rangoon, she wore a spectacular silver sheath, causing a customer to observe, "They call her Spot White," to which his companion sardonically replies, "It ought to be Spot Cash."

However distasteful her roles, Kay made no complaint until the release of *Wonderbar*, when stories circulated that her footage had been severely cut to expand Dolores Del Rio's. Kay, who'd been reluctant to accept the assignment, admitted that she was distressed to read that her dislike of the role was obvious by the way she played it. "I didn't scowl my way through the picture because I didn't like the part. I felt the woman would be spoiled, petulant and sullen, and I played her that way. I was trying to characterize," she explained. "I hope I'm too intelligent to let any dissatisfaction I may feel reflect in my work."

Then *Doctor Monica* opened to a mild reception. Instead of praise for her beauty, charm and wardrobe, Kay suddenly found herself "believable," "competent," and "okay within the limitations of the script."

Nor did it help her position that her next release, *British Agent*, in which Leslie Howard played an emmisary to Communist Russia and Kay a beautiful spy, was obviously a Howard vehicle.

Kay's run of bad luck and the rise of young Bette Davis had become so apparent that Louella Parsons began an item in her inimitable style: "Three cheers and a tiger! Kay Francis has got Frank Borzage to direct her next picture, *Living on Velvet*, by Jerry Wald and Julius Epstein. The story as told me by Jack Warner and Hal Wallis sounds like the sort of drama Kay should have and not those weak numbers in which she has no chance to display anything but her good looks."

George Brent played opposite Kay. Hopes for the film were so high that the Francis-Brent-Borzage combination was immediately assigned to *Stranded*. This was followed by another comedy, *The Goose and the Gander*, with Francis, Brent and Genevieve Tobin. "Kay and I made two films together, but we were not friends at all," Miss Tobin says. "I always felt she snubbed me, and at first I thought it mean of her. But later I decided that behind those velvety, tragic eyes there must have been some tragic thing that made it so she couldn't really be friends with anyone. I went to a party at her home when she was married to Ken MacKenna—whom we all loved and admired—but even then there was friction in the air. I couldn't understand her."

After seeing Kay in so many tearjerkers, critics were delighted to rediscover her comic flair in these three films, but audiences who had come to expect a fashion show and a good emotional storm stayed away. Given what they wanted in a maudlin tale of thwarted mother love called *I Found Stella Parish*, her fans happily returned to make the picture a commercial success. Unfortunately for Kay, beginning with *Stranded*, the New York *Times'* critics began making light of her lisp, which had heretofore been overlooked. But the question was now raised whether members of a steelworkers' strike meeting would be swayed by a chic young woman imploring them to "nevah wouse youah awwogance!" Reviewing *The Goose and the Gander*, André Senwald of the *Times* punned: "Its chief impediment to an evening pleasantly unimportant in the cinema comes from its insistence on cramming the dialogue with *r*'s which have an embarrassing habit of becoming *w*'s when Miss Francis goes to work on them." And again, with *I Found Stella Parish*: "Miss Francis' unfortunate lisp continues to plague this corner; it makes even more unbelievable the notion that London could regard Stella Parish as the Duse of her day."

Ironically, Warners had sent around a young writer to take care of that very problem in *Stranded*. He had worked as a property boy for director James Cruze and acted in eight films for MGM before beginning a long career that would include writing, directing and producing feature films. His name was Delmer Daves. He was six feet two, with wavy reddish-blond hair, thirty-one years old and unmarried. This is his recollection of what happened: "Hal Wallis was production head at Warner Brothers during the thirties, and it was he who was Mr. Fate with Kay and me—for he asked me, as a favor, since the writer of Kay's next film had left the lot, to go to her house and rewrite all the lines of the script that had the embarrassing *r*'s which Kay would turn into *w*'s in most instances—such as 'tomowwow' for 'tomorrow.' I hadn't even met her at that time, went to her house, introduced myself and the object of my visit, . . . and it became one of Cole's [Porter's] . . . 'one of those things,' for we hit it off so well I never left, and we were devoted to each other solely for the next three years, traveled together between films, to New York, Europe. . . . During those years Hedda and/or Louella (both close friends of ours and very tactful in their reportings of our wanders, etc.) would make us Best Bets in their annual Matrimonial Derby columns.''

The Frances-Daves relationship was played so low-key that when Kay went to London in 1935, newspapers speculated that she was actually on her way to France to marry Maurice Chevalier. When she entered a London nursing home to have an infected wisdom tooth and salivary gland removed, reporters sought out Chevalier to learn if the wedding would be postponed. He attempted to disabuse them of the notion. "Kay and I have a Franco-American friendship alliance—but that's all," he said, adding, "Please make it plain that she is one of my closest friends. But marriage—we're not even thinking of getting married—at least to each other."

Kay mysteriously took offense at the statement. It ended their friendship. "I could never understand it. I know she had various pieces of jewelry from him, and I noticed when he died there was a picture of Kay in his den," Dennis Allen says. "But she never saw him again, never, ever. She wouldn't even let me take her to his one-man show twenty years later."

In June Daves met Kay in New York upon her return from abroad, and after a few days they left for the privacy of Lake Louise in Canada. Kay traveled as "Mrs. Gibbs," Daves as Mr. Davis. But in mid-July, when she stepped off the train in Glendale, photographers were waiting. "Heavens, no! I certainly won't pose. I'm still on vacation," she said in response to a request for pictures. As for a romance with Daves, "My heavenly goodness, no!" And with that she scrambled into a taxi, leaving Daves to tell reporters, "I have nothing to say" as he gathered their luggage, hailed another cab and sped away.

Throughout 1933, 1934 and 1935 Kay often espoused her faith in the proposition that big studios "knew best." "We're so concerned whether our roles are fat ones that we lose perspective on the picture as a whole. The studio sees it as a complete unit—or should. The only fly in the ointment is that Warner's is primarily a man's studio. MGM is a woman's studio. They have the greatest stars, and their efforts are all directed toward exploiting them, '' she told an interviewer.

To another she rationalized: "If you are to be successful in pictures, your attitude toward them must be double-edged. Assuming an actress knows the artistic end—and she won't stay long if she doesn't—some understanding of the business side is also a necessity. The whole thing is an intricate organism, and all of it must be kept steadily moving. The important thing is to understand the viewpoint of others without losing your own. That can be fatal, too."

Secretly she was ambitious to widen her range. While she might shrug and comment that the only way to move once you reached the top was down, she nevertheless yearned for the heights. She urged Daves to write a script based on Mildred Cram's *Forever*. Although he thought it unwise to allow their careers to impinge upon their romantic relationship, he reluctantly agreed and was relieved to learn Norma Shearer owned the story. "Kay's greatest ambition was to do *Tristan and Isolde*, but I discouraged this, feeling her metier was modern life. I was certain the public wanted the more glamorous Kay Francis, the Kay with the wondrous husky voice, with or without her *r*'s," he later said.

But Kay, who occupied the number-two position on *Variety*'s popularity rating of Warner stars for 1935, was not to be dissuaded. She wanted a heavy dramatic role to regain the ground she had lost to Bette Davis, who had jolted the public with *Of Human Bondage* in 1934. To accomplish this, Mordaunt Shairp wrote a screenplay based on Lytton Strachey's astringent essay on Florence Nightingale. William Dieterle, with whom Kay had worked successfully, was assigned to direct.

But all the good intentions went awry in *The White Angel*. Shairp captured few of the iron-willed, strong-minded, sarcastic qualities with which Strachey had humanized the nurse's compassion and historic stature. The screenwriter's failure was underlined by Kay's reverential depiction of a noble personage. Emotions were suggested but seldom projected forcefully. Kay honored Florence Nightingale instead of acting her.

Facing the challenge she had begged for, she realized that she had no inkling how to make this legend a living, breathing human being. The middle ground that lay between a saintlike image and the modern characters she had played eluded her.

Kay's diary became an encyclopedia of woe. March 4: "Started Florence Nightingale. Terrible day. Del here for dinner. Bed early." March 6: "Terrible day at the studio. Scene on the stairs. Exhausted. Eyes ruined."

And so it went, one problem following another as intramural quarrels, accidents, psychosomatic and real illnesses beleaguered a woman who was attempting something beyond her range.

Finally, on April 22, the picture was finished, and she began to unwind. But she was truly relaxed only when drinking absinthe at the Herbert Marshalls', getting cockeyed drunk with Del or treating herself to "an enormous kind of drunk" at W. R. Hearst's birthday party, ignoring the fact that next day she was to report for a new film, *Sweet Alohes*, rechristened *Give Me Your Heart* at the request of exhibitors who were afraid it would be confused with *Sweet Alice*.

That filming, too, was punctuated with battles between Kay and director Archie Mayo, whom she berated for stupidly mishandling this fairly complex psychiatric study of frustrated mother love. What was really bothering her was fear of the reception her Nightingale characterization would receive.

On May 27 Louella Parsons invited Kay to act in *The White Angel* on her radio program. Kay was terrified of playing the role live. And when, in the last week of June, the film opened to disappointing reviews from New York critics, who had been led to expect another *Story of Louis Pasteur*, the diary was filled with anguish as she suffered from impacted wisdom teeth, hemorrhoids and psychosomatic complaints. "In bed all day—utter horror! Drs.!!!," Kay wailed. "Will this never stop? Script from studio—BAD! Too sweet—old hat."*

To complicate matters, Daves had an abscess lanced. Kay, who arrived at the hospital as he was anesthetized, later drove him home and nursed him. That evening the doctor looked in on both. "Christ! We are a pair!" she noted.

Daves quickly recovered, but Kay continued to suffer until July 2. "Doctors up nose to get fifth nerve—three times. Miserable." Nevertheless, five days later she dragged herself to the studio for wardrobe tests and on July 13 entered the hospital for two days to have an impacted wisdom tooth and a dry socket treated. A week later she began acting in *Stolen Holiday*, still another mediocre film.

Kay's nerves were so frazzled by the fall of 1936 that she was quarreling with Daves over such petty things as pinochle and berating herself for being stupid. "I'm getting to be a perfect harridan," she admitted in her diary.

She made only two films that year. *The White Angel*'s failure had se-

*Mistress of Fashion, eventually retitled *Stolen Holiday*.

riously harmed her since the studio had regarded this picture as her opportunity to score as a dramatic actress. Shairp had been kept on the set to rewrite any lines that gave trouble. They eliminated all *r*'s except the one in Florence which Kay practiced until she could enunciate it. "The only real trouble was when we got to the nurse's oath that was full of *r*'s," she said. "I learned it so every *r* came out clearly. When the picture was released, I waited for the notices. Always before some critic said something like 'the *r*-less Miss Francis is back in a new film.' This time the sillies wrote, 'Kay Francis complete with *r*'s in new film.' After that I gave up trying to overcome the lisp."

There would be no more *White Angels*, but even worse, *Give Me Your Heart* was advertised as:

THE PICTURE EVERY WOMAN WILL WANT TO SEE
    To all the women of the world who know—as no man can ever know—the anguish that is the glory of love, the despair that is the ecstasy, Warner Brothers give this amazing exploration of the heart of a girl faced with a fatal fascination—then driven by a tragic fate to share her baby's love with the woman who should have been its mother! See it and you will understand why famous feminine critics unite in calling this the finest picture of its type in recent years.

With this openly sexist appeal, an appeal that had always insured box-office returns, *Give Me Your Heart* failed.

Kay's dreams of playing Katharine Cornell roles were vanquished. She sank to portraying nobly suffering clotheshorses while Bette Davis had become the preeminent actress on the lot. Kay's response was to insist that she had never regarded acting as anything but a lucrative way to earn a living. Yet occasionally her growing bitterness spilled over. Discussing her frequent flights from Hollywood, she challenged an interviewer to ponder: with the finest talent in the world gathered in the film capitol, why had nothing great originated there? Why was the best always adapted from a successful play or book? Or, in the case of actors and directors, attracted from some other field? Ignoring Chaplin, she challenged the studios to name one finished artist developed by Hollywood. She said she only hoped that when her time came, she would have made a fortune and would have "sense enough to clear out."

It was a good ploy in 1937, when she still ranked sixth among *Varie-*

ty's listing of favorite feminine stars* and earned the highest salary of any star—$227,500 for forty weeks' work.†

Her films in 1937 included *Stolen Holiday,* which Bland Johnson in the New York *Daily Mirror* mischievously reviewed as a fashion show, followed by *Another Dawn,* with Errol Flynn, and *Confession.* Recently, William K. Everson reevaluated *Confession,* directed by Joe May, in *Films in Review.* Everson hailed it for its ambiguity, style and daring and described Kay as surprisingly good. At the time audiences were confused by its elliptic storytelling, and critics were hostile. Howard Barnes wrote in the New York *Herald Tribune*: "She [Kay] appears in three guises—as a brunette young matron, a bewigged and bespangled café singer and a blowsily blonde prisoner at the bar. It is hard to say which aspect of the characterization she makes most trying."

Sadly, when *First Lady* (Jane Cowl's prestigious Broadway hit by George S. Kaufman and Katherine Dayton) provided Kay with an opportunity, she was too dispirited to profit by it, causing a critic to assert: "The difference between the stage and screen versions of *First Lady* is approximately the difference between Jane Cowl and Kay Francis."

"I know that I've got one special quality to sell on the screen, as most actresses have," Kay alibied, ignoring earlier comedy hits. "Fans expect sincerity from me, a certain warmth, and if they don't get it, they howl. They didn't like me in *First Lady* worth a cent. They told me so by the hundreds."

With her career at a low ebb, Kay's relationship with Daves was also beginning to be troubled. During the first part of 1937 she recorded numerous fights and reconciliations. Then, on July 1, there is an enigmatic: "Hospital! Finally told Del," followed on July 2 by: "Operation. Feel fine. Del an angel." But thereafter she was more frequently critical of or hurt by him, suggesting conflicts engendered by the fact that his career was progressing while hers was faltering. In a youth-oriented society Kay, at thirty-two, began to feel used up and old hat. "I am sick of his superiority," she complained, reprising her allegations against MacKenna. A few days later they fought again, and she sent him home. "I told him I wouldn't see him Saturday and explained that

*She was preceded by Myrna Loy, Loretta Young, Claudette Colbert, Ginger Rogers and Alice Faye and followed by Barbara Stanwyck, Joan Crawford, Jeanette MacDonald and Janet Gaynor.

†In 1938 James Cagney topped the list with $234,000, followed by Kay at $224,000— approximately, it was pointed out, three times what the President of the United States earned, although in her case more than half went to the government for taxes.

his attitude toward me was getting too much. He hates 'brawls.' Bah!"

Daves later remembered their relationship as much more tranquil: "None of them* knew that Kay and I had a no-marriage pact between us; when our love affair started, I had been a bachelor with no permanent attachments for my thirty years, and Kay, on the contrary, had been married four times . . . and she laughed as she designated herself lousy-wife—happy-lover. Thus, our happy pact and our rather enchanted life for the next three years. We broke off in much the same manner—because my career had flourished. . . . Kay was accustomed to planning another adventure whenever she finished a film—and I was able to accompany her since I was a free-lance writer or a short-term contract writer during that period. But now my career was becoming increasingly important, my contractual obligations forbade the up-up-and-away life. So we had to face this change—and to do it without gossip columns; so I went to Europe alone—and suggested she find a new love while I was gone, so Louella and Hedda would write items such as 'Delmer had better cut that wander in Europe short, else he'll lose his Kay to a handsome wooer, etc., etc.''

Louella called on September 1, 1937, with something else in mind. She wanted to know whether, as a "little birdie" had told her, Kay was getting out of her contract. "Goodness, no," Kay assured her. "I'm starting a new picture."

Naturally Louella was furious when three days later Kay asked the court to dissolve her $5,250-a-week pact because Warner's had reneged on its promise to cast her as the exiled Russian princess turned maid in *Tovarich* as a reward for her signature on a three-year contract. To her chagrin the studio borrowed Claudette Colbert, an actress of her type, to appear in the "foolproof part . . . which would automatically enhance the reputation of anyone playing it." She also alleged that her employers had assigned her "parts and plays of inferior quality and had posted her name in a special interstudio register which kept other studios from bidding for her services."

Warners replied that they expected her to report at 9 A.M. on September 7 to begin a film, rather menacingly titled *Return from Limbo*. After a barrage of press releases from both sides announcement was made that Kay's federal court suit to annul her contract had been amicably settled. "Amicably" was a word that applied to neither side. Kay's bitterness increased as she was subjected to a series of humiliations. In upcoming attractions her employers threatened to co-star her

*Columnists, casual friends, reporters.

with the Mauch Twins in *A Prayer for My Sons.* The studio announced it had bought *The Sisters* to co-star Kay and Miriam Hopkins, but Bette Davis made the film. Jack Warner refused even to consider Kay for Empress Carlotta in *Juarez.*

There were accidents (for instance, a sandbag fell from the flies, landing nearby) which she suspected were designed to unnerve her. But now she stubbornly refused to abrogate the contract. When Warner's announced she was being assigned to Bryan Foy's cheapie unit, J. L. Warner sat back and waited for her to demand her release. Instead, she coldly informed him, "You can put me in B's, C's or Z's,

Warner, hard-nosed as he had threatened to be, assigned Kay to six quickies. And Kay, excellent poker player that she was, never showed her hand to co-workers. When her true feelings finally burst forth, she confirmed that the relentless campaign to scuttle her self-esteem had succeeded. Wallowing in self-flagellation, she claimed that during her entire career she had seen only one close-up of herself that she considered beautiful and even that was achieved by illusion. "In *One-Way Passage* cameraman Bob Kurle had taken so much pains, shifting the camera fifty different ways, experimenting with light and shadow until it was beautiful," she said. "When I saw that, I felt the one pang of pure pleasure I've ever experienced when I've looked at myself on the screen."

With the release of *Women Are Like That* her reasons for despair were justified. The dialogue was peppered with *r*'s and non sequiturs. *My Bill,* based on a decade-old Broadway play, damaged Kay's leading-lady image by casting her as the mother of four. When *Secrets of an Actress* opened, Howard Barnes cruelly observed: "Offhand I can think of no meaner assignment to give Miss Francis than that of impersonating an actress as she does in this show." But more perceptive critics such as Irene Thirer began shifting their attack, saying that when a Kay Francis production opened as the lower half of a double bill, it was a sorry state of affairs. "In spite of the definite B stamp, Kay is as ever the statuesque star who wears any old clothes with distinctive style," Miss Thirer wrote. Of *Comet over Broadway,* which supplanted *Secrets,* Bland Johnson ventured that women who liked "wifely sacrifice, fine clothes and hardy emotionalism" would be pleased with Kay's exploits as a woman of noble purpose.

While filming *Comet over Broadway,* Kay had constantly battled director Busby Berkeley. Halfway through it she had caved in under the pressures from all sides. She developed a kidney infection and had an allergic reaction to the drugs which made her look as if she had a bad case of measles. Warner's suspended her without pay, and she responded by drinking enough gin for the infection to flare again. Not much later she recorded: "Got tight for no good reason." On September 14 she wrote, "Don't know where or how or why I am going."

Women in the Wind was so atróciously written and directed that it evoked a wave of sympathy from critics, who went out of their way to remark on Kay's charm. A fan magazine lamented: "Poor Kay Francis gets another dirty deal in this one." But it remained for *King of the Underworld* to bring impartial reviewers to her defense. The picture was originally intended as a remake of *Doctor Socrates*, with the Paul Muni part rewritten as a new-woman role for Kay. Problems developed, and production was halted. Later new scenes were shot to turn the film into a Humphrey Bogart vehicle, with Kay in a supporting role.

Warner's vengefulness was so apparent that critics took the studio to task. In the *Times*, Bosley R. Crowther commented:

> Back in the old days of friendly panning, it never occurred to us that one day we might be the organizer of a Kay Francis Defense Fund. But after sitting through *King of the Underworld* at the Rialto, in which Humphrey Bogart is starred while Miss Francis, once the glamor queen of the studio, gets a poor second billing, we wish to announce publicly that contributions are now in order. Not that it wouldn't have been a great advantage to Miss Francis if her name had been omitted altogether from the billing; we simply want to go gallantly on record against what seems to us an act of corporate unpoliteness.
>
> For *King of the Underworld*, which is said to be the farewell appearance of Miss Francis (who evidently had no first-billing guarantee in her contract) in a Warner Brothers production, is not merely bad; it is, unless we are misled by all the internal evidence, deliberately bad. The scriptwriters, knowing as they perfectly well do that Miss Francis always has 'r' trouble, have unkindly written in the word "moronic." Indeed, considering the plot and everything, it is our settled conviction that meaner advantage was never taken of a lady.

Kay's treatment by Warner's also drew an open letter from Jimmy Fidler:

> Out here in the once-chivalrous West, the studio czars have a way—a sort of mean way, I might add—of "getting even" with players who have been quarrelsome and are about to leave their employ, either by mutual consent or because of a contract expiration. The bigwigs avenge their hurt pride by giving the departed star a thorough beating in the advertising.

For example, *King of the Underworld* is currently being screened. In the local theater ads, you have to read carefully to find the name of Kay Francis, in much smaller letters, buried way down in the reading matter. You grasp the psychology, of course. The intention is to make Kay feel very, very small indeed—as small, even as the type in which her name is printed. What the effect on the minds of the public may be is problematical—but I can imagine that Miss Movie Fan's opinion of Kay must have taken a certain slump when she reads that advertising.

It's all so absurd. Studios employing such tricks are like small boys, who, being displeased at something mama has done, sneak off around the corner and stick out their tongues.

After enduring such sadism, Kay must have been pleased that Carole Lombard insisted on RKO hiring her to play the other woman in *In Name Only*. By judicious casting, this film helped rehabilitate her reputation, which had been turned into an industry joke by Warner's. Basically, *In Name Only* was the familiar romantic triangle whose resolution rested on an arbitrary and coincidental crisis to break the stalemate. None of the characters was notably original, and the situations were circumscribed by restrictions of the Hays Code. Yet, because of the care and ingenuity with which it was written, directed and acted, the result was felicitious not only for Miss Lombard and Cary Grant, but also for Kay. Bosley Crowther could find only complimentary things to say about Kay's playing of "the model cat, suave, superior and relentless." Even today the acting seems spare, stylish and modern—completely devoid of the pseudo-sincerity that weighed down so many of Kay's Warner films.

At the beginning of June, 1937, Kay's personal life was a ruin. Like so many glamor girls before and after her, she made the mistake of assuming that at thirty-two her life was over. She could not cope. She generally either drank herself into unconsciousness or relied on sleeping pills to knock her out. Then, one evening at the home of Countess di Frasso (née Dorothy Taylor), she met Baron Raven Erik Angus Barnekow, a seemingly levelheaded German businessman.

Barnekow, who had been in the United States since 1922, insisted on being called Mr. Barnekow, but when pressed would acknowledge that he was heir to his father's castle and estates in Pomerania and through his mother to a share of Westeredeln potash mines. He was also proud that during World War I he had flown in the first Richthofen Pursuit Squadron for two years. There was some confusion about his current business—whether he was a broker, a maker of diesel engines or about to begin manufacturing commercial and military planes.

No matter. Kay soon found herself deeply in love with him, and, as planned, Delmer Daves slipped unobtrusively from the picture. Louella kept close track of the new pair, and Kay promised that this time LOP would be "first to know." Good as her word, at 10:30 P.M. on March 1, 1938, Kay authorized the columnist to announce her betrothal to the German nobleman and her imminent retirement from films. There is some confusion as to whether they ever wed. But upon debarking from a cruise steamer in San Juan in October, Kay described herself as "a former film star and future bride." Since Barnekow had returned to Germany the latter part of August, that would seem to preclude their marriage, although some of her friends remain convinced the couple were secretly married.

Kay's state of mind during their courtship could have been coped with only by a paragon of manhood—both supportive and tenderly understanding. The forty-six-year-old Barnekow was far from that. Spoiled as a child, he had grown into a stubborn, vain man. Attractive and charming when he wished to be, he was quarrelsome and suspicious when drinking. In his hotel suite he surrounded himself with photos of his aerial combat exploits "resulting in fifteen German victories" during World War I.

He lived in a male-oriented atmosphere in which women—even independent ones like Kay—were expected to be subservient. Kay and he quarreled because he criticized her for wearing makeup, insisting that German women "don't paint their faces." He forbade her to pry into his mysterious spur-of-the-moment trips. Kay complained about this to friends, and in the pre-World-War-II jittery atmosphere many suspected Barnekow of being a German agent.

Jessica and Richard Barthelmess, Kay's closest friends, worried that the baron would involve her in scandal. But when Jessica attempted to discuss the problem seriously, Kay refused to hear any criticism. "How could I sit there and let her say such things? I just gave way and had old-fashioned hysterics. Erik an angel," she wrote in her diary. The couples stopped seeing one another temporarily. An attempted Christmas Eve reconciliation resulted in Kay's spending Christmas Day alone, alienated from both Barnekow and the Barthelmesses.

Life increasingly assumed soap opera overtones. An unhappy Kay retreated into eating and drinking binges, and her slim 112-pound figure of 1930 ballooned to 142 by 1939. She resolved to get in shape for *In*

Name Only but only got tight and belligerent. In her cups she insulted her old friend Andy Devine and Jack Warner in a single evening. "So what?" she asked her diary. But when she saw her wardrobe tests, she recorded that she looked "frightening" and thereafter controlled herself long enough to lose twenty pounds.

She had a tiff with Dorothy di Frasso. When Barnekow learned about it, he accused Kay of carrying on with the countess' friend, Gerald Krech, son of a London financier, who, Barnekow said, was spreading unfounded rumors about him.

"What am I heading for?" Kay asked herself rhetorically on March 27. She quickly found out. Barnekow went to the DA and attempted to institute a suit for slander against the countess, saying she had called him a Nazi spy. Even if she had, said the DA, that fell within the jurisdiction of the Beverly Hills justice courts. Enraged, Barnekow took his case to the papers.

Kay was aghast to read that he had repeated the charge to reporters, claiming his witnesses against the countess were Gerald Krech and the Earl of Warwick, known in films as Michael Brooke.* Krech immediately denied ever having heard anything of the kind. Undaunted, Barnekow insisted he would press the case. "I am becoming an American citizen, and I am a manufacturer of motors, and such false remarks as this may damage my business."

"Someone must be mad. I never said anything of the sort," Countess di Frasso told reporters. "I haven't seen Baron Barnekow in weeks. I didn't know the baron in Europe or Germany. I do not know what his politics are, and I must say, I couldn't care less."

Fearful lest Barnekow be interned as an enemy alien, Kay attempted to persuade him to retire to Hawaii, explaining that she had accumulated enough money for both. He brusquely refused and three weeks later left for New York, ostensibly for a few days. When Kay heard indirectly that he was preparing to return to Germany, she telephoned him hysterically and exacted a promise he would not leave the country. But as the international situation worsened, Barnekow left for his homeland.

England declared war on Germany on September 3, and Kay self-centeredly scribbled: "Oh, dear God. Good-bye, Erik." As always when events were beyond her control, she began to crumble. She lost

---

*Earlier Kay had met Brooke, when he appeared at her door, thinking he was calling on the notorious madam Lee Frances—and Kay had strung him along before revealing her real identity.

an expensive emerald necklace and brooded until she became ill. Her doctor ordered her to bed, with nurses in twenty-four hour attendance. She kept both them and herself busy attempting to call Barnekow in Germany. When, after days of effort, the call was completed, Barnekow was cold and unresponsive.

Louella "Love's Undertaker" Parsons reported to readers on September 28:

> One of the most gallant women in Hollywood is Kay Francis, who has been frightfully worried over her fiancé Baron Erik Barnekow. Kay and Erik had made all plans to be married as soon as he returned from Europe. He had his reservations for the last of August and was ready to sail when war broke out and he was detained in Berlin. He had taken out his first citizenship papers, but nevertheless he still was a German subject. Kay talked to him on the telephone in Berlin. Of course a conversation in any country in wartime is difficult. She had been heartsick with worry but because she is a swell person she hasn't been weeping on her friends' shoulders.

Whether Louella scrambled the facts or Kay misled her, Barnekow had made no attempt to return to the United States. Kay finally faced the truth and began rebuilding her life. Still, on the anniversary of their meeting she asked her diary, "What is the sense?" took five codeine tablets and cried herself to sleep.

Between 1940 and 1942 there were eight films—hardly any of them worthy of her time, whatever salary she earned. At Universal she played Deanna Durbin's mother ("no ordinary mother role, but one of unusual importance," the press release stated) in *It's a Date*, and Randolph Scott's sweetheart in *When the Daltons Rode*. Next she went to RKO for a ludicrous production of *Little Men* (with Kay as Mrs. Jo) and *Play Girl*, in which she portrayed an aging adventuress instructing younger gold diggers. Then she checked in at Universal for *The Man Who Lost Himself* (never released in New York) and proceeded to Twentieth Century-Fox, where she played Donna Lucia to Jack Benny's Lord Babberly in *Charley's Aunt*. From there she went to MGM, where she acquitted herself with some distinction supporting Rosalind Russell in *The Feminine Touch*. But by 1942 she was reduced to mothering Gloria Warren in Warner's *Always in My Heart* and Diana Barrymore in Universal's *Between Us Girls*.

Her return to Warner's exemplifies her willingness to go anywhere for money, even to Warner's, although neither she nor Jack Warner ever forgave each other. Years later, when she was appearing in stock in Richmond, Virginia, a man came backstage and introduced himself as a Warner's representative. He told Kay that the studio was filming *The Helen Morgan Story*, with Judy Garland, and that Jack Warner wanted her for the mother. Something about the visitor's manner aroused Kay's suspicions, but she was so attracted by the proposed salary that she wired Jack Warner to find out whether the offer was legitimate. He promptly wired back: "No, Kay. We never even thought about you."

Kay led an empty existence in the "happy house" that she had built in the Santa Monica foothills. In January, 1942, half mad from insomnia that refused to be vanquished by pills, she decided she needed a change of scene. She went to New York to raise money in behalf of Bundles for Britain, then on to Washington, D. C., to sign up for a USO tour. In October, with Martha Raye, Mitzi Mayfair and Carole Landis, she flew to Bermuda, Northern Ireland and England before going to North Africa. There, averaging five hours' sleep each night, the four actresses entertained thousands of GIs. They were prevented from going to the front lines only by the official command.

At the wind-up of the tour Kay flew to Washington, D.C., where she dictated an official report. After a side trip to New York she returned to Hollywood, where she continued her war work. The result of this activity was a best-selling account of the girls' adventures *Four Jills in a Jeep*, which Twentieth Century-Fox made into a movie. Scriptwriter Snag Werris was assigned by Darryl Zanuck to be on the set daily for changes. "This was a true fun assignment," Werris says. "They were swell gals. Kay was a real pro and a joy to work with. Her troubles with r's were well known. So for a gag I was asked to bring in a new page of script. I don't recall the lines, but one was something like 'I ran into Ralph in Roanoke and rapidly wrung his neck.' When Kay got to it, she read it through and yelled, 'Where is that son of a bitch Snag? I'll kill him!' But none of the four took herself too seriously. They got along well—although the assistant director had orders to make sure the A.M. calls for all the girls were at the same time."

Having finished *Four Jills*, Kay forgot her talk about welcoming retirement. She hung around, awaiting another good offer, became more cordial to the press and even granted fan magazine interviews, explaining how pressures of stardom had caused her former antagonism. The reformation produced nary a nibble.

Against all advice she signed to co-produce her own films at that graveyard of burned-out stars, Monogram. Her associate was a feisty little Cockney named Jeffrey Bernerd. He had been brought to Hollywood by Steve Broidy, who liked Bernerd's "up-yours" attitude. Broidy had hired him to produce exploitation films, including, among many others, *Where Are Your Children?* and *Are These Our Parents?*

Kay's deal called for one picture per year for three years. Bernerd, who remembered her royal treatment in her heyday, was surprised by her penny-pinching approach. She insisted on searching for low-budget vehicles and took a hand in rewriting their first script, *Allotment Wives*. She also persuaded Otto Kruger and Paul Kelly to work for less than usual. The picture had a ten-day shooting schedule, and the object was to make money. The result was that once again a beautifully gowned Kay appeared in a hopeless vehicle. A. H. Wieler of the *Times* felt she looked "far too genteel for her job"—i.e., collecting allotment checks on several GIs. Her final two Monogram films, *Divorce* and *Wife Wanted*, were never exposed to the withering blasts of New York critics.

Thus, she ended her career as an elegant walkie-talkie doll, wandering endlessly through sumptuous sets, mindlessly repeating banal sentiments. She recognized that she had become a self-caricature. But never having learned to act, she could only reproduce external signals indicating emotion. The work had long ago become boring. Yet, because she mistakenly believed that money could solve problems, she persisted in subjecting herself to the monotony. Year after year the refrain became: "Home dead. Dinner on tray in bed. Bone-tired. . . . Finished picture. Thank God. . . . Where will this end? Where am I headed? What am I doing?"

Sadly, the same notation recurred over the years: "Showed Del *One-Way Passage*. He loved it." "Erik very moved by *One-Way Passage*." "Ran *One-Way Passage* for Don."

Saddest of all, among her sixty-eight films only *Girls About Town*, *One-Way Passage*, *Trouble in Paradise*, *In Name Only* and a couple of others seemed worth the effort.

While working on *Allotment Wives*, Kay had agreed to appear in silent star Patsy Ruth Miller's play *Windy Hill*, which Ruth Chatterton was directing. The first reading was held in New York on August 3, and Kay decided that henceforth there would only be the play. But in spite of the three former film favorites' "after-you-darling" approach, nerves frayed, and rehearsals were punctuated by seething exchanges and quiet sulking. The 10-day rehearsal allowed summer stock tryouts proved insufficient. Kay's throat closed the day before the Montclair, New Jersey, opening, but she somehow got through the premiere.

The next day reworking began, but audience response was poor. Miss Miller left town, and Miss Chatterton skipped watching many performances. Things continued to go awry in New Haven, Philadelphia and Pittsburgh. Playwright John Van Druten saw the show and made suggestions for improvement which caused Kay to blow up and break four bottles of Ballantine scotch.

In Pittsburgh the bogey that supposedly haunts doomed theatrical ventures hit. Leading man Roger Pryor found the door jammed, and no amount of tugging would loosen it. With the substantial-looking walls seemingly hit by a second San Francisco quake, Pryor finally entered through a door that had been firmly established as leading to a clothes closet. The audience yelped with delight. The cast broke up, and the curtain fell on pandemonium. A moment later it inexplicably rose to reveal the elegant Kay, arms akimbo, stamping her tiny foot and screaming, "Shit on this production!"

Rewrites were discarded, and new material was added without noticeable improvement, but wherever they went, the attraction did good business on the strength of the star names. They closed on May 25.

Hating what she had been through and what lay ahead, Kay returned to Hollywood to begin *Wife Wanted*. She was five days into shooting when she received a call from producer Leland Hayward, who asked her to replace Ruth Hussey in *State of the Union* on Broadway. "So excited," Kay wrote about a project for the first time in years.

Filming completed, she went to New York to rehearse for her first leading role on Broadway. Stage manager Howard "Hap" Graham saw to it that everything ran smoothly, explaining Kay's moves and business so that she was prepared when director Howard Lindsay began rehearsing her.

The thirty-six-year-old stage manager had begun to assume a central place in Kay's life even before her Broadway opening. Her diaries for August and September contain daily entries about "Happy" bouncing in for tea, a drink, dinner or coming back after the show. As always with romantic attachments, Kay's life revolved around her lover for about eight months. Then, in April, the entries began to change. Noting that they had seen *Finian's Rainbow*, she added, "Came home and read. Knock-out fight. Whew!"

That marked the beginning of a period when all the self-destructive strains of Kay's personality joined, making a spectacular eruption of headlines inevitable. In June Kay and Hap temporarily broke off. She spent the day alone "taking many pills" and considering whether or not to forgive him. Finally, she decided she could not face the upcoming road tour alone. They reconciled, but the bloom was off both the professional engagement and the love affair.

In the fall the play opened in Wilmington, played Philadelphia for a week and then moved to Newark, Harrisburg (where the mayor's *wife* presented the key to the city), up through New York State and into Michigan. Kay's loathing of touring, perhaps because it stirred memories of traumatic childhood experiences, made her impossible to please. The only balm was that from Philadelphia to Peoria the play was a box-office bonanza. But even that consolation disappeared in Witchita Falls, Texas. She wrote in the diary, "Just dead. Horror show. Nobody there."

The company abandoned Texas, moving to Evansville, Indiana, as Kay's mood darkened. "Box lunch on horror coach with everybody and his brother on it," she complained. Nor was Graham proving a pillar of strength. "Hap completely out of order and terrible. Too tired and too afraid of another fight," she recorded. She decided instead to avoid him while mulling over the situation and the following day informed him that their mutually deplorable behavior had ruined their affair.

The tour continued through Springfield, Rockford and other Illinois towns, in one instance playing to 6,200 people in an enormous auditorium. Gradually, out of boredom and loneliness, Kay resumed seeing Hap.

Then, during the Columbus, Ohio, engagement, on January 22, 1948, in Kay's words, "all hell broke loose." That evening, suffering from a cold, she called the hotel and ordered soup from room service for after the performance. She detested warm rooms, but since the kitchen had no heat lamps to keep the soup hot, she ordered her radiator turned on and the soup placed atop it.

Kay and Hap had several drinks in her dressing room, and she downed some sleeping pills before going to the hotel. Hap left about 2:30 A.M. At 6:30 she called, saying she had taken more pills and feared an overdose. Hap called a doctor, who suggested cold air and hot coffee until he arrived. Hap opened the window and put Kay's head outside. Attempting to feed her hot coffee, he inadvertently scalded her neck. She suddenly seemed to faint, and he became aware that the radiator was burning her legs.

At 7 A.M. Kay was admitted to White Cross Hospital, where her stomach was pumped and treatment was begun for second-degree burns extending from her knees to her hips. Regaining consciousness five hours later, she was distressed to learn from detectives that Hap was in jail, booked for "investigation of intent to kill," and had been subjected to five hours of intensive grilling. She exonerated him at once.

Humilated by the headlines, she insisted on leaving the hospital. With the help of Jessica Barthelmess, who had flown in from New York, another old friend, Winsor French, the Cleveland columnist, and her devoted maid, Eunice, she retreated to novelist Louis Bromfield's farm until arrangements could be make to take her to New York.

At New York's Cornell Medical Center she began undergoing tedious treatment for second-degree burns, treatment made all the more difficult by complications arising from the delay. As days passed, she won the admiration and friendship of the hospital staff for the stoicism she exhibited as she awaited the outcome of the painful skin grafts. She also began making plans for getting back to work.

Soon after her release from the hospital in June, 1948, Kay, wearing heavy elastic stockings and a long girdlelike garment to reinforce the damaged muscles, booked a short tour of summer theaters to prove that she was still capable of holding a stage. As vehicle she chose *The Last of Mrs. Cheyney*, a play in which she wore long gowns that hid her medical supports. Soon her leading man, a dark-haired matinee-idol type named Joel Ashley, had replaced Hap Graham in her affections. In 1949 she and Ashley did a full-summer tour in *Let Us Be Gay* and in 1950, a minitour of *Good-bye, My Fancy* before undertaking a dramatization of Thomas Wolfe's *The Web and the Rock*. Using only a small section of the sprawling novel, playwright Lester Cohen still had difficulty scaling it down to the limitations of the stage. Kay, Ashley and director Richard Barr hoped that the tryout would reveal a script worthy of Broadway production. It was not to be. *Variety* was complimentary to Ashley and Barr, but their reviewer seemed confused by Kay's characterization, observing that she "underplayed until in the powerful scenes she seemed to be overplaying."

That winter Kay read *Mirror, Mirror*, George Oppenheimer's adaptation of G. B. Stern's novel *The Back Seat*. She decided that it had good roles for her and Ashley and that, despite its failure in a previous tryout, with some rewriting it might be the vehicle to bring her back to Broadway. She began a series of meetings with Oppenheimer and Barr, who was to direct.

"Before rehearsal began, we rented a house in Westhampton with the idea of whipping the script into shape," Oppenheimer recalls. "And I really don't know what to say. Kay was great fun. Charming. I was very fond of her. She was a good scout—a good scout and a bad actress.

"The play wasn't a very good play, and the result was chaos. She wasn't the greatest person to work with because she couldn't remember lines easily. She was drinking in those days, too. She always claimed that she never drank when she worked, but she'd quit at eight and start again at eleven.

"Kay was more or less the manager. After the thing opened, she wanted to go on with it, but there was very little money, and she wanted me to continue touring and rewriting without expense money. I said, 'Thank you very much, but no.' That was more or less the end of our friendship. But I have a nice picture of her in the dressing room and remember her as a nice dame."

The following winter her agents, Robert Mayberry and Lee Wallace, booked Kay into Winter Park, Florida, to do Somerset Maugham's *Theater*. Richard Barr and Joel Ashley were otherwise occupied, but Barr suggested that Dennis Allen direct and appear opposite her. Allen, a tousle-haired blond young man of catlike grace, had previous experience with the Melvyn Douglas unit of Special Services during World War II and had since appeared with Flora Robson in *Suspect*, Jean Parker in *Candlelight* and Diana Barrymore in the bus-and-truck company of *Joan of Lorraine*.

Kay and Dennis' meeting marked the beginning of an intense, long-lasting and—for Kay, final—romantic liaison. Dennis admired her extravagantly. He saw her as a member of a school of stylish actresses that included Hope Williams, Jane Cowl and Katharine Cornell. "Kay was a clotheshorse, and she had mannerisms. Her entrances and exits were studied, but she knew exactly what she was doing, and she always got ovations," he says. "A great deal has been made of the lisp, but it was so slight as to be charming. And I had a hunch she ought to be doing Shaw and Wilde. I began convincing her to try them—or at least Coward. If she had—who knows what direction her career might have taken?"

In Winter Park, soon after he got the actors on their feet, Dennis began worrying about the production, not because it would be seen by anyone who could affect Kay's career, but because she aroused a curious protective feeling in him. "There wasn't a trace of vanity you'd expect," he said years later. "I guess everyone who'd seen her movies expected her to be chic in private life. You'd go into a stock theater, and the kids were appalled at the way she dressed. She always wore the same thing—a denim wrap-around skirt, a blouse and little wedgies. Of course, we're talking about the private Kay—not when she was on display. She had fantastic taste when she chose to use it. But she didn't have any illusions about her position."

In *Theater* Dennis was confronted with what he considered a dreary third-act curtain. The actress has scored a triumph, her confidence is restored, and her husband arrives after the premiere to take her to supper. After mulling over the ending, Dennis decided to change the staging so that the actress exited through the front of the house, ostensibly to avoid the fans at the stage door. He told Kay about his idea, which he felt would provide audiences with the excitement of rubbing elbows with a celebrity. She responded, "Don't worry. I'll dress it."

Dress it she did. Everyone who saw the production still talks of the flash of those final moments. Stage manager Jerry O'Brien, who has worked with many of the great glamor stars, including Vivien Leigh, maintains that Kay created one of the most visually exciting pictures he has every witnessed in the theater. "She entered on empty stage lighted with that brown jell she liked so much," he says. "There was only a rickety old chair. And she was wearing this black dornfelt cape with a little ermine collar. She moved as if she were bone-weary and sank onto a chair, saying, 'Oh, my God, I'm so tired,' or whatever the line is. Then, suddenly, she threw off the cape, which was lined with ermine. She was in black chiffon and her diamond necklace, bracelet and earrings. And it was POW! Like every light in the world had suddenly been turned on."

Dennis agrees. He says it made no difference that the scene was weak, because once Kay opened the cape no one heard the dialogue. "My God, there was an ovation for this woman every night," he recalls. "I don't know how her technique would hold up in the theater now. I don't think they produce vehicles for people like Kay today. But this was an era when a star was expected, as Jerry says, to be POW! And Kay was."

Word of the production's effectiveness spread, and Kay's agents booked it extensively from Bermuda to Skowhegan—and points far afield. Now that the pressure was off, Kay made touring a lark. She, Dennis and her general factotum, Eunice, would set out in Kay's station wagon, leaving one engagement, bound for the next. With them would be a picnic hamper and a thermos of martinis. Life assumed the proportions of one big party.

Eunice, who was half Indian, half black and had bleached blond hair, is almost inexplicable to those who have never observed the unorthodox relationships that develop between theater maids and actresses. The maids often become both employees and friends. The actresses and maids bicker, complaining about each other, and yet remain deeply loyal.

In one sense, Eunice was a paragon. She served as Kay's dresser and greatest fan in the theater. At home she was maid, laundress, cook, secretary and surrogate mother. She assumed an intensely proprietary air that protected Kay well when she'd taken one drink too many or wished to avoid unwanted attentions. "Miss Kay's having a nap," or "Miss Kay's stepped out," Eunice would say, unless she recognized the caller as a friend. Then she'd whisper, "She can't come to the phone. She's got that *flu* again, but she'll be all right tomorrow."

In another sense, Eunice was a trial. She liked to drink, and only a little alcohol was required to turn her into a wild woman. "It's the Indian in me," she explained. "It turns me savage."

"For a long time I couldn't figure out why Kay put up with her, and I finally decided Kay thrived on tempestuous relationships," says a friend. "She'd made so many of those B movies for Warner's that life had become a soap opera to her."

"Eunice is being naughty again," was Kay's usual comment. Once, when Kay, Dennis and Eunice were to return from a Bermuda engagement, Kay agreed to pose for photos to publicize the airline with which they were traveling. This necessitated arriving at the airport two hours early. It was apparent before they set out that Eunice had found friends the previous night and was already inebriated. "When we got to the airport, Eunice was supposed to watch the luggage," Dennis recalls. "But she hit the bar instead and by plane time was blind-assed drunk. We all got on, except Eunice, who couldn't make the steps. The next thing we knew the pilot had bumped her. I went down to talk with him and got nowhere. Kay came down and explained, but no go. So we left without Eunice.

"Unfortunately, when we got to New York International, we had a case of liquor, and Eunice had the declaration slips in her purse. Well, Kay had had enough. She kept saying, 'I did publicity for the airport, and they bumped my maid, and now you expect me to pay to bring this liquor in!' The charge was something like fifteen dollars. She screamed and yelled and finally slammed the money on the counter. Then she ostentatiously opened the boxes and passed out every last bottle before sailing out, clutching her handbag containing her rubies, diamonds and emeralds—which they hadn't even bothered to look at."

During the tour Dennis kept urging Kay to read Shaw and Wilde, but she was in no mood to undertake demanding assignments. She liked being well paid—with only an occasional challenge from an unexpected development. In Skowhegan, Maine, during a quick change in the wings, she somehow got both feet through one of the wide legs of lounging pajamas. A moment after her entrance she realized she was trailing the other pajama leg, but before the audience noticed, she executed a graceful twirl, tossing the unused material around her shoulders and transforming it into a stole. "Now that's class in dress," Dennis says. "She had learned her business thoroughly and was effective. And she did it solely for money."

During Kay's theater tours her agents, Mayberry and Wallace, diligently searched for radio and television roles for her, no easy task since it was tacitly understood that when she appeared it was on her terms. Producers and directors invariably came to her to iron out script, casting and wardrobe problems. Choosing what to wear developed into a ritual for her. "After a drink and small talk Kay would turn to Eunice and say, 'Bring out the blue,'" Mayberry recalls. "And Eunice brought the blue dress and a little tray which held shoes dyed to match plus a sapphire necklace, bracelet and earrings. In other words, accessories. If the blue wouldn't do, Kay'd ask for 'the brown'— which meant a brown dress, shoes and her rubies and topazes. That wardrobe was part of her business, and she appreciated it as that, but she wasn't ever silly or drooling over clothes. It was just a straightforward reaction."

Having signed for a role, Kay would analyze the character and then begin assembling possible wardrobe by digging out surviving outfits from her Warner days—such as the Orry-Kelly lounging pajamas she wore in *Theater.* When something new was needed, she'd consult with Bernie Newman at Bergdorf's, describe the character in detail and choose those outfits that best suited her purposes. She realized better than anyone else that what she offered was theatrical chic, and she worked tirelessly to achieve it.

Kay had an opportunity to buy an apartment at 32 East Sixty-Fourth Street in late 1951. Considering her accumulated capital, the outlay required was modest, but she vacillated. Finally, she called her longtime friend Stephie Wiman and asked her to inspect it. "It had been a big apartment that was divided into two. It was lovely, perfectly lovely," Mrs. Wiman said. "A big bedroom, an enormous bathroom, a hallway, tiny kitchenette, lovely library and a huge drawing room. They were only asking eleven thousand dollars for it. After we'd looked it over, she asked, 'Do you think that's too much?' And I almost fainted.''

By the time Kay moved from 31 East Sixty-First Street to her new home it had been transformed into a small jewel, containing only choice pieces from her previous residences, plus a large collection of bibelots, boxes and other objets d'art. About these Kay proved as meticulous as she was known to be punctual, causing Dennis teasingly to call her "Craig's wife.'' No matter, if anything was an inch from its intended place, she could not rest until it was restored to where it belonged.

Many people believe that at this time she consciously turned her back on Hollywood acquaintances. "I don't think that was the case,'' says L. Arnold Weissberger, her attorney and friend. "I think the movie people forgot about her after she was no longer in the swim. It was especially true in those days that you were as important as your last picture and how much money you were earning.''

For whatever reason, film people and early-day New York associates—with the exception of Stephie Wiman—disappeared from her life. Others came and went. A few stayed. She became particularly fond of art galley owner Allan Brandt and his wife, Priscilla; director Richard Barr; hospital administrator Eva Patton; Clay Shaw, the New Orleans businessman and cultural entrepreneur whose life was ruined when he was accused of conspiring to assassinate John F. Kennedy; Hilda Coppage, who operated an inn on Cape Cod; and actor Paul Lipson. At Goldie's, an intimate East Side club, she struck up a friendship with the piano duo Goldie Hawkins and Wayne Saunders, with whom she founded the Monday Night Hookin' Society—Kay Francis, Chief Hooker—and turned out some beautiful rugs.

Her closeness with Goldie cooled when he rebuked her for an unkind remark about a mutual friend. Enraged, she accused him of using her to get publicity for the club, only to be told, "Listen, sweetie, at this point I could get more publicity with Dixie Dunbar's name than yours.'' Saunders, however, remained faithful, calling her at least once each day until her death.

Perhaps Kay's favorite new acquaintance was Weissberger's mother, Anna, whom Kay found at once amusing and relaxing. At one point she suggested that Mrs. Weissberger be included as an executor. When Weissberger expressed surprise, Kay informed him, "I think the most important thing in an executor is common sense, and Anna has more common sense than all of you lawyers put together.'' Weissberger finally dissuaded her from the proposal.

With the years her behavior became increasingly self-destructive as she resented her physical condition and advancing age. During a summer stock engagement, while angry and in her cups, she turned on Eunice, calling her a "nigger." Eunice, also in her cups, retaliated by beating Kay so severely with a shoe that hospitalization was required.

In the next few years Kay also lost a lung and a kidney surgically. She fractured a bone in her ankle and injured her back by falling in the bathtub, thereafter requiring a brace.

No longer able or willing to work, she spent her summers on Cape Cod. One winter she went to St. Thomas, where Dennis opened a nightclub, but that proved unsatisfactory since there was no place, by day or by night, where she could find amusement.

The two of them returned to New York, where Kay's infirmities increased. Dennis secured a job at Bronzini's selling ties. For a couple of years he remained there, making no effort to find theatrical employment. After work he would go home to dine with Kay. Their quarrels became more frequent, and at last friends began to drift away, unable to put up with the scenes. "The whole thing was psychologically bad," Dennis said years later, "and I honestly believe that she broke off with me because she realized that otherwise I'd sit there and dedicate my life to her. I loved her deeply, and I think in the beginning, she loved me." But by the summer of 1961 relations were so strained that Kay spent the summer on Cape Cod while Dennis went to Fire Island to work for Goldie Hawkins. There he met a younger woman whom he eventually was to marry.

When he returned to the city, Kay terminated their association. "Frankly, I'm glad it was her decision and that she did it. My life is much better. She may have sensed that. She was seventeen years older than me—that's a lot. If we'd continued, I could never have had a life other than sitting around holding the hand of a sick old lady," he says. "That fall, when I came back from Goldie's, my stuff was packed, and it was all over—*closed*. I could never get her on the phone or anything else again."

Others who had once been intimates dropped away because of Kay's drinking. The last time Charles Baskerville saw her, Kay invited him and another half dozen guests to dinner at the Valeria at Fifty-fifth Street and Madison Avenue. "When we were ready to leave, she just measured her length on the floor of the restaurant. Which broke our hearts," Baskerville says. "We'd hoped that this once she was going to get out of the restaurant without making a terrible disaster of the evening."

Beatrice Ames Stewart, who had taken a position at Bergdorf's, was stunned when she encountered Kay there one afternoon. They had not seen each other in years. "Well, I hardly recognized her. She had salt-and-pepper hair skinned back in a bun like Grant Wood's 'Woman with a Plow.' She was enormous and rolling drunk. She wanted Bernie Newman. I told her he'd be right down and took her into a fitting room, where she eventually bought a beautiful mink stole—and this was the middle of July. It was terribly sad. I loved her very much, and I'd known her since we were girls, but the drinking was too much for me."

Occasionally, Kay played poker or hooked rugs with those friends whom she would still see and who would see her. Then it was discovered that she had breast cancer, and a masectomy was performed. Thereafter she preferred to conduct her friendships by telephone while she remained in bed, reading, watching television, drinking and taking medication.

"No bouquets to me, but I was probably the only old friend she had had for—well, God, it would be fifty years—that went to see her," Stephie Wiman said. "I'd go over at three or three thirty, and she'd want me to have a drink, and I'd say, 'No, I don't drink at this time of day.' She'd insist, and as I drink vodka, I'd have a glass of water.

"But she was so alone. There was no family. And in those last years, when she was so sick, she'd get frightened at times. She'd call, and I'd go down there at three or four in the morning. She had my private unlisted number in my bedroom. I'd get up, leave a note for the maid where I was and go down there. It was just awful, having her die there alone."

Kay died on August 26, 1968, and when her will was filed, her bequests included her emeralds to Mrs. Wiman; Picasso's "Guitar Player" to Mrs. Allan Brandt; drawings by Leo and Jo Mielziner to Arnold Weissberger; and the major portion of her almost $2,000,000 estate to Seeing Eye, Inc., of Morristown, New Jersey. A vice-president of the foundation, contacted by a reporter of the New York *Daily News*, described the bequest as a "splendid if mysterious surprise," adding that no one at Seeing Eye had been aware of Kay's interest in their work. But Weissberger says that Kay had thought about it and decided loss of sight was the most tragic fate that could befall anyone—hence the gift. She had also emphatically stated that she had no living relatives—laying to rest rumors of an estranged half sister. She directed that her body be cremated and that the undertaker dispose of her ashes in any manner determined by him, but that those ashes under no circum-

233

stances be retained in an urn or interred or scattered to the seven seas. Nor was there to be a funeral, memorial service, monument or other remainder that she had ever graced this earth.

Early on, Kay Francis' (née Katie Gibbs) life had promised to turn out gloriously. In the best *Hattie* Alger tradition she had been a poor but beautiful teenager who flourished on the periphery of society during World War I. She had seemingly married well before invading the theatrical world just as Broadway was flowering. Then, turning to the newly thriving talkies, she had grown rich and famous as their highest-paid glamor star. In her heyday she had been idolized by audiences, sought out by rich and sophisticated friends and pursued by innumerable dashing suitors.

Where had it all gone wrong?

Perhaps Kay unwittingly gave the answer during a summer stock engagement in Ogonquit, Maine, when Bette Davis dropped by after a performance. The two actresses went out for drinks and fell into a discussion of the contemptuous treatment they had received when their usefulness to the studio had diminished. Bette Davis told of the embarrassing circumstances surrounding the filming of her final picture, *Beyond the Forest*, while Kay more than matched those stories as she recalled the series of harassments and humiliations she had suffered as the movie czars had attempted to force her to break her high-paying contract. Eventually, Bette Davis asked Kay why she had endured this treatment for so long.

"I didn't give a shit," Kay said. "I wanted the money."

Bette Davis shook her head. "I didn't," she said. "I wanted the career."

And in that exchange is pinpointed not only the difference in talent but in aspiration as well.

LORETTA YOUNG

The Manipulator

At the end of 1933 Loretta Young had every reason to feel optimistic. Having started in silent pictures as a preteenager, Loretta represented the archetype of Hollywood's manufactured and packaged star. At various times her employers had supplied padding for calves, thighs, buttocks and breasts to enhance her figure. They had also provided complete technical knowledge, enabling her to project her beauty—natural or otherwise—for fullest visual impact. Her mannequinlike perfection had long ago established her as a favorite with thousands of fans who did not know or care whether she could act. To them she was the symbol of purity and refinement in generally raffish surroundings. Had they heard that censors had rejected the original ending of *A Man's Castle*, a story laid in a Hooverville on the banks of the East River, they would have rejoiced. Any character Loretta played deserved the happiness of wedlock before the fade-out. Even if critics complained that the addition of nuptial bliss brought the film to a happy ending and an artistic muddle, no such thought would have occurred to most of her fans.

Loretta had worked hard in nine films during 1933. All the long hours and nervous strain had taken their toll. During the November shooting of a swimming scene in *Born to Be Bad* she developed a fever and a cough which dictated going to Palm Springs to regain her health instead of taking a long-planned trip to Europe. Near the end of her recuperation she received a call from the studio setting an early starting date for *The House of Rothschild*, in which she was to play George Arliss' daughter. Most actresses would have been pleased at the opportunity to observe the working methods of the screen's leading male character star. Not so Loretta, who sulked because her postponed European vacation had to be canceled. Ironically, in view of her screen image, to her the only benefit lay in the fact that as 1933 turned into 1934 she would be near the man she was in love with, Spencer Tracy.

Loretta's prospects had begun improving early in 1933, when she had won court approval of a term contract with Darryl Zanuck's Twentieth Century, Inc. She was to receive an increase of $731 a week more than the $1,000 she had been earning at Warner Brothers. Not bad for a girl of twenty at a time when most Americans were grateful to draw forty cents an hour.

"Now we really have something," fledgling tycoon Zanuck asserted as he made plans to groom Loretta to replace that most appealing of all screen ingenues, Janet Gaynor.

Nor was Zanuck alone in his opinion. During the filming of *A Man's Castle*, which Loretta made on loan to Columbia Pictures, Spencer Tracy described her as one of the finest actresses on the screen.

Director Frank Borzage wasn't quite so extravagant in his assessment of her abilities, but after directing her in *A Man's Castle*, he called Loretta "most promising," adding, "She hasn't the faintest notion of what her possibilities and her talents are! She is just now maturing, but she has not matured enough to know what she has."

The usually astrigent George Jean Nathan, in a commentary on acting, noted, "There is no woman on our stage, incidentially, who couldn't profitably take lessons in this business of looking—hearing and everything with eyes as well as ears—from the young girl in films named Loretta Young."

By the end of 1933 Helen Brown Norden (now known as Helen Lawrenson) was preparing a feature on Loretta as the only one of the 1929 Wampas Baby Stars* who had fulfilled her promise. "After years of vapid sugar-and-water roles, she suddenly in pictures such as *Zoo in Budapest* and *A Man's Castle* has blossomed forth from a stereotyped ingenue into a sensitive actress of more than ordinary promise," Miss Norden wrote.

Why had it taken Loretta four years to evoke this excitement?

The answer lay in the pre-1933 Gretchen—as her friends continued to call her. She was a slim, graceful teenager of infinite poise and self-engrossment which camouflaged the fact that she was as devoid of

*A group of starlets chosen by the industry as stars of tomorrow.

emotional depth as a windup doll. Blessed with an unusually mature appearance and naturally wavy hair that framed a triangular-shaped face punctuated by luminous eyes, prominent cheekbones and a dazzling smile, she was a cameraman's delight. Her matchstick-thin figure could be padded to become any character needed to support an important leading man in a male-oriented vehicle. In an undertaking that was dedicated more to industry than art Loretta was, until 1933, an unexceptional but useful and popular commodity.

What set her apart, in addition to her voracious appetite for success, whas her unrealized potential. Directors quickly discovered that simple emotions could be simulated by training the camera on her face. Intuitively, Loretta soon learned to employ something akin to Stanislavsky's sense-memory technique to re-create an emotion. In her first leading role at fourteen she was called upon to register passionate feelings for her leading man. She produced acceptable fake lust by concentrating on her craving for "luscious ice-cream sundaes."

Her years in front of the camera had taught her technical tricks that served her well in her subsequent career. If she was uninterested in the aesthetics of filmmaking, she took pains to absorb complete knowledge of the mechanics of makeup, costuming, lighting and camera angles. Later, when one of her sisters appeared in a film, wearing an unbecoming coiffure, Loretta demanded why she had agreed to it. Her sister said the hairdresser had recommended it. To which Loretta sniffed, "If you don't know more than your hairstylist, you don't deserve to have one."

Loretta herself so completely mastered the externals of moviemaking that she could reputedly sense by the degree of heat on her face whether the scene was being lit to her maximum advantage. Like the industry of which she was a part, she dedicated herself to the business of entertaining the masses and left masterpieces to others. Even after *Zoo in Budapest* and *A Man's Castle*, which demonstrated her potential, Loretta opted for journeyman productions rather than join such fighters as Bette Davis and Olivia De Havilland in the battle for challenging roles. The result was that she squandered her talent on parts rejected by more combative personalities.

From the beginning Loretta stirred conflicting reactions. Some regarded her as, if not Saint Loretta, at least the most honest and selfless star in Hollywood; while detractors saw her as an obsessive opportunist who fully qualified for the derogatory descriptions that have dogged her—"The Steel Butterfly," "Gretch, the Wretch" and "The

Chocolate-Covered Black Widow.'' But neither fans nor disparagers denied that from the beginning she observed, analyzed and skillfully created an image that appealed to audiences.

In 1917 Gladys Royal Young and her four youngsters—all under the age of ten—arrived in Los Angeles from Salt Lake City to eke out a living. Gladys' husband, John Earle Young, a traveling auditor for the Denver, Rio Grande and Western Railroad, had simply traveled on without them—not to be heard from for twenty years.

In Los Angeles Gladys, a strong-minded woman, borrowed $1,000 from a Catholic bishop, rented a rambling old structure at Ninth and Greer streets and opened a boarding house. There, however dire their straits, she saw to it that Polly Ann, Elizabeth Jane (Sally Blane), Gretchen (Loretta) and Jack attended mass regularly and lived by the Ten Commandments. She also did her best to instill in them a sense of obligation to others, hoping to eradicate any inherited weakness from their likable but unstable father.

Their situation was sometimes grim. In 1948 a former boarder recalled that it was often necessary to advance rent money to forestall having the gas cut off or to provide food for the table. At other times, pressed for cash, Mrs. Young would rent one of the children's rooms, and a woman boarder would return home late at night to find a displaced child sharing her bed.

Mrs. Young's brother-in-law, who was a supervisor at Famous Players-Lasky, helped her by arranging for the children to supplement their mother's income by working as film extras. The first to benefit from this mild form of nepotism was Gretchen. In Fanny Ward's *The Only Way* she played a brief bit as a hysterical child crying piteously on the operating table. Even at four she was remarkably self-possessed and enjoyed working in front of the camera. When she turned over her $3.50 salary to her mother, the precocious miss, who had obviously analyzed the star, confided that Miss Ward was pretty, but that she (Gretchen) liked her better as an old lady.

The four children were hired for *Sirens of the Sea* and Rudolph Valentino's *The Son of the Sheik*, but only Gretchen seemed to take acting seriously. As a six-year-old she already envisioned herself as destiny's tot, telling an aunt, ''When I'm a star, I'll buy you a new broom.''

During one financial crisis Mrs. Young became desperate enough to send Jack to live with friends. Shortly after this, glamorous Mae Murray spotted Gretchen among a group of extras and decided she would make a wonderful daughter for a star. She proposed adopting her. Mrs.

Young refused but agreed her daughter could "visit" Miss Murray and her husband for a year. Gretchen refused to go alone. Since Miss Murray felt the other Young girls looked too mature to pose as a glamor girl's children, their cousin, Colleen Traxler, accompanied Gretchen. For a year and a half the two of them were tutored by a German governess, attended ballet school, and learned the art of curtsying and sitting quietly to avoid annoying their volatile "mama." Suddenly Miss Murray tired of the responsibility, and the charade ended, with the girls returning to their real homes. Not, however, before Gretchen had developed an "I'm-a-ballerina" complex that was to depersonalize so many of her early performances.

Having obtained a divorce and married businessman George U. Belzer in 1923, Gladys Young Belzer enrolled Gretchen in the Alhambra Convent School and later at Immaculate Heart in Hollywood. While attending them, Gretchen may have been away from the camera in body but not in spirit. On visits home she hated doing household chores but would work tirelessly at a neighbor's or anywhere else where she had an audience that might reward her efforts with soul-satisfying "ooohs" and "ahhhs."

Elizabeth Jane, renamed Sally Blane, meanwhile had begun working as a film extra in a Billy Haines college comedy at MGM. "Milton Bren, the producer, was just a boy then, a second assistant director. And the studio was worried about finding young people who had enough enthusiasm for this dance sequence," Miss Blane recalls. "Milton said, 'I'll fill the bill,' and he did. He came to a tea dance and took us to the studio. Of course, I was so thrilled I'd have done it for nothing. It didn't seem like work. It was fun.

"I happened to meet Mike Romanoff, who was a horseman on a Dolores Costello picture, and I got Polly Ann a job doubling for her. While Polly was away, a phone call came from First National, and Gretchen answered. She didn't say, 'Polly isn't here.' She just put on long stockings, went over and got the job. Isn't that funny, you know, for a girl of twelve and a half to do that? And to be able to pull it off?"

Gretchen was obviously already aware that ingenuity was a prerequisite of stardom. When she arrived at the gate, she said that she was Miss Young and she thought Mr. Mervyn LeRoy wanted to see her. She presented herself to LeRoy and persuaded him that she could handle the proposed part in *Naughty but Nice*.

She quickly attracted the attention of Colleen Moore, star of the film. "She had huge gray eyes that seemed to be watching everything and everyone, and she listened as though the director were talking only to her,'' Miss Moore said. Impressed with Gretchen's potential, the star went to Al Rockett, head of talent, and suggested that the studio put the youngster under contract.

The moguls were unenthusiastic. They objected to the name "Gretchen" as too Dutch. Miss Moore suggested substituting Lorita—after a favorite doll she owned. Lorita sounded foreign. Miss Moore proposed adding another *t* and changing the *i* to an *e*. That did it. Gretchen later claimed she found out she was "Loretta" only after reading about it in the papers. Having signed her, the studio gave her an unbilled part in *Her Wild Oat* to keep her working and to allow her to become accustomed to the camera until a real part came along.

"Loretta, bless her, made herself loved immediately,'' Sally Blane says. "You see, she was so bright. In one scene the director placed a camera at both ends of a hall. The girls raced to one end, turned around and ran back to the other. Loretta would run like the devil so that she'd be sure to be in the forefront and get her face on the screen. Then she'd slow down and let the others pass her so that when they ran the other way, she'd be out front again. Isn't that bright? You see, the instinct to survive was built in.

"The rest of us didn't have it. All the time we were breaking into pictures, Clara Bow was the rage, and most girls were trying to imitate her. I know I did. Now my older sister, Polly Ann, was too sweet, too genuine, too much of a lady to do that. That would have been beneath her. And Loretta was intelligent enough to use the daintiness and the ballerina glamor to make herself into something original.

"Sweet Loretta—she never doubted that what she was doing was right for her. As a child she made costumes, and she and I would try out for stage productions. We didn't have a routine or a real scene. Imagine! We just kind of made it up as we went along. I always played the male. It must have been awful. Naturally, we were never chosen. That deflated me, but it angered her. I'd be so crushed, and she'd say, 'Wht do they know! They're not going to depress me.'

"You know, we all have our strengths. And Loretta didn't seem to mind rejection like I did. She didn't take it personally. I think I wanted to be in films as much as she did, maybe more. I'm being very honest now: I can look back and remember wanting a part so badly that when I didn't get it, I'd be ill for two or three weeks. After I'd got clobbered too often, it wasn't worth it anymore to me. Any rejection she got just made Loretta more determined.''

Upon signing with the studio, Loretta left school to be privately tutored. After her unbilled appearance in *Her Wild Oat* she was entrusted with a small part in *Whip Woman*. Her brief moments on the screen attracted the attention of MGM director Herbert Brenon, who had already tested forty-seven other girls for the role of the childlike Simonetta, opposite Lon Chaney in *Laugh, Clown, Laugh*. He contacted First National and arranged to test Loretta. After looking at her scene many times, he was of two minds about it. One evening he took it to his Malibu cottage to show it to his dinner guests Anna Q. Nilsson and Claire DuBrey. "When Herbert ran the test, his ninety-year-old mother put her feet on the mantel and closed her eyes while he fidgeted," Miss DuBrey remembers. "As we watched, we realized why he was in doubt. It was a circus story, requiring Loretta to wear tights. She had unbelievably thin legs, very knobby knees, and she was as slim as Twiggy. But she had a pretty face and beautiful eyes. Herbert wanted our opinions, and Anna and I reassured him. He asked, 'But what about those knees?' and we told him that her face was so beautiful no one would notice her legs. If we'd said, 'My God, those knees! They'll laugh her off the screen!' who knows what would have happened? But we didn't, and indirectly that evening led to her long career."

Having won a leading role, Loretta began to understand the demands of professionalism. When she played a scene to the best of her ability, only to be asked to change her approach and try again, she could no longer shrug off the criticism with her what-does-he-know attitude. Brenon was a perfectionist and a tyrant who sometimes drove veteran actors to despair. Almost daily he reduced his inexperienced leading lady to tears. When at last she fled from the set and threw herself on the floor, sobbing, Lon Chaney followed and soothed her, explaining that if she met only half of Brenon's demands, she would deliver a performance worth all the pain and frustration she was experiencing. Loretta obviously listened to the star's counsel. For no matter what her private feelings may have been, she seldom again indulged in emotional outbursts that delayed production. This almost superhuman self-control was a major factor in sustaining her long career.

Laugh, Clown, Laugh turned out to be only mildly successful. Critical attention focused on Chaney. Loretta emerged relatively unscathed. Louella Parsons voiced the opinion of many in her review:

> A charming child is Loretta Young, girlish and winsome, and with some of the appeal that has made Betty Bronson such an enjoyable little actress. Little Miss Young, who plays Simonetta, is still inexperienced

and a trifle self-conscious, but she will overcome that in time. She is a promising little actress with a screen personality that is different from the average bobbed-hair flapper. . . .

After her starring role Loretta reverted to playing conventional ingenues in her remaining three features that year. *The Squall,* her first release in 1929, provided the opportunity to demonstrate that she possessed a "microphone voice." The plot concerned the experiences of a Hungarian family that takes a gypsy lass to live with them. Myrna Loy, sporting brown makeup and speaking in broken English, had the pivotal role while Loretta was cast as the daughter in the family. Critics found the dialogue less from Hungary than hunger and ridiculed the production. Its only importance then or now was that it established that both Loretta and Miss Loy would survive the transition from silence to sound.

Loretta was again promoted to leading lady status in *The Glass Booth* and performed effectively enough that the studio decided to build her and Douglas Fairbanks, Jr., as a romantic team in the Janet Gaynor-Charles Farrell tradition. But three negligible scripts and Loretta's cool detachment doomed the attempt. The extent of her impact might be capsuled by a recurring adjective from reviews of the Fairbanks-Young films: she was "decorative."

Nevertheless, somebody up there was impressed. By the time she was sixteen she had been assigned her own wardrobe woman, hairdresser and makeup man. Although still not a star, she behaved like one at the studio and at home. "Polly and I were filled with doubt," Sally Blane says. "If Loretta was, she never let us realize it. I don't mean this in a negative way—but no one really knew her. She was always acting, always. She had been only twelve and a half at the time she worked with Colleen Moore, so we didn't pay any attention to her airs. But now, when she came home and pulled her leading-lady act—no way were we going to let her get away with it. So when she acted as if everything were hers, we'd strike back.

"We'd call her the Duchess and things like that. I put a star on her bedroom door, and did she hate me for that! Later she said I'd hurt her terribly, and I think I probably did. While the studio encouraged or at least tolerated her little princess behavior, we'd level with her, and that was a very cruel thing for sisters to do, I suppose."

It did achieve results. Once Loretta heard that Kay Francis went directly to bed upon arriving home from the studio, dined from a tray, studied her script and switched off the light by 9 P.M. She decided to emulate the star. But the moment the room was dark, Polly, Sally and their friends rushed in and at 9:05 routed Loretta from bed, ending the experiment—if not Loretta's impulse to observe and imitate the reigning stars of the day.

Loretta's private life developed at almost the same clip as her career. On January 26, 1930, she and her leading man, Grant Withers, who had been playing love scenes both on- and offscreen during the making of *The Second Story Murder,* chartered a plane and eloped to Yuma, Arizona. Loretta had turned seventeen only twenty days earlier and, despite her association with the film industry, was as unworldy as her fiercely protective family could keep her. She later ruefully observed that she had been so shielded from ordinary boy-girl relationships that she knew nothing of puppy love. When she'd found herself physically attracted to Withers, she had mistakenly thought she was in the grip of the indestructible passion poets sing about.

Withers, seemingly a dashing adventurer, but whose devil-may-care air hid a weakling's insecurities, was Arrow-collar handsome. Although more sophisticated members of the film colony regarded him as a likable ne'er-do-well, Loretta saw him as her white knight. He was seven years older than she, divorced and the father of an eight-year-old son. He had reached Los Angeles on a wave of publicity as the heroic rescuer of flood victims in a Colorado catastrophe. When the publicity had failed to bring him the anticipated film offers, he had driven a truck and worked briefly as a reporter. Finally, he succeeded in obtaining work as an extra and eventually landed a contract at Warner's.

Warned by actor Carrol Nye that Withers was "not solid husband material," Loretta replied that she loved him—and anyway, she had to find out what "it was all about." The couple surreptitiously rented a honeymoon hideaway at the El Royale Apartments at 450 North Rossmore and furnished it. "What a lark it was. We would sneak over separately to examine our furniture and draperies," Loretta said shortly after her marriage. "Oh, what a happy time!" When the furnishing was completed, Loretta and Withers eloped.

Upon their return Loretta'a mother was at the airport to whisk her daughter away from Withers, insisting that annulment proceedings be instituted immediately. The distraught groom drove off alone and several hours later become involved in an auto accident, injuring three girls and a boy.

A family conference convened the following day. Included were the young couple and their mothers. Gladys Belzer was determined to annul the civil ceremony, and Mrs. Norma Withers, who had already managed to break up her son's first marriage, supported Mrs. Belzer.

The next morning a press conference was held on the set, at which Loretta was almost too acquiescent. "You see, my mother thinks we were too impulsive," she explained. "She thinks we should wait until I am old enough to assume the responsibilites of marriage. She thinks marriage would interfere with my career."

The reporters inquired what Withers felt. "We aren't especially happy about it, but, of course, we will defer to Loretta's mother," he said, bowing to Mrs. Belzer, who had stationed herself in a director's chair on the set to keep the couple under surveillance while they were filming love scenes.

Meanwhile, other troubles developed. Inez Withers, Grant's ex-wife, petitioned to have his child support payments increased from $60 to $300 a month. She contended that he was a $150-a-month extra when they divorced and that he now earned $3,000 per month. She needed extra money for their son's medical and military school expenses.

Despite Withers' and Loretta's seeming docility, they suddenly disappeared on February 5. Mrs. Belzer made no comment. The manager of the El Royale denied that the couple were occupying the apartment they had rented prior to the wedding, but a handyman volunteered to reporters that Mr. and Mrs. Withers were only out for the evening. And Loretta's stepfather, George Belzer, fumed to newsmen, "The apparent friendliness of Withers and Loretta toward the annulment proceedings was nothing but an attempt to fool Mrs. Belzer. They had that friendly talk last Sunday just so they could disappear as they have done."

The next day the Witherses appeared at the studio to resume filming, and Mrs. Belzer's attorney conceded that legal proceedings had been dropped since girls could legally marry at fifteen in Arizona.

"My happiness is the only thing at stake," Loretta told newsmen. "We intend to remain man and wife. We are deeply in love with each other, and I am extremely happy. I love my mother, but I love Grant and he loves me, and that's all that matters." In another interview she said, "I'm very much in love with Grant. So much in love that I couldn't do my best work if we were not married." Exhibiting a characteristically practical quality, she added, "If I had thought marriage would have harmed my career, I might have considered further!"

As Mrs. Belzer had predicted, domesticity soon began to weigh on the couple. To complicate the situation, Withers' popularity did not keep pace with his wife's, and he was forced to accept a vaudeville tour. While he was gone, Loretta moved in with her mother, announcing that she had decided to end the marriage, although there would be no quick divorce. "If I do decide to divorce Grant in the end, I shall never, never go to Reno for it! I wouldn't dream of such a thing!" She made it clear that marrying in haste was one thing, but dissolving even a civil ceremony quickly was not proper.

Informed that Withers was inconsolable over her decision, Loretta sniffled, "Nobody need worry about Grant. He's getting along quite nicely."

Stung, Withers conferred upon Loretta the epithet that was to cling to her ever after when he bitterly described her as the Steel Butterfly. (As it turned out, Loretta was mistaken about Wither's ability to get along. He drifted into alcoholism and in 1954 narrowly escaped death from an overdose of sleeping pills. Three years later he was hospitalized with second-degree burns, having set the bed afire after falling asleep with a lighted cigarette in his hand. Finally, on March 27, 1959, he scribbled a message: "Please forgive me, my family. I was so unhappy. It's better this way. Thanks to all my friends. Sorry I let them down." Without bothering to sign his name, he gulped down a lethal dose of barbiturates.)

At the eventual divorce hearing, Loretta testified that her husband had provided her with only one dress during the marriage while she had paid for all their housing and their food. Mrs. Belzer followed her daughter to the stand, confirming that Withers had covered only a few minor expenses.

The demands of Loretta's career might have destroyed the relationship without any interference. During 1930 and 1931 Loretta appeared in fourteen pictures. Neither the films nor her performances were memorable. Her acting was bland. It neither marred the picture nor contributed anything beyond the pleasure to be derived from her fresh beauty. In several of these features she supported major stars, including John Barrymore and Otis Skinner, who were past their prime. Occasionally she was lent to another studio. For example, Warner's decided it added box-office stature for her to appear opposite Ronald Colman in *The Devil to Pay* at the Goldwyn Studios. But there were also dangers involved in being lent out. When she reported to Columbia to play a newspaper reporter in *Platinum Blonde*, her unobtrusive working girl role could hardly be expected to compete for audience response with Jean Harlow's flamboyant histrionics as, of all things, a society girl. Mostly she was used in movies whose modest ambitions are suggested by their very titles: *Loose Ankles, I Like Your*

Nerve or *Too Young to Marry*, a feature whose chief claim to the public's attention was that it exploited Loretta's personal life by teaming her with her by then estranged husband.

Still, the advantages of the contract sytem are vividly illustrated by Loretta's career between 1931 and 1933. She and scores of her contemporaries under this arrangement benefited from the opportunity to learn, fail, move forward, fail again and eventually develop a style and master their craft. In the meantime, whether the films in which she appeared were strong stories—such as James Cagney's *Taxi*—or ludicrous mishaps—such as Edward G. Robinson's *The Hatchet Man*, in which he and Loretta played Orientals—she was developing a box-office following that identified with her on a level that had little to do with her professional accomplishments. Unlike the instant novas of the 1950s, 60s, and 70s, she and her contemporaries were not immediately starred and subsequently tossed aside after a disappointing performance or two. Unlike Maggie McNamara, Millie Perkins or Doria Halpern, Loretta, Kay and Ginger were allowed what now seems a staggering number of pictures to demonstrate their strengths and weaknesses.

Occasionally, as in *Life Begins*, a script inspired Loretta to make an unusual effort. The picture was set in a maternity hospital, and Loretta's growing ambition and enthusiasm for the part led her to spend a week in a similar institution to observe details and absorb the psychological atmosphere. As she matured, she began to tire of her colorless assignments. Executives were typecasting her as a conventional ingenue. The meatier roles were awarded to actresses who had delivered performances of impact. Having served her apprenticeship, Loretta requested a leave of absence in 1932. She proposed to appear in an outdoor stage production of *Romeo and Juliet* which was to be produced for the benefit of Greater California Charities. Cooler heads persuaded her that a leading role in a Shakespearean play was hardly an appropriate choice for a rising screen personality who had neither training nor experience in the living theater. While refusing permission, Warner's executives promised that she would receive assignments with more depth. Loretta's rebellion was aborted, but she became increasingly vocal in her complaints and pressed the studio for action. "It seems to me I'm always doing parts I don't like, but I never feel that is an excuse for poor work," she said, then added, "I don't feel I've ever done anything particularly striking, but I hope to do something really good."

Warner's-First National was unable or unwilling to trust her with the type of role she was campaigning for, but when Jesse L. Lasky sought

246

to borrow her for *Zoo in Budapest* at Fox, permission was granted. And under the guidance of director Roland V. Leigh Loretta was encouraged to abandon the walls of reserve, to take the risk of allowing trickles of emotion to spill onto the nation's screens. As the runaway girl who hid out in a cave at the zoo Loretta elicited sympathy for all the sensitive misfits of the world. This strangely touching fantasy—set entirely within the zoo, where human beings and animals converse—showed that after thirty-odd undistinguished performances Loretta was capable of projecting a character of some emotional depth.

Encouraged by this achievement, Loretta marshaled all her intelligence, determination and charm in mounting a campaign to secure the leading role opposite Leslie Howard in another fantasy, *Berkeley Square*. She was plunged into gloom when Heather Angel was selected. During one of Loretta's tirades about her misfortune, her mother brought her up short, telling her that she was squandering valuable emotional energy on negative feelings instead of saving it for her screen roles.

Loretta kept her mother's advice in mind when she was lent to MGM for *Midnight Mary*, with Franchot Tone. Although critics were unimpressed with the result, audiences flocked to see Mary's fall, her suffering and her redemption through the love of a good man. It marked another step in Loretta's rise from the synthetic little beauty to an authentic screen personality.

In her struggle to progress, Loretta also began to exhibit new idiosyncrasies during filming. Victor Jory recalls that he was playing one of his first leads opposite her in *The Devil's in Love*. "Now Loretta had been a star at seventeen or eighteen, and I still wasn't a star at twenty-five. So this gloriously beautiful and capable creature was not happy to be loaned to Fox to work with somebody of inferior stature to her," he says. "As a result, the picture has a peculiar love scene in which we didn't actually kiss. It may have looked as if we did, but if you study it closely you'll see she didn't allow any such intimacy." Jory paused, then added, "And on the set she seldom bothered to speak to me. Although many people in my profession have great respect for Loretta, that was my experience with her as a young star. Of course, I understand when you reach a certain plateau while you're very young, you want to maintain that plateau. The only way you can go is down."

Lyle Talbot, who worked with her in *She Had to Say Yes* around this time, found Loretta far less remote and had a little romance with her. "It was Buzz Berkeley's first nonmusical directorial job, and the studio insisted on protecting itself by making George Amy co-director,"

Talbot says. "Amy had been a film editor. Both guys resented it, and a power struggle developed. Somehow Amy got Loretta on his side. She had the idea that this magnificent musical choreographer and director didn't know what he was doing. I didn't particularly want to get involved until I noticed poor Buzz was having a sandwich sent in to spend time working on the script. My God, it was just a simple little picture, not *Gone with the Wind* or anything. So I finally leveled with Loretta. I said, 'Listen, give the guy a break. Don't work against him and so forth,' and I must say, after I told her what was going on, she did cooperate with Buzz. The picture didn't turn out very well, but the parts we were doing didn't call for talent. Most parts in those days didn't. I liked Loretta and Kay Francis and Ginger, at the time I worked with her. Of the three, I suppose Ginger would be the best actress, the most versatile. But I don't know whether any of them could be considered inspired in the way Stanwyck sometimes was."

About a month before *A Man's Castle* was placed in production, Spencer Tracy and his wife, Louise, separated, and the actor moved to a hotel. What tormented him most, he confessed, was that the separation was not caused by any failing of his wife's but rather by something within himself that he couldn't analyze or even talk about. He began to drink heavily to assuage his loneliness and the guilt he felt at leaving her with the reponsibility for rearing their two small children.

After filming commenced, his problems mounted. Studio employees were regularly deployed to find him, throw him under a cold shower, pour black coffee down his throat and bring him to the studio to resume shooting. Tracy was trouble. But when he acted, his genius in depicting character made his self-destructive behavior seem all the more tragic. For a strong-willed, resolute woman such as Loretta had become the attractions were multifaceted. She admired his talent, responded to his craggy masculinity and was infinitely moved by his soul-wracking torment.

She began to invent excuses to keep him from returning to his empty hotel room or from joining drinking buddies after work. One evening she suggested they dine together to explore a particularly difficult scene scheduled for the next day. On another occasion she claimed that her car was unavailable. Would it be too troublesome for him to drive her home? And when they arrived, she invited him to meet her mother and her sisters. From there nature took its course. They found themselves deeply in love and took few pains to conceal it. They dined in Hollywood's popular restaurants, danced at leading nightclubs and attended the theater together. They saw each other's current films and admired each other's performances.

Naturally, the romance stirred gossip. Loretta, who had earlier given a lighthearted interview in which she claimed she always fell in "love" with co-workers, estimated that since she had been in films she had been in "love" at least fifty times. She lived to regret her levity. Tracy heard about her remarks—and just as he later told Katharine Hepburn not to worry about being taller, he's soon cut her down to his size—he called Loretta to say he hoped he wasn't "just the fifty-first guy in line."

When *A Man's Castle* was finished, the romance intensified. By the beginning of 1934 Loretta was openly discussing her feelings. "In many ways," she told interviewer Jack Grant, immediately correcting herself: "many, many ways Spencer measures up to my standards of a man. I was first attracted to him by my profound respect for his ability as an actor. Yet there is nothing actorish about him. He even scorns greasepaint."

She found Tracy continuously interesting and totally lacking in conceit. What seemed to her a rare quality in a male, she said, exhibiting a bit of feminist chauvinism, was a "refined mind."

Her family approved of Tracy, and she hoped that he was the man whom she had been waiting for since the dissolution of her marriage to Withers. She would know whether this was true by the time that Tracy was free to talk of love and marriage.

"I am not at all ashamed of my affection for Spencer Tracy," Loretta told Grant. "I haven't said anything about it until now, but I am sick and tired of being referred to as 'the woman in Spencer's life.'" Never having paid attention to reports linking her to or even having her engaged to men she hardly knew, she was disturbed to be regarded as "a designing wench who had broken up Tracy's marriage."

Loretta's life focused on Tracy—on what already was and what would be. Then it suddenly dawned on her that she was daydreaming when she talked of becoming Mrs. Tracy. Both she and Tracy were Catholics, and although hers had been a civil ceremony, the Tracys had been married in church. Shortly afterward Loretta advised Tracy to return to his wife and refused to see him again.

Having broken off the relationship, Loretta set out on her first European trip, accompanied by her mother. She later confessed that she had been unable to stop thinking of Tracy until she picked up a newspaper in London and saw that he had reconciled with his wife.

A few months later Helen Louise Walker inquired during an interview whether Loretta felt her "experience" had deepened or helped her to mature. "Loretta gazed at me with wide, shocked eyes. 'It isn't just an *experience*,' she protested in a horrified voice, and I realized my term for her had been a desecration. . . . I had been irrelevant," Miss Walker wrote. "Something cosmic and permanent had happened to her. No one knows what will come of it. But it has left permanent marks on Loretta."

To backtrack, Loretta's 1934 releases under her new contract with Twentieth Century, Inc., or on loan-out were disappointing. She remained a leading lady in prestigious productions and co-starred in programmers. In *Born to Be Bad* Marguerite Tazelaar of the New York *Herald Tribune* found her portrayal of the callous unwed mother a refreshing change from the usual treacle she was cast in. "Miss Young gives a good performance of a bad heroine," Miss Tazelaar wrote. But that film was an exception. In Ronald Colman's *Bulldog Drummond Strikes Back* and *Clive of India,* and Charles Boyer's *Caravan* and *Shanghai* Loretta almost erased the interest aroused by *Zoo in Budapest* and *A Man's Castle.* Her most notable contribution to the pageantry of Cecil B. DeMille's *The Crusades*, with Henry Wilcoxon, was a flattering blond wig. Though there was scant praise in the reviews for her, this teaming with top leading men attracted large audiences, including a growing number of people who were won over by her ladylike bearing, ripening beauty and attractive speaking voice.

To be cast in *Call of the Wild* as the co-star of Clark Gable, who had just won an Academy Award for his performance in *It Happened One Night,* further enhanced Loretta's reputation. In addition, the chemistry between the two seemed perfect for the screen. The soft, ultrarefined daintiness that was her trademark worked as an excellent contrast to the good-natured, fearless, yet somehow suave roughnecks that Gable played so well. Since he was already emotionally, if not in fact, estranged from his wife, Ria, it was inevitable that during the location shooting, columnists should regularly report a sizzling romance between Hollywood's preeminent male sex symbol and a woman who easily qualified as one of Hollywood's ten most beautiful women. The love affair was taken so seriously that there was even speculation that Gable would divorce his wife and marry Loretta.

It must have seemed odd to her, therefore, that upon the film's release reviewers complained that the Gable-Young love scenes lacked fire.

Both Loretta and Gable denied that there was anything more than an enduring friendship between them. In November, when he moved out of the home he shared with Ria and into the Beverly Hills Hotel, he specifically denied reports linking him to three women, including Loretta, whom he said he hadn't "ever been out with."

The previous August, Twentieth Century, Inc., had assigned Loretta the title role in *Ramona* but then announced that she was withdrawing because of ill health. Since she had been plagued by illness previously, the report drew only cursory attention until certain overemphatic gossip column items led puzzled readers to conclude that lurid rumors must be circulating. For instance, on October 29 columnist Lloyd Pantages lectured: "Stuff and nonsense! I very much fear that Loretta Young's illness will necessitate her retirement from the screen for at least a year. Her unfortunate case proves the old adage 'the show must go on' is foolishness personified. She hasn't been feeling well for over a year now, and still she goes on making picture after picture until her health is sapped."

Two days later, in the October 31 issue of the *Hollywood Reporter,* another ominous item appeared: "Loretta Young's ill-health, which has already forced her out of 'Ramona,' 20th-Fox's first full-color picture, is expected to lead to the announcement shortly that the studio will retire the star from the screen for a full year."

Stuff and nonsense, as Pantages put it. Who decided the exact length of Loretta's incapacitation? Why a full year? And what was the exact nature of her illness? Is it any wonder that sensational rumors abounded about "the real" reason for her seclusion? Dorothy Manners spelled out some of what was being bruited about in the January, 1936, issue of *Photoplay.* In an article innocuously titled "Fame, Fortune and Fatigue" Miss Manners entered a blanket denial that Loretta was (1) suffering from an incurable illness; (2) marred by a secret accident; (3) penniless and supported by kind friends; (4) the secret bride of a secret marriage and in retirement to have a secret child. Actually, Miss Manners contended, Loretta was building up strength to prepare for major surgery that she must eventually undergo. "For this is the truth about Loretta Young's mysterious illness," she concluded.

Mysteriously, a month after the magazine (with its long deadline and predating a month ahead) was off the stands, Loretta, who "had had such a long and dangerous illness," was looking "more beautiful than ever." No further mention was made of the major surgery Miss Manners had stressed. Fans were now assured that Loretta had recovered entirely from what suddenly became "the cough and cold that kept her in seclusion for so many months." Whatever the studio's intentions, these conflicting releases served only to arouse further suspicions.

Adding fuel to the speculation was the fact that she rushed into two minor films one after another and followed them with *Ramona*. In postponing the picture until she was able to make it, Zanuck, who had guided her career from early on at Warner's, demonstrated his unflagging faith in her box-office appeal. If further evidence of his belief in her future was needed, it came in her next film, when he trusted her to equal the impact of such powerhouse personalities as Janet Gaynor, Constance Bennett and a new French import, Simone Simon. In this film, *Ladies in Love*, Zanuck tentatively teamed Loretta with the handsomest newcomer of the decade, Tyrone Power. The reaction was so positive that the studio publicized them as the only love team on the screen—ignoring Rogers and Astaire, Ruby Keeler and Dick Powell, Kay Francis and George Brent and Jeannette MacDonald and Nelson Eddy.

The romance with Gable and Loretta's subsequent illness were almost forgotten by May 11, 1937, when she made a move that revived earlier speculation. Despite stringent California laws restricting adoption of a child by a single person, Loretta began proceedings to obtain two children. She said that she had lost her heart to them while decorating a Christmas tree in an orphanage in San Diego.

Once again confusion arose. The children were first described as boys; then a boy, James, three, and a girl, Judy, twenty-three months. James turned out to be Jane, who was later said to have been reclaimed by her natural parents. Subsequently, all mention of the mysterious James-Jane was omitted.

Over the years numerous writers alluded to the "real" reason for Loretta's illness. The underground version—and the most widely accepted one—was that Loretta and Gable had had a romance during the filming of *Call of the Wild*. Discovering that she was pregnant, and devout Catholic that she was, she had refused to consider an abortion. As she later said about the girls at St. Anne's, an adoption service for unwed mothers, "Bad girls don't have babies." In any case, scandal sheets periodically revived the rumor that Loretta had actually adopted her natural-born child. And in any discussion of her with associates some allusion to the story usually pops up.

One of her former representatives says that Loretta and Gable had "a mild romance" during the making of the film and recalls sitting on the edge of the bed discussing business with them one morning. Asked whether she became pregnant, he says he has no way of knowing and wouldn't tell if he did. He requests that his name not be mentioned.

Another former co-worker claims that when she was ill after the birth of her second child, she employed a nurse who told her, "Loretta didn't adopt that child. She's hers." The nurse claimed to have worked on the staff of the hospital where the child was born. "Now that nurse was a good Catholic woman who had nothing against Loretta, and there was no reason for her to lie."

Another business acquaintance of the I'll-tell-you-but-don't-use-my-name school says she visited the star and her daughter in Lake Tahoe many years ago while the child was recovering from cosmetic surgery on her ears.

A chum of Judy's has said she was once told by Judy that she had not been informed of her real father's identity until she reached the age of sixteen. And a friend of later years claims that one evening, while he was with Judy, an actress, emboldened by alcohol, asked point-blank whether Gable was Judy's father. How had Judy reacted? She simply gave an enigmatic little laugh.

Needless to say, there is no way to prove that Judy is Loretta's child. But when the late William Wellman, director of *Call of the Wild*, was asked whether the rumor was true, the irrepressible Wellman said, "All I know is that Loretta and Clark were very friendly during the picture, and it was very cold up there. When the filming was finished, she disappeared for a while and later showed up with a daughter with the biggest ears I ever saw except on an elephant."

"There's nothing wrong with Loretta having a child," a former studio head says. "And her way of expiating has been to raise a great deal of money for that home for unwed mothers. As Loretta said once—bad girls don't have their babies."

In today's permissive society the flap about the child appears grotesquely out of proportion—especially since Loretta long ago listed among things that had no interest to her that old bogey: "What will people say?"

Which was probably lucky because being a beautiful, spirited, unmarried Hollywood star caused "people" to spread numerous stories about her relationships with, to name only a few, George Brent, Gilbert Roland, Ricardo Cortez, Wayne Morris, Herbert Somborn, directors Eddie Sutherland, Joseph Mankiewicz and Gregory Ratoff; writers John McClain and Robert Riskin; tennis star Fred Perry; socialite Jock Whitney; Tyrone Power, Jimmy Stewart, Cesar Romero, David Niven and playboy William Buckner.

Loretta met the thirty-year-old Buckner, who claimed to be the nephew of Thomas A. Backer, chairman of the board of the New York Life Insurance Company, in 1937. The handsome, colorful, free-spending Buckner made a splash in Hollywood, where he was variously identified in the press as a "wealthy young broker," "a playboy," "a financier," "a socialite" and a "young tycoon." Loretta liked him immediately, and after he asked to take her to mass, she began dating him exclusively. When some of her cautious friends mentioned that Buckner had approached them with what seemed questionable financial schemes, Loretta impulsively brushed aside their warnings and rushed ahead with the friendship.

As usual, she introduced Buckner to her family, whose reactions were so favorable that she invited him to move into her guest house. When she and Buckner were apart, she wired and wrote of her deepening affection for him. There was little question about whom she was thinking when she told an interviewer, apparently having forgotten her resolutions when divorcing Withers, "When I fall in love again, I'll marry the man immediately. Long engagements are stuffy and have nothing to do with marital happiness."

She must have been somewhat shaken when Buckner was arrested on charges of mail fraud and attempting to defraud buyers of Philippine Railway bonds of $100,000. He immediately called to tell her not to worry, and she was loyal and ingenuous enough to release a statement that the charges would not affect their friendship. The moment he gained his freedom on $5,000 bail, he posted an additional $2,000 bond, enabling him to fly to California to attend church with Loretta.

During his New York trial Loretta's love letters to him—with some of "the more vivid incidents" deleted—and letters by his associates, revealing that he had initially courted her with the intention of borrowing money and then fallen in love with her, were introduced into evidence. Embarrassing as their contents must have been to her, Loretta stood by Buckner, testifying in his behalf. He was found guilty and sentenced to serve a prison term.

Loretta's eventful private life far outstripped the monotony of the inconsequential pictures Zanuck assigned her. By this time she was more than adequate in roles that were beneath or beyond criticism. Plots were almost interchangeable, and once the studio czar discovered a salable title, he was quick to recycle it for her. When *Love Is News* turned out to be popular, he came up with *Love Under Fire;* just as *Wife, Doctor and Nurse* inevitably begot *Wife, Husband and Friend.* Miracle of miracles, *Suez* was not followed by *Zeus.*

Zanuck's decision to cast Loretta as Empress Eugenie to Ty Power's

Ferdinand de Lesseps focused her growing dissatisfaction. Power's role was obviously the more important. Stories abound relating her tactics—growing distractingly long fingernails, waving a handkerchief and other scene-stealing tricks—to protest the downgrading of her stature. Veteran director Allan Dwan dismisses these tales. "I suppose like all actresses she worried whether her talents were being properly utilized or whether she was being mistreated, but I didn't allow her to get away with anything that detracted from the picture. She'd kicked around a good deal in films. She was experienced, even though she was young.

"She fitted the part of Eugenie like a glove—an ambitious woman who took advantage of the situation and married the king. Never mind the young man who loved her and whom she loved. Will to succeed took precedence over love. She understood that. Loretta was always above everything, you know. And she used that quality in Eugenie, of having complete control over her situation and being vastly superior to everybody. It came naturally for her to make you feel that everyone she came in contact with was far beneath her."

In *Kentucky* Loretta was teamed with Richard Greene, another actor who, like Power, was almost as pretty as she was. But it was gravel-voiced, craggy-faced Walter Brennan who stole the spotlight from her and Greene and won an Oscar as the best actor of the year in a supporting role.

Despite her $4,000 per week earnings,* Loretta became increasingly disenchanted. By 1939 even the enthusiasm she aroused as a light comedienne left her unhappy at Zanuck's reluctance to trust her with complex roles. And when her longtime mentor insisted she play the deaf wife in *The Story of Alexander Graham Bell* starring Don Ameche, Loretta began talking seriously with agent Phil Berg about the advisability of free-lancing. Berg agreed.

"I suppose the family contributed to her discontent," Sally Blane says. "I know I was always completely frank with her. When she was good, I was impressed and told her so. And when she wasn't, I used to tell her that I didn't think the picture was worthy of her. Because I don't believe she even realized at that point how gifted she was. She knew I wasn't doing it to hurt her. But I was her sister, and I was convinced that she was capable of so much more. The trouble was she didn't associate with the kind of people who would have pushed her to greatness. Great! Great! Great! No, greatness wasn't their goal. The talent was there, but it was being wasted on the nonsense, the re-

*Including radio compensation.

worked stories, the posing and the clothes. All the studio cared about was making a profit.''

The pervasive influence of the major studios is demonstrated by what happened to Loretta after she terminated her contract. Columnist Jimmy Fidler accused her of greed and ingratitude and advised her to return to the fold, predicting Zanuck would welcome her. Word spread that she had grown temperamental and generally uncooperative. In the year when 3,000 independent theater owners selected her as the most popular star, offers for parts in major productions were notably scarce. She occupied a place on a gray list of shunned stars.

Seven months elapsed between the release of *Alexander Graham Bell* and the premiere of Walter Wanger's production of *Eternally Yours*, co-starring David Niven. This thin little comedy was an inauspicious beginning for Loretta's free-lance career.

Worse still, she was forced to cut her salary from $150,000 to $50,000 per picture* before Harry Cohn could be persuaded to bring her to Columbia for two pictures of the same genre: *The Doctor Takes a Wife,* with Ray Milland, and *He Stayed for Breakfast,* opposite Melvyn Douglas. In the Douglas disaster, rich American Loretta sets out to convert the USSR's Douglas to her point of view. Critics jeered at her character's approach to the ideological struggle between Capitalism and Communism, the jingoistic philosophizing and the reduction of life to the sexual equation—i.e., "You are always talking about the poor and the rich. There are only two kinds of people—male and female.''

At the time Loretta probably saw nothing simplistic about the script. After an early marriage and a parade of suitors she had finally met a man who made her want to believe that love solved all problems. As her film work diminished, she had increased network radio appearances. While working in radio, she met Thomas H. A. Lewis, a thirty-eight-year-old New Englander who had gained considerable success in radio and advertising.

Lewis, who had previously dated Bette Davis, was ending a relationship with Glenda Farrell. In any case, he initially did not interest Loretta. When he phoned in his official capacity to set an 11 A.M. Sunday rehearsal, Loretta announced that she always attended mass at that hour. Like Buckner, Lewis immediately scored points by proposing they attend an early one together and then rehearse the show. It was a fortuitous suggestion because Loretta, who had founts of holy water on the

*In 1939, the $75,000 figure was given, but it was later emended to $50,000.

wall beside each doorway in her home, found in Lewis someone even more conscientious about observing rituals than she was.

This peerless couple was wed at the Church of St. Paul in Westwood on July 3, 1940. Attempting to ensure a decorous atmosphere, the bride and groom limited attendance to their families and intimate friends. Loretta's brother, Jack, gave her away, and her half sister, Georgiana, was maid of honor. The groom's brother, Dr. Charles Lewis, served as best man. After the marriage ceremony, performed by one priest, a second celebrated the nuptial mass.

Outside the church a mob of 3,000 had gathered. However reverent and dignified Loretta had hoped to keep her wedding, the crowd was not to be denied. When she and Tom emerged from the church, her fans burst through the barricades and swarmed around the couple, showering them with rice. In the joyous turmoil four overemotional women swooned and had to be carried to the rectory, while five policemen sweated and fought to clear a path allowing the bridal limousine to move away.

After a wedding breakfast-reception Loretta and Tom left for a secret honeymoon. But soon she was back in Hollywood, delivering opinions about the marital state: "Marriage is the only real career for a mature woman, and I'm glad I will no longer be referred to as a 'bachelor girl,' " she told one reporter.

"If Tom wanted me to stop being Loretta Young and become just Mrs. Tom Lewis, I'd do it in a minute," she assured a columnist. "Maybe you think I'm kidding, but I'm not."

But Tom had no intention of asking her to abandon her career, even though his own work as an advertising executive kept him in New York six months out of twelve. As a free-lancer Loretta made two films annually while she and Lewis were in California and spent the remainder of the year in New York with him. Even so, she earned the equivalent of what she had received under Twentieth Century-Fox. "Best of all, I can choose my films," she told columnist Sheilah Graham. "I don't have to do twelve bad pictures for every good one."

But her marital Eden was soon disrupted when America entered World War II and Lewis enlisted. At loose ends, Loretta signed for a picture. Movie attendance in 1941 had reached 85,000,000 weekly and was growing. Almost every film made a profit, but Loretta played it extra safe by agreeing to do her first Western, a genre that never lost money. She chose Universal's *The Lady from Cheyenne,* opposite Robert Preston.

She then returned to Columbia for three pictures. In *The Men in Her*

Life she played a circus performer transformed into a ballerina. She delivered a performance of such narcissism that a disgusted Bosley Crowther flatly stated that she was not a good actress and that her lack of resemblance to a dancer was laughable.

She followed with *Bedtime Story*. Harry Cohn had reluctantly granted her billing over Fredric March, but when she attempted to charge the studio $300 for a dress she was providing, Cohn, who had fought his way up from poverty row, refused to pay and tried to rescind her top billing. Loretta promptly retaliated by turning up for fittings on her substitute gown so late in the day that wardrobe workers had to be paid overtime. Although subsequently she made *A Night to Remember* for Columbia, she and Cohn stopped speaking to each other before *Bedtime Story* started shooting. Not until several years later did she impetuously slip up behind him at a party, put her hands over his eyes and whisper, "I'm sorry. I was wrong."

Both *A Night to Remember* and *Bedtime Story* further eroded Loretta's standing. *Bedtime Story,* a frivolous piece about an actress-wife who leaves her playwright-husband because he thwarts her retirement by writing new roles for her, had the bad luck to follow Tracy and Hepburn's *Woman of the Year* into Radio City Music Hall. Since *Woman of the Year* also dealt with what was known as the battle of the sexes, comparison was inevitable. Loretta's sulking, self-righteous actress was no match for Hepburn's political pundit who could tell generals how to plan a battle but couldn't crack an egg without breaking the yolk.

It began to seem doubtful that Loretta would choose one good role in twelve—or even twenty-four. Whether the studio was Columbia, Paramount or Universal, whether the hero was as flamboyant as Orson Welles or as understated as Gary Cooper, Loretta fared poorly. Not only they, but also Frederic March, David Niven and Brian Aherne dominated the pictures she chose. Her playing of the deaf girl opposite Ladd in *And Now Tomorrow* brought this blast from Bosley Crowther: "As the lady, Miss Young gives a performance which may best be compared to a Fannie Brice imitation of a glamorous movie queen. Whatever it was that this actress never had, she still hasn't got it."

It appeared that what Warner's had inflicted on Kay Francis, Loretta was managing to do to herself. Was it poor judgment in scripts or something else? *And Now Tomorrow* had been based on Rachel Field's best-selling novel. *The Perfect Marriage,* a play by Samson Raphaelson, who had written so wittily for Lubitsch, had been adapted by a highly regarded screenwriter, Leonard Spigelgass. That many of the difficulties were of Loretta's making can be gleaned from Spigelgass' recollection of the preparations for a troublesome scene. "There were all kinds of problems because she didn't want to mention the word 'divorce,'" he says. "I'd written this one forty different ways, using 'separation' and every other synonym you can imagine. Finally I came down to the set to read her a new version, and when I finished, she looked at me with those large moist eyes and said, 'Oh, I think it's one of the loveliest scenes ever written.' Then she added, 'I just wish I were a good enough actress to play it.'

"Now what a wonderful put-down. It was such a clever way of getting us to do what she wished and at the same time not make us feel bad."

How had he handled it?

"Oh, we had all kinds of tricks in those days," he says. "We'd cut the line or have her mumble. Or in this case we gave the exposition to David Niven in a close-up so she didn't have to be on the set when he said it. The whole play was about a divorce she never got. That's why she agreed to do it. But she wouldn't say 'divorce.' She'd say 'separation,' but not 'divorce.' Very funny when you think of what they say now."

By such shenanigans Loretta contrived to bring her career to an all-time low. Yet, strangely, throughout all this self-defeating behavior and the disastrous pictures she managed to retain a respectable following. Stranger still, in spite of major and minor scandals that had swirled around her, she continued to enjoy the image of an ethereal, almost other-wordly creature, far, far removed from the hurly-burly of Hollywood.

If the war years were professionally a low point for Loretta, she never allowed herself to sink into the slough of despond. In spite of her many years in the film industry, it had remained her business and only a portion of her life. With her mother she bought, remodeled, decorated and sold houses. She was deeply involved in religious and charitable work and led an active social life. She could commit herself just as wholeheartedly to battling Bugsy Siegel in court, when she discovered that termites had once infested the foundations of the Holmby Hills house that she and Lewis had purchased from the mobster, as she could to fighting Harry Cohn over the price of a dress. And she could take just as much pride in her husband's service to his country as in an increase in salary her agent might wangle for her. The security of marriage had somewhat diminished the urge to be in front of the camera.

But it didn't diminish the urge for self-dramatization. When she learned that she was pregnant, she commissioned designers Adrian and Howard Greer to create what she called an *enceinte trousseau*—which would allow her to lead an active social life without violating her sense of decorum. Pregnancy gave her a new role to play. Moving in stately grace, Loretta was enjoying a party at Claudette Colbert's on August 1, 1944, when she went into labor and had to be rushed directly to the hospital. A few hours later she gave birth to Christopher Paul. Less than a year later, on July 15, a second son, Peter, was born. Meanwhile, Lewis had adopted Judy, completing their family group.

Lewis was discharged from the service in 1946, and the family had every reason to anticipate a happy future. For a few months Loretta professed to be entirely content to devote herself to her home, archly confessing to Louella Parsons that Chris and Peter were two leading men she didn't mind being upstaged by.

At this time Loretta actually seemed to glow with happiness. Many people, through no fault of hers, were made a little uneasy by it. Writer Therese Lewis recalls that she was surprised to find how often she subconsciously compared herself to Loretta. "Not that she invited it," says Miss Lewis. "She was amiable, intelligent and entertaining. Her physical beauty was beyond dispute, and her clothes by Irene were worn with greatest presence. She was a wonderful hostess. But through no failing of hers, Loretta gave many people a great sense of inferiority. I wasn't poor by any means, and I was fairly successful as a writer, but I just never felt in her league."

Loretta was ecstatic about her husband ("one of the finest men who ever lived") and made it clear that her inactivity was voluntary. Tom Lewis was in no way threatened by her career and reassured her that he had married her in spite of her being a star. If she had a goal, he didn't want to interfere. On the other hand, if she wished to retire, that would please him, too. "Oh, I'm a fortunate girl in finding a man like Tom," she declared, explaining his admirable qualities in almost the same words she had used to describe Spencer Tracy a dozen years before. "He's completely masculine, yet he also has delicacy and intuition usually found only in women. Those qualities I really need with my personality."

The Lewises attended mass together daily during this blissful period. The entire family could occasionally be glimpsed kneeling humbly at a dusty roadside shrine—if they were not at the fashionable church whose parishioners included Rosalind Russell, Irene Dunne and Louella Parsons, causing some wag to nickname it Our Lady of the Cadillacs.

Among their friends the Lewises were admired for the way they counterbalanced and complemented each other. Tom was intelligent, well educated and, most important of all, successful enough in his field to take pride in and not be threatened by Loretta's worldwide fame.

It seemed a perfect match, but some acquaintances were disturbed by what they interpreted as an overzealousness. For instance, the head of a studio, also a Catholic, attended a funeral of a popular star in a Protestant church. Leaving afterward with the Lewises, he was surprised to hear Lewis chide Loretta for "participating in the services." "Did I? I'm sorry," she said, only to have him respond. "Yes, you did. You shouldn't have done that." In telling the story, the executive shook his head. "Tom was such a phony, such a phony. Here he was excoriating her for participating in the service. What was she supposed to do? Sit there like a klutz? It's especially funny now. The last time I saw him was on a television show of Kathryn Kuhlman's.

"I've always liked Loretta, but she's a strange lady in many ways, too. She's always had the ability to close off certain areas, to keep herself austere and detached. I don't think she was in very close touch with reality about Tom—or a lot of other things, for that matter."

Diana Serra Cary, author of *The Hollywood Posse* and famous as Baby Peggy in silent films, converted to Catholicism in the 1940s and came to know Lewis through a shared interest in founding a liberal Catholic magazine. She began to be disillusioned with him when he told a priest and her that on a recent holy day he had asked God what he could do to demonstrate his humility. Almost immediately he noticed that rocks lining the long drive leading to his home were in need of paint. Digging out an old shirt, faded shorts and tennis shoes, he got down on his hands and knees and set about his humble task. As he worked, often wiping his brow, he became grimy and paint-splattered. When he was at his worst, he looked up to find an obviously important person at his side. The stranger inquired where he could find Mr. Lewis. Struggling with an impulse to conceal his identity, Lewis reluctantly identified himself. Only subsequently did he realize that God had granted his appeal. "It was then I knew I was dealing with the Madison Avenue mind," Miss Cary says.

Later Lewis brought out what he called "candid" photos of his wife. "They were almost Madonnalike," Miss Cary says, "and Tom's attitude toward Loretta was reverent as if she were the Blessed Virgin."

On another occasion Lewis led Miss Cary to a room that he felt illustrated what a wonderful woman his wife was. This sitting room was done in French Provincial with a great deal of blue, including blue walls. He waited for her reaction beyond how attractive it was. When none was forthcoming, he inquired whether she couldn't see what Loretta had done. Miss Cary couldn't. "Why, she has the whole room in the particular shade of blue that is most flattering to all women. That's the kind of person she is," Lewis said, beaming. The straightforward Miss Cary had had more than enough and withdrew from the publishing venture.

For a time Loretta apparently convinced herself that she welcomed simple domestic existence. But she would have been more saintly than even Lewis believed her to be had she resisted the repeated blandishments of producer Dore Schary. Schary was convinced that all she needed was a good script and a firm directorial hand to repair the damage to her career. He was certain he had the script and was eager to persuade her to sign for the package he and David O. Selznick were putting together for RKO.

Like Ginger Rogers, who had at first rejected *Kitty Foyle,* which earned her an Oscar, Loretta read and turned down *Katie.* She said that she didn't feel qualified to attempt a Swedish accent, that the role required a blonde and that, anyway, she was happy to remain a wife and mother.

Schary, a veteran in manipulating star egos, replied, "You're an actress, aren't you?" He assured her that she could acquire the accent and bleach her hair, but that a part as rich in opportunities as this came along once in a career. "It's a gamble," he admitted. "You may flop badly. But if you really play the part, you'll win an Oscar."

It was the proper tack—challenge, reassurance, a fleeting reference to risk and prediction of worldwide acclaim. Loretta accepted the assignment, resolving to be more Swedish than Ingrid Bergman and Garbo.

She hired Ruth Roberts, who had helped Bergman erase her Swedish accent, to assist her in acquiring one. The two women worked eight hours a day for six weeks, and at Miss Roberts' suggestion Loretta read extensively, familiarizing herself with Swedish immigrant psychology. Once production was under way, Lorreta performed beyond her customary level, spurred on by Ethel Barrymore, Joseph Cotten and director H. C. Potter. When the film was shown, audiences were surprised at her deft performance, which had humor, passion and sincerity. *Katie,* retitled *The Farmer's Daughter,* was a comedy hit which vied with *The Best Years of Our Lives* and *The Egg and I* as the top box-office attraction of 1947. At Academy Award time Loretta, Joan Crawford, Susan Hayward, Dorothy McGuire and Rosalind Russell emerged as nominees for the outstanding performance given by a woman in a leading role.

Miss Russell was such an odds-on favorite that Loretta was tempted not to attend the ceremonies. When her name was called, she seemed not to hear it. After she finally reached the stage, she reduced many emotional spectators to tears by reminding them of all her—and by extension their—years of struggle and disappointment as she grasped the statuette and sighed, "At long last!"

Afterward, the Lewises celebrated until 7 A.M., but she characteristically arose in time to go to mass to give thanks for answered prayers. A few weeks later Louella Parsons wrote, "I think it's indicative of Loretta's character that in spite of all the excitements of the Academy Award, she went into retreat which she planned before she won her Oscar. She's consistent on all things—her religion, her marriage and her career."

Possibly true, but impetuousness sometimes made her appear pretentious. In November, 1947, *The Bishop's Wife,* in which she played opposite Cary Grant, was chosen for a Royal Command Performance as part of the festivities celebrating the wedding of Princess Elizabeth and Prince Philip. Loretta, Tom and Judy set off for England in proper fairy-tale fashion, taking with them seven trunks—one entirely filled with soap and other necessities with which Loretta intended to play lady bountiful in an England still in the grip of post-World War II shortages.

Upon her return to the United States in January, 1948, Loretta held a press conference, giving one of her most maudlin performances as she recounted heart-rending stories of conditions in Britain, including a tale about a small girl who asked, when given a chocolate bar, "Do I lick or bite?" She cited an executive who was forced to cut out cardboard soles for his shoes, factory workers who fainted from hunger at 11 A.M. and a shipping reporter who wore a beard because he was unable to buy razor blades.

The London press picked up and spoofed "Life with Loretta in England," but the head of the British Tourist and Holiday Board criticized her sharply. Since she had been ill and confined to her room most of the time she was abroad, how had she seen things he had never seen?

Loretta lamely defended her stories but admitted the information had come secondhand. Nevertheless, she tried to put on a good face by snapping that if her British sources were "fictionalizing," she was glad.

Loretta's halo was tipped slightly askew again in 1948, three months after she won the Academy Award and thirty-one years after John Earl Young had deserted his family. The story broke that on June 6, a man who called himself John V. Earle had died in Los Angeles County General Hospital of a stroke. Polly Ann and Sally attended the simple Christian Science service for him, but Loretta was "too busy with a film assignment."

She did issue a response to queries: "As far as I know, this man may have been my father.

"I never saw him.

"Ten or twelve years ago my parish priest came to me and said that a man who called himself Jack Earle and who said he was my father had come to him needing help.*

"I asked the priest what I should do, and he said that the man's story seemed clear. So I told him to send the man to see my lawyer.

"An arrangement was made for me to contribute to his support, and I have done so ever since. I never heard further from him or about him until just before the funeral."

Her contributions to Earle's support had been known only to the priest and her paternal grandmother, who deplored her son's behavior.

At the time of his demise Gladys Belzer also issued a statement: "I have not seen the children's father since he left us thirty-one years ago. If the man who died under the name of John Earle was really he, I respect his desire to die in the identity he chose and maintained during his life." Nevertheless, his reemergence in death traumatized his ex-wife to the extent that she and George Belzer separated.

In later years Loretta expressed regret that she had sat in judgment of her father, admitting that her behavior was one aspect of her life that she wished she had the power to change. She said that he had been brushed off by the family and that she now felt it had been unforgivable of them all.

Loretta began the last lap of her feature-film career with the ambitious *Rachel and the Stranger* in 1948. She played a bondswoman from the early 1800s who lives with an indifferent husband (William Hol-

---

*An artificial leg.

den)—he married her because he needed a mother for his son—and who is tempted by a dashing Indian scout (Robert Mitchum). Filmed on location near Eugene, Oregon, under the direction of Loretta's brother-in-law, Norman Foster, the picture represented a laudable attempt to dispense with glamorous gowns and to create a powerful character study. In *Rachel* Loretta saw an opportunity to earn a second Academy Award.

On the set she was pleasant but serious. Mitchum, whose wicked sense of humor and peculiar low-key style had unnerved earlier co-workers, began his scene-stealing magic at once. Loretta smiled sweetly and said that lots of leading men had tried to upstage her, but that he was the first to downstage her. Mitchum got the message.

Discarding her mannerisms, Loretta endowed Rachel with simple, honest reactions, foregoing the temptation to overplay her big scenes. The result was one of her most moving performances. Reporters speculated that she might receive another Oscar nomination, but this time she was overlooked.

If *Rachel* roused hope that Loretta had at last abandoned the unambitious type of film that represented the major part of her work, it was a false expectation. She returned to melodramas and slick comedies at once. Most popular of these was Clare Booth Luce's sentimental comedy *Come to the Stable,* in which two naive and unwordly nuns in God's service charm and outwit everyone from crusty businessmen to gangsters. Loretta and Celeste Holm played the leading roles. On the set, a few days into the shooting, public relations man Frank Liberman asked Miss Holm, "Which sister are you?" The witty actress smiled. "The one that's slightly out of focus."

Strangely, where Loretta had been overlooked for her work in *Rachel,* she received a second Oscar nomination for Sister Margaret, but lost to Olivia de Havilland in *The Heiress.* Nevertheless, it remains her favorite role.

While co-starring in *Key to the City* at MGM with her old friend Clark Gable, Loretta collapsed and was rushed to Queen of Angels Hospital. After completing an examination, her beaming physician announced that she was pregnant and ordered her to remain in the hospital for observation. In spite of all precautions, Loretta lost the baby two weeks later.

After she finished the formula-ridden *Key to the City,* the Lewises decided to make a picture together. Doubling as co-author and producer of *Cause for Alarm,* Lewis, with the help of director Tay Garnett, produced a modestly budgeted but carefully wrought suspense film about a paranoid invalid who commits suicide after posting a letter accusing his wife and his doctor of murder.

Lewis wrote the role of the semiglamorous wife in a way that showcased Loretta's dramatic strength while avoiding the perils of excessive emotionalism. Many of her fans consider *Cause for Alarm*—not *The Farmer's Daughter*—her best performance. What the picture reemphasizes are the advantages accruing to an actress when the person in control understands and is committed to furthering her best interests.

After this success Loretta made four more pictures—none worthy of discussion. Yet it would be a serious underestimation of Loretta's steely will to conclude her life's work had come to a sorry end. In a career extending over a quarter of a century probably no other actress ever survived so many devastating reviews. Yet she consistently had the discipline and courage to pull herself together and get on with her work. If a real star is defined as someone the public will come to see even if she chooses to squander her talents reading something approximately as interesting as the Chinese telephone book, then Loretta is a STAR.

In the late 1940s themes that were subsequently so often struck began to echo and reecho: Loretta's eternal youth, her good works, her ideal family life, and her religiosity. Certain reporters approached this tongue in cheek. Jim Marshall in *Collier's*, for instance, observed that Loretta had "in the tradition of film dieties taken to giving out like the Delphic Oracle on a variety of subjects, mainly love, courtship, marriage and how to use leftovers. . . . Miss Young herself is on record," he reported, "concerning love (favorable); hate (the world could well do without it); the most important thing in life (health); her worst fault (forgetting people's names); . . . the greatest influence in her life (mother); what causes divorce (lack of understanding)."

Elsa Maxwell, on the other hand, found Loretta totally admirable, insisting that "even the star's mistakes had made her an actress of greater depth and understanding, sharpening her sense of humor and coloring her personality." Every day in every way, according to Elsa, Loretta was getting better and better.

As president of St. Anne's Foundation, an adoption service for unwed mothers, Loretta raised $41,000 for the institution by staging a four-day charity auction in 1949. Presumably this earned her the Sienna Medal as an outstanding woman and a Golden Apple lapel pin from the Hollywood Women's Press Club at "the most cooperative actress." Through the vigilance of her personal press agent, Helen Ferguson ("I can give a better Loretta Young interview than Loretta"), the actress piled up more honors than any other performer, including some dubious ones such as a "special award" as the first star to appear twenty-five times on the *Lux Radio Theater.*

On the surface, then, she was a woman who had the best of everything. She and Tom moved with heady grace through the upper echelons of the entertainment world. They were blessed with a beautiful family. Although some friends questioned the advisability of buying a house, settling in, selling, uprooting the children and moving every few years, none of the Lewises seemed to object. Yet *home* was hardly a cozy place, whether it happened to be in Beverly Hills, Ojai, Malibu or West Hollywood. Years later Loretta's elder son, Christopher, granted an interview, after his arrest on charges of filming hard-core pornography. To reporter John Marvin of *The Advocate*, he described in a curiously impersonal way his boyhood, when the family occupied a 400-acre ranch on the edge of Beverly Hills and lived in a three-story, twenty-bedroom house.

"My brother and sister and I didn't really come into contact with a lot of other kids," he said. "My parents were always afraid of kidnappings and things like that, and so they were always trying to safeguard us. We had three or four good friends that were shipped in from good families, but like at our birthday parties, we had a whole circus one time. I remember a horse, a polka-dotted horse, that would do tricks. Dogs would jump over and under it and all that stuff.

"And I've got pictures of all our friends that would come around. Alfred Hitchcock and people like that. I remember Clark Gable was a good friend of my mother's, and I kind of remember Carole Lombard. Rosalind Russell was a close friend and Irene Dunne, who's my brother's godmother. And Duke Wayne. Darryl Hickman used to come over and throw us in the pool."

When the interviewer referred to the "wonderland" that set the Lewises apart from other kids, Christopher indicated he hadn't been aware of it. Nor did he exhibit any particular warmth or resentment over the relatively detached existence that was forced on him and his brother and sister by the next development of their mother's career.

As the postwar film audiences grew younger and more discriminating, Loretta's conventional beauty, ladylike demeanor and her prefabricated 99 and 99/100 percent pure heroines no longer coincided with the prevailing mood of neorealism. The antihero or antiheroine now enjoyed acceptance by critics and at the box-office.

Still, Loretta and Tom were shrewd enough to realize that the fans who preferred storybook naïveté in which goodness vanquished evil had not disappeared. They had merely transferred their attention to the new mass medium—television.

In a period when "togetherness" was being merchandised by the media as a panacea for family ills, Loretta and Tom might have served as its symbol. They lived, loved, worshipped and, in 1951, began planning to work together.

Analyzing the blizzard of fan mail that arrived after each showing of a kinescoped dramatic segment Loretta had performed on *The Ken Murray Show,* they devised a format; an anthology of 30-minute programs ranging from comedy to romance to fantasy to melodrama. The premise for each script was to be culled from the fan mail. Everyone connected with the Lewises contributed refinements to the plan, including Helen Ferguson's secretary, who suggested calling the show *Letters to Loretta.*

The company was incorporated as Lewislor Enterprises, Inc., and gambled $30,000 on a pilot film. Using their own considerable experience and employing the most skilled professional talent available, they created a half-hour pilot that was bought by Procter and Gamble, the first sponsor to view it, within forty-eight hours of the initial showing.

On August 21, Loretta announced that she was deserting films for an NBC TV show. As the first major star to make the transition from silent to sound to a weekly television series, Loretta received an exceptional amount of coverage. Much was made of her youthful appearance and her enthusiasm for the new medium. "Right now I'm strictly a television girl, and I love every minute of it," she stated, praising the intimacy of the medium and repeatedly expressing joy at being blessed with a husband who was creative and experienced. "There's an unhealthy trend today to turn vice into virtue and virtue into vice. Morality is being turned upside down," she lectured, sounding for all the world like Ginger Rogers. Loretta wanted to fight for goodness and light. Each week she would play a different role during the first thirty-nine shows, and her repertory would find her in a gingham housedress one week and a Jean Louis gown the next. To guard against the possibility that some viewers, seeing her in a character role, might conclude she had aged overnight, she developed her "trademark" entrance, whirling through the famous doorway each week. Perhaps no one ever described it more vividly than columnist Harriet Van Horne, who wrote, "She doesn't simply walk in beauty like the night. She sweeps and darts like a humming bird at high noon. I often tune in just to watch lovely Loretta's lovely entrance."

From the beginning, the series enjoyed immense popularity, despite reservations that it often teetered over into soap opera. In the first flush of success, Loretta and Tom's minds seemed to function as one. "That couldn't last," says a former agent of Loretta's. "I would say she was a real pro from the time she was a kid—and tough. I don't mean tough in a vulgar way. I mean—she had a great deal of fiber. And in many ways is actually masculine in her attitudes. She has taken over all the guys she's been with, every time. She's a very complex mixture. I never figured her out."

A woman writer who worked with her agrees with the agent. "Although it's well known she had many romances, she was actually more comfortable working with women than men. It seemed to me she felt threatened by men," she says. "Loretta wanted them to dominate her, and if they didn't, she had no respect for them. But at the same time she set out to undercut them.

"Tom was the producer. I found him an intelligent, darling, sweet guy to work for. But I soon realized she could overrule him anytime she wanted. And maybe she was more knowledgeable about films than he was. I don't know. I just know that I sensed very quickly that he wouldn't last as producer, even though he was a major stockholder."

By the end of the first season Loretta had achieved a popularity that exceeded anything she had ever known in films. She was the First Lady of dramatic television. She received the first of seven nominations by the Television Academy of Arts and Sciences as the "Best Female Star in a Series" and won three Emmys. The readers of *TV-Radio Mirror* found her worthy of six consecutive gold medals as "Favorite Dramatic Actress in Television," and she received special "Star of the Year" award in 1961. She also became the first television actress ever to collect a Grand Prix at the Cannes Film Festival.

Riding high, the Lewises began developing a number of young leading men, including Hugh O'Brian, Jock Mahoney, Craig Stevens and Bill Campbell, on the show, while putting George Nader under personal contract, with vague plans of forming a stable of contractual players.

It soon became apparent that Loretta found it difficult to adjust to her husband as her producer. "His" people were gradually replaced by "her" people. While both Loretta and Lewis denied that there was friction, she increasingly took over the reins to guide production.

On Easter Sunday, 1955, Loretta entered St. John's Hospital in Oxnard, California, where two and a half months later she underwent four-hour surgery with six doctors in attendance. Wild rumors spread when it was learned that her mother, sister Sally and close friends Josie and John Wayne were at the hospital, even though Lewis issued a statement thanking God that she had come through "in strong condition." He asserted that adhesions had been removed and nothing else found. Still, she was not released for two months, when she went to her Ojai residence for additional convalescence. With Loretta unable to begin filming for the new season, Rosalind Russell, Dinah Shore, Lucille Ball, Barbara Stanwyck, Groucho Marx and Van Johnson, among others, stood in for her—although she allowed none of them to come whirling through her doorway.

At this point it was assumed that she had terminal cancer. Attempting to refute the rumor, Loretta held a press conference which inspired a columnist searching for an exclusive angle to comment:

> No one will give out a statement as to the nature of Loretta's illness, but close friends report that she and her husband had a difference of views on some very major matters. Since Loretta has always put her marriage before her career any discord automatically sets Hollywood gossips to discussing Tom and Loretta—illness or no. During this tense time, Loretta went down to under 100 pounds and only now is beginning to approach her normal weight. Since she is dearly beloved by the whole industry, Hollywood is rooting for her.

Upon Loretta's return to the set it became apparent that she was in full control. Tom Lewis resigned at Loretta's request on May 11, 1956, and moved to New York, taking Christopher with him while Peter remained with his mother. (Judy was already living in New York.) Both Loretta and Lewis insisted that his absence was attributable to his acceptance of a position to develop properties for the C. S. LaRoche Advertising firm.

Loretta now embarked on a seven-day sunrise-to-long-after-sunset regimen. *The Loretta Young Show* reflected only the viewpoints of the sponsor, the network and the actress. She involved herself directly in publicity, promotion, meetings with the agency and approval of stories. She also introduced every show and rehearsed and starred in a majority of them.

Not content to mind the condition of her soul, she meddled in the morals of co-workers and insisted that an air of decorum prevail around her sound stage. This brought into existence the famed "penalty box," which she used to discipline the profane or merely vulgar. For example, a "hell" or a "damn" cost a quarter. Gamier expressions ranged from fifty cents to a dollar. All proceeds went to Loretta's favorite charity, St. Anne's.

Many co-workers resented Loretta's interference, but it remained for a famed Broadway star with the vocabulary of a truck driver to defy her. While appearing on the show, pretending to be unaware of Loretta's presence, the guest star swore mildly. Loretta waggled a finger, saying, "That's a no-no! You're fined fifty cents." Without batting an eyelash, the guest pulled out a bill, saying, "Here's ten bucks. Now fuck off, Loretta!"

Others joked about Loretta's much-publicized piety. Once, when producer Ross Hunter visited Joan Crawford, he was about to seat himself when his hostess cried in mock alarm, "Not in that chair! Loretta was just sitting there. It probably has the mark of the cross on the seat."

And at a roast for *Variety*'s Jack Hellman, Hellman was presented with a bowl of water upon which Loretta Young once had walked.

If Loretta was puritanical in outlook, she also subscribed wholeheartedly to the Puritan work ethic. Sustained by vitamins, one good meal a day and a chain of lighted cigarettes, she compulsively applied herself to the job at hand. "You have to put on blinders if you want to get anywhere," she once observed. Following her own advice, she limited her social activity and even slept at the studio on nights when she was scheduled to film the next day. Unable to relax, she spent any spare time perusing magazines, searching for stories suitable for her program. In assessing herself, she said she did not claim the genius of Bette Davis or Lucille Ball, that the only difference between her and other contemporaries was that she had worked harder and longer and disciplined herself more rigidly.

Writer-director Richard Morris once explained working conditions on the show to writer Jane Wilkie: "It's simply that Loretta is in absolute control," he said. "The fact that she's both star and owner doesn't make for the usual director-actress relationship because you're aware of this when you take the job. She's fascinating to direct because she's such a challenge. To work with Loretta, you must realize that the show is the most important thing in the world to her, but she'll listen to ideas with an open mind.

"She's difficult when she's tired, but that only happens when personal problems sap her strength, and then her eyes fill with tears of exhaustion. I don't think she's aware the crew spoils her or that there's a reason no one crosses her."

Someone surprising challenged her on March 13, 1958. On this day Tom Lewis filed a civil suit in Superior Court requesting the dissolution of their television company. In the suit Lewis charged his wife, as president, Robert F. Shewalter, as secretary-treasurer, and both, as directors and stockholders, with "dishonesty, persistent mismanagement, abuse of authority and unfairness toward him" in conducting Lewislor Inc.'s business. He further charged that they had exercised complete control, denying him a voice in operating the corporation, and asserted that no dividends had been paid from 1955 through 1957, although the company had shown a profit of $95,430.73. During this period Loretta and Shewalter had increased their salaries by $20,293.30 each.

Attempts by reporters to clarify the issues brought forth intentional obfuscation:

Lewis initially contended that his suit was a corporate matter instituted as much to protect his wife as himself against small stockholders.

Loretta retreated behind a no-comment policy.

Her lawyer regretted that the suit was "unfortunately too strongly worded."

She later explained that the court action reflected no personal animosity but was strictly a business move to clarify a clouded business situation.

Helen Ferguson admitted to Louella Parsons that the nature of the charges had come as a "surprise." When she was cornered by another persistent reporter and was asked whether there was a separation, she replied, "Not as far as Loretta's concerned." Would there be a divorce? "They are both practicing Catholics," Miss Ferguson reminded the writer.

By 1961 *The Loretta Young Show*, after seven seasons, had run its course and was canceled by NBC. Meanwhile, Loretta and Helen Ferguson collaborated on Loretta'a autobiography, *The Things I Had to Learn*, which was poorly received ("a type of literary output that can quickly drown in its own treacle," according to *Variety*), but sold well. For the 1962–63 season she switched to CBS for a short-lived series, *The New Loretta Young Show*, portraying, against all advice, a widow with several children. It was a disaster. By early November a romantic interest for her was introduced in an attempt to inject interest. The move failed. Amusingly, Loretta agreed to all suggested changes except discarding her "trademark" entrance, anachronistic though it seemed.

Even after both series were off prime time, she sometimes used her entrance in real life. Once Ted Montague, who worked with Mrs. Belzer in her decorating business, was talking to Judy Lewis at a party given by his employer. Well into the evening, the door flew open, and a late-arriving Loretta came whirling into the room, showing off her gown. Startled guests broke into applause, and Loretta bowed graciously before joining the guests. Judy crinkled her nose, shrugged and sighed with amused resignation: "That's my mother!"

After the demise of the new TV show Loretta went into self-imposed retirement in 1963. Three years later she granted one of her rare interviews to AP columnist Bob Thomas. Asked about her absence from sound stages, she explained, "I haven't liked the things that they—the producers—have offered, and they haven't liked the things I've offered. So we're at an impasse."

Not that she was inactive. She traveled. (It was rumored and denied that she had visited the Vatican in an unsuccessful attempt to arrange an annulment of her marraige to Lewis.) She continued her charitable work. She enjoyed herself.

She moved to a Manhattan apartment overlooking Central Park South in 1967. At this time she associated herself with Brides International Showcase, Incorporated, a company designed to provide elaborate traditional bridal gowns and accessories at a time when young couples were rebelling against ostentation and opting for simple ceremonies of their own composition in natural settings—or simply not bothering to marry at all. The project failed. She also talked of making her Broadway debut, but never found a script to her liking.

A friend of both Loretta and her estranged husband recalls this period with sadness. "Such a tearing, hacking relationship had developed," she says. "Loretta would call and suggest getting together for girl talk, which always turned out to be about Tom. And the intensity of the bitterness was so strong that you got the feeling that this couldn't be so important unless there was some residual feeling. Then, a few days later, I'd lunch with Tom, and he'd deliver a diatribe against her. Finally, I stopped seeing them. I just couldn't take it."

Loretta moved back to Los Angeles and in November, 1968, carried out her excruciating decision to divorce Lewis. Her corroborating witness was Josie Wayne, who testified that Lewis had said he wanted to be finished with the whole family.

The previous month, after ten years of litigation, a financial settlement had been reached. In 1959 Loretta and Lewis had secretly agreed on a split of $1,400,000 for sale of *The Loretta Young Show* to NBC. They now agreed to divide assets, including two adjacent apartment buildings, located at Flores Street and Fountain Avenue in Hollywood, valued at $500,000 each. Thus the way was cleared that on October 21, 1969, the woman who had refused even to utter the word "divorce" on screen was granted a decree charging Lewis with desertion and was awarded $1 token alimony.

Nor was this her only appearance in court. The year before, she had sued Brides International for $53,322.46 for use of her name and likeness, personal appearances and consultant fees. And in August, 1970, she obtained an injunction to prevent clips of her "don't move—don't even breathe" scene in *The Story of Alexander Graham Bell* from being included in Twentieth Century-Fox's *Myra Breckenridge.* If the studio insisted on using the scene, Loretta threatened to sue for $10,000,000. The studio removed the clips. Two years later she was back in court to collect $559,000 from NBC for violating a 1959 agreement guaranteeing to excise her introductions in 239 segments of *The Loretta Young Show* when it was syndicated. Her contention: the dated gowns and hairdos harmed her image as a fashionable woman. Incidentally, during the five-week trial Loretta never wore the same dress twice.

Amid all this, Loretta announced that she was resigning from St. Anne's (too rich to need her anymore), selling her home and moving to Arizona to establish the Loretta Young Youth Project of Phoenix, Inc., which was intended to aid "not only the poorest, but those poor enough to live in the wrong place."

"It will succeed. I am not accustomed to failure," she confidently predicted. But after investing a good deal of time and energy in the undertaking, she was forced to admit that the demands were too great. She returned to Beverly Hills and took up residence on Ambassador Avenue. Asked why Loretta had come back, an old acquaintance speculated: "I suppose she went in search of her soul again. I've always felt that whether she was aware of it or not, she'd gone through all the rituals and done her charity work as a means of assuaging guilt. And I suppose she found her soul was no different in Arizona from here."

For a period of almost a year she was rarely seen in public, but in 1974 she again began attending parties and public events with a series of escorts, including producers Frank McCarthy and William Frye, executive Duny Cashion and tycoon Mark Taper.

Late in 1975 there were rumor that she would return to the screen, playing a former Ziegfeld girl or an ex-film star in a film version of Hal Prince's Broadway musical *Follies*. Nothing came of it. But in 1976 she began negotiating for a reported $1,000,000 to play Mother Cabrini, the first American to be granted sainthood.

Whether or not Loretta returns to the screen depends on how successfully the attitudes of old and new moviemakers can be melded. Director Martin Scorsese has said he views Mother Cabrini as "an unsaintly saint who hustled in the streets and clawed her way through society." Loretta, on the other hand, has long believed that her spiritual beauty, captured by the camera, has been responsible for her long-term popularity. "She will never agree to appear unless she can be photographed attractively," says someone who is close to her. "That I know for a fact. The only one of the great stars who doesn't mind looking just as she looks today is Ingrid Bergman. But I've watched Gretchen squirm when she's seen Ingrid looking frankly middle-aged. It hurts her, you see. And that's wrong. You wouldn't want your intellect to be the same. Or your soul to be the same. Or your capacity to love. So why should you want your face to remain unchanged? You want everything to grow, develop. Otherwise, what in *hell* have you been on earth for?"

Yet there is no doubt that if Loretta ever agreed to play Scorsese's Mother Cabrini, she would be capable of projecting the tenacity he is looking for. Probably the most meaningful insight into Loretta I found was provided by the curtain of silence she succeeded in dropping between herself and the outside world. When I wrote, requesting a meeting, my letter went unacknowledged. Nor, in twenty-five years of interviewing, have I ever encountered so many friends and former co-workers who refused to talk. Most amusing perhaps were the score of people who discussed her at length and then said, in effect, "But for God's sake, don't attribute any of this to me." A formidable lady—Miss Loretta Young.

IRENE BENTLEY

The Dropout

Irene Bentley was the leading—and only—lady in Will James' *Smoky* at the Mayfair Theater on New Year's Day, 1934. As such, she must have been seen by millions of Americans since this was the most successful film of the horse-picture genre up to that time.

Critics liked Irene. The New York *Times* praised her work in her first feature, *My Weakness*, a musical starring Lew Ayres and Lilian Harvey. Both *Variety* and *Billboard* alerted exhibitors to watch for her in *Smoky*. The *Times* carried her photograph to illustrate its review of her third movie, *Frontier Marshal*. She had made a beginning that Loretta Young, Kay Francis or Ruth Etting would have been pleased with.

Yet, she never made another film after *Frontier Marshal*, and within a year she had dropped completely out of sight.

What had happened? I decided to find out.

I called the Screen Actors' Guild. They were sorry, but no such member was listed. When had she last worked? 1933 or '34! SAG hadn't even been formed then.

I called George Cukor to tap his encyclopedic knowledge of Hollywood. He didn't remember her. What the hell was the point in trying to find her? Lots of girls had made a few pictures and quit.

I telephoned Richard Lamparski, who writes the *Whatever Became of?* series and makes it his business to know the whereabouts of everyone from Spanky McFarland to Vera Hruba Ralston. Did he have an address on Irene Bentley? Long pause. "Irene who?"

The Academy of Motion Picture Arts and Sciences Library provided dribs and drabs of information:

276

A photo from an unidentified fan magazine was captioned "IRENE BENTLEY—The Girl Fox Studios Believes In."

A clip from Grace Kingsley's movie news column in the Los Angeles *Times* of June 24, 1933, announced: "Irene Bentley arrives in Hollywood under contract to Fox. She's one of those tired-of-it-all girls. She's twenty-two and has brown eyes. She is the niece of Harry B. Smith, playwright. One of her ancestors, Stephen Allen, was one of the early mayors of New York."

The Los Angeles *Times* printed a notice that she was playing the second lead in *My Weakness*.

A full page was devoted to her in the February, 1934, *Photoplay*. The caption repeated the old saw about how this girl had gone along to watch a friend make a screen test, agreed as a lark to help out and wound up with a contract.

Items from Fox's press kit claimed she was a member of the Daughters of the American Revolution, "being a direct descendant of David Crane, a corporal in the rebel army" and "a prominent member of New York's social circle before she decided on a career" and "the wife of socialite broker George S. Kent."

The Academy library also provided a photo of Irene with Victor Jory. With her lively eyes sparkling from beneath surprising, thin-line eyebrows, she appeared to be as pretty or prettier than many who became popular favorites. Her heart-shaped face was emphasized by a dark widow's peak, and her smile was friendly. Statistics revealed that she was five feet four inches tall and weighed one hundred pounds.

I left the library, confident that these leads would enable me to find Miss Bentley. Then I began to wonder. In the early 1930s, publicity departments manufactured a *proper* background for every starlet—until an exasperated Louella Parsons finally publicly thanked a studio for signing a young actress without identifying her as "a socialite."

I enlisted the aid of friends.

Alys Aker checked the index of the Los Angeles *Times* and called to say that on January 31, 1935, INS and Universal wire services both carried stories that Irene and George S. Kent were obtaining a Mexican divorce on grounds of mutual incompatibility. They had been separated for eight months.

Samuel Stark, a theatrical historian who lives in Pebble Beach, California, sent a clipping dated February 10, 1935: "Miss Irene Bentley and Richard C. Hemingway, a film actor, were married at San Bernardino after a whirlwind courtship. Miss Bentley's first husband was George S. Kent, a New York broker."

No more press clippings detailing Irene's adventures could be located. But a letter to the San Bernardino County Recorder's Office brought an offer of a certified copy of the Richard C. Hemingway/Alexina Kent marriage license application for a $2 fee. From it, I learned that Irene's real name was Alexina Bentley and her age 28, not 24. She had been born in New York, was the daughter of Charles E. Bentley and Josephine Jones Bentley and in 1935 was living at 132 South Oakhurst Drive, Beverly Hills. Her father had been born in Maryland; her mother, in New York. Under "Occupation" Irene had written "None."

Her new husband, described in the news as an actor, listed himself as sales manager of a paint company.

Intrigued, I checked the Beverly Hills telephone directory for their names and then all the other Los Angeles directories. Dead end.

I studied the license application for clues. Why the "none"? Had she been dropped at option time? Had she decided to retire? Who could say?

I telephoned David Butler, who had directed *My Weakness,* and said I'd like to talk to him about Irene Bentley.

"Who's that? Irene who?"

I explained she had appeared in *My Weakness.*

"She must have been one of the Goldwyn Girls we borrowed for the picture."

I told him that was unlikely since she was only five feet four inches and had played the second lead, but he did not recall her.

I called Lew Ayres. Ayres: "That's a very remote picture. It wasn't a great success, and I don't remember anything about Irene Bentley but the name. Now would she have been older than I? . . . An ingenue. In her twenties and five four. Well, that's certainly the right age and size. I ought to remember her. Of course, I was married at the time. . . . No, not to Lola [Lola Lane]. To another actress [Ginger Rogers]. . . . I'll tell you, I certainly worked with Irene Bentley, but it's been so long ago I just can't recall her at the moment."

Ayres kindly suggested I contact William Bakewell, who had appeared in *All Quiet on the Western Front* and some fifty other films. Bakewell: "Irene Bentley? I certainly do remember her. A beautiful girl. I took her out a couple of times. A model type. . . . I don't know how I met her, but she was very sweet. Had an air of refinement. Obviously from a nice background but a novice compared to, say, Miriam Hopkins. Irene didn't do an awful lot. So many girls are like that. They do a picture or two, and that's it. . . . There was nothing serious between us. I'll bet I hadn't thought of her in thirty years. Nice girl. I hope she's happy.''

I sent an inquiry to the Social Register Association in New York and received this: "In reply to Mr. Eells' letter the Association wishes to state that there is no record of the Kent or Bentley families in the files.''

From the Daughters of the American Revolution: "In checking our files, we find no record of Mrs. Alexina Bentley Kent Hemingway as being a member of the DAR. We have checked under all the names you have given us. We have even checked under her mother's maiden and married names to see if maybe she was a member.

"We are sorry we could not be of more assistance.''

Through talent agent Richard Segel I learned that his client Ruth Gillette had never met Miss Bentley. True, they had both appeared in *Frontier Marshal*, but they had no scenes together.

Victor Jory remembered Irene well. "We were on location for five weeks with *Smoky* in Arizona," he said. "That picture made a fortune, but, in all fairness, you'd have to say the horse was the star.

"Irene, as I recall, had a child and was separated from her husband who, I think—you have to remember this was thirty or forty years ago—was back east. She worked hard and always appeared on time. She photographed beautifully, and she was easy to work with, but she needed reassurance and encouragement. She required the help of professionals, but she was able to distinguish between good and bad advice. She gave, I'd say, a commendable performance. But she was a girl, as compared to Kay Francis, who was a woman. How she got into pictures or why she didn't continue I couldn't tell you.''

I wrote to the only Hemingway in the San Bernardino telephone book, reasoning that perhaps that was why she and Hemingway had chosen to marry there. It might be his hometown. I also placed ads in the weekly *Variety*, *Daily Variety*, and the *Hollywood Reporter* and wrote a letter requesting information from readers of *Films in Review*.

The ads drew not a single response. The letter to *Films in Review* corrected me concerning the identity of the leading lady in *My Weakness*. A nice letter from the San Bernardino Hemingway informed me that he was not related to Richard C. Hemingway, but that perhaps I'd be interested to know that his ancestors had been among the first forty black pioneers to cross the Rockies. Dead end.

What *had* happened to this rising starlet? I began to look in the East.

The Theater Collection of the Library of Performing Arts at Lincoln Center in Manhattan had an Irene Bentley clipping folder. It contained two references to Irene/Alexina and several others pertaining to musical comedy star Irene Bentley, including an obituary notice which named her as the widow of Harry Bach Smith.

Harry Bach Smith? Harry B. Smith! Irene/Alexina, according to the Fox release, was his niece.

I made a quick check of the 1921 *Who's Who in America,* unearthing the information that in 1906 Smith had married Irene Bentley of Maryland—where, according to Irene/Alexina's marriage license, her father had been born. I speculated that Irene Bentley, the musical star, had been the sister of Irene/Alexina's father. *Who's Who* also identified Harry B. Smith as a lyricist for Victor Herbert and a contributor to the *Ziegfeld Follies.* Wasn't it logical to assume that Irene/Alexina might be an heir to his royalties?

I contacted the American Society of Composers and Publishers and learned that Smith had been a member of the organization and that his estate was still active. Unfortunately, ASCAP policy prohibited providing addresses of any heirs. I could, however, address a letter to Mr. Smith in care of ASCAP and it would be forwarded. I immediately did so.

A few days later attorney William H. Peck of Oyster Bay, New York, phoned me to say he had never heard of Alexina/Irene but had forwarded my request for information to his client, Mrs. Spencer Bentley, one of Smith's heirs. She was living in Mexico and might or might not respond.

A month went by.

Then a letter arrived from Cuernavaca:

July 13, 1975

Dear Mr. Eells:

I received this note from Mr. Peck and will tell you all I know of Irene Bentley. In this letter I'll refer to Irene Bentley Smith as "Aunt Irene" and Harry B. Smith as "Uncle Harry." I married into the family in 1931.

The Bentley family was of Baltimore. There Aunt Irene first married the son of a well-known doctor—divorced—and brought her mother and two younger brothers to New York, and Aunt Irene became quite a star in the very early 1900s because of her talent and remarkable beauty.

Her mother's name was Alexina—her elder brother, Charles B. Bentley, the father of Irene II, the younger brother was Wilmer H. Bentley, whose son was W. Spencer Bentley, my late husband.

Aunt Irene married Harry B. Smith later—in 1906—and she retired from the stage and they bought a magnificent home at 107th Street and

Riverside Drive, where they both lived the rest of their lives. Uncle Harry passed on in 1935 and Aunt Irene in 1940.

Irene II visited Aunt Irene at their summer home in Allenhurst, New Jersey, one summer and there met a young man from Pittsburgh, I believe, the son of a man in the banking business. The name was Nieman, I am sure. They married and had one son. Later divorced, and when I first came into the family in 1931—Irene II was married to George Kent, living in New York. I believe he was in the insurance business. No children. Irene wanted to try the movies, and it was through Uncle Harry that a screen test was arranged through his friends the Shuberts and Walter Vincent. At any rate, she went to Hollywood and then divorced George Kent.

There were few communications between her and Aunt Irene. I thought Richard Hemingway was a sort of a "bit" actor, but I really don't know. I met them once and thought him an extremely nice guy. Shortly after that Aunt Irene died in 1940 and we, my husband and I, never saw them again. Something seems to recall "Florida," but I'm not sure.

I'm sorry that I cannot give you more help. I might suggest, however, that you go to the Museum of the City of New York and see what they have catalogued under the Harry B. Smith and Irene Bentley Smith Collection. When we came to Mexico to live—I sent much of the theatrical memorabilia to the Museum and there are probably old photographs of Irene II.

Good luck in your new book and let me know if I can be of any further assistance.

Sincerely,
Betty Bentley
(Mrs. Spencer Bentley)

Dead end.

On the trail again. Letters to every Nieman currently listed in the Pittsburgh telephone book, inquiring whether any of them knew a Nieman who had married Alexina Bentley in the late 1920s, brought no reply.

A check of the telephone directories of every major city in Florida turned up only one lead: an A. B. Hemingway in Jacksonville. I at once placed a person-to-person call to Alexina Bentley Hemingway. A woman answered. When the operator asked for Alexina Bentley Hemingway, the woman asked, "Who?"

"Alexina Bentley Hemingway."

"This must be a bad connection," she said.

"Irene Bentley Hemingway," I cut in.

"Irene who?"

Dead end.

I returned to Hollywood, and upon hearing of my difficulties in locating Miss Bentley, producer Hunt Stromberg, Jr., became intrigued. "If none of those people will admit knowing her, there must be some reason. Are they covering up?" he asked. "People don't just disappear."

"What about Judge Crater?"

"Other than Judge Crater. You obviously haven't been getting to the right people. I'll help."

He contacted Leonard Spigelgass, a story editor at Fox in the early 1930s. Spigelgass drew a blank, but he suggested checking to see whether Irene Bentley's name hadn't been changed to Irene Purcell. He also supplied numbers for people who had been on the Fox lot about that time.

Irene Purcell was eliminated as a possibility since she had made her film debut eight years before Irene B arrived in Hollywood.

Marguerite Roberts, executive secretary to producers Sol Wurtzel and Winfield Sheehan in the early 1930s, was reached in Santa Barbara. Irene Bentley? "Never heard of her."

Janet Gaynor, a top Fox star, recalled the name but not the face.

Failure fired Stromberg's imagination. Wasn't it possible people chose not to remember? Had there been a scandal? Had Irene married a big-time mobster?

I contacted Lois Moran, living in Sedona, Arizona. Unfortunately, she had left Fox for Broadway by 1933.

Fifi D'Orsay's answering service took my name and number. The next day the inimitable Fifi called to say she was 'sooooo sorrreeee I nevaire met zis Miss Bentley. God bless."

Claire Trevor was unavailable.

More calls. More dead ends.

Phil Berg, a top agent in 1933, recalled Irene as promising but hadn't heard her name in years. There were thousands like her. Why did I want her anyway?

I checked the Museum of the City of New York and ran down other leads. But I never encountered anyone who could tell me what the future had held for the girl Fox Studios had believed in so much. I discovered no private triumphs, no shattered dreams.

She remains a question mark.

"Nice girl," Bill Bakewell had said of her. "I hope she's happy."

Why did she suddenly withdraw from the scene? Did she lack Ginger's persistence and love of the spotlight—qualities which would have enabled her to survive? Or was there within her personality some of the rebelliousness that ultimately defeated Miriam? She had no past achievements to barter as Ruth had. Nor, presumably, was she willing to sacrifice her dignity and personal pride for monetary reward as Kay was. It is also questionable that she was endowed with the manipulative shrewdness of Loretta. Unwilling to submit to the discipline and demands of stardom—including surrender of her privacy and freedom—she simply disappeared. The price was obviously too great. She may have shared Sally Blane's view: "Every star and would-be star paid dearly for any good part, fame or money she got. They arose early and worked hard all day, making believe while the real world went on around them. To me that was intolerable because it meant sacrificing things that are meaningful and joyful in order to pretend."

But rather than forget Irene, let her stand for all the girls who made it inside the dream factories and were disillusioned to discover that factories were factories, whether they processed daydreams or dynamite; and that actresses, while better paid, worked longer and harder in those days than assembly-line girls, arriving at the studios at sunrise and returning home after sunset, too exhausted to enjoy what they had earned, working six days a week—when it wasn't seven.

Let her stand, too, for those who married well, or badly, or went into other professions because they wouldn't or couldn't cope emotionally or physically.

Let her stand also for all those bright-eyed hopefuls—beauty contest winners, society girls, dime store clerks, showgirls, schoolteachers, playgirls, nurses, jazz babies and jitterbugs—all the untrained beauties who yearned to escape their humdrum lives, to be transformed into MOOOOOVIE STARS and to live what they imagined as the sweet life of celebrity.

APPENDIXES

GINGER ROGERS

Various Short Subjects

CAMPUS SWEETHEART, with Rudy Vallee, Radio, 1922
A NIGHT IN A DORMITORY, Pathé, 1929
A DAY OF A MAN OF AFFAIRS, Columbia-Victor Gems, 1929
OFFICE BLUES, Paramount, 1930
HOLLYWOOD ON PARADE NO. 1, Jack Oakie, Paramount, 1932

Feature Films of Ginger Rogers

Dates are for New York City Release

(1) YOUNG MAN OF MANHATTAN
  Paramount, April 19, 1930   Directed by Monta Bell
Screenplay by Robert Presnell; adapted from Katharine Brush's novel
  Songs by Irving Kahal and Sammy Fain

Cast: Norman Foster, Claudette Colbert, Charles Ruggles, Leslie Austin, H.
  Dudley Hawley, Aalbu Sisters
Paramount Theater

(2) THE SAP FROM SYRACUSE
Paramount, July 26, 1930   Directed by Edward Sutherland
Screenplay by Gertrude Purcell; based on story by John Wray, Jack O'Don-
  nell, John Hayden
Songs by E. Y. Harburg, John Green, Vernon Duke
Cast: Jack Oakie, Granville Bates, George Barbier, Sidney Riggs, Betty Star-
  buck, Veree Teasdale, J. Malcolm Dunn, Bernard Jukes, Walter Fenner,
  Jack Daley
Paramount Theater

(3) QUEEN HIGH
Paramount, August 9, 1930   Directed by Fred Newmeyer
Screenplay by Laurence Schwab, B. G. DeSylva and Lewis Gensler, taken
  from Edward Henry Peple's *A Pair of Sixes*

Songs by Arthur Schwartz and Ralph Rainger; DeSylva and Gensler; E. Y. Harburg and Henry Souvain; Dick Howard and Ralph Rainger
Cast: Frank Morgan, Charles Ruggles, Stanley Smith, Helen Carrington, Theresa Maxwell Conover, Betty Garde, Nina Olivette, Rudy Cameron, Tom Brown
Paramount Theater

(4) FOLLOW THE LEADER
Paramount, December 6, 1930   Directed by Norman Taurog
Screenplay by Irene Purcell and Sid Silvers; adapted from William K. Wells' *Manhattan Mary*
Songs by Ray Henderson, Lew Brown, B. G. DeSylva, George White, E. Y. Harburg, Arthur Schwartz, Irving Kahal, Sammy Fain
Cast: Ed Wynn, Stanley Smith, Lou Holtz, Lida Kane, Ethel Merman, Bobby Watson, Donald Kirke, William Halligan, Holly Hall, Preston Foster, James C. Morton Jack LaRue, William Gargan
Times Square and Brooklyn Paramount Theaters

(5) HONOR AMONG LOVERS
Paramount, February 28, 1931   Directed by Dorothy Arzner
Screenplay by Austin Parker and Irene Purcell; story by Austin Parker
Cast: Claudette Colbert, Fredric March, Monroe Owsley, Charles Ruggles, Avonne Taylor, Pat O'Brien, Janet McLeay, John Kearney, Ralph Morgan, Jules Epailly, Leonard Carey
Times Square and Brooklyn Paramount Theaters

(6) THE TIP-OFF
RKO-Pathe, October 26, 1931   Directed by Alfred Rogell
Screenplay by Earl Baldwin; story by George Kibbe Turner
Cast: Eddie Quillan, Robert Armstrong, Joan Peers, Ralf Harolde, Charles Sellon, Mike Donlin, Ernie Adams, Jack Herrick, Cupid (Helen) Ainsworth
Broadway Theater

(7) SUICIDE FLEET
RKO-Pathe, November 26, 1931   Directed by Albert Rogell
Screenplay by Lew Lipton and F. McGrew Wills; based on a story by Commander Herbert A. Jones
Cast: Bill Boyd, Robert Armstrong, James Gleason, Harry Bannister, Frank Reicher, Ben Alexander, Henry Victor, Hans Joby
Mayfair Theater

(8) CARNIVAL BOAT
RKO-Pathe, March 21, 1932   Directed by Albert Rogell
Screenplay by James Seymour; from a story by Marion Jackson and Don Ryan

Cast: Bill Boyd, Fred Kohler, Hobart Bosworth, Marie Prevost, Edgar Kennedy, Harry Sweet, Charles Sellon, Walter Percival, Jack Carlyle, Eddie Chandler, Bob Perry
Hippodrome Theater

(9) THE TENDERFOOT

First National, May 23, 1932   Directed by Ray Enright
Screenplay by Arthur Caesar, Monty Banks, Earl Baldwin; from George S. Kaufman's hit play *The Butter and Egg Man*
Cast: Joe E. Brown, Lew Cody, Vivian Oakland, Robert Greig, Wilfred Lucas, Spencer Charters, Ralph Ince, Mae Madison, Marion Byron, Lee Kohlmar, Harry Seymour, Richard Cramer, Douglas Gerrard, Jill Dennett
Warners' Strand Theater

(10) THE THIRTEENTH GUEST

Monogram, 1932 (not reviewed in New York)   Directed by Albert Ray
Screenplay by Francis Hyland, Arthur Hoerl and Armitage Trail
Cast: Lyle Talbot, J. Farrell MacDonald, James Eagles, Eddie Phillips, Erville Alderson, Robert Klein, Crauford Kent, Frances Rich, Ethel Wales, Paul Hurst, William Davidson, Phillips Smalley, Harry Tenbrook, John Ince, Allan Cavan, Alan Bridge, Tom London, Henry Hall, Tiny Sanford, Kit Guard

(11) HAT CHECK GIRL

Fox, October 8, 1932   Directed by Sidney Lanfield
Screenplay by Philip Klein and Barry Conners; based on a story by Rian James
Cast: Ben Lyon, Sally Eilers, Monroe Owsley, Arthur Pierson, Noel Madison, Dewey Robinson, Harold Goodwin, Eulalie Jensen, Purnell Pratt, Eddie Anderson, Dennis O'Keefe, Joyce Compton, Bill Elliott, Astrid Allwyn
Roxy Theater

(12) YOU SAID A MOUTHFUL

First National, November 18, 1932   Directed by Lloyd Bacon
Screenplay by Robert Lord and Bolton Mallory; from a story by William B. Dover
Cast: Joe E. Brown, Preston S. Foster, Sheila Terry, Guinn Williams, Harry Gribbon, Oscar Apfel, Edwin Maxwell, Walter Walker, William Burgess, Frank Hagney, Selmer Jackson, Mia Marvin, Harry Seymour, James Eagles, Arthur S. Byron, Anthony Lord, Bert Morehouse, Farina, Wilfred Lucas, Don Brodie
Winter Garden Theater

(13) BROADWAY BAD

Fox, March 6, 1933   Directed by Sidney Lanfield
Screenplay by Arthur Kober and Maude Fulton; from a story by William R. Lipman and A. W. Pezet

Cast: Joan Blondell, Ricardo Cortez, Adrienne Ames, Allen Vincent, Victor Jory, Philip Tead, Francis McDonald, Spencer Charters, Ronald Cosbey, Margaret Seddon, Donald Crisp, Frederick Burton
Palace Theater

(14) 42nd STREET
Warner Brothers, March 10, 1933   Directed by Lloyd Bacon
Screenplay by James Seymour and Rian James; from a novel by Bradford Ropes
Songs by Al Dubin and Harry Warren
Choreography by Busby Berkeley; costumes by Orry-Kelly
Cast: Warner Baxter, Bebe Daniels, George Brent, Una Merkel, Ruby Keeler, Guy Kibbee, Ned Sparks, Dick Powell, Allen Jenkins, Henry B. Walthall, Edward J. Nugent, Harry Akst, Clarence Nordstrom, Robert McWade, George E. Stone, Al Dubin, Harry Warren, Toby Wing, Jack LaRue, Patricia Ellis, Louise Beavers, Lyle Talbot
Strand Theater

(15) GOLD DIGGERS OF 1933
Warner Brothers, June 8, 1933   Directed by Mervyn LeRoy
Screenplay by David Boehm, Ben Markson, Erwin Gelsey, James Seymour; based on Avery Hopwood's *Gold Diggers*
Songs by Al Dubin and Harry Warren
Choreography by Busby Berkeley; gowns by Orry-Kelly
Cast: Warren William, Joan Blondell, Aline MacMahon, Ruby Keeler, Dick Powell, Guy Kibbee, Ned Sparks, Clarence Nordstrom, Robert Agnew, Tammany Young, Sterling Holloway, Ferdinand Gottschalk, Lynn Browning, Billy Barty, Fred Toones, Theresa Harris, Hobart Cavanaugh, Dennis O'Keefe, Busby Berkeley, Frank Mills, Etta Moten, Billy West, Bill Elliott
Strand Theater

(16) PROFESSIONAL SWEETHEART
RKO-Radio, July 14, 1933   Directed by William Seiter
Screenplay and story by Maurine Watkins
Cast: Norman Foster, Zasu Pitts, Frank McHugh, Allen Jenkins, Gregory Ratoff, Edgar Kennedy, Lucien Littlefield, Franklin Pangborn
Radio City Music Hall

(17) A SHRIEK IN THE NIGHT
M. H. Hoffman Productions, July 24, 1933   Directed by Albert Ray
Screenplay by Frances Hyland; story by Kurt Kempler
Cast: Lyle Talbot, Arthur Hoyt, Purnell Pratt, Harvey Clark, Lillian Harmer, Maurice Black, Louise Beavers
Cameo Theater

(18) DON'T BET ON LOVE

Universal, July 31, 1933   Directed by Murray Roth

Screenplay by Murray Roth and Howard Emmett Rogers; from story by Murray Roth

Cast: Lew Ayres, Charles Grapewin, Shirley Grey, Merna Kennedy, Thomas Dugan, Robert Emmett O'Connor, Lucille Webster Gleason

Rialto Theater

(19) SITTING PRETTY

Paramount, December 2, 1933   Directed by Harry Joe Brown

Screenplay by Jack McGowan, S. J. Perelman and Lou Breslow; based on a story suggested by Nina Wilcox Putnam

Songs by Mack Gordon and Harry Revel

Choreography Larry Ceballos

Cast: Jack Oakie, Jack Haley, Thelma Todd, Gregory Ratoff, Lew Cody, Harry Revel, Jerry Tucker, Mack Gordon, Hale Hamilton, Walter Walker, Kenneth Thomson, William Davidson, Lee Moran, Pickens Sisters, Arthur Jarrett, Virginia Sale, Fuzzy Knight, Stuart Holmes, Irving Bacon,

Times Square and Brooklyn Paramount Theaters

(20) FLYING DOWN TO RIO

RKO-Radio, December 22, 1933   Directed by Thorton Freeland

Screenplay by Cyril Hume, H. W. Hanemann, Erwin Gelsey; based on a play by Anne Caldwell taken from an original story by Lou Brock

Songs by Vincent Youmans, Edward Eliscu and Gus Kahn

Choreography by Dave Gould; music director: Max Steiner: costumes; Walter Plunkett

Cast: Dolores Del Rio, Gene Raymond, Raul Roulien, Fred Astaire, Blanche Frederici, Walter Walker, Etta Moten, Roy D'Arcy, Maurice Black, Armand Kaliz, Paul Porcasi, Reginald Barlow, Eric Blore, Franklin Pangborn, Luis Alberni, Jack Goode, Jack Rice, Eddie Borden, Clarence Muse, The Brazilian Turunas, The American Clippers Band, Betty Furness

Radio City Music Hall

(21) CHANCE AT HEAVEN

RKO-Radio, December 26, 1933   Directed by William Seiter

Screenplay by Julian Josephson and Sarah Mason; based on a story by Vina Delmar

Cast: Joel McCrea, Marian Nixon, Andy Devine, Virginia Hammond, Lucien Littlefield, Ann Shoemaker, George Meeker, Betty Furness, Herman Bing

Rialto Theater

(22) 20 MILLION SWEETHEARTS

First National, April 27, 1934   Directed by Ray Enright

Screenplay by Warren Duff and Harry Sauber; from a story by Jerry Wald and Paul Finder Moss

Music and lyrics by Harry Warren and Al Dubin

Cast: Pat O'Brien, Dick Powell, Allen Jenkins, Grant Mitchell, Joseph Cawthorne, Joan Wheeler, Henry O'Neil, Johnny Arthur, Four Mills Brothers, Ted Fio Rito and His Orchestra, Radio Rogues, Leo Forbstein, Bill Ray,

Strand Theater

(23) RAFTER ROMANCE

RKO-Radio (not reviewed in New York)   Directed by William Seiter

Screenplay by H. W. Hanneman, Sam Mintz and Glenn Tryon; story by John Wells

Cast: Norman Foster, George Sidney, Robert Benchley, Laura Hope Crews, Guinn Williams

(24) FINISHING SCHOOL

RKO-Radio, April 30, 1934

Directed by Wanda Tuchock and George Nicholls, Jr.

Screenplay by Wanda Tuchock and Laird Doyle; based on a story by David Hempstead

Cast: Frances Dee, Billie Burke, Bruce Cabot, John Halliday, Beulah Bondi, Sara Haden, Marjorie Lytell, Adalyn Doyle, Dawn O'Day (aka Anne Shirley), Claire Myers, Susanne Thompson, Edith Vale, Rose Coghlan, Irene Franklin, Ann Cameron, Caroline Rankin

Casino Theater

(25) CHANGE OF HEART

Fox, May 11, 1934   Directed by John G. Blystone

Screenplay by Sonya Levien, James Gleason and Samuel Hoffenstein; based on Kathleen Norris' novel *Manhattan Love Song*

Cast: Janet Gaynor, Charles Farrell, James Dunn, Beryl Mercer, Gustav von Seyffertitz, Irene Franklin, Kenneth Thomson, Theodor von Eltz, Drue Leyton, Nella Walker, Shirley Temple, Barbara Barondess, Fiske O'Hara, Jane Darwell, Mary Carr

Radio City Music Hall

(26) UPPER WORLD

Warners, May 25, 1934   Directed by Roy Del Ruth

Screenplay by Ben Markson; from story by Ben Hecht

Cast: Warren William, Mary Astor, Andy Devine, Dickie Moore, Henry O'Neill, J. Carrol Naish, Sidney Toler, Theodore Newton, Robett Barrat, Ferdinand Gottschalk, Robert Greig

Strand Theater

289

(27) THE GAY DIVORCEE
RKO-Radio, November 16, 1934   Directed by Mark Sandrich
Produced by Pandro S. Berman.
Screenplay by George Marion, Jr., Dorothy Yost and Edward Kaufman; from
    Dwight Taylor's stage libretto based on J. Hartley Manner's play
Musical adaptation by Kenneth Webb and Samuel Hoffenstein; dances by
    Dave Gould; songs by Cole Porter, Con Conrad and Herb Magidson, Harry
    Revel and Mack Gordon; costumes by Walter Plunkett
Cast: Fred Astaire, Alice Brady, Edward Everett Horton, Erik Rhodes, Eric
    Blore, Lillian Miles, Charles Coleman, William Austin, Betty Grable, Paul
    Porcasi, E. E. Clive
Radio City Music Hall

(28) ROMANCE IN MANHATTAN
RKO-Radio, January 18, 1935   Directed by Stephen Roberts
Produced by Pandro S. Berman
Screenplay by Jane Murfin and Edward Kaufman; story by Norman Krasna
    and Don Hartman
Cast: Francis Lederer, Arthur Hohl, Jimmy Butler, J. Farrell MacDonald, Hel-
    en Ware, Eily Malyon, Lillian Harmer, Donald Meek, Sidney Toler, Oscar
    Apfel, Reginald Barlow, Andy Clyde
Radio City Music Hall

(29) ROBERTA
RKO-Radio, March 8, 1935   Directed by William A. Seiter
Produced by Pandro S. Berman
Screenplay by Jane Murfin and Sam Mintz; additional dialogue by Allan Scott
    and Glenn Tryon; from stage musical by Otto Harbach and Jerome Kern
    based on Alice Duer Miller's novel *Gowns by Roberta*
Dances by Fred Astaire; assistant dance director: Hermes Pan; gowns by Ber-
    nard Newman
Songs by Jerome Kern with lyrics by Otto Harbach, Bernard Dougall, Oscar
    Hammerstein II-Dorothy Fields and Jimmy McHugh
Cast: Irene Dunne, Fred Astaire, Randolph Scott, Helen Westley, Claire
    Dodd, Victor Varconi, Luis Alberni, Ferdinand Munier, Torben Meyer,
    Adrian Rosley, Bodil Rosing, Johnny (Candy) Candido, Muzzi Marcellino,
    Gene Sheldon, Howard Lally, William Carey, Paul McLarind, Hal Borne,
    Charles Sharpe, Ivan Dow, Phil Cuthbert, Delmon Davis, William Dunn,
    Lucille Ball
Radio City Music Hall

(30) STAR OF MIDNIGHT
RKO-Radio, April 12, 1935   Directed by Stephen Roberts

Screenplay by Howard J. Green, Anthony Veiller and Edward Kaufman; based on novel by Arthur Somers Roche
Cast: William Powell, Paul Kelly, Gene Lockhart, Ralph Morgan, Leslie Fenton, J. Farrell MacDonald, Russell Hopton, Vivian Oakland, Frank Reicher, Robert Emmett O'Connor, Francis McDonald, Paul Hurst, Sidney Toler, Spencer Charters, George Chandler, Charles McMurphy, Hooper Atchley, John Ince
Radio City Music Hall

(31) TOP HAT
RKO-Radio, August 30, 1935   Directed by Mark Sandrich
Produced by Pandro S. Berman
Screenplay by Dwight Taylor and Allan Scott; story by Dwight Taylor
Dances by Fred Astaire and Hermes Pan; gowns by Bernard Newman
Songs by Irving Berlin
Cast: Fred Astaire, Edward Everett Horton, Helen Broderick, Erik Rhodes, Eric Blore, Donald Meek, Florence Roberts, Gino Corrado, Peter Hobbs, Edgar Norton, Leonard Mudie, Lucille Ball, Dennis O'Keefe
Radio City Music Hall

(32) IN PERSON
RKO-Radio, December 13, 1935   Directed by William A. Seiter
Produced by Pandro S. Berman
Screenplay by Allan Scott; from a novel by Samuel Hopkins Adams
Music and lyrics by Oscar Levant and Dorothy Fields
Cast: George Brent, Alan Mowbray, Grant Mitchell, Samuel S. Hinds, Joan Breslau, Louis Mason, Spencer Charters, Bob McKenzie, Lee Shumway, Lew Kelly, William B. Davidson
Radio City Music Hall

(33) FOLLOW THE FLEET
RKO-Radio, February 21, 1936   Directed by Mark Sandrich
Produced by Pandro S. Berman
Screenplay by Dwight Taylor and Allan Scott; adapted from Hubert Osborne's play *Shore Leave*
Dances by Hermes Pan; gowns by Bernard Newman
Songs by Irving Berlin
Cast: Fred Astaire, Randolph Scott, Harriet Hilliard, Astrid Allwyn, Harry Beresford, Russell Hicks, Brooks Benedict, Ray Mayer, Lucille Ball, Betty Grable, Joy Hodges, Jeanne Grey, Addison Richards, Edward Burns, Frank Mills, Frank Jenks, Jack Randall, Tony Martin, Jane Hamilton, Maxine Jennings, Herbert Rawlinson
Radio City Music Hall

(34) SWING TIME

RKO-Radio, August 28, 1936   Directed by George Stevens

Produced by Pandro S. Berman

Screenplay by Howard Lindsay and Allan Scott

Songs by Jerome Kern and Dorothy Fields

Dances by Fred Astaire and Hermes Pan

Cast: Fred Astaire, Victor Moore, Helen Broderick, Eric Blore, Betty Furness, Georges Metaxa, Landers Stevens, John Harrington, Pierre Watkin, Abe Reynolds, Gerald Hamer, Edgar Deering, Harry Bernard, Ralph Byrd, Charles Hall, Jean Perry, Olin Francis, Floyd Shackleford, Fern Emmett, Howard Hickman, Ferdinand Munier, Joey Ray, Frank Jenks, Jack Goode, Donald Kerr, Ted O'Shea, Frank Edmunds, Bill Brand, Harry Bowen, Jack Rice

Radio City Music Hall

(35) SHALL WE DANCE

RKO-Radio, May 14, 1937   Directed by Mark Sandrich

Produced by Pandro S. Berman

Screenplay by Allan Scott and Ernest Pagano; based on Lee Loeb and Harold Buchman's *Watch Your Step*

Dances by Fred Astaire, Hermes Pan and Henry Losee

Songs by George and Ira Gershwin

Cast: Fred Astaire, Edward Everett Horton, Eric Blore, Jerome Cowan, Ketti Gallian, William Brisbane, Ann Shoemaker, Harriet Hoctor, Ben Alexander, Emma Young, Sherwood Bailey, Pete Theodore, Marek Windheim, Rolfe Sedan, Charles Coleman, Frank Moran

Radio City Music Hall

(36) STAGE DOOR

RKO-Radio, October 8, 1937   Directed by Gregory La Cava

Produced by Pandro S. Berman

Screenplay by Morrie Ryskind and Anthony Veiller; adapted from Edna Ferber and George S. Kaufman's play *Stage Door*

Cast: Katharine Hepburn, Adolphe Menjou, Gail Patrick, Constance Collier, Andrea Leeds, Samuel S. Hinds, Lucille Ball, Franklin Pangborn, William Corson, Pierre Watkin, Grady Sutton, Frank Reicher, Phyllis Kennedy, Eve Arden, Ann Miller, Margaret Early, Jean Rouverol, Elizabeth Dunne, Norma Drury, Jane Rhodes, Peggy O'Donnell, Harriet Brandon, Katharine Alexander, Ralph Forbes, Mary Forbes, Huntley Gordon, Jack Carson, Fred Santley, Lynton Brent, Theodor Von Eltz, Jack Rice, Harry Strang, Bob Perry, Larry Steers, Mary Board, Frances Gifford

Radio City Music Hall

(37) VIVACIOUS LADY
RKO-Radio, June 3, 1938   Directed and produced by George Stevens
Screenplay by P.J. Wolfson and Ernest Pagano; based on a story by I. A. R. Wylier
Cast: James Stewart, James Ellison, Beulah Bondi, Charles Coburn, Frances Mercer, Phyllis Kennedy, Franklin Pangborn, Grady Sutton, Jack Carson, Alec Craig, Willie Best, Lee Bennett, June Johnson, Tom Quinn, Vinton Haworth, Frank M. Thomas, Spencer Charters, Maude Eburne, Hattie McDaniel, Lloyd Ingraham, Ed Mortimer
Radio City Music Hall

(38) HAVING A WONDERFUL TIME
RKO-Radio, July 8, 1938   Directed by Alfred Santell
Produced by Pandro S. Berman
Screenplay by Arthur Kober; adapted from his hit play
Cast: Douglas Fairbanks, Jr., Peggy Conklin, Lucille Ball, Lee Bowman, Eve Arden, Dorothea Kent, Richard (Red) Skelton, Ann Miller, Donald Meek, Jack Carson, Kirk Windsor, Grady Sutton, Shimen Ruskin, Leona Roberts, Harlan Briggs, Inez Courtney, Juanita Quigley, Clarence H. Wilson, Dorothy Tree, Hooper Atchley, Ronnie Rondell, Dean Jagger, George Meeker
Radio City Music Hall

(39) CAREFREE
RKO-Radio, September 23, 1938   Directed by Mark Sandrich
Produced by Pandro S. Berman
Screenplay by Allan Scott and Ernest Pagano; story and adaptation by Dudley Nichols and Hagar Wilde
Dances by Fred Astaire and Hermes Pan; songs by Irving Berlin
Cast: Fred Astaire, Ralph Bellamy, Luella Gear, Jack Carson, Clarence Kolb, Franklin Pangborn, Walter Kingsford, Kay Sutton, Tom Tully, Hattie McDaniel, Robert B. Mitchell, St. Brendan's Boys Choir
Radio City Music Hall

(40) THE STORY OF VERNON AND IRENE CASTLE
RKO-Radio, March 31, 1939   Directed by H.C. Potter
Produced by George Haight and Pandro S. Berman
Screenplay by Richard Sherman; adaptation by Oscar Hammerstein II and Dorothy Yost of Irene Castle's *My Husband* and *My Memories of Vernon Castle*
Dances by Astaire and Pan, based on those of the Castles consultant, Irene Castle
Cast: Fred Astaire, Edna Mae Oliver, Walter Brennan, Lew Fields, Etienne Girardot, Rolfe Sedan, Janet Beecher, Robert Strange, Leonid Kinskey,

293

Clarence Derwent, Victor Varconi, Frances Mercer, Donald MacBride, Douglas Walton, Sonny Lamont, Marge Champion
Radio City Music Hall

(41) BACHELOR MOTHER

RKO-Radio, June 30, 1939   Directed by Garson Kanin
Produced by B. G. De Sylva
Screenplay by Norman Krasna; from a story by Felix Jackson
Cast: David Niven, Charles Coburn, Frank Albertson, E. E. Clive, Elbert Coplen, Jr., Ferike Boros, Ernest Truex, Leonard Penn, Paul Stanton, Gerald Oliver-Smith, Leona Roberts, Dennie Moore, June Wilkins, Frank M. Thomas, Edna Holland
Radio City Music Hall

(42) FIFTH AVENUE GIRL

RKO-Radio, August 25, 1939   Directed and produced by Gregory La Cava
Screenplay by Allan Scott
Cast: Walter Connolly, Verree Teasdale, James Ellison, Tim Holt, Kathryn Adams, Franklin Pangborn, Cornelius Keefe Ferike Boros, Manda Lane, Theodore von Eltz, Louis Calhern, Alexander D'Arcy, Robert Emmett Kean, Jack Carson
Radio City Music Hall

(43) PRIMROSE PATH

RKO-Radio, March 23, 1940   Directed and produced by Gregory La Cava
Screenplay by Allan Scott and La Cava; adapted from Robert L. Buckner and Walter Hart's dramatization of Victoria Lincoln's *February Hill*
Cast: Joel McCrea, Marjorie Rambeau, Henry Travers, Miles Mander, Queenie Vassar, Joan Carroll, Vivienne Osborne, Carmen Morales
Roxy Theater

(44) LUCKY PARTNERS

RKO-Radio, September 6, 1940   Directed by Lewis Milestone
Produced by George Haight
Screenplay by Allan Scott and John Van Druten; adapted from Sacha Guitry's story "Bonne Chance"
Cast: Ronald Colman, Jack Carson, Spring Byington, Cecilia Loftus, Harry Davenport, Hugh O'Connell, Brandon Tynan, Leon Belasco, Eddie Conrad, Walter Kingsford, Helen Lynd, Lucile Gleason, Helen Lynd, Otto Hoffman, Alex Melesh, Dorothy Adams, Frank Mills, Murray Alper, Billy Benedict, Al Hill, Robert Dudley, Grady Sutton, Nora Cecil, Harlan Briggs
Radio City Music Hall

(45) KITTY FOYLE

RKO-Radio, January 9, 1941   Directed by Sam Wood
Produced by David Hempstead
Screenplay by Dalton Trumbo; additional dialogue by Donald Ogden Stewart;
    from Christopher Morley's novel *Kitty Foyle*
Cast: Dennis Morgan, James Craig, Eduardo Ciannelli, Ernest Cossart, Gladys
    Cooper, Odette Myrtil, Mary Treen, Katharine Stevens, Walter Kingsford,
    Cecil Cunningham, Nella Walker, Edward Fielding, Kay Linaker, Richard
    Nichols, Florence Bates, Heather Angel, Tyler Brooke, Frank Milan,
    Charles Quigley, Ray Teal, Joey Ray, Joe Bernard, Tom Herbert, Hilda Plo-
    wright, Helen Lynd, Spencer Charters, Franks Mills
Rivoli Theatre

(46) TOM, DICK AND HARRY

RKO-Radio, July 18, 1941   Directed by Garson Kanin
Produced by Robert Sisk
Screenplay and story by Paul Jarrico
Cast: George Murphy, Alan Marshal, Burgess Meredith, Joe Cunningham,
    Jane Seymour, Lenore Lonergan, Vicki Lester, Phil Silvers, Betty Brecken-
    dridge, Sidney Skolsky, Edna Holland, Jack Briggs, Jane Patten, Jane
    Woodworth, Gus Glassmire, Netta Packer, Ellen Lowe, Sarah Edwards,
    Gertrude Short, Edward Colebrook, Gayle Melott, Dorothy Lloyd, Lurene
    Tuttle, Maurice Brierre
Radio City Music Hall

(47) ROXIE HART

20th Century-Fox, February 20, 1942   Directed by William Wellman
Written and produced by Nunnally Johnson; adapted from Maurine Watkins's
    play *Chicago*
Cast: Adolphe Menjou, George Montgomery, Lynne Overman, Nigel Bruce,
    Phil Silvers, Sara Allgood, William Frawley, Spring Byington, Helene Rey-
    nolds, George Chandler, George Lessey, Iris Adrian, Milton Parsons, Mi-
    chael North, Helene Reynolds, Charles D. Brown, Morris Ankrum, Billy
    Wayne, Charles Williams, Leon Belasco, Lee Shumway, Jim Pierce, Phillip
    Morris, Pat O'Malley, Stanley Blystone, Frank Orth, Alec Craig, Edward
    Clark, Larry Lawson, Harry Carter, Jack Norton, Arthur Aylesworth, Mar-
    garet Seddon
Roxy Theatre

(48) THE MAJOR AND THE MINOR

Paramount, September 17, 1942   Directed by Billy Wilder
Produced by Arthur Hornblow, Jr.
Screenplay by Charles Brackett and Billy Wilder; suggested by a play by Ed-
    ward Childs Carpenter and a story by Fannie Kilbourne

Cast: Ray Milland, Rita Johnson, Robert Benchley, Diana Lynn, Edward Fielding, Frankie Thomas, Jr., Raymond Roe, Charles Smith, Larry Nunn, Billy Dawson, Stanley Desmond, Lela Rogers, Aldrich Bowker, Boyd Irwin, Byron Shores, Richard Fiske, Norma Varden, Getl Dupont, Dell Henderson, Ed Peil, Sr., Ken Lundy, Ethel Clayton, Gloria Williams, Marie Blake, Mary Field, Will Wright, William Howell, Tom Dugan, Carlotta Jelm, George Anderson, Stanley Andrews, Emory Parnell, Guy Wilkerson, Milton Kibbee, Archie Twitchell, Alice Keating, Billy Ray, Don Wilmot, Jack Lindquist, Billy Glauson, John Borgden, Bradley Hall
Paramount Theater

(49) TALES OF MANHATTAN

Twentieth Century-Fox, September 25, 1942   Directed by Julien Duvivier
Omnibus of short stories with all-star cast; Ginger played opposite Henry Fonda
Cast: Henry Fonda, Cesar Romero, Gail Patrick, Roland Young, Marian Martin, Frank Orth, Connie Leon
Radio City Music Hall

(50) ONCE UPON A HONEYMOON

RKO-Radio, November 13, 1942   Directed and produced by Leo McCarey
Screenplay by Sheridan Gibney; from a story by Gibney and McCarey
Cast: Cary Grant, Walter Slezak, Albert Dekker, Albert Basserman, Ferike Boros, Harry Shannon, John Banner, Natasha Lytess, Alex Melesh, Peter Seal, Major Nichols, Dina Smirnova, Alex Davidoff, Leda Nicova, Ace Bragunier, Emil Ostlin, Otto Reichow, Henry Guttman, Johnny Dime, Dell Henderson, Carl Ekberg, Fred Niblo, Oscar Lorraine, Claudine De Luc, Brandon Beach, Eddie Licho, Joseph Kamaryt, Walter Stahl, Joe Diskay, Eugene Marum, Gordon Clark, Jack Martin, Manart Kippen, George Sorel, Walter Bonn, Bill Martin, Lionel Royce, Jacques Vanaire, Frank Alten, Boyd Davis, Emory Parnell
Radio City Music Hall

(51) LADY IN THE DARK

Paramount, February 23, 1944   Directed by Mitchell Leisen
Produced by B.G. DeSylva
Screenplay by Frances Goodrich and Albert Hackett; based on the Moss Hart-Kurt Weill musical play; lyrics by Ira Gershwin; additional song by Johnny Burke and Jimmy Van Husen; Robert E. Dolan; Clifford Grey and Victor Schertzinger
Sets and costumes by Raoul Pene du Bois
Cast: Ray Milland, Jon Hall, Warner Baxter, Barry Sullivan, Mischa Auer, Mary Phillips, Phyllis Brooks, Edward Fielding, Don Loper, Mary Parker, Catherine Craig, Marietta Canty, Virginia Farmer, Fay Helm, Gail Russell,

Kay Linaker, Harvey Stephens, Rand Brooks, Pepito Perez, Charles Smith, Audrey Young, Eleanor DeVan, Jeanne Straser, Arlyne Varden, Angela Wilson, Dorothy O'Kelly, Betty Hall, Fran Shore, Lynda Grey, Christopher King, Maxine Ardell, Alice Kirby, Louise LaPlanche, Paul Pierce, George Mayon, James Notaro, Jacques Karre, Byron Poindexter, Kit Carson, Bunny Waters, Susan Paley, Dorothy Ford, Mary MacLaren, Paul McVey, Marten Lamont, Tristram Coffin, Dennis Moore, Jack Mulhall, Murray Alper, Dorothy Granger, Emmett Vogan, Lester Dorr, Grandon Rhodes, Johnnie Johnson, John O'Connor, Buster Brodie, Herbert Corthell, Herb Holcomb, Charles Bates, Theodore Marc, Armand Tanny, Stuart Barlow, Leonora Johnson, Harry Bayfield, Larry Rio, Buz Buckley, Priscilla Lyon, Marjean Neville, Billy Dawson
Paramount Theater

(52) TENDER COMRADE
RKO-Radio, June 2, 1944   Directed by Edward Dmytryk
Produced by David Hempstead
Screenplay and story by Dalton Trumbo
Cast: Robert Ryan, Ruth Hussey, Patricia Collinge, Mady Christians, Kim Hunter, Jane Darwell, Mary Forbes, Richard Martin, Richard Gaines, Patti Brill, Euline Martin, Edward Fielding, Claire Whitney, Donald Davis, Robert Anderson
Capitol Theater

(53) I'LL BE SEEING YOU
Selznick International-UA, April 6, 1945   Directed by William Dieterle
Produced by Dore Schary
Screenplay by Marion Parsonnet; based on a Charles Martin story
Cast: Joseph Cotten, Shirley Temple, Spring Byington, Tom Tully, Chill Wills, Dare Harris, Kenny Bowers, John Derek, John James
Capitol Theater

(54) WEEKEND AT THE WALDORF
MGM, October 5, 1945   Directed by Robert Z. Leonard
Produced by Arthur Hornblow, Jr.
Screenplay by Sam and Bella Spewack; adapted from a play by Vicki Baum
Songs by Sammy Fain, Ted Koehler and Pepe Guizar
Choreography by Charles Walters
Cast: Lana Turner, Walter Pidgeon, Van Johnson, Edward Arnold, Phyllis Thaxter, Keenan Wynn, Robert Benchley, Leon Ames, Lina Romay, Samuel S. Hinds, Constance Collier, Leon Ames, Warner Anderson, Porter Hall, George Zucco, Bob Graham, Michael Kirby, Cora Sue Collins, Rosemary DeCamp, Jacqueline DeWit, Frank Puglia, Charles Wilson, Irving Bacon, Miles Mander, Nana Bryant, Russell Hicks, Ludmilla Pitoeff, Naomi Chil-

ders, Moroni Olsen, William Halligan, John Wengraff, Ruth Lee, Jack Luden, Jean Carpenter, Ethel King, Rex Evans, Harry Barris, Byron Foulger, Arno Frey, Gordon Richards, Dorothy Christy, Dick Hirbe, Shirley Lew, Billie Louie, Bess Flowers, Sandra Morgan, Dick Gordon, Oliver Dross, Ella Ethridge, Charles Madrin, Kenneth Cutler, Frank McClure, Estelle Ettere, Barbara Powers, Xavier Cugat and His Orchestra
Radio City Music Hall

(55) HEARTBEAT
RKO-Radio, May 11, 1946   Directed by Sam Wood
Produced by Robert and Raymond Hakim
Based on the screenplay by Hans Wilhelm, Max Kolpe and Michel Duran; adapted by Morrie Ryskind, with additional dialogue by Rowland Leigh
Cast: Jean Pierre Aumont, Adolphe Menjou, Basil Rathbone, Eduardo Ciannelli, Mikhail Rasumny, Melville Cooper, Mona Maris, Henry Stephenson
Palace Theater

(56) MAGNIFICENT DOLL
Universal, December 9, 1946   Directed by Frank Borzage
Produced by Jack H. Skirball and Bruce Manning
Screenplay by Irving Stone
Cast: David Niven, Burgess Meredith, Horace McNally, Peggy Wood, Frances Williams, Robert Barrat, Grandon Rhodes, Henri Letondal, Joe Forte, Erville Alderson, Francis McDonald, Emmett Vogan, George Barrows, Arthur Space, Byron Foulger, Joseph Crehan, Larry Blake, Pierre Watkin, John Sheehan, Ruth Lee, George Carleton, Jack Ingram, Olaf Hytten, Sam Flint, Boyd Irwin, Lee Phelps, Lois Austin, Harlan Briggs, John Hines, Ferris Taylor, Eddy Waller, Stanley Blystone, Stanley Price, Victor Zimmerman, Ja George, Ethaln Laidlaw, Mary Emery, Carey Hamilton, Dick Dickson, Larry Steers, Frank Erickson, Grace Cunard, Tom Coleman, Pietro Sosso, Jack Curtis, Harry Denny, Garnett Marks, Jerry Jerome, John Michael
Loew's Criterion Theater

(57) IT HAD TO BE YOU
Columbia, December 8, 1947   Directed by Don Hartman and Rudolph Mate
Produced by Don Hartman
Screenplay by Norman Panama and Melvin Frank; from a story by Don Hartman and Allen Boretz
Cast: Cornel Wilde, Spring Byington, Ron Randell, Thurston Hall, Charles Evans, William Bevan, Frank Orth, Percy Waram, Harry Hays Morgan, Douglas Wood, Mary Forbes, Nancy Saunders, Douglas D. Coppin, Michael Towne, Fred Sears, Paul Campbell, Carol Nugent, Judy Nugent, Mary Patterson, Myron Healey, Harlan Warde, Anna Q. Nilsson, George Chandler,

Edward Harvey, Allen Wood, Vera Lewis, Cliff Clark, Victor Travers
Roxy Theater

(58) THE BARKLEYS OF BROADWAY
MGM, May 5, 1949   Directed by Charles Walters
Produced by Arthur Freed
Screenplay by Betty Comden and Adolph Green
Songs by Harry Warren and Ira Gershwin, plus "They Can't Take That Away from Me"
Astaire's choreography by Hermes Pan; other choreography by Robert Alton
Cast: Fred Astaire, Oscar Levant, Billie Burke, Gale Robbins, Jacques Francois, George Zucco, Clinton Sundberg, Inez Cooper, Carol Brewster, Wilson Wood, Laura Treadwell, Allen Wood, Margaret Bert, Alphonse Martell, Howard Mitchell, Marcel de la Brosse, Wilbur Mack, Larry Steers, Lillian West, Forbes Murray, Bess Flowers, Lois Austin, Betty Blythe, Bill Tannen, Betty O'Kelly, Pat Miller, Bobbie Brooks, Charles Van, Richard Winters, Mickey Martin, Dick Barron, Lorraine Crawford, Mahlon Hamilton, Dee Turnell, Reginald Simpson, Hans Conreid, Sherry Hall, Frank Ferguson, George Boyce, John Albright, Butch Terrell, Edward Kilroy, Nolan Leary, Joe Granby, Esther Somers, Helen Eby-Rock, Joyce Mathews, Bob Purcell, Max Willenz, Jack Rice, Roger Moore, Wheaton Chambers, Roberta Jackson
Loew's State Theater

(59) PERFECT STRANGERS
Warner Brothers, March 11, 1950   Directed by Bretaigne Windust
Produced by Jerry Wald
Screenplay by Edith Sommer; adapted by George Oppenheimer from Charles MacArthur and Ben Hecht's *Ladies and Gentlemen*, which was based on an L. Bush-Fekete drama
Cast: Dennis Morgan, Thelma Ritter, Margalo Gillmore, Anthony Ross, Howard Freeman, Alan Reed, Paul Ford, Harry Bellaver, George Chandler, Frank Conlan, Charles Meredith, Frances Charles, Marjorie Bennett, Paul McVey, Edith Evanson, Whit Bissell, Sumner Getchell, Ford Rainey, Sarah Selby, Alan Wilson, Ronnie Tyler, Isabelle Withers, Max Mellenger, Boyd Davis, Ezelle Poule, Creighton Hale, John Albright, Frank Marlowe, Ed Coke, Dick Kipling
Strand Theater

(60) STORM WARNING
Warner Brothers, March 3, 1951   Directed by Stuart Heisler
Produced by Jerry Wald
Screenplay by Daniel Fuchs and Richard Brooks
Cast: Ronald Reagan, Doris Day, Steve Cochran, Hugh Sanders, Lloyd

Gough, Raymond Greenleaf, Ned Glass, Paul E. Burns, Walter Baldwin, Lynn Whitney, Stuart Randall, Sean McClory, Dave McMahon, Robert Williams, Charles Watts, Charles Phillips, Dale Van Sickel, Anthony Warde, Paul Brinegar, Len Hendry, Ned Davenport, Frank Marlowe, Leo Cleary, Alex Gerry, Charles Conrad, Lillian Albertson, Eddie Hearn, Harry Harvey, Janet Barrett, Lloyd Jenkins, King Donovan, Tommy Walker, Dewey Robinson, Gene Evans
Strand Theater

(61) THE GROOM WORE SPURS

Fidelity Pictures-Universal, March 14, 1951 Directed by Richard Whorf
Produced by Howard Welsch
Screenplay by Robert Carson, Robert Libott and Frank Burt; based on Robert Carson's story *Legal Bride*
Cast: Jack Carson, Joan Davis, Stanley Ridges, James Brown, John Litel, Victor Sen Yung, Mira McKinney, Gordon Nelson, George Meader, Kemp Niver, Robert B. Williams
Criterion Theater

(62) WE'RE NOT MARRIED

Twentieth Century-Fox, July 12, 1952 Directed by Edmund Goulding
Produced by Nunnally Johnson
Screenplay by Nunnally Johnson; adaptation by Dwight Taylor of a story by Gina Kaus and Jay Dratler
Cast: Fred Allen, Victor Moore, Marilyn Monroe, David Wayne, Eve Arden, Paul Douglas, Eddie Bracken, Mitzi Gaynor, Louis Calhern, Zsa Zsa Gabor, James Gleason, Paul Stewart, Jane Darwell, Alan Bridge, Harry Golder, Victor Sutherland, Tom Powers, Kay English, Lee Marvin, O. Z. Whitehead, Marjorie Weaver, Dabbs Greer, Forbes Murray, Maurice Cass, Margie Liszt, Maude Wallace, Richard Buckley, Alvin Greenman, Eddie Firestone, Phyllis Brunner, Steve Pritko, Robert Dane, James Burke, Robert Forrest, Bill Hale, Ed Max, Richard Reeves, Ralph Dumke, Harry Antrim, Byron Foulger, Harry Harvey, Selmer Jackson, Harry Carter, Emile Meyer, Henry Faber, Larry Stamps
Roxy Theater

(63) DREAMBOAT

Twentieth Century-Fox, July 26, 1952 Directed by Claude Binyon
Produced by Sol C. Siegel
Screenplay by Claude Binyon; based on a story by John D. Weaver
Cast: Clifton Webb, Anne Francis, Jeffrey Hunter, Elsa Lanchester, Fred Clark, Paul Harvey, Ray Collins, Helene Stanley, Richard Garrick, Jay Adler, George Barrows, Marietta Canty, Emory Parnell, Laura Brooks, Gwen Verdon, Matt Mattox, Frank Radcliffe, May Wynn, Vickie Raaf, Bar-

bara Wooddell, Robert B. Williams, Tony De Mario, Steve Carruthers, Joe Recht, Victoria Horne, Bob Nichols, Alphonse Martel, Mary Treen, Fred Graham, Richard Karlan, Jean Corbett
Roxy Theater

(64) MONKEY BUSINESS

Twentieth Century-Fox, September 6, 1952   Directed by Howard Hawks
Produced by Sol C. Siegel
Screenplay by Ben Hecht, Charles Lederer and I. A. L. Diamond; from a story by Harry Segall
Cast: Cary Grant, Charles Coburn, Marilyn Monroe, Hugh Marlowe, Henri Letondal, Robert Cornthwaite, Larry Keating, Douglas Spencer, Esther Dale, George Winslow, Emmett Lynn, Gil Stratton, Jr., Faire Binney, Harry Carey, Jr.
Roxy Theater

(65) FOREVER FEMALE

Paramount, January 14, 1954   Directed by Irving Rapper
Produced by Pat Duggan
Screenplay by Julius J. Epstein and Philip G. Epstein; from a play by J. M. Barrie
Cast: William Holden, Paul Douglas, Pat Crowley, James Gleason, Jesse White, Marjoie Rambeau, George Reeves, King Donovan, Vic Perrin, Russell Gaige, Marian Ross, Richard Shannon, Sally Mansfield, Kathryn Grant, Rand Harper, Henry Dar, Victor Romito, Hyacinthe Railla, Alfred Paix, Joel Marston, Almira Sessions, Michael Darrin
Victoria Theater

(66) BLACK WIDOW

20th Century-Fox, October 28, 1954
Written, produced and directed by Nunnally Johnson; from a story by Patrick Quentin
Cast: Van Heflin, Gene Tierney, George Raft, Peggy Ann Garner, Reginald Gardiner, Virigina Leith, Otto Kruger, Cathleen Nesbitt, Skip Homeier, Hilda Simms, Harry Carter, Geraldine Wall, Richard Cutting, Mabel Albertson, Aaron Spelling, Wilson Wood, Tony De Mario, Virginia Maples, Frances Driver, Michael Vallon, James F. Stone
Roxy Theater

(67) TWIST OF FATE

UA, 1954 (not reviewed in New York)   Directed by David Miller
Produced by Maxwell Setton and John R. Sloan
Screenplay by Robert Westerby and Carl Nystrom; from a story by Rip Van Ronkel and David Miller

Cast: Herbert Lom, Jacques Bergerac, Stanley Baker, Margaret Rawlings, Eddie Byrne, Lily ,Kann, Coral Browne, Lisa Gastoni, John Chandos, Ferdy Mayne, Rudolph Offenbach

(68) TIGHT SPOT

Columbia, March 19, 1955   Directed by Phil Karlson
Produced by Lewis J. Rachmil
Screenplay by William Bowers; based on Leonard Cantor's play *Dead Pigeon*
Cast: Brian Keith, Edward G. Robinson, Katherine Anderson, Lorne Greene, Eve McVeagh, Allen Nourse, Peter Leeds, Lucy Marlowe, Helen Wallace, Frank Gentle, Gloria Ann Simpson, Robert Shield, Norman Keats, Kathryn Grant, Will J. White, Patrick Miller, Bob Hopkins, Kenneth N. Mayer, Dean Cromer, Tom de Graffenried, Joseph Hamilton, Robert Nichols, Alfred Linder, Ed Hinton, John Larch
Palace Theater

(69) TEENAGE REBEL

Twentieth Century-Fox, November 17, 1956   Directed by Edmund Goulding
Produced by Charles Brackett
Screenplay by Walter Reisch and Charles Brackett; adapted from Edith Sommer's play *Roomful of Roses*
Cast: Michael Rennie, Betty Lou Keim, Mildred Natwick, Lili Gentle, Louise Beavers, Irene Hervey, John Stephenson, Warren Berlinger, Diane Jergens, Rusty Swope, Susan Luckey, James O'Rear, Gary Gray, Pattee Chapman, Richard Collier, Wade Dumas, James Stone, Sheila James, Joan Freeman, Gene Foley
Globe Theater

(70) THE FIRST TRAVELING SALESLADY

RKO-Radio, 1956 (not reviewed in New York)
Directed and produced by Arthur Lubin
Screenplay by Devery Freeman and Stephen Longstreet
Cast: Barry Nelson, Carol Channing, David Brian, James Arness, Clint Eastwood, Frank Wilcox, Robert Simon, Daniel M. White, Harry Chesire, John Eldredge, Robert Hinkle, Jack Rice, Kate Drain Lawson, Edward Cassidy, Fred Essler, Bill Hale, Lovyss Bradley, Nora Bush, Ann Kunde, Hans Herbert, Lynn Noe, Joan Tyler, Janette Miler, Kathy Marlowe, Roy Darmour, Peter Croyden, Al Cavens, Paul Bradley, Hal Taggart, Ian Murray, Robert Easton, Lester Dorr, Frank Soannel, Paul Keast, Mauritz Hugo, Julius Eyans, Stanley Farrer, Lane Chandler

(71) OH, MEN! OH, WOMEN!

Twentieth Century-Fox, February 22, 1957
Directed and produced by Nunnally Johnson; from Edward Chodorov's play

Cast: Dan Dailey, David Niven, Barbara Rush, Tony Randall, Rachel Stephens, John Wengraf, Cheryl Clark, Charles Davis, Natalie Schafer, Clancy Cooper, Joel Fluellen, Franklin Pangborn, Franklin Farnum, Hal Taggart
Roxy Theater

(72) HARLOW
Bill Sargent-Magna, May 15, 1965   Directed by Alex Segal
Produced by Lee Savin.   Screenplay by Karl Tunberg
Cast: Carol Lynley, Barry Sullivan, Efrem Zimbalist, Jr., Lloyd Bochner, John Williams, Jack Kruschen, Michael Dante, Hermione Baddeley, Audrey Christie, Hurd Hatfield, Audrey Totter, Celia Lovsky, Robert Strauss, James Dobson, Sonny Liston, Nick Demitri, Cliff Norton, Paulle Clark, Jim Plunkett, John Fox, Joel Marston, Christopher West, Fred Conte, Catherine Ross, Buddy Lewis, Danny Francis, Frank Scannell, Maureene Gaffney, Ron Kennedy, Harry Holcombe, Lola Fisher, Fred Klein
Paramount Theater

(73) THE CONFESSION
Golden Eagle, 1964 (not released)   Directed by William Dieterle
Produced by William Marshall
Screenplay by Allan Scott; based on a story by William Marshall
Cast: Ray Milland, Barbara Eden, Carl Schell, Michael Ansara, Elliot Gould, Walter Abel, Vinton Hayworth, David Hurst, Pippa Scott, Cecil Kellaway, Michael Youngman, Julian Upton, Mara Lynn, Carol Ann Daniels, Leonard Cimino

Long Play Record

Ginger Rogers, Silver Screen Series

Ginger Rogers' Stage Career

1926: Texas Charleston Champion. Began vaudeville tour as "Ginger Rogers and Her Redheads."

1929: Top Speed. Ginger's first Broadway role in musical comedy as Babs Green, the second lead. Opened December 25 at Chanin's 46th Street Theater

1930: Girl Crazy. Ginger was the leading lady in the Gershwin hit, but Ethel Merman stole the show. Opened October 14 at the Alvin.

1951: *Love and Let Love.* Trouble-plagued play by Louis Verneuil became more of a fashion show than a comedy. Opened October 19 at the Plymouth.

1957: *Bells Are Ringing.* Ginger toured in the role orginated by Judy Holliday.

1959: *The Pink Jungle.* Leslie Steven's story of the cosmetics business opened in San Francisco October 14 on what was billed as a pre-Broadway tour. After playing Detroit and Boston, it closed for revamping. It never reopened.

1960: *Annie Get Your Gun.* Summer stock production with Ginger in the Merman role.

1963: *The Unsinkable Molly Brown.* Summer production with Ginger in the part originated by Tammy Grimes.

1964: *Tovarich.* Summer production with Ginger as the White Russian reduced to working as a maid. The role in this musical was originated by Vivien Leigh.

1965: *Hello, Dolly!* Ginger succeeded Carol Channing as Dolly Gallagher Levi, played the role eighteen months on Broadway, then joined the national company, playing Dallas, San Diego, Denver, Los Angeles, San Francisco, Las Vegas, etc.

1969: *Mame.* Ginger played the title role in the London production, opening February 21 at the Theatre Royale. Earned mixed notices and the highest salary ever paid a performer on the London stage.

1971: *Coco.* National tour in which Ginger played Katharine Hepburn's role.

1972: *Our Town.* Ginger played the part of the stage manager in this student production which was part of dedication ceremonies for the $2,000,000 Ida Green Communications Center at Austin College in Sherman, Texas.

1974: *No, No, Nanette.* Summer production.

1974: *Forty Carats.* Ginger "had the honor" of opening the new Drury Lane Theater East in Chicago with this Broadway comedy.

1975: *Forty Carats.* Summer circuit.

1976: Kicked off her fiftieth year in show business in a nightclub revue designed for New York, Las Vegas, Los Angeles and spots in between.

MIRIAM HOPKINS

Films of Miriam Hopkins

Dates are for New York City release

(1) FAST AND LOOSE
Paramount, December 1, 1930   Directed by Fred Newmeyer
Screenplay by Preston Sturges, Doris Anderson and Jack Kirkland; adapted
from Avery Hopwood and David Gray's play *The Best People*
Cast: Frank Morgan, Carole Lombard, Charles Starrett, Henry Wadsworth,
Winifred Harris, Herbert Yost, David Hutcheson, Ilka Chase, Herschel
Mayall
Paramount Theater

(2) THE SMILING LIEUTENANT
Paramount, May 23, 1931   Directed by Ernst Lubitsch
Screenplay by Ernest Vajda and Samson Raphaelson; adapted from Hans Mül-
ler's novel *Nux der Prinzgemahl* and the Leopold Jacobson, Felix Dormann,
Oscar Strauss operetta *A Waltz Dream*.
Music by Oscar Strauss and Clifford Grey
Cast: Maurice Chevalier, Claudette Colbert, George Barbier, Hugh O'Connell,
Charles Ruggles, Robert Strange, Janet Reade, Con MacSunday, Elizabeth
Patterson, Harry Bradley, Werner Saxtorph, Karl Stall, Granville Bates
Criterion Theater

(3) TWENTY-FOUR HOURS
Paramount, October 3, 1931   Directed by Marion Gering
Screenplay by Louis Weitzenkorn; based on Louis Bromfield's novel *24 Hours*
Cast: Clive Brook, Kay Francis, Regis Toomey, George Barbier, Adrienne
Ames, Charlotte Granville, Minor Watson, Lucille La Verne, Wade Boteler,
Robert Kortman, Malcolm Waite, Thomas Jackson
Times Square and Brooklyn Paramount Theaters

(4) DR. JEKYLL AND MR. HYDE
Paramount, January 2, 1932   Directed and produced by Rouben Mamoulian
Screenplay by Samuel Hoffenstein and Percy Heath; based on Robert Louis
Stevenson's story

Cast: Fredric March, Rose Hobart, Holmes Herbert, Halliwell Hobbes, Edgar Norton, Arnold Lucy, Colonel MacDonnell, Tempe Pigott
Rivoli Theater

(5) TWO KINDS OF WOMEN
Paramount, January 16, 1932   Directed by William C. de Mille
Screenplay by Benjamin Glazer; adapted from Robert E. Sherwood's play *This Is New York*
Cast: Phillips Holmes, Wynne Gibson, Stuart Erwin, Irving Pichel, Stanley Fields, James Crane, Vivienne Osborne, Josephine Dunn, Robert Emmett O'Connor, Larry Steers, Adrienne Ames, Claire Dodd, Terrence Ray, June Nash, Kent Taylor, Edwin Maxwell, Lindsay McHarris
Times Square and Brooklyn Paramount Theaters

(6) DANCERS IN THE DARK
Paramount, March 19, 1932   Directed by David Burton
Screenplay by Herman J. Mankiewicz; adapted by Brian Marlow and Howard Emmett Rogers from James Creelman's play *Jazz King*
Cast: Jack Oakie, William Collier, Jr. Eugene Pallette, Walter Hiers, Lyda Roberti, George Raft, Maurice Black, Frances Moffett, DeWitt Jennings, Alberta Vaughn, Paul Fix, Kent Taylor,
Times Square and Brooklyn Paramount Theaters

(7) THE WORLD AND THE FLESH
Paramount, May 7, 1932   Directed by John Cromwell
Screenplay by Oliver H. P. Garrett; based on Phillip Zeska and Ernest Spitz's play
Cast: George Bancroft, Alan Mowbray, George E. Stone, Emmett Corrigan, Mitchell Lewis, Oscar Apfel, Harry Cording, Max Wagner, Reginald Barlow, Ferike Boros
Times Square and Brooklyn Paramount Theaters.

(8) TROUBLE IN PARADISE
Paramount, November 9, 1932   Directed and produced by Ernst Lubitsch
Screenplay by Samson Raphaelson and Grover Jones; based on Laszlo Aladar's play *The Honest Finder*
Songs by Leo Robin and W. Franke Harling
Cast: Kay Francis, Herbert Marshall, Charles Ruggles, Edward Everett Horton, C. Aubrey Smith, Robert Greigh, George Humbert, Rolfe Sedan, Luis Alberni, Hooper Atchley
Rivoli Theater

(9) THE STORY OF TEMPLE DRAKE
Paramount, May 6, 1933   Directed by Stephen Roberts

Screenplay by Oliver H. P. Garrett; based on William Faulkner's *Sanctuary*
Cast: Jack LaRue, William Gargan, William Collier, Jr., Irving Pichel, Sir Guy
Standing, Elizabeth Patterson, Florence Eldridge, James Eagles, Harlan E.
Knight, James Mason, Jobyna Howland, Henry Hall, John Carradine, Oscar
Apfel, Kent Taylor
Paramount Theater

(10) THE STRANGER'S RETURN
MGM, July 28, 1933   Directed by King Vidor
Screenplay by Brown Homes and Phil Stong; based on a novel by Phil Stong
Cast: Lionel Barrymore, Franchot Tone, Stuart Erwin, Irene Hervey, Beulah
Bondi, Grant Mitchell, Tad Alexander, Aileen Caryle
Capitol Theater

(11) DESIGN FOR LIVING
Paramount, November 23, 1933   Directed by Ernst Lubitsch
Screenplay by Ben Hecht; loosely based on Noel Coward's play
Cast: Fredric March, Gary Cooper, Edward Everett Horton, Franklin Pang-
born, Isabel Jewell, Harry Dunkinson, Helena Phillips, Jane Darwell,
Adrienne d'Ambricourt, Emile Chautard, Rolfe Sedan
Criterion Theater

(12) ALL OF ME
Paramount, February 5, 1934   Directed by James Flood
Screenplay by Sidney Buchman and Thomas Mitchell; adapted from Rose Al-
bert Porter's play *Chrysalis*
Music and lyrics by Leo Robin and Ralph Rainger
Cast: Fredric March, George Raft, Helen Mack, Nella Walker, William Col-
lier, Jr., Gilbert Emery, Blanche Frederici, Kitty Kelly, Guy Usher, John
Marston, Edgar Kennedy
Times Square and Brooklyn Paramount Theaters

(13) SHE LOVES ME NOT
Paramount, September 8, 1934   Directed by Elliott Nugent
Produced by Benjamin Glazer
Screenplay by Benjamin Glazer; from novel by Edward Hope and play by
Howard Lindsay
Music: "Love In Bloom" by Leo Robin and Ralph Rainger; "After All, You're
All I'm After" by Edward Heyman and Arthur Schwarz; "Straight from the
Shoulder," "I'm Hummin', I'm Whistlin', I'm Singin'" and "Put a Little
Rhythm in Everything You Do" by Mack Gordon and Harry Revel
Cast: Bing Crosby, Kitty Carlisle, Edward Nugent, Henry Stephenson, War-
ren Hymer, Lynne Overman, Judith Allen, George Barbier, Henry Kolker,

307

Maude Turner Gordon, Margaret Armstrong, Ralf Harolde, Matt McHugh, Franklyn Ardell, Vince Barnett
Paramount Theater

(14) THE RICHEST GIRL IN THE WORLD
RKO-Radio, September 21, 1934   Directed by William A. Seiter
Produced by Pandro S. Berman
Screenplay and story by Norman Krasna
Cast: Joel McCrea, Fay Wray, Henry Stephenson, Reginald Denny, George Meeker, Wade Boteler, Fred Howard, Herbert Bunston, Burr McIntosh, Edgar Norton, Beryl Mercer
Radio City Music Hall

(15) BECKY SHARP
Pioneer Pictures Production; released by RKO-Radio, June 14, 1935
Directed by Rouben Mamoulian.   Produced by Kenneth Macgowan
Screenplay by Francis Edward Faragoh; adaptation of Langdon Mitchell's play, which was based on Thackeray's *Vanity Fair*
Color designs for first three-color technicolor film by Robert Edmond Jones
Cast: Frances Dee, Sir Cedric Hardwicke, Billie Burke, Alison Skipworth, Nigel Bruce, Alan Mowbray, Colin Tapley, G. P. Huntley, Jr., William Stack, George Hassell, William Faversham, Charles Richman, Doris Lloyd, Leonard Mudie, Bunny Beatty, Charles Coleman, May Beatty, Finis Barton, Olaf Hytten, Pauline Garon, James Robinson, Elspeth Dudgeon, Tempe Pigott, Ottola Nesmith, Pat Ryan (to become Pat Nixon in 1940)
Radio City Music Hall

(16) BARBARY COAST
Samuel Goldwyn-UA, October 14, 1935   Directed by Howard Hawks
Screenplay by Charles MacArthur and Ben Hecht
Edward G. Robinson, Joel McCrea, Walter Brennan, Frank Craven, Brian Donlevy, Clyde Cook, Harry Carey, Matt McHugh, Otto Hoffman, Rollo Lloyd, J. M. Kerrigan, Donald Meek, Fred Vogeding, Dave Wegren, Anders Van Haden, Jules Cowles, Cyril Thorton, Roger Gray, David Niven, Herman Bing, Jim Thorpe
Rivoli Theater

(17) SPLENDOR
Samuel Goldwyn-UA, November 23, 1935   Directed by Elliott Nugent
Screenplay and story by Rachel Crothers
Cast: Joel McCrea, Paul Cavanagh, Helen Westley, Billie Burke, Katharine Alexander, Ruth Weston, David Niven, Ivan Simpson, Arthur Treacher, Torben Meyer, Reginald Sheffield
Rivoli Theater

(18) THESE THREE
Samuel Goldwyn-UA, March 19, 1936   Directed by William Wyler

Screenplay by Lillian Hellman; from her play *The Children's Hour*
Cast: Merle Oberon, Joel McCrea, Catherine Doucet, Alma Kruger, Bonita Granville, Marcia Mae Jones, Carmencita Johnson, Margaret Hamilton, Marie Louis Cooper, Walter Brennan
Rivoli

(19) MEN ARE NOT GODS
Alexander Korda-UA, January 19, 1937   Directed by Walter Reisch
Screenplay by C. B. Stern, Iris Wright and William Hornbeck; story by Walter Reisch
Cast: Gertrude Lawrence, Sebastian Shaw, Rex Harrison, A. E. Matthews, Val Gielgud, Laura Smithson, Lawrence Grossmith, Sybil Grove, Winifred Willard, Wally Patch, James Harcourt, Rosamund Greenwood, Noel Howlett, Paddy Morgan, Nicholas Nadejin, Michael Hogarth
Rivoli Theater

(20) THE WOMAN I LOVE
RKO-Radio, April 16, 1937   Directed by Anatol Litvak
Produced by Albert Lewis
Screenplay by Ethel Borden; from Joseph Kessel's novel *L'Equipage*
Cast: Paul Muni, Louis Hayward, Colin Clive, Minor Watson, Elizabeth Risdon, Paul Guilfoyle, Wally Albright, Mady Christians, Alec Craig, Owen Davis, Jr., Sterling Holloway, Vince Barnett, Adrian Morris, Donald Barry, Joe Twerp, William Stelling
Radio City Music Hall

(21) WOMAN CHASES MAN
Samuel Goldwyn-UA, June 11, 1937   Directed by John Blystone
Screenplay by Dorothy Parker, Alan Campbell and Joe Bigelow; from a story by Lynn Root and Frank Fenton
Cast: Joel McCrea, Charles Winninger, Erik Rhodes, Ella Logan, Leona Maricle, Broderick Crawford, Charles Halton, William Jaffrey, George Chandler, Alan Bridge, Monte Vandergrift, Jack Baxley, Walter Soderling, Al K. Hall, Dick Cramer
Radio City Music Hall

(22) WISE GIRL
RKO-Radio, January 10, 1938   Directed by Leigh Jason
Produced by Edward Kaufman
Screenplay by Allan Scott; from story by Allan Scott and Charles Norman
Cast: Ray Milland, Walter Abel, Henry Stephenson, Alec Craig, Guinn Williams, Betty Philson, Marianna Strelby, Margaret Dumont, Jean de Briac, Ivan Lebedeff, F. Rafael Storm, Gregory Gaye, Richard Lane, Tom Kennedy, James Finlayson
Rivoli Theater

(23) THE OLD MAID

Warner Brothers, August 12, 1939   Directed by Edmund Goulding
Produced by Hal Wallis
Screenplay by Casey Robinson; from play by Zoë Akins, based on Edith
  Wharton's novel
Cast: Bette Davis, George Brent, Jane Bryan, Donald Crisp, Louise Fazenda,
  James Stephenson, Jerome Cowan, William Lundigan, Cecilia Loftus, Rand
  Brooks, Janet Shaw, DeWolf (Bill) Hopper, Frederick Burton, Doris Lloyd
Strand Theater

(24) VIRGINIA CITY

Warner Brothers, March 23, 1940   Directed by Michael Curtiz
Executive producer: Hal Wallis
Screenplay by Robert Buckner
Cast: Errol Flynn, Randolph Scott, Humphrey Bogart, Frank McHugh, Alan
  Hale, Guinn Williams, John Litel, Russell Hicks, Russell Simpson, Thurston
  Hall, Charles Middleton, Victor Kilian, Ward Bond, Spencer Charters, De-
  Wolfe (Bill) Hopper, George Reeves
Strand Theater

(25) LADY WITH RED HAIR

Warner Brothers, December 6, 1940   Directed by Kurt Bernhardt
Screenplay by Charles Kenyon and Milton Krims; story by N. Brewster Morse
  and Norbert Faulkner, based on Mrs. Leslie Carter's memoirs
Cast: Claude Rains, Richard Ainley, Laura Hope Crews, Helen Westley, John
  Litel, Mona Barrie, Victor Jory, Cecil Kellaway, Fritz Lieber, Johnny Rus-
  sell, Selmer Jackson, Halliwell Hobbs, William Davidson, Doris Lloyd,
  Alexis Smith, William (DeWolfe) Hopper, Russell Hicks, Florence Shirley
Palace Theater

(26) A GENTLEMAN AFTER DARK

Edward Small-UA, April 17, 1942   Directed by Edwin L. Marin
Screenplay by Patterson McNutt and George Bruce; based on Richard Wash-
  burn Child's *A Whiff of Heliotrope*
Cast: Brian Donlevy, Preston Foster, Harold Huber, Philip Reed, Gloria Hol-
  den, Douglas Dumbrille, Sharon Douglas, Bill Henry, Ralph Morgan, Jack
  Mulhall
Loew's State Theater

(27) OLD ACQUAINTANCE

Warner Brothers, November 3, 1943   Directed by Vincent Sherman
Produced by Henry Blanke
Screenplay by John Van Druten and Lenore Coffee; from Van Druten's play
Cast: Bette Davis, Gig Young, John Loder, Dolores Moran, Philip Reed,

Roscoe Karns, Anne Revere, Esther Dale, Francine Rufo, Leona Maricle
Hollywood Theater

(28) THE HEIRESS
Paramount, October 7, 1949　　　　Directed and produced by William Wyler
Screenplay by Ruth and Augustus Goetz; from the Goetzs' play, based on
　Henry James' *Washington Square*
Cast: Olivia de Havilland, Montgomery Clift, Ralph Richardson, Venessa
　Brown, Mona Freeman, Ray Collins, Betty Linley, Selena Royle, Paul Lees,
　Harry Antrim, Russ Conway, David Thursby
Radio City Music Hall

(29) THE MATING SEASON
Paramount, April 12, 1951　　　　Directed by Mitchell Leisen
Produced by Charles Brackett
Screenplay by Charles Brackett, Walter Reisch and Richard Breen
Cast: Thelma Ritter, John Lund, Gene Tierney, Jan Sterling, Larry Keating,
　James Lorimer, Cora Witherspoon, Malcolm Keen, Gladys Hurlburt, Ellen
　Corby, Billie Bird, Mary Young, Samuel Colt, Jean Acker, Ben Flowers
Paramount Theater

(30) THE OUTCASTS OF POKER FLAT
Twentieth Century-Fox, May 16, 1952　　　　Directed by Joseph M. Newman
Produced by Julian Blaustein
Screenplay by Edmund H. North; from a story by Bret Harte
Cast: Anne Baxter, Dale Robertson, Cameron Mitchell, Craig Hill, Barbara
　Bates, Billy Lynn, Dick Rich, Tom Greenway, Russ Conway, John Ridgely,
　Harry T. Shannon, Harry Harvey, Sr., Lee Phelps, Kit Carson, Bob Adler
Mayfair Theater

(31) CARRIE
Paramount, July 17, 1952　　　　Directed and produced by William Wyler
Screenplay by Ruth and Augustus Goetz; based on Theodore Dreiser's *Sister
　Carrie*
Cast: Laurence Olivier, Jennifer Jones, Eddie Albert, Basil Ruysdael, Ray
　Teal, Barry Kelley, Sara Berner, William Regnolds, Mary Murphy, Harry
　Hayden, Charles Halton, Walter Baldwin, Dorothy Adams, Jacqueline de
　Wit, Harlan Briggs, Melinda Plowman, Donald Kerr, Lester Sharpe, Don
　Beddoe, John Alvin, Royal Dano, Snub Pollard
Capitol Theater

(32) THE CHILDREN'S HOUR
UA, March 15, 1962　　　　Directed and produced by William Wyler
Screenplay by John Michael Hayes; adapted by Lillian Hellman from her play

Cast: Audrey Hepburn, Shirley MacLaine, James Garner, Fay Bainter, Karen Balkin, Veronica Cartwright, Jered Barclay
Astor Theater, Trans-Lux 52nd Street Theater

(33) FANNY HILL
Pan World, December 2, 1965   Directed by Russ Meyer
Produced by Al Zugsmith
Screenplay by Robert Hill; based on John Cleland's novel
Cast: Letitia Roman, Walter Giller, Alex D'Arcy, Helmut Weiss, Ulli Lommel, Chris Howland, Christiane Schmidtmer, Cara Garnett, Albert Zugsmith, Patricia Houston, Karen Evans, Heidi Hansen, Erica Erikson
Released in neighborhood theaters

(34) THE CHASE
Columbia, February 19, 1966   Directed by Arthur Penn
Produced by Sam Spiegel
Screenplay by Lillian Hellman; based on Horton Foote's novel and play
Cast: Marlon Brando, Jane Fonda, Robert Redford, E. G. Marshall, Angie Dickinson, Janice Rule, Martha Hyer, Robert Duvall, Henry Hull, Diana Hyland, James Fox, Jocelyn Brando, Richard Bradford, Katherine Walsh, Malcolm Atterbury, Clifton James, Nydia Westman, Bruce Cabot, Paul Williams, Marc Seaton
Victoria and Sutton Theaters

(35) COMEBACK
Congdon (never released)   Directed and produced by Donald Wolfe
Executive producer: J. Talmadge Congdon
Screenplay by Donald Wolfe
Cast: Gale Sondergaard, John Garfield, Jr., Minta Durfee Arbuckle, Joe Besser, Katina Garner, Virginia Wing, Bud Douglass, Eddie Baker, Morris Reese

Miriam Hopkins' Stage Career

1919: The Fascinating Fanny Brown. Miriam made her stage debut in the senior class play at Goddard Seminary, Barre, Vermont.

1921: Music Box Revue. Miriam was one of the "Eight Silver Notes," a kind of superchorine, in this Irving Berlin revue.

1922: The Tavern. Miriam played Sally in stock.

1923: Little Jessie James. Miriam was cast as Juliette in Harlan Thompson and

Harry Archer's musical at the Longacre Theater. The opening on August 15 marked her Broadway debut in a speaking role.

1924: *High Tide.* Opened and closed in Washington, D.C.

1925: *Puppets.* Miriam succeeded Claudette Colbert out of town. Opened with Fredric March at Selwyn Theater, March 10.
The Enemy. Miriam was fired during the pre-Broadway tour of this Channing Pollock melodrama.
Lovely Lady. Miriam played in it only briefly.
The Matinee Girl. Another short run for Miriam.

1926: *Gentlemen Prefer Blondes.* Miriam was fired during rehearsals. Too intelligent to play Lorelei Lee.
An American Tragedy. Miriam played Sondra in Patrick Kearney's dramatization of Dreiser's novel. Opened at the Longacre to glowing notices.

1927: *The Home Towners.* Miriam played it in stock at the Four Cohans Theater in Chicago, where she filed for divorce.
Thou Desperate Pilot. Short run in Zoe Akins' play in March at the Morosco Theater.
The Last of Mrs. Cheyney, Is Zat So?, Applesauce and others, as leading ingenue with the famous Cukor-Kondolf Lyceum Players in Rochester, New York.
Garden of Eden. Lasted only twenty-three performances on Broadway.
Excess Baggage. Miriam made it big in the leading female role of this play about vaudeville. Opened December 26 at the Ritz Theater.

1928: *John Ferguson.* Experimental matinee, January 18.

1929: *Flight.* Miriam scandalized critics by stripping to her teddies. but the show closed anyway. Opened February 18 at the Lyceum.
The Camel through the Needle's Eye. Miriam opened in this Theatre Guild production on April 16 and played 72 performances.
The Bachelor Father. In September, London reviewers liked Miriam but not the play.

1930: *Ritzy.* Miriam and Ernest Truex couldn't save this trifle that opened February 10.
Lysistrata. Miriam created a sensation as Kalonika, a part written for her, in this classic. The role led to her film debut.
His Majesty's Car. Miriam and Ernest Truex had no better luck than in *Ritzy* in this Shubert production, which opened to tepid reviews October 24.

1931: The Affairs of Anatol. Miriam played Mimi in this all-star production, which opened to friendly reviews and a short run.

1933: Jezebel. Miriam returned from Hollywood to take over a role originally designed for Tallulah Bankhead, who was ill and unable to appear that season. Opened December 19 at the Ethel Barrymore.

1937: The Wine of Choice. S. N. Behrman's weak play wasn't helped by Miriam's endless "helpful" suggestions. She withdrew during pre-Broadway tryout.

1940: Battle of Angels. Miriam played the leading role in the first major production of a Tennessee Williams play. It opened and closed in Boston.

1943: The Skin of Our Teeth. Miriam followed Tallulah Bankhead as Sabina in Thornton Wilder's then-controversial drama on Broadway. Reviews were mixed.

1944: The Perfect Marriage. Samson Raphaelson's concoction about a divorce that didn't happen lacked the Lubitsch touch to put it over. Co-star Victor Jory felt Miriam was miscast.

1945: St. Lazare's Pharmacy. Eddie Dowling's production of this offbeat fantasy failed to repeat his 1944 success with Tennessee Williams' memory play, *The Glass Menagerie*. In its pre-Broadway tour, beginning in Montreal and ending in Chicago, Miriam created more drama off- than onstage.

1946: Laura. Hunt Stromberg, Jr., produced this vehicle for Miriam. Neither she nor Tom Neal lived up to expectations.

1947: Message for Margaret. Miriam, Mady Christians and Roger Pryor were caught in a five-performance disaster at the Plymouth Theater on April 16.
There's Always a Juliet. Miriam played it on the summer circuit.

1948: Happy Birthday. Anita Loos' comedy for Helen Hayes was taken on the road in November by Miriam.

1949: The Heiress. Miriam showed summer theatregoers that, though perhaps reduced to character parts in films, she could still do leading lady roles on the stage.

1952: A Night at Mme. Tussaud's. Miriam tried out this script in summer stock with Peter Lorre but decided it wouldn't do.

1953: Hay Fever. Miriam directed and starred in Noel Coward's play in summer stock.

1957: The Old Maid. Miriam co-starred with Sylvia Sidney in this summer package.

1958: Look Homeward, Angel. Miriam emerged triumphant as a replacement for Jo Van Fleet and took the play on tour in 1959.

1964: Riverside Drive. Miriam was replaced in this two-character play before the opening at the Theatre DeLys. Sylvia Sidney played her role.

RUTH ETTING

Feature Films of Ruth Etting

Dates are for New York City release

(1) ROMAN SCANDALS
Samuel Goldwyn-UA, December 25, 1933, Directed by Frank Tuttle
Screenplay by William Anthony McGuire, with additional dialogue by George
  Oppenheimer, Arthur Sheekman and Nat Perrin; from a story by George S.
  Kaufman and Robert E. Sherwood
Songs by Harry Warren, Al Dubin and L. Wolfe Gilbert
Choreography by Busby Berkeley
Cast: Eddie Cantor, Gloria Stuart, David Manners, Veree Teasdale, Edward
  Arnold, Alan Mowbray, Jack Rutherford, Grace Poggi, Lucille Ball,
Rivoli Theater

(2) HIPS, HIPS HOORAY
RKO-Radio, February 24, 1934 Directed by Mark Sandrich
Screenplay by Harry Ruby, Bert Kalmar and Edward Kaufman
Story, music and lyrics by Harry Ruby and Bert Kalmar
Choreography by Dave Gould
Cast: Bert Wheeler, Robert Woolsey, Thelma Todd, Dorothy Lee, George
  Meeker, James Burtis, Matt Briggs, Spencer Charters
Roxy Theater

(3) GIFT OF GAB
Universal, September 26, 1934 Directed by Karl Freund
Screenplay by Philip G. Epstein; based on a story by Jerry Wald and Philip G.
  Epstein
Music by Albert von Tilzer, Con Conrad and Charles Tobias
Cast: Edmund Lowe, Gloria Stuart, Phil Baker, Ethel Waters, Alice White,
  Alexander Woollcott, Victor Moore, Hugh O'Connell, Helen Vinson, Gene
  Austin, Thomas Hanlon, Henry Armetta, Andy Devine, Wini Shaw, Marion
  Byron, Sterling Holloway, Sid Walker, Skins Miller, Jack Harling, Edwin
  Maxwell, Leighton Noble, Maurice Block, Tammany Young, James Flavin,
  Billy Barty, Florence Enright, Richard Elliott, Warner Richmond
Rialto Theater

RUTH ETTING'S CAREER

1918–1926: CHICAGO

Chorus girl in show starring Sophie Tucker and Bill "Bojangles" Robinson at
  Marigold Gardens cabaret. Ruth steps in for baritone Bobby Roberts,
  dressed in tails and top hat, to sing "Hats Off to the Polo Girl."
Featured ingenue in Ernie Young's *The Passing Parade* at Marigold Gardens
Palais Royale
Fred Mann's Million Dollar Rainbo Gardens—shows: "Rainbo Trail," "In
  Rainbo Land," "Rainbo Blossoms"
Montmartre Café
Terrace Gardens (with Sam and Henry, later known as "Amos 'n' Andy")
Green Mill (with Helen Morgan)
Big Jim Colosimo's Café
College Inn (with Abe Lyman's Orchestra)
Granada

Radio spots on KYW, WQJ
WLS—billed as "Chicago's Sweetheart of the Air"

Ruth signed Columbia Recording contract in 1925.

Personal appearances in film palaces, including McVicker's Theater (Jazz
  Week, 1926); Palace Theater; Oriental Theater (with Paul Ash).

1927:

Paul Whiteman Club, New York City, unpublicized tryout, February

Official Manhattan debut at Paramount Theater with Paul Whiteman, June

ZIEGFELD FOLLIES OF 1927   August 16, 1927
Sketches by Harold Atteridge and Eddie Cantor
Score by Irving Berlin
Cast: Eddie Cantor, Andrew Tombes, Harry McNaughton, Dan Healy, Claire
  Luce, Irene Delroy, Franklyn Baur, Cliff "Ukulele Ike" Edwards, Brox Sis-
  ters, Edgar Fairchild and Ralph Rainger
(R. E. scored with "Shaking the Blues Away.")

1928:

Toured Pantages Circuit in the West

(1) RUTH ETTING   1 reel songs
Directed by Joseph Santley   Paramount-Astoria Studios
Short consisted of R. E. singing "Roses of Yesterday" and "Because My
Baby Don't Mean Maybe"
(In *Variety*, Land. observed, "She photographs like a million dollars.")
(2) PARAMOUNT MOVIETONE   1 reel songs
Directed by Joseph Santley   Paramount-Astoria Studios
R. E. sang "That's Him Now" and "My Mother's Eyes"
(*Billboard*: ". . . stands a fine chance of becoming a decided favor-
ite . . . as she is on the phonograph, where her billing is 'The Sweetheart
of Columbia Records.' ")

STAGE

WHOOPEE
Produced by Florenz Ziegfeld, Jr.   December 5
Book by William Anthony McGuire; adapted from Owen Davis' *The Nerv-
ous Wreck*
Music by Walter Donaldson; lyrics by Gus Kahn; staged by William An-
thony McGuire
Cast: Eddie Cantor, Ethel Shutta, Gladys Glad, Walter Hackett, Mary
Jane
(R. E. stopped the show with "Love Me or Leave Me.")

1929:

MOVIE SHORT SUBJECTS continued

(3) RUTH ETTING   with Phil Ohman-Victor Arden, twin pianos
Vitaphone 886   7 minutes   songs and piano
Directed by Murray Roth   Vitaphone Studios, Brooklyn
(Land. of *Variety* applauded "improvement in method and technique in
the making of shorts as contrasted with, say, a year ago.")

(4) GLORIFYING THE POPULAR SONG   Ohman-Arden, twin pianos
Vitaphone 894   1 reel songs and piano
Directed by Murray Roth   Vitaphone Studios, Brooklyn
Songs: "Wonderful Boy Friend," instrumental and "All I Want Is
Y-O-U"

(5) THE BOOK OF LOVERS
Illustrated version of the words to R. E.'s recording of "Deep Night."
Ruth did not appear.

MOVIE SHORT SUBJECTS continued

(6) BROADWAY'S LIKE THAT   WB Vitaphone Variety 960   1 reel
Directed by Arthur Hurley   Vitaphone Studios, Brooklyn
Cast: Joan Blondell, Humphrey Bogart, Mary Phillips
Plot: Ruth, demonstrator of popular songs in a Broadway music shop, falls
madly in love with a handsome customer. But he constantly finds ways to
sidestep marriage. Obligatory scene reveals he is already married to a bur-
lesque chorus cutie.
Songs: "Where Is the Man I Love" and "From the Bottom of My Heart"

(7) ROSELAND   WB Vitaphone Variety 2 reels
Directed by Roy Mack   *Cast:* Donald Cook
Plot: trials of a dance hall hostess
Songs: "Ten Cents a Dance," "Let Me Sing and I'm Happy," "Dancing
with Tears in My Eyes"

(8) ONE GOOD TURN   WB Vitaphone 112–23 2 reels
No director credited   *Cast:* Jay Velie
Plot: Singing star coaches her accompanist, who leaves to become a star in
his own right, then sinks to oblivion. Ruth is the only one who turns up to
sing at a benefit for him. They reconcile.
Songs: "The Kiss Waltz," "Don't Tell Her What's Happened to Me" and
"If I Could Be with You"
(Comment: "Best of the new crop," Rush, *Variety*)

STAGE

9:15 REVUE   February 11
Produced by Ruth Selwyn   George M. Cohan Theater
Sketches by Anita Loos, Ring Lardner, Eddie Cantor, Robert Riskin
Songs by George and Ira Gershwin, Rudolf Friml, Victor Herbert, Harold
Arlen and Ted Koehler, Kay Swift and Paul James, Vincent Youmans
(Ruth scored in this short-lived revue with Arlen and Koehler's "Get Hap-
py" and Kay Swift and Paul James' "Up Among the Chimney Pots.")

SIMPLE SIMON   February 18
Produced by Florenz Ziegfeld, Jr.
Book by Ed Wynn and Guy Bolton
Songs by Richard Rogers and Lorenz Hart
Staged by Zeke Colvan

319

Cast: Ed Wynn, Will Ahern, Bobbe Arnst, Harriet Hoctor, Helen Walsh, Hazel Forbes
(Ruth introduced "Ten Cents a Dance.")

VAUDEVILLE

Ruth and Lou Holtz headlined the Palace for a week in July, then completely changed their acts when held over for the second week.

Ruth returned to the Palace to kick off a vaudeville tour in October.

RADIO

Frequent guest shots. Some major ones included:
   First guest star on Walter Winchell's very first radio broadcast
   Frequent appearances with Rudy Vallee
   Majestic Hour

1931:

MOVIE SHORT SUBJECTS continued

(9) FRESHMAN LOVE   WB Vitaphone Varieties 1204–5   2 reels
Directed by Roy Mack   *Cast*: Jeanie Lang, Don Tomkins
Plot: Smitten college boy writes Ruth. Friends fake answers from her. Boy meets Ruth, who helps him turn tables on his tormentors.
Songs: "She's Funny That Way," "Love Is Like That"

(10) RADIO SALUTES   Paramount 1 reel
Nathaniel Shilkret and His Orchestra   Frederick Rogers
Ruth sang "You're Always Sure of My Love."

(11) WORDS AND MUSIC WB Vitaphone No 1288–9 20 mins 2 reels
Directed by Roy Mack   Written by Don Tomkins
Cast: Don Tomkins, Marjorie Lytell, Maurice Barrett, Blaire Kent, Byron Russell, Frank McNellis, Ralph Hertz and Harry Vokes
Plot: Ruth attempts to help country bumpkin outwit city slickers and break into the song writing racket.
Songs: "I'm Falling in Love with Love," "Now That You've Gone"

(12) SEASONS GREETINGS   WB Vitaphone 1 reel
Directed by Arthur Hurley
Cast: Joe Penner, Ted Husing, Robert L. Ripley, Thelma White, Billy Hayes, Fanny Watson, Mr. and Mrs. Jack Norworth

(13) OLD LACE   WB Vitaphone   2 reels 18 mins skit
Directed by Roy Mack   Written by Burnet Hershey and Stanley Rauh
Cast: Mabel Louis Andrews, Margaret Lee, Max Hoffman Jr., Shirley
Oliver, Arthur Donaldson, Patricia Lynn
Plot: One-time actress—now a ladies' maid—Ruth attempts to keep a star
from jilting her true love for a wastrel. In flashback, Ruth reveals she's
done that—and look at her now. Tag: that old boyfriend has become the
actress's chauffeur. Period ranged from Gay Nineties to the 1930s.
Songs: "Good Old Summertime," "She's Only a Bird in a Gilded Cage,"
"Let Me Call You Sweetheart" and "Pretty Baby."

STAGE

ZIEGFELD FOLLIES OF 1931   July 1, 1931
Produced by Florenz Ziegfeld, Jr.
Music and sketches: Gene Buck, Mark Hellinger, Dave Stamper, Walter
Donaldson and Dr. Hugo Riesenfeld
Dances by Bobby Connolly
Cast: Helen Morgan, Harry Richman, Jack Pearl, Hal LeRoy, Gladys
Glad, Ethel Borden, Albert Carroll, Faith Bacon and others
Songs: Ruth re-created "Shine On, Harvest Moon" and made it a hit
again; "Cigarettes, Cigars," etc.

ROXY CHRISTMAS SHOW
Ruth, the Mills Brothers and Patricia Bowman substituted for this Depres-
sion-time stage show at the Roxy, which had always featured a spectacle.
Held over.

1932:

MOVIE SHORT SUBJECTS continued

(14) A REGULAR TROUPER   WB Vitaphone 6032   19 mins
Skit and songs
Directed by Roy Mack   *Cast:* Wanda Perry, Edward Leiter
Plot: Ruth, who is engaged to the manager of a touring show, is jilted by
the manager for her younger sister.
Songs: "Without That Gal," "Why Did it Have to Be Me?"

(15) A MAIL BRIDE   WB Vitaphone   2 reels   19 mins
Directed by Roy Mack
Plot: Maid of singing star Ruth sends Ruth's photo to a matrimonial co-
lumn. Maid's suitor sends photo of a famous singer instead of one of him-

self. Both suitor and singing star arrive at the same time, but Ruth untangles the situation.

Songs: "Can't We Talk It Over," "When We're Alone," "Auf Wiedersehn"

(16) ARTISTIC TEMPERAMENT (also *Artistic Temper*)   WB Vitaphone
2 reels
Directed by Roy Mack
Cast: Wilfred Lytell, Lucille Sears, Johnny Dale, Victor Killian, Frank McNellis
Plot: Ruth rises from kitchen to Broadway stardom but returns to the kitchen—for love.
Songs: "Loveable," "What a Life," "That's What Heaven Means to Me"

(17) THE MODERN CINDERELLA   WB Vitaphone   2 reels
Directed by Roy Mack
Cast: Adrian Rosley, Barbara Child, Brian Donlevy, Merwin Light, Al Downing, Frank and Jean, Ralph Sumpter
Plot: not located
Songs: "Masquerade," "Dinah," "It Was So Beautiful," "Pretty Cinderella"

RADIO

Chesterfield's Music That Satisfies,   WABC and CBS network
(Norman Brokenshire, announcer). Ruth was with the program 1 year and 15 weeks.
Various combinations split the six weekly broadcasts, each taking two:
  R. E., Boswell Sisters, Nathaniel Shilkret Orchestra with Alex Gray
  R. E., Boswell Sisters, Arthur Tracy, accompanied by Shilkret
  R. E., Bing Crosby, Tom Howard and George Shelton, accompanied by Lenny Hayton and His Orchestra
  R. E., Bing Crosby, Jane Frohman

1933:

MOVIE SHORT SUBJECTS continued

(18) BYE-GONES   WB Vitaphone   18 minutes
Directed by Alf Goulding
Cast: Frank McNellis, Fritz and Jean Hubert, Embassy Boys
Plot: Singing star Ruth Etting tells kids of a thwarted romance. Flashback to a Western camp where she meets her sweetheart. They were separated

by World War I. They met briefly in France and were at last reunited when he saw her from a theater box while she performed on Broadway.

Songs: "Smiles," "Smile for Me," "I'll Follow You," "Melancholy Baby," "When My Baby Smiles at Me"

(Comment by exhibitor in *Motion Picture Herald*'s "What the Picture Did for Me" column, January 13, 1934: "A fine musical short that everyone liked. The best Miss Etting I have exhibited." Gladys E. McArdle, Owl Theater, Lebanon, Kansas. Small-town patronage.)

(19) ALONG CAME RUTH   WB Vitaphone 2 reels
Directed by Joseph Henabery
Written by Burnet Hershey and A. Adrian Otovos
Cast: Sam Wren, Charles Altholff, Chester Clute, Ruth DeQuincy
Plot: based on incidents from Ruth Etting's life
Songs: "Daisy," "Shine On, Harvest Moon," "Sidewalks of New York"

(20) CRASHING THE GATE   WB Vitaphone   2 reels
Directed by Joseph Henabery   July 1, 1933
Cast: Tony Sarg's Famous Marionettes; Roy Atwell, radio comic; Adler and Bradford, adagio dancers
Plot: struggle for success
Songs: "St. Louis Blues," "Play, Fiddle, Play," "Sitting on a Rainbow"
(Comment: *Motion Picture Herald*'s "What the Picture Did for Me," January 13, 1934: "Some very fine singing by the star. A good story and very interesting. Better than average short subject." Bert Silver, Silver Family Theater, Greenville, Michigan. General Patronage.)

(21) KNEE-DEEP IN MUSIC   RKO-Radio   22 minutes
Directed by Alf Goulding
Cast: Nat Carr, Garry Owen, Edward Elischu, Harry Akst, Eddie Borden, Hal Findlay, Betty Farrington, Jo Trent, Sylvester Scott
Plot: Ruth is hired as star of a new radio show, bought by Carr, who owns a dried-fish plant. Search is made for a new theme song. Studio is inundated by would-be songwriters when call is issued for material. In the end Ruth retains her old theme song.
Songs: "Shine On, Harvest Moon," "You've Got Me Crying Again," "We Couldn't Do Better Than That."

(22) CALIFORNIA WEATHER   RKO-Radio 20 1/2 minutes
Directed by Alf Goulding   Dec 15, 1933
Cast: Arthur Treacher, Luis Alberni, Bud Jamison, Eddie Borden, Harry Bowen
Plot: Musical genius Luis Alberni is trying to write an opera and also searching for "the perfect voice" of Ruth Etting. He's distracted from

writing by someone's voice. It turns out to belong to Ruth Etting.
Songs: "Shine On, Harvest Moon," "Stormy Weather," "Isn't This a Night for Love?"

RADIO: Jimmy Durante, Ruth, Rubinoff and His Violin headlined the *Chase and Sanborn Hour,* coast-to-coast WABC from Hollywood, Sundays at eight, for thirteen weeks.

1934:

MOVIE SHORT SUBJECTS continued

(23) HOLLYWOOD ON PARADE   Paramount
Shots of famous film faces, including Ruth Etting's.

(24) A TORCH TANGO   RKO-Radio
Reviewed in *Motion Picture Herald,* February 23, 1934
Cast: Will Ahern, Adrian Rosley, Eddie Hart, Mathilde Comont
Plot: not given
Songs: "Shine On, Harvest Moon," "Don't Blame Me," "Just a Kiss at Midnight"

(25) DERBY DECADE   RKO-Radio   22 minutes
Directed by Alf Goulding, produced by Lou Brock   July 12, 1934
Cast: Tom Kennedy, Eddie Baker, Harry Bowen, Eddie Borden, Leslie Goodwin, Jean Fontaine, Charlie Hall
Plot: Saloon owner Tom Kennedy hires Ruth to give some class to his Bowery saloon. Ruth draws uptowners, and a battle ensues between the low-class Boweryites and the uptown reformers—while Ruth sings and sings.
Songs: "Only a Bird in a Gilded Cage," "After the Ball," "When You Were Sweet Sixteen"

(26) THE SONG OF FAME   WB Vitaphone
Directed by Joseph Henaberry
Cast: Eddie Bruce, Arthur Donaldson, Jackson Halliday, Minor and Root, Pat West
Plot: Ruth plays a cigarette girl who is trying to get cast by a big producer but is stymied by an inept agent. Ruth finally corners the producer in a barber's chair and gets a part in the show.
Songs: "Shine On, Harvest Moon"

(27) SOUTHERN STYLE   RKO-Radio
Directed by Alf Goulding

Cast: Spencer Charters, Phyllis Ludwig, Jack McGuire, Bob Graves, John Larkin
Songs: "Just a Bird's-Eye View of My Old Kentucky Home," "Swanee Shore"

(28) BANDITS AND BALLADS — RKO-Radio
Directed by Frederick Hollander
Cast: Jack Mulhall, Phil Dunham, Jack Rice, Bill Franey, Ernest Young
Songs: "Comin' Through the Rye," "In the Shade of the Old Apple Tree," "Love Is a Bandit"

STAGE: Six-week tour of Balaban-Katz picture houses

RADIO: *Oldsmobile Show*, CBS (Ted Husing, announcer)
Ruth Etting and Johnny Green's Orchestra, starting May, for thirteen weeks, Tuesdays and Fridays

1935:

MOVIE SHORT SUBJECTS continued

(29) NO CONTEST — WB Vitaphone
Directed by Joseph Henaberry
Cast: Charles Lawrence, Elmer Brown, Bert Matthews, Betty Jane Cooper, Lathrop Brothers
Songs: "Easy Come, Easy Go," "Shine On, Harvest Moon," "Dancing in the Moonlight," "A Thousand Good-nights"

(30) AN OLD SPANISH ONION — RKO-Radio
Directed by Alf Goulding
Cast: Mario Alvarez, Renee Torres, Eumenio Blanco, Emilia Leovalli, Carlos Villaias, Harry Vejar
Plot: Ruth visits an old friend in old Mexico and saves a young girl from losing her fiancé—first by impersonating the girl at a masked festival, then by singing from the balcony to the girl's lover while the girl moves her lips appropriately.
Songs: "Those Endearing Young Charms," "Ay, Ay, Ay"

(31) TICKET OR LEAVE IT — RKO-Radio
Directed by Alf Goulding
Cast: Luis Alberni, Lloyd Hughes, Doris McMahon, Edith Craig, Jack Rice
Songs: "When I Lost You," "Lazy," "Blue Skies," "All Alone," "Always"

(32) TUNED OUT   RKO-Radio
Directed by Alf Goulding
Cast: Herbert Rawlinson, Irving Bacon, Renee Whitney, Vernon Dent
Songs: "Shine On, Harvest Moon," "Dinah," "Opened My Eyes," "I'll See You in My Dreams"

RADIO: Kellogg College Prom, Ruth Etting and Red Nichols, 1935–36, at 7:45 EST

1936:

MOVIE SHORT SUBJECTS continued

(33) ALADDIN FROM MANHATTAN   RKO-Radio
Cast: Ray Mayer, Frank Mills, Charles Withers, Isabell Lamal, Bud Jamison
Songs: "I Cried over You," "What Can I Say After I Say I'm Sorry?" "Just a-Wearyin' for You"

(34) MELODY IN MAY   RKO-Radio
Directed by Ben Holmes
Cast: Frank Coghlan, Jr., Margaret Armstrong, Joan Sheldon, Kenneth Howell, Robert Meredith
Songs: "St. Louis Blues," "It Had to Be You"

(35) SLEEPY TIME   RKO-Radio
Directed by Ben Holmes
Cast: Billy Dooley, Vivian Reid, Libby Taylor, Eddie Conrad, Darby Jones
Songs: "A Shady Tree," "I Wish I Hadn't Said Hello," "Mighty Like a Rose"

STAGE

TRANSATLANTIC RHYTHM   Adelphi Theatre, London
Directed by Edward Clark Lilley   October 2, 1936
Produced by Felix Ferry and Jimmy Donahue
Sketches and lyrics by Irving Caesar, music by Raymond Henderson
Cast: Lou Holtz, Lupe Velez, Buck and Bubbles

1937: Ruth announces retirement

1939: Ruth and Myrl Alderman booked for variety appearances in England. Tour canceled by World War II

1946: Comeback guesting on *Rudy Vallee Hour*, drawing 400 fan letters

1947: Copacabana nightclub engagement, New York, beginning March 27

RADIO: Ruth Etting Show, with Myrl Alderman, WHN 15 minutes, five days a week

Ruth Etting Discography

1924:

Vocal, piano accompaniment: You're in Kentucky Sure As You're Born; My Sweetie's Sweeter Than That (Chicago)

1926:

Co 580-D Nothing Else to Do (141670)/Let's Talk About My Sweetie (141671)

Co 633-D Could I? I Certainly Could (141969)/So Is Your Old Lady (141964)

Co 644-D But I Do, You Know I Do (141970)/Lonesome and Sorry (141968)

Co 675-D What a Man! (141962)/You'veGot Those Wanna-Go-Back-Again Blues (141963)

Co 692-D That's Why I Love You (142400)/I Ain't Got Nobody (142401)

Co 716-D Hello, Baby (142449-2)

Co 722-D Precious (142418)/Her Beaus Are Only Rainbows (142419)

Co 764-D Stars (142402)/There's Nothing Sweeter Than a Sweet, Sweet Sweetie (141961)

Co 827-D Thinking of You (142960)/Just a Bird's-Eye View of My Old Kentucky Home (142959)

Co 865-D 'Deed I Do (142974)/There Ain't No Maybe in My Baby's Eyes (142975)

1927:

Co 908-D Sam, the Old Accordian Man (143564)/It All Depends on You (143551)

Co 924-D Hoosier Sweetheart (143550)/Wistful and Biue (142958)

Co 979-D On A Dew-Dew-Dewy Day (143548)/Wherever You Go, Whatever You Do (143549)

Co 995-D My Man (143561)/After You've Gone (143563)

Co 1052-D At Sundown (144402)/Sing Me a Baby Song (144403)

Co 1075-D Swanee Shore (144366)/Just Once Again (144367)

Co 1104-D I'm Nobody's Baby (143562)/You Don't Like It—Not Much! (144418)

Co 1113-D Shaking the Blues Away (R. E.'s big hit from the *Ziegfeld Follies of 1927*) (144592)/It All Belongs to Me (also from the *Follies*) (144593)

Co 1196-D The Song Is Ended (144969-2)/Together, We Two (144968)

Co 1208-D Blue River (144953-6)/Just a Little Bit of Heaven (144970)

Co 1237-D The Varsity Drag (145413)/Good News

Co 1242-D Keep Dusting the Cobwebs Off the Moon (145395-2) (with Ted Lewis and His Band)

1928:

Co 1288-D When You're with Somebody Else (Phil Schwartz on piano) (145466-2)/Back in Your Own Backyard (145465-2)

Co 1312-D I Ain't Got Nobody (144952)/Don't Leave Me, Daddy (144981)

Co 1352-D Ramona (145848)/Say "Yes" Today (145851)

Co 1393-D Bluebird, Sing Me a Song (145849-2)/I Must Be Dreaming (145850-3)

Co 1420-D Beloved (146347-4)/Because My Baby Don't Mean Maybe Now (146346)

Co 1454-D Happy Days and Lonely Nights (146340-3)/Lonely Little Bluebird (146341)

Co 1563-D I Still Keep Dreaming of You (147017-3)/Sonny Boy (147018-1)

Co 1595-D My Blackbirds Are Bluebirds Now (147092)/You're in Love and I'm in Love (147093-2)

Co 1680-D I'm Bringing a Red, Red Rose (147710-1)/Love Me or Leave Me (147711-2)

1929:

Co 1707-D You're the Cream in My Coffee (147779-3)/To Know You Is to Love You (147780-3)

Co 1733-D Glad Rag Doll (147781)/I'll Get By (147955-3)

Co 1762-D Mean to Me (148030)/Button Up Your Overcoat (148029-3)

Co 1801-D Deep Night (148193)/Maybe—Who Knows? (148194)

Co 1830-D The One in the World (148404-2)/I'm Walkin' Around in a Dream (148405-1)

Co 1883-D I Want to Wander in the Meadow (148701)/Now I'm in Love (148702-6)

Co 1958-D Ain't Misbehavin' (148805-6)/At Twilight (148906-7)

Co 1998-D What I Wouldn't Do for That Man (149098-1)/Right Kind of
Man (149099-1)
Co 2038-D More Than You Know (149412)/A Place to Call Home (149413)
Co 2066-D The Shepherd's Serenade/Charming
Co 2073-D If He Cared (149705-2)/Crying for the Carolines (149706-2)

1930:

Co 2146-D Ten Cents a Dance (150062-3)/Funny, Dear, What Love Can Do
(150063-2)
Co 2172-D Let Me Sing and I'm Happy (150118)/A Cottage for Sale (150119)
Co 2199-D and Epic Sn 6059 It Happened in Monterey (150512)/Exactly
Like You (150513)
Co 2207-D and CB-128 I Remember You from Somewhere (150437) (Ben Sel-
vin's Orchestra)
Co 2206-D and CB-119 Dancing with Tears in My Eyes (150438) (Ben Selvin's
Orchestra)
Co 2216-D I Never Dreamt (150560)/Dancing with Tears in My Eyes (150561-3)
Co 2257-D Good Night, Sweetheart/That's Something to Be Thankful For
Co 2280-D Don't Tell Her What's Happened to Me (150740-3)/The Kiss Waltz
(150741-3)
Co 2300-D Body and Soul (150844)/If I Could Be with You (150826-3)
Co 2307-D I'll Be Blue Just Thinking of You (150744-6)/Just a Little Closer
(150743-7) (DB-341)
Co 2318-D and DB-409 I'm Yours (150742-3)/Laughing at Life (150845-3)

1931:

Co 2377-D Overnight (151203)/Reaching for the Moon (151202)
Co 2398-D You're the One I Care For (151227)/Love Is Like That
(151204-3)
Co 2445-D Falling in Love Again (151515)/Were You Sincere? (151516)
Co 2454-D Out of Nowhere (151519)/Say a Little Prayer for Me (151520)
Co 2470-D Faithfully Yours (151569)/Moonlight Saving Time (151570-2)
Per 12732, Dec F-2483, Imp 2625 and EBW 5373 Without That Gal
(10692-2)/Nevertheless (10693-2) (all labels same)
Co 2505-D I'm Good for Nothing but Love (151688)/I'm Falling in Love
(151689)
Ban 32231, Or 2311, Per 12739, Rom 1681 and Pic 846 Just One More Chance
(10738-3) (Imp 2579)/Have You Forgotten? (10739-3) (Imp 2601)
Ban 32229, Or 2308 and Per 12737 Cigars, Cigarettes! (10724)/Shine On, Har-
vest Moon (10725)
Co 2529-D Guilty (151761) Now That You've Gone (151762)

CQ 7828, Per 12754 and Imp 2625 Love Letters in the Sand (10798-3)/CQ 7828, Per 12754 and Imp 2601 Me!

Ban 32289, Per 12757 and Imp 2645 If I Didn't Have You (10827-1)/Let Me Call You Sweetheart (10828-1) (not reissued on Imp)

Co 2557-D and MR-458 A Faded Summer Love (151858)/Good Night, Sweetheart (151859) (not reissued on MR)

Co 2580-D and MR-507 Too Late (152037-2)/Cuban Love Song (152038-3)

CQ 7918, Per 12771 and Imp 2652 All of Me (11064-3)/Home (11065-2)

1932:

Co 2630-D When We're Alone (152123)/Kiss Me Good Night (152124)

Mt M-12352 and Per 12791 Love, You Funny Thing! (11419)/Can't We Talk It Over? (11420)

Mt M-12375, Per 12809 and Imp 2769 Happy-Go Lucky You (11791)/Mt M-12375 and Per 12809 That's What Heaven Means to Me (11792)

Co 2660-D That's Something to Be Thankful For (152190)/The Voice in the Old Village Choir (152191)

Mt M-12394, Cq 8042, Per 12810 and Re 233 Lazy Day (11889-2)/With Summer Coming On (11890-1)

Co 2681-D and DB-945 Holding My Honey's Hand (152229-2)/The Night When Love Was Born (152230-2)

Mt M-12450, Broadway 4021, Cq 7997, Per 12828 and Imp 2769 It Was So Beautiful (12115-1)/I'll Never Be the Same (all except Imp 2769)

Ban 32595, Cq 8075, Mt M-12528, Per 12855 I'll Follow You (12503-1)/I'll Never Have to Dream Again (12504-1)

Ban 32634, Mt M-12563 and Per 12869 Take Me in Your Arms (12688)/Some Day We'll Meet Again (12689)

1933:

Mt M-12625, Cq 8122, Per 12887 and Imp 2480 Hey, Young Fella (13039-1)/Try a Little Tenderness (13040-1)

Ban 32714, Cq 8123, Mt M-12643, Or 2663, Per 12896 and Rom 2036 How Can I Go On Without You? (13105)/Linger a Little Longer in Twilight (13106)

Ban 32739, Cq 8154, Mt M-12668, Or 2679, Per 12904 and Rom 2052 You've Got Me Crying Again (13185)/Hold Me (13186)

Br 6657 and 01614 Summer Is Over (LA-11-A)/Close Your Eyes (LA-13-A)

Br 6697 and 01674 No More Love (LA-5-A)/Build a Little Home (LA-6-A)

Br 6719 and 01634 Everything I Have Is Yours (LA-12-A)/Dancing in the Moonlight (LA-8-A)

BR 6671 and 01634 You're My Past, Present and Future (LA-7-A)/What Is Sweeter? (LA-10-A)

1934:

Br 6761 and 01740 Tired of It All (B-14667-A)/Keep Romance Alive
(B-14668-A)

Br 6769 This Little Piggie Went to Market (B-14817-A)/Smoke Gets in
Your Eyes (B-14868-A) (Br 6769 and 01879)

Br 6892 and 01794 Riptide (B-15188-A)/Easy Come, Easy Go (B-15189-A)

Br 6914 and 01829 With My Eyes Wide Open (B-15190-A)/Were Your Ears
Burning? (B-15191-A)

Co 2954-D Talkin' to Myself (LA-196)/Tomorrow Who Cares? (LA-197) (Jimmy Grier's Orchestra)

Co 2955-D and DB-1499 What About Me? (LA-198-A)/Out in the Cold Again
(LA-199)

Co 2979-D and DB 1499 Stay as Sweet as You Are (Co-16349-1)/DB 1512 A
Needle in a Haystack (Co-16350-1)

Co 2985-D Am I To Blame? (Co-16351-1)/Co 2985-D and DB-1512 I've Got an
Invitation to a Dance (Co-16352)

1935:

Co 3014-D and DB 1539 Things Might Have Been So Different (Co-16841-3)/Co
3014-D and DB-1539 March Winds and April Showers (Co-16842-1)

Co 3031-D and FB-1140 It's Easy to Remember (Co-17249)/Life Is a Song
(Co-17250)

Co 3085-D Ten Cents a Dance (Co-17751)/Shine On, Harvest Moon (Co-17752)

Co 3070-D I Wished on the Moon (Co-17774)/Why Dream? (Co-17775)

1936:

LONDON RECORDINGS

Rex 8852 You (F-1940-1)/It's Love Again (F-1941-1)

Rex 8853 It's a Sin to Tell a Lie (F-1942-1-2)/Take My Heart (F-1943-2)

Rex 8881 Holiday Sweethearts (F-1990-2)/Who'll Buy My Song of Love?
(F-1943-2)

USA RECORDINGS

Br 7646 and 02218 Lost (B-18895-1)/It's Been So Long (B-18896)

Dec 1084, and F-6257 In the Chapel in the Moonlight (61478)/There's
Something in the Air (61479-A) (F-6294)

Dec 1107 and F-6294 Good Night, My Love (61477-A)/Dec 1107 and
F-6257 May I Have the Next Romance with You? (61480)

Dec 1212 and Br 02446 It's Swell of You (62090-A)/Br02446 There's a Lull in My Life (62092-A)
Dec 1259 and Br 02420 On a Little Dream Ranch (62091-A)/A Message from the Man in the Moon (62103-A)

LONG PLAY ALBUMS

The Original Recordings of Ruth Etting, Columbia ML5050
Ruth Etting Sings Again, Jay 3011
Hello, Baby, Biograph BLP-C-11

KAY FRANCIS

FILMS OF KAY FRANCIS

Dates are for New York City release

(1) GENTLEMEN OF THE PRESS

Paramount, May 13, 1929   Directed by Millard Webb

Screenplay by Bartlett Cormack; from Ward Morehouse's Broadway play

Cast: Walter Huston, Charles Ruggles, Betty Lawford, Norma Foster, Duncan Penwarden, Lawrence Leslie. Kay was billed as Katherine Francis

Paramount Theater   Silent and sound versions

(2) THE COCOANUTS

Paramount, May 25, 1929   Directed by Joseph Santley and Robert Florey

Screenplay by Morrie Ryskind; based on the Broadway hit by George S. Kaufman

Music by Irving Berlin

Cast: Four Marx Brothers, Mary Eaton, Oscar Shaw, Margaret Dumont, Cyril Ring, Basil Ruysdael, Sylvan Lee, and others. Kay was billed as Katherine

Rialto Theater

(3) DANGEROUS CURVES

Paramount, July 15, 1929   Directed by Lothar Mendes

Screenplay by Donald Davis, Florence Ryerson and Viola Brothers Shore; story by Lester Cohen

Cast: Clara Bow, Richard Arlen, David Newell, Anders Randolph, May Boley, T. Roy Barnes, Joyce Compton, Charles D. Brown, Stuart Erwin, Jack Luden

Paramount Theater   Silent and sound versions

(4) ILLUSION

Paramount, September 28, 1929   Directed by Lothar Mendes

Screenplay by E. Lloyd Sheldon; based on a story by Arthur Train; titles by Richard H. Digges

Cast: Charles "Buddy" Rogers, Nancy Carroll, June Collyer, Regis Toomey, Knute Erickson, Eugene Besserer, Maude Turner Gordon, William Austin,

Emelie Melville, Frances Raymond, Katherine Wallace, John E. Nash, Eddie Kane
Paramount Theater   Silent and sound versions

(5) THE MARRIAGE PLAYGROUND
Paramount, December 14, 1929   Directed by Lothar Mendes
Screenplay by J. Walter Reuben; adaptation and dialogue by Doris Anderson; based on Edith Wharton's *The Children*
Cast: Mary Brian, Fredric March, Lilyan Tashman, Huntley Gordon, William Austin, Seena Owen, Philippe de Lacy, Anita Louise, Little Mitzi, Billy Seay, Ruby Parsley, Donald Smith, Jocelyn Lee, Maude Turner Gordon, David Newell, Armand Kaliz, Joan Standing, Gordon DeMain
Paramount Theater

(6) BEHIND THE MAKEUP
Paramount, January 18, 1930   Directed by Robert Milton
Screenplay by George Manker Watters and Howard Eastbrook; based on the story *The Feeder* by Mildred Cram
Cast: Hal Skelly, William Powell, Fay Wray, E. H. Calvert, Paul Lukas, Agostino Borgato
Paramount Theater

(7) STREET OF CHANCE
Paramount, February 3, 1930   Directed by John Cromwell
Scenario by Howard Eastbrook; story and dialogue by Oliver H. P. Garrett
Cast: William Powell, Jean Arthur, Regis Toomey, Stanley Fields, Brook Benedict, Betty Francisco, John Risso, Joan Standing, Maurice Black, Irving Bacon
Rialto Theater

(8) PARAMOUNT ON PARADE
Paramount, April 21, 1930   11 directors, supervised by Elsie Janis
Revue by various writers
Cast: Maurice Chevalier, Helen Kane, Ruth Chatterton, Clive Brook, George Bancroft, Nino Martini, William Powell, Clara Bow, Leon Errol, Jack Oakie, Mitzi Green, Nancy Carroll, Harry Green, Skeets Gallagher, Warner Oland, Eugene Pallette
Rialto Theater

(9) A NOTORIOUS AFFAIR
First National, April 26, 1930   Directed by Lloyd Bacon
Produced by Robert North
Screenplay by J. Grubb Alexander; based on a play by Audrey and Waverly Carter

Cast: Billie Dove, Basil Rathbone, Montague Love, Kenneth Thomson
Warners' Strand Theater

(10) FOR THE DEFENSE
Paramount, July 19, 1930   Directed by John Cromwell
Screenplay by Oliver H. P. Garett; from a story by Charles Furthman
Cast: William Powell, Scott Kolk, William B. Davidson, John Elliott, Thomas
    Jackson, Harry Walker, James Finlayson, Charles West, Charles Sullivan,
    Ernest S. Adams, Bertram Marbugh and Edward LeSaint
Paramount Theater

(11) RAFFLES
Goldwyn-UA, July 25, 1930   Directed by Harry D'Arrast
Screenplay by Sidney Howard; based on stories by E. W. Hornung
Cast: Ronald Colman, Bramwell Fletcher, Frances Dade, David Torrance, Al-
    ison Skipworth, Frederick Kerr, John Rogers, Wilson Benge
Rialto Theater

(12) LET'S GO NATIVE
Paramount, August 30, 1930   Directed by Leo McCarey
Screenplay by George Marion, Jr., and Percy Heath
Cast: Jeanette MacDonald, Jack Oakie, Skeets Gallagher, James Hall, William
    Austin, David Newell, Charles Sellon, Eugene Pallette
Paramount and Brooklyn Paramount Theaters

(13) THE VIRTUOUS SIN
Paramount, November 2, 1930   Directed by George Cukor and Louis Gasnier
Screenplay by Martin Brown; scenario by Louise Long; based on the play *The
    General* by Lajos Zilahy
Cast: Walter Huston, Kenneth McKenna, Jobyna Howland, Paul Cavanaugh
Paramount Theater

(14) PASSION FLOWER
MGM, December 22, 1930   Directed and produced by William C. de Mille
Screenplay by Martin Flavin; based on a Kathleen Norris story
Cast: Charles Bickford, Zasu Pitts, Kay Johnson, Winter Hall, Lewis Stone,
    Dickie Moore
Capitol Theater

(15) SCANDAL SHEET
Paramount, February 9, 1931   Directed by John Cromwell
Screenplay by Vincent Lawrence and Max Marcin; based on a story by Vin-
    cent Lawrence

Cast: George Bancroft, Clive Brook, Lucien Little Field, Gilbert Emery, Regis Toomey
Paramount Theater

(16) LADIES' MAN
Paramount, May 1, 1931   Directed by Lothar Mendes
Screenplay by Herman J. Mankiewicz; based on a story by Rupert Hughes
Cast: William Powell, Carole Lombard, Gilbert Emery, Olive Tell, Martin Burton, John Holland, Frank Atkinson, Maude Turner Gordon
Times Square and Brooklyn Paramount Theaters

(17) THE VICE SQUAD
Paramount, June 6, 1931   Directed by John Cromwell
Screenplay and story by Oliver H. P. Garrett
Cast: Paul Lukas, Helen Johnson, William B. Davidson, Rockliffe Fellowes, Esther Howard, Monte Carter, G. Pat Collins, Phil Tead, Davison Clark, Tom Wilson, James Durkin, William Arnold
Times Square and Brooklyn Paramount Theaters

(18) TRANSGRESSION
RKO-Radio, June 15, 1931   Directed by Herbert Brenon
Based on a story by Kate Jordon
Cast: Paul Cavanagh, Ricardo Cortez, Nance O'Neil, John St. Polis, Adrienne d'Ambricourt, Cissy Fitzgerald, Doris Lloyd, Augustion Borgato
Mayfair Theater

(19) GUILTY HANDS
MGM, August 29, 1931   Directed by W. S. Van Dyke
Screenplay and story by Bayard Veiller
Cast: Lionel Barrymore, Madge Evans, William Bakewell, C. Aubrey Smith, Polly Moran, Alan Mowbray, Forrester Harvey, Charles Crockett, Henry Barrows
Capitol Theater

(20) TWENTY-FOUR HOURS
Paramount, October 3, 1931   Directed by Marion Gering
Screenplay by Louis Weitzenkorn; based on Louis Bromfield's novel
Cast: Clive Brook, Miriam Hopkins, Regis Toomey, George Barbier, Adrienne Ames, Charlotte Granville, Minor Watson, Lucille La Verne, Wade Boteler, Robert Kortman, Malcolm Waite, Thomas Jackson
Times Square and Brooklyn Paramount Theaters

(21) GIRLS ABOUT TOWN
Paramount, November 2, 1931   Directed by George Cukor

Screenplay by Raymond Griffith; story by Zoë Akins, based on her play *The Greeks Had a Word for It*

Cast: Joel McCrea, Lilyan Tashman, Eugene Pallette, Alan Dinehart, Lucile Webster Gleason, Anderson Lawler, Lucille Brown, George Barbier, Robert McWade, Louise Beavers, Adrienne Ames, Hazel Howell, Claire Dodd, Patricia Caron, Judith Wood

Times Square and Brooklyn Paramount Theaters

(22) THE FALSE MADONNA

Paramount, 1932 (no New York review)   Directed by Stuart Walker

Screenplay by Arthur Kober and Roy Harris; based on a story by May Edgington

Cast: William "Stage" Boyd, Conway Tearle, John Breeden, Marjorie Gateson

(23) STRANGERS IN LOVE

Paramount, March 5, 1932   Directed by Lothar Mendes

Screenplay by William Slavens McNutt and Grover Jones; based on William J. Locke's *The Shorn Lamb*

Cast: Fredric March, Stuart Erwin, Juliette Compton, George Barbier, Sidney Toler, Earle Foxe, Lucien Littlefield, Leslie Palmer, Gertrude Howard, Ben Taggart, John M. Sullivan

Times Square and Brooklyn Theaters

(24) MAN WANTED

Warner Brothers, April 16, 1932   Directed by William Dieterle

Screenplay by Charles Kenyon; story by Robert Lord

Cast: David Manners, Andy Devine, Una Merkel, Kenneth Thomson, Claire Dodd, Charlotte Merriam, Edward Von Sloan, Robert Greig, Guy Kibbee

Warner's Strand Theater

(25) STREET OF WOMEN

Warner Brothers, May 30, 1932   Directed by Archie Mayo

Screenplay by Mary McCall, Jr., and Charles Kenyon; based on a novel by Polan Banks

Cast: Alan Dinehart, Marjorie Gateson, Roland Young, Gloria Stuart, Allen Vincent, Louise Beavers, Adrienne Dore

Warner's Strand Theater

(26) JEWEL ROBBERY

Warner Brothers, July 23, 1932   Directed by William Dieterle

Screenplay by Laszlo Fodor; based on his play

Cast: William Powell, Hardie Albright, André Luguet, Henry Kolker, Lee Kohlmar, Spencer Charters, C. Henry Gordon, Robert Greig, Helen Vinson,

Lawrence Grant, Jacques Vanaire, Harold Minjur, Ivan Linow, Harold Walridge, Charles Coleman, Herman Bing, Ruth Donnelly, Charles Wilson
Warner's Strand Theater

(27) ONE WAY PASSAGE

Warner Brothers, October 14, 1932   Directed by Tay Garnett
Screenplay by Wilson Mizner and Joseph Jackson; based on a story by Robert Lord
Cast: William Powell, Aline MacMahon, Frank McHugh, Warren Hymer, Frederick Burton, Douglas Gerrard, Herbert Mundin
Warner's Strand Theater

(28) TROUBLE IN PARADISE

Paramount, November 9, 1932   Directed and produced by Ernst Lubitsch
Screenplay by Grover Jones and Samson Raphaelson; based on Laszlo Aladar's play *The Honest Finder*
Cast: Miriam Hopkins, Herbert Marshall, Charles Ruggles, Edward Everett Horton, C. Aubrey Smith, Robert Greig, George Humbert, Rolfe Sedan, Luis Alberni
Rivoli Theater

(29) CYNARA

Samuel Goldwyn-UA, December 26, 1932   Directed by King Vidor
Screenplay by Frances Marion and Lynn Starling; from H. M. Harwood and Robert Gore-Brown's play *Cynara*, based on Gore-Brown's novel *An Imperfect Love*
Cast: Ronald Colman, Phyllis Barry, Henry Stephenson, Viva Tattersall, Florine McKinney, Clarissa Selwyn, Paul Porcasi, George Kirby, Donald Stewart, Wilson Benge
Rivoli Theater

(30) THE KEYHOLE

Warner Brothers, March 31, 1933   Directed by Michael Curtiz
Screenplay by Robert Presnell, based on Alice D. G. Miller's story *Adventuress*
Cast: George Brent, Glenda Farrell, Allen Jenkins, Monroe Owsley, Helen Ware, Henry Kolker
Radio City Music Hall

(31) STORM AT DAYBREAK

MGM, July 22, 1933   Directed by Richard Boleslavsky
Screenplay by Bertram Milhauser; adapted from Sandor Hunyady's play *Black-Stemmed Cherries*

Cast: Nils Asther, Walter Huston, Phillips Holmes, Eugene Pallette, C. Henry Gordon, Louise Closser Hale, Jean Parker
Capitol Theater

(32) MARY STEVENS, M. D.
Warner Brothers, August 5, 1933   Directed by Lloyd Bacon
Screenplay by Rian James and Robert Lord; based on a novel by Virginia Kellogg
Cast: Lyle Talbot, Glenda Farrell, Thelma Todd, Una O'Connor, Charles Wilson, Hobart Cavanaugh
Strand theater

(33) I LOVED A WOMAN
First National, September 22, 1933   Directed by Alfred E. Green
Screenplay by Charles Kenyon and Sidney Sutherland; based on the novel by David Krasner
Cast: Edward G. Robinson, Genevieve Tobin, J. Farrell MacDonald, Henry Kolker, Robert Barrat, George Blackwood, Murray Kinnell, Robert McWade, Walter Walker, Henry O'Neill, Lorena Layson, Sam Godfrey, E. J. Ratcliffe, Paul Porcasi, William V. Mong
Strand Theater

(34) THE HOUSE ON 56th STREET
Warner Brothers, December 2, 1933   Directed by Robert Florey
Screenplay by Austin Parker and Sheridan Gibney; based on a novel by Joseph Santley
Cast: Ricardo Cortez, Gene Raymond, John Halliday, Margaret Lindsay, Frank McHugh, Sheila Terry, William Boyd, Hardie Albright, Philip Reed, Philip Faversham, Henry O'Neill, Walter Walker, Nella Walker
Hollywood Theater

(35) MANDALAY
First National, February 15, 1934   Directed by Michael Curtiz
Screenplay by Austin Parker; based on a story by Paul Henry Fox
Cast: Ricardo Cortez, Warner Oland, Lyle Talbot, Ruth Donnelly, Reginald Owen, Hobart Cavanaugh, David Torrence, Rafaela Ottiano, Halliwell Hobbes, Etienne Girardot, Lucien Littlefield
Strand Theater

(36) WONDER BAR
First National, March 1, 1934   Directed by Lloyd Bacon
Screenplay by Earl Baldwin; an adaptation of the play by Geza Herczeg, Karl Farkas and Robert Katscher

Music and lyrics by Harry Warren and Al Dublin
Cast: Al Jolson, Dolores Del Rio, Ricardo Cortez, Dick Powell, Hal LeRoy, Guy Kibbee, Ruth Donnelly, Hugh Herbert, Louise Fazenda, Fifi D'Orsay, Merna Kennedy, Henry O'Neill, Robert Barrat, Henry Kolker
Strand Theater

(37) DR. MONICA

Warner Brothers, June 21, 1934   Directed by William Keighley
Screenplay by Charles Kenyon; adapted from a play by Maria Morozowicz Szczepkowska
Cast: Warren William, Jean Muir, Verree Teasdale, Phillip Reed, Emma Dunn, Herbert Bunston, Ann Shoemaker, Virginia Hammond, Hale Hamilton, Virginia Pine
Strand Theater

(38) BRITISH AGENT

First National, September 20, 1934   Directed by Michael Curtiz
Screenplay by Laird Doyle; suggested by R. H. Bruce Lockhart's book.
Cast: Leslie Howard, William Gargan, Philip Reed, Irving Pichel, Walter Byron, Ivan Simpson, Halliwell Hobbes, Arthur Aylesworth, J. Carrol Naish, Cesar Romero, Alphonse Ethier, Tenen Holtz, Doris Lloyd, Marina Schubert, George Pearce, Gregory Gaye, Paul Porcasi, Addison Richards, Walter Armitage
Strand Theater

(40) STRANDED

Warner Brothers, June 20, 1935   Directed by Frank Borzage
Screenplay by Delmer Daves, with additional dialogue by Carl Erickson; based on Frank Wead and Ferdinand Reyher's story *Lady with a Badge*
Cast: George Brent, Patricia Ellis, Donald Woods, Robert Barrat, Barton MacLane, Joseph Crehan, William Harrigan, Shirley Grey, June Travis, Henry O'Neill, Frankie Darro, John Wray
Strand Theater

(41) THE GOOSE AND THE GANDER

Warner Brothers, September 12, 1935   Directed by Alfred E. Green
Screenplay and story by Charles Kenyon
Cast: George Brent, Genevieve Tobin, John Eldredge, Claire Dodd, Ralph Forbes, Helen Lowell, Spencer Charters, William Austin, Eddie Shubert, Charles Coleman, Olive Jones, Gordon Elliott, John Sheehan, Wade Boteler
Strand Theater

(42) I FOUND STELLA PARISH

First National, November 4, 1935   Directed by Mervyn LeRoy

Screenplay by Casey Robinson; from a story by John Monk Saunders
Cast: Ian Hunter, Paul Lukas, Sybil Jason, Jessie Ralph, Barton MacLane, Harry Beresford, Joseph Sawyer, Eddie Acuff, Robert Strange, Walter Kingsford
Strand Theater

(43) THE WHITE ANGEL
First National, June 25, 1936   Directed by William Dieterle
Screenplay by Mordaunt Shairp; suggested by Lytton Strachey's essay in *Eminent Victorians*
Cast: Ian Hunter, Donald Woods, Nigel Bruce, Donald Crisp, Henry O'Neill, Billy Mauch, Charles Croker-King, Phoebe Foster, George Curzon, Ara Gerald, Halliwell Hobbes, Elly Maylon, Montagu Love, Ferdinand Munier, Lillian Cooper, Egon Brecher, Tempe Piggott, Barbara Leonard, Frank Conroy, Charles Irwin, Clyde Cook, Harry Allen, George Kirby, Harry Cording, Alma Lloyd, Georgia Kane
Strand Theater

(44) GIVE ME YOUR HEART
Warner Brothers, September 17, 1936   Directed by Archie L. Mayo
Screenplay by Casey Robinson; from Joyce Carey's play *Sweet Aloes*
Cast: George Brent, Roland Young, Patric Knowles, Henry Stephenson, Frieda Inescort, Helen Flint, Halliwell Hobbes, Zeffie Tilbury, Elspeth Dudgeon
New Criterion Theater

(45) STOLEN HOLIDAY
Warner Brothers, February 1, 1937   Directed by Michael Curtiz
Screenplay by Casey Robinson; story by Warren Duff and Virginia Kellogg
Cast: Claude Rains, Ian Hunter, Alison Skipworth, Alexander D'Arcy, Betty Lawford, Walter Kingsford, Charles Halton, Frank Reicher, Frank Conroy, Egon Brecher, Robert Strange, Kathleen Howard, Wedgewood Nowell
Strand Theater

(46) ANOTHER DAWN
Warner Brothers, June 18, 1937   Directed by William Dieterle
Screenplay and story by Laird Doyle
Score by Erich Wolfgang Korngold
Cast: Errol Flynn, Ian Hunter, Frieda Inescort, Herbert Mundin, G. P. Huntley, Jr., Billy Bevan, Richard Powell, Mary Forbes, Charles Austin, Ben Welden, David Clyde, Reginald Sheffield
Radio City Music Hall

(47) CONFESSION
First National, August 19, 1937   Directed by Joe May

Screenplay by Hans Rameau; adaptation by Julius J. Epstein and Margaret Levine

Cast: Ian Hunter, Basil Rathbone, Jane Bryan, Donald Crisp, Dorothy Peterson, Laura Hope Crews, Robert Barrat, Ben Welden, Veda Ann Borg

Strand Theater

(48) FIRST LADY

Warner Brothers, December 23, 1937   Directed by Stanley Logan

Screenplay by Rowland Leigh; adapted from a play by George S. Kaufman and Katharine Dayton

Cast: Preston Foster, Anita Louise, Walter Connolly, Vetree Teasdale, Victor Jory, Marjorie Rambeau, Marjorie Gateson, Louise Fazenda, Henry O'Neill, Grant Mitchell, Eric Stanley, Lucille Gleason, Sara Haden, Harry Davenport, Gregory Gaye, Olaf Hytton

Strand Theater

(49) WOMEN ARE LIKE THAT

Warner Brothers, April 11, 1938   Directed by Stanley Logan

Screenplay by Horace Jackson; based on a story by Albert H. Z. Carr

Cast: Pat O'Brien, Ralph Forbes, Melville Cooper, Thurston Hall, Grant Mitchell, Gordon Oliver, John Eldredge, Herbert Rawlinson, Hugh O'Connell, Georgia Caine, Joyce Compton, Sarah Edwards, Josephine Whittel, Lola Cheaney, Edward Broadley

Strand Theater

(50) MY BILL

Warner Brothers, July 7, 1938   Directed by John Farrow

Screenplay by Vincent Sherman and Robertson White; based on Tom Barry's play *Courage*

Cast: Dickie Moore, Bonita Granville, John Litel, Anita Louise, Bobby Jordan, Maurice Murphy, Elisabeth Risdon, Helena Phillips Evans, John Ridgely, Sidney Bracy, Bernice Pilot, Jan Holm

Strand Theater

(51) SECRETS OF AN ACTRESS

Warner Brothers, October 8, 1938   Directed by William Keighley

Screenplay by Milton Krims, Rowland Leigh and Julius J. Epstein

Cast: George Brent, Ian Hunter, Gloria Dickson, Isabel Jeans, Penny Singleton, Dennie Moore, Selmer Jackson, Herbert Rawlinson, Emmett Vogan, James B. Carson

Strand Theater

(52) COMET OVER BROADWAY

Warner Brothers, December 16, 1938   Directed by Busby Berkeley

Screenplay by Mark Hellinger and Robert Buckner; based on a story by Faith
   Baldwin
Cast: Ian Hunter, John Litel, Donald Crisp, Minna Gombel, Sybil Jason, Mel-
   ville Cooper, Ian Keith, Leona Maricle, Ray Mayer, Vera Lewis
Palace Theater

(53) KING OF THE UNDERWORLD
Warner Brothers, January 7, 1939   Directed by Lewis Seiler
Screenplay by George Bricker and Vincent Sherman; story by W. R. Burnett
Cast: Humphrey Bogart, James Stephenson, John Eldredge, Jessie Busley, Ar-
   thur Aylesworth, Raymond Brown, Harland Tucker, Ralph Remley, Charley
   Foy
Rialto Theater

(54) WOMEN IN THE WIND
Warner Brothers, April 13, 1939   Directed by John Farrow
Screenplay by Lee Katz and Albert DeMond; from a novel by Francis Walton
Cast: William Gargan, Victor Jory, Maxie Rosenbloom, Eddie Foy, Jr., Sheila
   Bromley, Eve Arden, Charles Anthony Hughes, Frankie Burke, John Dilson
Palace Theater

(55) IN NAME ONLY
RKO-Radio, August 4, 1939   Directed by John Cromwell
Produced by George Haight
Screenplay by Richard Sherman; from *Memory of Love,* a novel by Bessie
   Breuer
Cast: Carole Lombard, Cary Grant, Charles Coburn, Helen Vinson, Grady
   Sutton, Katherine Alexander, Jonathan Hale, Maurice Moscovich, Nella
   Walker, Peggy Ann Garner, Spencer Charters
Radio City Music Hall

(56) IT'S A DATE
Universal, March 23, 1940   Directed by William A. Seiter
Produced by Joe Pasternak
Screenplay by Norman Krasna; based on a story by Jane Hall, Frederick
   Kohner and Ralph Block
Cast: Deanna Durbin, Walter Pidgeon, Eugene Pallette, Lewis Howard, Samu-
   el S. Hinds, Cecilia Loftus, Fritz Feld, S. Z. Sakall, Henry Stephenson, Joe
   King, Virginia Brissac, Romaine Callendar, Harry Owens and his Royal Ha-
   waiians
Rivoli Theater

(57) WHEN THE DALTONS RODE
Universal, August 23, 1940   Directed by George Marshall

Screenplay by Harold Shumate; based on a story *When the Daltons Rode* by Emmett Dalton and Jack Jungmeyer, Sr.
Cast: Randolph Scott, Brian Donlevy, George Bancroft, Broderick Crawford, Stuart Erwin, Andy Devine, Frank Albertson, Mary Gordon, Harry Stephens, Edgar Deering, Quen Ramsey, Dorothy Grainger, Bob McKenzie, Fay McKenzie, June Wilkins, Walter Soderling
Loew's State Theater

(58) LITTLE MEN
RKO-Radio, December 9, 1940   Directed by Norman Z. McLeod
Produced by Gene Towne and Graham Baker
Screenplay by Mark Kelly and Arthur Caesar; based on a novel by Louisa May Alcott
Cast: Jack Oakie, George Bancroft, Jimmy Lydon, Ann Gillis, Charles Esmond, Richard Nichols, Casey Johnson, Francesca Santoro, Johnny Burke, Lillian Randolph, Sammy McKim, Edward Rice, Anne Howard, Jimmy Zaner, Bobby Cooper, Schuyler Standish, Paul Matthews, Tony Neil, Fred Estes, Douglas Rucker, Donald Rackerby, William Demarest, Sterling Holloway, Isabel Jewell, Elsie, the cow
Rivoli Theater

(59) PLAY GIRL
RKO-Radio, January 30, 1941   Directed by Frank Woodruff
Produced by Cliff Reid
Screenplay and story by Jerry Cady
Cast: James Ellison, Mildred Coles, Nigel Bruce, Margaret Hamilton, Katharine Alexander, George P. Huntley, Kane Richmond, Stanley Andrews, Selmer Jackson
Palace Theater

(60) THE MAN WHO LOST HIMSELF
Universal (no New York City review) 1941   Directed by Edward Lugwig
Cast: Brian Aherne, Henry Stephenson, S. Z. Sakall, Nils Asther, Henry Stephenson, Sig Rumann

(61) CHARLEY'S AUNT
Twentieth Century-Fox, August 2, 1941   Directed by Archie Mayo
Produced by William Perlberg
Screenplay by George Seaton; based on a play by Brandon Thomas
Cast: Jack Benny, James Ellison, Anne Baxter, Edmund Gwenn, Reginald Owen, Laird Cregar, Arleen Whelan, Richard Haydn, Ernest Cossart, Morton Lowry, Lionel Pape, Will Stanton, Montague Shaw, Claud Allister, William Austin, Maurice Case
Roxy Theater

344

(62) THE FEMININE TOUCH

MGM, December 12, 1941   Directed by W. S. Van Dyke

Produced by Joseph L. Mankiewicz

Screenplay by George Oppenheimer, Edmund L. Hartman and Ogden Nash

Cast: Rosalind Russell, Don Ameche, Van Heflin, Donald Meek, Gordon Jones, Henry Daniell, Sidney Blackmer, Grant Mitchell, David Clyde

Capitol Theater

(63) ALWAYS IN MY HEART

Warner Brothers, March 14, 1942   Directed by Jo Graham

Screenplay by Adele Comandini; suggested by a play by Dorothy Bennett and Irving White

Cast: Walter Huston, Gloria Warren, Patty Hale, Frankie Thomas, Una O'Connor, Sidney Blackmer, Armida, Frank Puglia, Russell Arms, Anthony Caruso, Elvira Curci, John Hamilton, Harry Lewis, Herbert Gunn, Borrah Minevitch and His Rascals

Strand Theater

(64) BETWEEN US GIRLS

Universal, September 25, 1942   Directed and produced by Henry Koster

Screenplay by Myles Connolly and True Boardman; based on *Le Fruit Vert*

Cast: Diana Barrymore, Robert Cummings, John Boles, Andy Devine, Guinn Williams, Scotty Beckett, Mary Treen, Ethel Griffies, Walter Catlett, Andrew Tombes, Peter Jamerson, Irving Bacon, Lillian Yarbo

Capitol Theater

(65) FOUR JILLS IN A JEEP

Twentieth Century-Fox, April 6, 1944   Directed by William A. Seiter

Produced by Irving Starr

Screenplay by Robert Ellis, Helen Logan and Snag Werris; from a story by Froma Sand and Fred Niblo, Jr.; based on actual experiences of Kay Francis, Carole Landis, Martha Raye and Mitzi Mayfair

Music by Jimmy McHugh and Harold Adamson

Cast: Carole Landis, Martha Raye, Mitzi Mayfair, Jimmy Dorsey and His Orchestra, Alice Faye, Carmen Miranda, Betty Grable, George Jessel, John Harvey, Phil Silvers, Dick Haymes, Lester Matthews, Glen Langan, Paul Harvey, Miles Mander, Winifred Harris, Mary Servoss, B. S. Pully

Roxy Theater

(66) DIVORCE

Monogram, August 18, 1945 (no New York City review)   Directed by William Nigh

Produced by Jeffrey Bernerd and Kay Francis

Cast: Bruce Cabot, Helen Mack, Craig Reynolds, Jean Fenwick, Larry Olsen

(67) ALLOTMENT WIVES (also known as ALLOTMENT WIVES, INC.)
Monogram, November 22, 1945   Directed by William Nigh
Screenplay by Harvey H. Gates and Sidney Sutherland; from an original story
  by Sutherland
Produced by Jeffrey Bernerd and Kay Francis
Cast: Paul Kelly, Otto Kruger, Gertrude Michael, Teala Loring, Bernard Ne-
  dell, Matty Fain, Anthony Ward, Jonathan Hale, Selmer Jackson, Evelyn
  Eaton
Ambassador Theater

(68) WIFE WANTED
Monogram (no New York review, release date unknown)
Directed by Phil Karlson
Produced by Jeffrey Bernerd and Kay Francis
Cast: Paul Cavanaugh, Robert Shayne, Veda Ann Borg, Teala Loring

Kay Francis' Stage Career

1921: Stage debut, class play *You Never Can Tell*, Cathedral School of St.
  Mary. Katherine Gibbs played male lead.

1925: Katherine Francis understudied Katharine Cornell in *The Green Hat*.
  Katherine Francis as player Queen in Basil Sidney's modern-dress
  Hamlet, November 9, Booth Theater.

1926: Stuart Walker Stock Companies in Indianapolis, Indiana, Cincinnati and
  Dayton, Ohio. May to September. *White Collars. Candida. Polly Preferred. Puppy Love*, etc.

1927: *Crime*, starring Sylvia Sidney. Katherine Francis played Marjorie Gray.
  February 22, Eltinge Theater. *Venus* by Rachel Crothers. December 25,
  Masque Theater.

1928: *Elmer, the Great* by Ring Lardner. Starred Walter Huston. September
  24, Lyceum Theater.

1945: *Windy Hill* by Patsy Ruth Miller. Directed by Ruth Chatterton. Starred
  Kay. Tour. Opened August 13.

1946: *Windy Hill*. Tour, January to May. *State of the Union*. Kay replaces
  Ruth Hussey in New York company. Lyceum, Hudson, September 3.

1947: *State of the Union.* New York, January to September; tour, September.

1948: *State of the Union* tour. Closed by accident January 22. *The Last of Mrs. Cheyney*, with Joel Ashley. Summer circuit.

1949: *Let Us Be Gay*, with Joel Ashley. Summer circuit.

1950: *Good-bye, My Fancy*, with Ashley. Minitour, summer circuit. Tryout of Thomas Wolfe's *The Web and the Rock* on summer circuit.

1951: *Mirror, Mirror* by George Oppenheimer. Summer circuit. *Theater* by Somerset Maugham. Winter stock, with Dennis Allen.

1952: *Theater*, with Dennis Allen. Summer circuit. *Portrait in Black*, with Dennis Allen. Summer circuit

LORETTA YOUNG

Films of Loretta Young

Dates are for New York City release

(1) THE ONLY WAY   Fanny Ward, Theodore Roberts
Extra as child on the operating table.

(2) SIRENS OF THE SEA   Extra

(3) THE SON OF THE SHEIK Rudolph Valentino   Arab child

(4) NAUGHTY BUT NICE
First National, July 5, 1927   Directed by Millard Webb
Screenplay by Carey Wilson; based on Lewis A. Browne's *The Bigamists*
Cast: Colleen Moore, Donald Reed, Claude Gillingwater, Kathryn McGuire,
    Hallam Cooley, Edythe Chapman, Clarissa Selwynne, Burr McIntosh
Mark Strand Theater

(4) HER WILD OAT
First National, February 6, 1928   Directed by Marshall Neilan
Adapted from a story by Howard Irving Young
Cast: Colleen Moore, Lary Kent, Hallam Cooley, Gwen Lee, Martha Mattox,
    Charles Giblin, Julanne Johnston
Paramount Theater

(5) THE WHIP WOMAN
First National, February 13, 1928   Directed by Joseph C. Boyle
Produced by Allan Dwan
Screenplay by Earle Roebuck; from a story by Forrest Halsey and Leland
    Hayward
Cast: Estelle Taylor, Antonio Moreno, Lowell Sherman, Hedda Hopper, Ju-
    lanne Johnston
Greenwich Village Theater

(6) LAUGH, CLOWN, LAUGH
MGM, May 28, 1928   Directed by Herbert Brenon

348

Screenplay by Elizabeth Meehan; adapted from David Belasco and Tom Cushing's play
Cast: Lon Chaney, Bernard Siegel, Cissy Fitzgerald, Nils Asther, Gwen Lee
Capitol Theater

(7) THE MAGNIFICENT FLIRT
Paramount, June 25, 1928   Directed by Harry D'Abbie D'Arrast
Screenplay by Jean de Limur and D'Arrast; from the story "Maman"
Cast: Florence Vidor, Albert Conti, Matty Kemp, Marietta Millner, Ned Sparks
Paramount Theater

(8) THE HEAD MAN
First National (not reviewed in New York)   Directed by Eddie Cline
Screenplay by Harvey Thew and Harry Green; based on a play by Harry Leon Wilson
Cast: Charlie Murray, Larry Kent, Lucien Littlefield, E. J. Ratcliffe, Irving Bacon, Harvey Clark, Sylvia Ashton, Dot Farley, Martha Mattox, Rosa Gore

(9) SCARLETT SEAS
First National, December 31, 1928   Directed by John Francis Dillon
Screenplay by Bradley King; based on a story by W. Scott Darling
Cast: Richard Barthelmess, Betty Compson, James Bradbury, Sr., Jack Curtis, Knute Erickson
Mark Strand Theater

(10) THE SQUALL
First National, May 10, 1929   Directed by Alexander Korda
Screenplay by Bradley King; from the play by Jean Bart (aka Marie Antoinette Sarlabous)
Cast: Myrna Loy, Richard Tucker, Alice Joyce, Carroll Nye, Harry Cording, Zasu Pitts, Nicholas Souseanin, Knute Erickson, George Hackathorne (Loretta's first sound picture)
Central Theater

(11) THE GIRL IN THE GLASS CAGE
First National (no New York review)   Directed by Ralph Dawson
Screenplay by James Gruen; adapted from George Kibbe Turner's novel
Cast: Carroll Nye, Matthew Betz, Lucien Littlefield, Ralph Lewis, George E. Stone, Julia Swayne Gordon, Mabel Coleman, Charles Sellon, Robert Haines

(12) FAST LIFE
First National, August 17, 1929   Directed by John Francis Dillon
Screenplay by John Goodrich; based on a play by Samuel Shipman and John B. Hymer
Cast: Douglas Fairbanks, Jr., William Holden, Frank Sheridan, Chester Morris, Ray Hallor, John St. Polis, Purnell Pratt
Central Theater

(13) THE CARELESS AGE
First National, September 21, 1929   Directed by John Griffith Wray
Screenplay by Richard A. Rowland; from John Van Druten's play *Diversion*
Cast: Douglas Fairbanks, Jr., Carmel Myers, Holmes Herbert, Kenneth Thomson, George Baxter, Wilfred Noy, Ilka Chase, Doris Lloyd, Raymond Lawrence
Mark Strand Theater

(14) THE SHOW OF SHOWS
Warner Brothers, November 21, 1929   Directed by John G. Adolfi
Produced by Darryl Zanuck   Musical revue.
Among the sister acts were Sally Blane and Loretta. Richard Barthelmess introduced the "sisters," some of which, such as Ann Sothern and Marion Byron, were not related. John Barrymore spoke for the first time in talking pictures. Cast of seventy-seven.
Winter Garden Theater

(15) THE FORWARD PASS
First National, November 29, 1929   Directed by Eddie Cline
Screenplay by Harvey Gates and Howard E. Rogers
Cast: Douglas Fairbanks, Jr., Guinn Williams, Phyllis Crane, Bert Rome, Lane Chandler, Marion "Peanuts" Byron, Allen Lane
Warner's Strand Theater

(16) THE MAN FROM BLANKLEY'S
Warner Brothers, May 29, 1930   Directed by Alfred E. Green
Screenplay by Harvey Thew and Joseph Jackson; based on a play by F. Anstey
Cast: John Barrymore, William Austin, Albert Gran, Emily Fitzroy, Dick Henderson, Edgar Norton, Dale Fuller, D'Arcy Corrigan, Louise Carver, Yorke Sherwood, Diana Hope, Tiny Jones, Angella Mawby
Central Theater

(17) THE SECOND-STORY MURDER
Warner Brothers, May 3, 1930   Directed by Roy Del Ruth
Screenplay by Joe Jackson; based on Earl Derr Bigger's novel *The Agony Column*

Cast: Grant Withers (top billing), Claude King, John Loder, Crauford Kent, H. B. Warner, Clair McDowell
Warner's Beacon Theater

(18) LOOSE ANKLES
First National (no New York review)   Directed by Ted Wilde
Screenplay by Gene Towne; from a play by Sam Janney
Cast: Douglas Fairbanks, Jr., Louise Fazenda, Ethel Wales, Otis Harlan, Daphne Pollard, Inez Courtney, Eddie Nugent, Raymond Keane

(19) ROAD TO PARADISE
First National, September 30, 1930   Directed by William Beaudine
Screenplay by F. Hugh Herbert; adapted from Dodson Mitchell's play *Cornered*
Cast: Jack Mulhall, Raymond Hatton, George Barraud, Kathlyn Williams, Purnell Pratt, Fred Kelsey, Dot Farley, Winter Hall, Ben Hendricks, Jr., Georgette Rhodes
Hippodrome Theater

(20) KISMET
First National, October 31, 1930   Directed by John Francis Dillon
Screenplay by Howard Eastbrook; adapted from Edward Knoblock's play
Cast: Otis Skinner, Mary Duncan, David Manners, Sidney Blackmer, Ford Sterling, Edmund Breese, Blanche Frederici, Montagu Love, Richard Carlyle, John St. Polis, John Sheehan, Otto Hoffman
Hollywood Theater

(21) THE TRUTH ABOUT YOUTH
First National, December 13, 1930   Directed by William A. Seiter
Screenplay by W. Harrison Orkow; from Harry V. Esmond's play *When We Were Twenty-One*
Cast: Conway Tearle, David Manners, J. Farrell MacDonald, Harry Stubbs, Myrtle Stedman, Myrna Loy, Ray Hallor, Dorothy Matthew, Yole D'Avril
Strand Theater

(22) THE DEVIL TO PAY
Samuel Goldwyn-UA, December 19, 1930   Directed by George Fitzmaurice
Screenplay by Benjamin Glazer and Frederick Lonsdale; based on Frederick Lonsdale's play *Monarch of the Field*
Cast: Ronald Colman, Florence Britton, Frederick Kerr, David Torrence, Mary Forbes, Paul Cavanaugh, Crauford Kent, Myrna Loy
Gaiety Theater

(23) BEAU IDEAL
RKO-Radio, January 19, 1931   Directed and produced by Herbert Brenon
Screenplay by Paul Schofield and Elizabeth Meehan; based on Percival Christopher Wren's novel
Cast: Ralph Forbes, Lester Vail, Don Alvarado, Otto Matieson, Irene Rich, Paul MacAllister, George Rigas, Leni Stengel, Hale Hamilton, Myrtle Stedman, Frank McCormack, Bernard Seifel, John M. St. Polis, Joseph Di Steffani
Mayfair Theater

(24) THE RIGHT OF WAY
Warner Brothers, March 24, 1931   Directed by Frank Lloyd
Screenplay by Francis Faragoh; based on Sir Gilbert Parker's novel
Cast: Conrad Nagel, Fred Kohler, William Janney, Snitz Edwards, George Pierce, Halliwell Hobbes, Olive Tell, Brandon Hurst, Yola d'Avril
Warner's Theater

(25) THREE GIRLS LOST
Fox, May 2, 1931   Directed by Sidney Lanfield
Screenplay by Bradley King; from Robert D. Andrews' story
Cast: John Wayne, Lew Cody, Joyce Compton, Joan Marsh, Kathrin Clare Ward, Paul Fix
Roxy Theater

(26) TOO YOUNG TO MARRY
First National, May 4, 1931   Directed by Mervyn LeRoy
Screenplay by Francis Faragoh; adapted from Martin Flavin's *Broken Dishes*
Cast: Grant Withers, O. P. Heggie, Emma Dunn, J. Farrell MacDonald, Lloyd Neal, Richard Tucker, Virginia Sale, Aileen Carlisle
Warner's Theater

(27) BIG BUSINESS GIRL
First National, June 12, 1931   Directed by William A. Seiter
Screenplay by Robert Lord; based on a story by Patricia Reilly and H.N. Swanson
Cast: Frank Albertson, Ricardo Cortez, Joan Blondell, Frank Darion, Dorothy Christy, Mickey Bennett, Bobby Gordon, Nancy Dover, Virginia Sale, Oscar Apfel
Strand and Brooklyn Strand Theater

(28) I LIKE YOUR NERVE
First National, September 12, 1931   Directed by William McGann
Screenplay by Huston Branch; based on a story by Roland Pertwee
Cast: Douglas Fairbanks, Jr., Edmund Breon, Henry Kolker, Claude Allister,

Ivan Simpson, Paul Porcasi, André Cheron, Boris Karloff, Henry Bunston
Warner's Strand and Brooklyn Strand Theaters

(29) PLATINUM BLONDE

Columbia, October 31, 1931   Directed by Frank Capra
Screenplay by Jo Swerling, Robert Riskin and Dorothy Howell; based on a story by Harry E. Chandlee and Douglas W. Churchill
Cast: Robert Williams, Jean Harlow, Louise Closser Hale, Donald Dillaway, Reginald Owen, Walter Catlett, Edmund Breese, Halliwell Hobbs, Claude Allister
Strand Theater

(30) THE RULING VOICE

First National, November 5, 1931   Directed by Rowland V. Lee
Screenplay by Robert Lord; based on a story by R. V. Lee and Donald W. Lee
Cast: Walter Huston, Doris Kenyon, David Manners, John Halliday, Dudley Digges, Gilbert Emery, Willard Robertson, Douglas Scott
Winter Garden Theater

(31) TAXI

Warner Brothers, January 8, 1932   Directed by Roy Del Ruth
Screenplay by Kubec Glasman and John Bright; based on Edward Caulfield's play *Blind Spot*
Cast: James Cagney, George E. Stone, Dorothy Burgess, Ray Cooke, Matt McHugh, Leila Bennett, David Landau, Guy Kibbee, George MacFarlane, Nat Pendleton, Polly Walters, Berton Churchill, Lee Phelps, George Raft
Warner's Strand Theater

(32) THE HATCHET MAN

First National, February 4, 1932   Directed by William A. Wellman
Screenplay by J. Grubb Alexander; from David Belasco and Achmed Abdullah's play *The Honorable Mr. Wong*
Cast: Edward G. Robinson, Dudley Digges, Leslie Fenton, Edmund Breese, Tully Marshall, Noel Madison, Blanche Frederici, J. Carrol Naish, Toshia Mori, Charles Middleton, Ralph Ince, Otto Yamioka, Evelyn Selbie, E. Allyn Warren, Eddie Piel, Willie Fung, Anna Chang
Winter Garden Theater

(33) PLAY GIRL

Warner Brothers, March 19, 1932   Directed by Ray Enright
Screenplay by Maurine Watkins
Cast: Winnie Lightner, Norman Foster, Guy Kibbee, Noel Madison, Polly Walters, Dorothy Burgess, Mae Madison, Eileen Carlisle, Rene Whitney,

James Ellison, Adrienne Dore, Harold Waldridge, Charles Coleman, Nat Pendleton
Warner's Strand Theater

(34) WEEKEND MARRIAGE

First National, June 4, 1932   Directed by Thornton Freeland
Screenplay by Sheridan Gibney; based on Faith Baldwin's novel *Part-Time Marriage*
Cast: Norman Foster, George Brent, Aline MacMahon, Vivienne Osborne, Sheila Terry, J. Farrell MacDonald, Louise Carter, Grant Mitchell, Harry Holman, Louis Alberni, J. Carrol Naish, Richard Tucker
Warner's Strand Theater

(35) LIFE BEGINS

First National, August 26, 1932   Directed by James Flood and Elliott Nugent
Screenplay by Earl Baldwin; based on a play by Mary McDougal Axelson
Cast: Eric Linden, Aline MacMahon, Glenda Farrell, Dorothy Peterson, Vivienne Osborne, Frank McHugh, Gilbert Roland, Hale Hamilton, Herbert Mundin, Preston Foster, Walter Walker, Clara Blandick, Gloria Shea, Helena Phillips, Reginald Mason, Ruthelma Stevens, Elizabeth Patterson, Dorothy Tree, Mary Phillips, Terrance Ray
Hollywood Theater

(36) THEY CALL IT SIN

First National, October 21, 1932   Directed by Thornton Freeland
Screenplay by Lillie Hayward and Howard Green; from a novel by Alberta Stedman Eagan
Cast: George Brent, David Manners, Louis Calhern, Una Merkel, Joseph Cawthorne, Helen Vinson, Nella Walker, Mike Marito, Erville Alderson, Elizabeth Patterson
Winter Garden Theater

(37) EMPLOYEES' ENTRANCE

First National, January 21, 1933   Directed by Roy del Ruth
Screenplay by Robert Presnell; based on a story by David Boehm
Cast: Warren William, Wallace Ford, Alice White, Albert Gran, Allen Jenkins, Marjorie Gateson, Hale Hamilton, Ruth Donnelly, Zita Moulton, Frank Reicher, Berton Churchill, Charles Sellon, Helen Mann, H. C. Bradley
Capitol and Loew's Metropolitan Theaters

(38) GRAND SLAM

First National, February 22, 1933   Directed by William Dieterle
Screenplay by Erwin Gelsey and David Boehm; from B. Russell Hertz' novel
Cast: Paul Lukas, Frank McHugh, Glenda Farrell, Helen Vinson, Walter By-

ron, Ferdinand Gottschalk, Joseph Cawthorne, Paul Porcasi, Mary Doran, Lucien Prival, Tom Dugan, Maurice Black, Lee Morgan, Ruthelma Stevens, Emma Dunn, Reginald Barlow
Winter Garden Theater

(39) ZOO IN BUDAPEST
Fox, April 28, 1933   Directed by Rowland V. Lee
Screenplay by Dan Totheroh, Louise Long and Rowland V. Leigh; based on a story by Melville Baker and Jack Kirkland
Cast: Gene Raymond, O. P. Heggie, Wally Albright, Paul Fix, Murray Kinnell, Ruth Warren, Roy Stewart, Frances Rich, Niles Welch, Lucille Ward, Russ Powell, Dorothy Libaire
Radio City Music Hall

(40) THE LIFE OF JIMMY DOLAN
Warner Brothers, June 14, 1933   Directed by Archie Mayo
Screenplay by Erwin Gelsey and David Boehm; based on a play by Bertram Milhauser and Beulah Marie Dix
Cast: Douglas Fairbanks, Jr., Aline MacMahon, Guy Kibbee, Lyle Talbot, Fifi D'Orsay, Harold Huber, Shirley Grey, George Meeker, David Durand, Farina, Mickey Rooney, Dawn O'Day (aka Anne Shirley), Arthur Hohl
Rialto Theater

(41) MIDNIGHT MARY
MGM, July 15, 1933   Directed by William Wellman
Screenplay by Gene Markey and Kathryn Scola; story by Anita Loos
Cast: Ricardo Cortez, Franchot Tone, Andy Devine, Una Merkel, Frank Conroy, Warren Hymer, Ivan Simpson
Capitol and Loew's Metropolitan Theaters

(42) HEROS FOR SALE
First National, July 22, 1933   Directed by William Wellman
Screenplay by Robert Lord and Wilson Mizner
Cast: Richard Barthelmess, Aline MacMahon, Gordon Westcott, Robert Barrat, Charles Grapewin, Berton Churchill, Grant Mitchell, James Murray, Robert McWade, Ward Bond, Dewey Robinson
Strand Theater

(43) THE DEVIL'S IN LOVE
Fox, July 28, 1933   Directed by William Dieterle
Screenplay by Howard Estabrook; based on a story by Harry Hervey
Cast: Victor Jory, Vivienne Osborne, David Manners, C. Henry Gordon, Herbert Mundin, J. Carrol Naish
Radio City Music Hall

355

(44) SHE HAD TO SAY YES
First National, July 29, 1933   Directed by Busby Berkeley and George Amy
Screenplay by Rian James and Don Mullaly; from John F. Larkin's story
Cast: Lyle Talbot, Winnie Lightner, Regis Toomey, Hugh Herbert, Ferdinand
Gottschalk
Strand Theater

(45) A MAN'S CASTLE
Columbia, December 30, 1933   Directed by Frank Borzage
Screenplay by Jo Swerling; based on a play by Lawrence Hazard
Cast: Spencer Tracy, Glenda Farrell, Walter Connolly, Arthur Hohl, Marjorie
Rambeau, Dickie Moore
Rialto Theater

(46) THE HOUSE OF ROTHSCHILD
Twentieth Century-UA, March 15, 1934   Directed by Alfred Werker
Screenplay by Nunnally Johnson; based on an unproduced play by George
Hembert Westley
Cast: George Arliss, Boris Karloff, Robert Young, C. Aubrey Smith, Arthur
Bryon, Helen Westley, Reginald Owen, Florence Arliss, Alan Mowbray,
Holmes Herbert, Paul Harvey, Ivan Simpson, Noel Madison, Murray Kin-
nell, Georges Renavent, Oscar Apfel, Lumsden Hare, Gilbert Emery, Wil-
liam Strauss, Matthew Betz, Leonard Mudie, Ethel Griffies
Astor Theater

(47) BORN TO BE BAD
Twentieth Century-UA, May 31, 1934   Directed by Lowell Sherman
Screenplay and original story by Ralph Graves
Cast: Cary Grant, Jackie Kelk, Henry Travers, Russell Hopton, Andrew
Tombes, Harry Green, Marion Burns, Howard Lang, Paul Harvey, Matt
Briggs, Geneva Mitchell, Charles Coleman
Rivoli Theater

(48) BULLDOG DRUMMOND STRIKES BACK
Twentieth Century-UA, August 16, 1934   Directed by Roy del Ruth
Screenplay by Nunnally Johnson; taken from H. C. McNeile's novel
Cast: Ronald Colman, Warner Oland, Charles Butterworth, Una Merkel, C.
Aubrey Smith, Kathleen Burke, Arthur Hohl, George Regas, Ethel Griffies,
Mischa Auer, Douglas Gerrard, Halliwell Hobbes, E. E. Clive, Lucille Ball
Rivoli Theater

(49) CARAVAN
Fox, September 28, 1934   Directed by Erik Charell
Screenplay by Samson Raphaelson; based on a story by Melchior Lengyel

Songs by Werner Richard Heymann and Gus Kahn

Cast: Charles Boyer, Jean Parker, Phillips Holmes, Louise Fazenda, Eugene Pallette, C. Aubrey Smith, Charles Grapewin, Noah Beery, Dudley Digges, Richard Carle, Lionel Belmore, Billy Bevan, Armand Kaliz, Harry C. Bradley

Radio City Music Hall

(50) THE WHITE PARADE

Fox, November 10, 1934   Directed by Irving Cummings

Produced by Jesse Lasky

Screenplay by Sonya Levien and Ernest Pascal; adapted by Jesse Lasky, Jr., and Rian James from Rian James' novel

Cast: John Boles, Dorothy Wilson, Muriel Kirkland, Astrid Allwyn, Frank Conroy, Jane Darwell, Frank Melton, Walter Johnson, Sara Haden, Joyce Compton, June Gittleson, Polly Ann Young, Ben Bard, Rheta Hoyt, Ann Darcy

Paramount Theater

(51) CLIVE OF INDIA

Twentieth-UA, January 18, 1935   Directed by Richard Boleslavski

Screenplay by W. P. Lipscomb and Rubeigh Minney; adapted from their play

Musical score by Alfred Newman

Cast: Ronald Colman, Colin Clive, Francis Lister, C. Aubrey Smith, Cesar Romero, Montagu Love, Lumsden Hare, Ferdinand Munier, Gilbert Emery, Leo G. Carroll, Etienne Girardot, Robert Greig, Ian Wolfe, Herbert Bunston, Mischa Auer, Ferdinand Gottschalk, Wyndham Standing, Doris Lloyd, Edward Cooper, Ann Shaw, Vernon Downing, Neville Clark, Peter Shaw, Pat Somerset, Eily Malyon, Keith Kenneth, Desmond Roberts, Joseph Tozer, Phyllis Clare, Connie Leon, Leonard Mudie, Phillip Dare, Charles Evans, Vesey O'Davern, Lila Lance, Don Ameche

Rivoli Theater

(52) SHANGHAI

Paramount, July 20, 1935   Directed by James Flood

A Walter Wanger Production

Screenplay and story by Gene Towne, Graham Baker, and Lynn Starling

Cast: Charles Boyer, Warner Oland, Fred Keating, Charles Grapewin, Alison Skipworth, Libby Taylor, Josephine Whittel, Walker Kingsford, Olive Tell, Arnold Korff, Willie Fung, Keye Luke

Paramount Theater

(53) CALL OF THE WILD

Twentieth Century-UA, August 15, 1935   Directed by William Wellman

Screenplay by Gene Fowler and Leonard Braskins, from Jack London's novel

357

Cast: Clark Gable, Jack Oakie, Frank Conroy, Reginald Owen, Sidney Toler, Katherine DeMille, Lalo Encinas, Charles Stevens, James Burke, Duke Green
Rivoli Theater

(54) THE CRUSADES
Paramount, August 22, 1935   Directed by Cecil B. DeMille
Screenplay by Harold Lamb, Dudley Nichols and Waldemar Young
Cast: Henry Wilcoxon, Ian Keith, Katherine DeMille, C. Aubrey Smith, Joseph Schildkraut, Alan Hale, C. Henry Gordon, George Barbier, Montagu Love, Hobart Bosworth, William Farnum, Lumsden Hare, Ramsey Hill, Pedro de Cordoba, Paul Satoff, Mischa Auer, J. Carrol Naish, Ann Sheridan
Astor Theater

(55) THE UNGUARDED HOUR
MGM, April 4, 1936   Directed by Sam Wood
Produced by Lawrence Weingarten
Screenplay by Howard Emmett Rogers and Leon Gordon, based on a play by Ladislas Fodor
Cast: Franchot Tone, Lewis Stone, Roland Young, Jessie Ralph, Dudley Digges, Henry Daniell, Robert Greig, E. E. Clive, Wallace Clark, John Buckler, Aileen Pringle
Capitol Theater

(56) PRIVATE NUMBER
Twentieth Century-Fox, June 12, 1936   Directed by Roy del Ruth
Screenplay by Gene Markey and William Conselman; based on Cleves Kinkhead's play *Common Clay*
Cast: Robert Taylor, Basil Rathbone, Patsy Kelly, Joe Lewis, Marjorie Gateson, Paul Harvey, Jane Darwell, Paul Stanton, John Milijan, Monroe Owsley, George Irving
Radio City Music Hall

(57) RAMONA
Twentieth Century-Fox, October 7, 1936   Directed by Henry King
Produced by Sol M. Wurtzel
Screenplay by Lamar Trotti; from Helen Hunt Jackson's novel
Cast: Don Ameche, Kent Taylor, Pauline Frederick, Jane Darwell, Katherine DeMille, Victor Killian, John Carradine, J. Carrol Naish, Pedro deCordoba, Charles Waldron, Claire DuBrey, Russell Simpson, William Benedict, Robert Spindola, Chief Thunder Cloud
Criterion Theater

(58) LADIES IN LOVE
Twentieth Century-Fox, October 29, 1936   Directed by Edward H. Griffith
Screenplay by Melville Baker; based on a play by Ladislaus Bus-Fekete
Cast: Janet Gaynor, Constance Bennett, Simone Simon, Don Ameche, Paul
    Lukas, Tyrone Power, Jr., Alan Mowbray, Wilfrid Lawson, J. Edward
    Bromberg, Virginia Field, Frank Dawson, Egon Brecher, Vesey O'Davoren,
    John Bleifer, Eleanor Wesselhoeft
Rivoli Theater

(59) LOVE IS NEWS
Twentieth Century-Fox, March 6, 1937   Directed by Tay Garnett
Screenplay by Harry Tugend and Jack Yellen; story by William Lipman and
    Frederick Stephani
Cast: Tyrone Power, Don Ameche, Slim Summerville, Dudley Digges, Walter
    Catlett, Jane Darwell, Stepin Fetchit, George Sanders, Pauline Moore, Eli-
    sha Cook, Jr., Frank Conroy, Paul McVey, Edwin Maxwell, Charles Wil-
    liams, Julius Tannen, George Hurbert, Frederick Burton
Roxy Theater

(60) CAFÉ METROPOLE
Twentieth Century-Fox, April 29, 1937   Directed by Edward H. Griffith
Produced by Nunnally Johnson
Screenplay by Jacques Deval; story by Gregory Ratoff
Cast: Tyrone Power, Adolphe Menjou, Gregory Ratoff, Charles Winninger,
    Helen Westley, Ferdinand Gottschalk, Christian Rub, Georges Renavent,
    Leonid Kinskey, Hal K. Dawson, Paul Porasi, Andre Cheron, Andre
    Beranger, Frederik Vogeding
Rivoli Theater

(61) LOVE UNDER FIRE
Twentieth Century-Fox, August 28, 1937   Directed by George Marshall
Produced by Nunnally Johnson
Screenplay by Gene Fowler, Allen Rivkin and Ernest Pascal; from a play by
    Walter Hackett
Cast: Don Ameche, Borrah Minevitch and His Gang, Frances Drake, Walter
    Catlett, John Carradine, Sig Rumann, Harold Huber, Katherine DeMille,
    E. E. Clive, Don Alvarado, Georges Renavent, Clyde Cook, George Regas,
    Claude King, Francis McDonald, David Clyde, Egon Brecher, Juan Toreno,
    Holmes Herbert, George Humbert
Roxy Theater

(62) WIFE, DOCTOR AND NURSE
Twentieth Century-Fox, October 11, 1937   Directed by Walter Lang

Produced by Raymond Griffith
Screenplay by Kathryn Scola, Darrell Ware and Lamar Trotti
Cast: Warner Baxter, Virginia Bruce, Jane Darwell, Sidney Blackmer, Maurice Cass, Minna Gombel, Margaret Irving, Gordon Elliott, Elisha Cook, Jr., Brewster twins, Paul Hurst, Hal Dawson, George Ernst, Georges Renavent, Spencer Charters, Claire DuBrey, Lon Chaney, Jr., Charles Judels, Stanley Fields, Olin Howland, Jan Duggan
Rivoli Theater

(63) SECOND HONEYMOON
Twentieth Century-Fox, November 13, 1937   Directed by Walter Lang
Produced by Raymond Griffith
Screenplay by Kathryn Scola and Darrell Ware; based on a magazine story by Philip Wylie
Cast: Tyrone Power, Stuart Erwin, Claire Trevor, Marjorie Weaver, Lyle Talbot, J. Edward Bromberg, Paul Hurst, Jayne Regan, Hal K. Dawson, Mary Treen, Lon Chaney, Jr., Robert Lowery
Roxy Theater

(64) FOUR MEN AND A PRAYER
Twentieth Century-Fox, May 7, 1938   Directed by John Ford
Produced by Kenneth MacGowan
Screenplay by Richard Sherman, Sonya Levien and Walter Ferris; based on a book by David Garth
Cast: Richard Greene, George Sanders, David Niven, C. Aubrey Smith, J. Edward Bromberg, William Henry, John Carradine, Alan Hale, Reginald Denny, Berton Churchill, Barry Fitzgerald, Claude King, Cecil Cunningham, Frank Dawson, John Sutton, Lina Basquette, Frank Baker, William Stack, Peter Lorre, Harry Hayden, Will Stanton, Winter Hall, Lionel Pape, Brandon Hurst, John Spacy, C. Montague Shaw
Roxy Theater

(65) THREE BLIND MICE
Twentieth Century-Fox, June 18, 1938   Directed by William A. Seiter
Produced by Darryl Zanuck and Raymond Griffith
Screenplay by Brown Holmes and Lynn Starling; based on a play by Stephen Powys
Music and lyrics by Lew Pollack and Sidney B. Mitchell
Cast: Joel McCrea, David Niven, Stuart Erwin, Marjorie Weaver, Pauline Moore, Binnie Barnes, Jane Darwell, Leonid Kinskey, Spencer Charters, Franklin Pangborn, Herb Heywood
Roxy Theater

(66) SUEZ
Twentieth Century-Fox, October 15, 1938   Directed by Allan Dwan
Associate producer: Gene Markey
Screenplay by Philip Dunne and Julien Josephson; from a story by Sam Duncan
Cast: Tyrone Power, Annabella, J. Edward Bromberg, Joseph Schildkraut, Henry Stephenson, Sidney Blackmer, Maurice Moscovich, Sig Rumann, Nigel Bruce, Miles Mander, George Zucco, Leon Ames, Rafaela Ottiano, Victor Varconi, Georges Renavent, Frank Reicher, Carlos de Valdez, Jacques Lory, Albert Conti, Brandon Hurst, Marcelle Corday, Odette Myrtil, Victor Varconi
Roxy Theater

(67) KENTUCKY
Twentieth Century-Fox, December 24, 1938   Directed by David Butler
Produced by Darryl F. Zanuck
Screenplay by Lamar Trotti and John Taintor Foote; based on Foote's story "The Look of the Eagles"
Cast: Richard Greene, Walter Brennan, Douglas Dumbrille, Karen Morley, Moroni Olsen, Russell Hicks, Willard Robertson, Charles Waldron, George Reed, Bobs Watson, Delmar Watson, Leona Roberts, Charles Lane, Charles Middleton, Harry Hayden, Robert Middlemass, Madame Sui-Te-Wan, Cliff Clark, Meredith Howard, Fred Burton, Charles Trowbridge, Eddie Anderson, Stanley Andrews
Roxy Theater

(68) WIFE, HUSBAND AND FRIEND
Twentieth Century-Fox, February 25, 1939   Directed by Gregory Ratoff
Screenplay by Nunnally Johnson; from a James Cain novel
Songs by Samuel Pokrass, Walter Bullock and Armando Hauser
Cast: Warner Baxter, Binnie Barnes, Cesar Romero, George Barbier, J. Edward Bromberg, Eugene Pallette, Helen Westley, Ruth Terry, Alice Armand, Iva Stewart, Dorothy Dearing, Helen Erickson, Kay Griffith, Harry Rosenthal, Edward Cooper, René Riano, Laurence Grant, Howard Hickman, George Irving, Harry Hayden
Roxy Theater

(69) THE STORY OF ALEXANDER GRAHAM BELL
Twentieth Century Fox, April 1, 1939   Directed by Irving Cummings
Produced by Darryl F. Zanuck
Screenplay by Lamar Trotti; based on a story by Ray Harris
Cast: Don Ameche, Henry Fonda, Charles Coburn, Gene Lockhart, Spring Byington, Sally Blane, Polly Ann Young, Bobs Watson, Russell Hicks, Paul

Stanton, Jonathan Hale, Harry Davenport, Elizabeth Patterson, Charles Trowbridge, Jan Duggan, Claire DuBrey, Harry Tyler, Ralph Remley, Zeffie Tilbury, Georgiana Young, Beryl Mercer, Jack Kelly, Crauford Kent
Roxy Theater

(70) ETERNALLY YOURS
Walter Wanger-UA, October 7, 1939   Directed and produced by Tay Garnett
Screenplay by Gene Towne and Graham Baker
Cast: David Niven, Hugh Herbert, Billie Burke, C. Aubrey Smith, Virginia Field, Broderick Crawford, Raymond Walburn, Zasu Pitts, Eve Arden, Ralph Graves, Lionel Pape, Dennie Moore, May Beatty, Douglas Wood, Leyland Hodgson, Herman, the rabbit, Frank Jacquet, Fred Keating, Paul LePaul, Ralph Norwood, Billy Wayne, Edwin Stanley, Franklin Parker, Mary Field, Granville Bates, Tay Garnett, George Cathrey, Lieutenant Pat Davis
Roxy Theater

(71) THE DOCTOR TAKES A WIFE
Columbia, June 15, 1940   Directed by Alexander Hall
Produced by William Perlberg
Screenplay by George Seaton and Ken Englund; based on a story by Aleen Leslie
Cast: Ray Milland, Reginald Gardiner, Gail Patrick, Edmund Gwenn, Frank Sully, Georges Metaxa, Gordon Jones, Charles Halton, Joseph Eggenton, Paul McAllister, Chester Clute, Hal K. Dawson, Edward Van Sloan
Roxy Theater

(72) HE STAYED FOR BREAKFAST
Columbia, August 31, 1940   Directed by Alexander Hall
Produced by B. P. Schulberg
Screenplay by P. J. Wolfson, Michael Fessier and Ernest Vajda; based on Sidney Howard's adaption of Michel Duran's play *Liberte Provisoire*
Cast: Melvyn Douglas, Alan Marshall, Eugene Pallette, Una O'Connor, Curt Bois, Leonid Kinskey, Grady Sutton, Trevor Bardette, Frank Sully, William Castle, Vernon Dent, Walter Merrill, Joseph Karnryt
Roxy Theater

(73) THE LADY FROM CHEYENNE
Universal, April 18, 1941   Directed and produced by Frank Lloyd
Screenplay by Kathryn Scola and Warren Duff; original story by Jonathan Finn and Theresa Oaks
Cast: Robert Preston, Edward Arnold, Gladys George, Frank Craven, Jessie Ralph, Samuel S. Hinds, Willie Best, Stanley Fields, Spencer Charters, Clare Verdera, Alan Bridge, Joseph Sawyer, Ralph Dunn, Harry Cording,

Dorothy Granger, Marion Martin, Iris Adrian, Gladys Blake, Sally Payne, June Wilkins, Roger Imhof
Roxy Theater

(74) THE MEN IN HER LIFE
Columbia, December 12, 1941   Directed and produced by Gregory Ratoff
Screenplay by Frederick Kohner, Michael Wilson and Paul Trivers; based on Lady Eleanor Smith's novel *Ballerina*
Cast: Conrad Veidt, Dean Jagger, Eugenie Leontovich, John Sheppard, Otto Kruger, Paul Baratoff, Ann Todd, Billy Rayes, Ludmila Toretzka, Tom Ladd
Radio City Music Hall

(75) BEDTIME STORY
Columbia, March 20, 1942   Directed by Alexander Hall
Produced by B. P. Schulberg
Screenplay by Richard Flournoy; from a story by Horace Jackson and Grant Garrett
Cast: Fredric March, Robert Benchley, Allyn Joslyn, Eve Arden, Helen Westley, Joyce Compton, Tim Ryan, Olaf Hytten, Dorothy Adams, Clarence Kolb, Andrew Tombes, Grady Sutton, Emmett Vogan, Spencer Charters
Radio City Music Hall

(76) A NIGHT TO REMEMBER
Columbia, January 1, 1943   Directed by Richard Wallance
Produced by Samuel Bischoff
Screenplay by Richard Flournoy and Jack Henley; from a story by Kelley Roos
Cast: Brian Aherne, Jeff Donnell, William Wright, Sidney Toler, Gale Sondergaard, Donald MacBride, Lee Patrick, Don Costello, Blanche Yurka, Richard Gaines, James Burke, Billy Benedict
Loew's State Theater

(77) CHINA
Paramount, April 22, 1943   Directed by John Farrow
Produced by Dick Blumenthal
Screenplay by Frank Butler; based on a play by Archibald Forbes
Cast: Alan Ladd, William Bendix, Philip Ahn, Jessie Tai Sing, Richard Loo, Sen Yung, Iris Wong, Marianne Quon, Irene Tso, Ching Wan Lee, Soo Yong, Barbara Jean Wong
Paramount Theater

(78) LADIES COURAGEOUS
Universal, March 16, 1944   Directed by John Rawlins

Produced by Walter Wanger

Screenplay and story by Norman Reilly Raine and Doris Gilbert; suggested by Virginia Spencer Cowles' book *Looking for Trouble*

Cast: Geraldine Fitzgerald, Richard Fraser, Anne Gywnne, Diana Barrymore, Evelyn Ankers, David Bruce, June Vincent, Lois Collier, Philip Terry, Samuel S. Hinds, Kane Richmond, Marie Harmon, Janet Shaw, Billy Wayne, Ruth Roman, Matt McHugh, Steve Brodie, Blake Edwards, Samuel S. Hinds

Lowe's Criterion Theater

(79) AND NOW TOMORROW

Paramount, November 23, 1944   Directed by Irving Pichel

Produced by Fred Kohlmar

Screenplay by Frank Partos and Raymond Chandler; from Rachel Field's novel

Cast: Alan Ladd, Susan Hayward, Barry Sullivan, Beulah Bondi, Cecil Kellaway, Grant Mitchell, Helen Mack, Anthony Caruso, Jonathan Hale, George Carleton, Connie Leon, Darryl Hickman, Conrad Binyon, Leon Bulgakov, Mae Clarke, Doris Dowling, Doodles Weaver, Ann Carter

Paramount Theater

(80) ALONG CAME JONES

International Pictures-RKO, July 19, 1945   Directed by Stuart Heisler

Produced by Gary Cooper

Screenplay by Nunnally Johnson; from Alan LeMay's novel *The Useless Cowboy*

Cast: Gary Cooper, William Demarest, Dan Duryea, Frank Sully, Russell Simpson, Willard Robertson, Arthur Loft, Erville Alderson

Palace Theater

(81) THE STRANGER

International Pictures-RKO, July 11, 1946   Directed by Orson Welles

Produced by S. P. Eagle (Sam Spiegel)

Screenplay by Anthony Veiller and John Huston; story by Victor Trivas and Decla Dunning

Cast: Edward G. Robinson, Orson Welles, Philip Merivale, Billy House, Richard Long, Konstantin Shayne, Martha Wentworth, Byron Keith, Pietro Sosso

Palace Theater

(82) THE PERFECT MARRIAGE

Hal B. Wallis-Paramount, January 16, 1947   Directed by Lewis Allen

Screenplay by Leonard Spigelgass; from Samson Raphaelson's play

Cast: David Niven, Eddie Albert, Charlie Ruggles, Virginia Field, Rita John-

son, Zasu Pitts, Nona Griffith, Nana Bryant, Jerome Cowan, Luella Gear, Howard Freeman, Catherine Craig, John Vosper, Ann Doran, Carol Coombs, Jimmie Dundee
Paramount Theater

(83) THE FARMER'S DAUGHTER
RKO-Radio, March 26, 1947　　　　　　　Directed by H. C. Potter
Produced by Dore Schary
Screenplay by Allen Rivkin and Laura Kerr
Cast: Joseph Cotten, Ethel Barrymore, Charles Bickford, Rose Hobart, Rhys Williams, Harry Davenport, Tom Powers, William Harrigan, Lex Barker, Harry Shannon, Keith Andes, Thurston Hall, Art Baker, Don Beddoe, James Arness, Anna Q. Nilsson, Cy Kendall, William B. Davidson, William Bakewell
Rivoli Theater

(84) THE BISHOP'S WIFE
Samuel Goldwyn/RKO-Radio, December 10, 1947　　Directed by Henry Koster
Produced by Samuel Goldwyn
Screenplay by Robert E. Sherwood and Leonardo Bercovici; from a novel by Robert Nathan
Cast: Cary Grant, David Niven, Monty Woolley, James Gleason, Gladys Cooper, Elsa Lanchester, Sara Haden, Karolyn Grimes, Tito Vuolo, Regis Toomey, Sara Edwards, Margaret McWade, Ann O'Neal, Almira Sessions, Claire DuBrey, Isabel Jewell
Astor Theater

(85) RACHEL AND THE STRANGER
RKO-Radio, September 20, 1948　　　　　Directed by Norman Foster
Produced by Dore Schary and Richard Berger
Screenplay by Waldo Salt; from the story *Rachel* by Howard Fast
Cast: William Holden, Robert Mitchum, Gary Gray, Tom Tully, Sara Haden, Frank Ferguson, Walter Baldwin, Regina Wallace
Mayfair Theater

(86) THE ACCUSED
Hal B. Wallis-Paramount, January 13, 1949　　　Directed by William Dieterle
Screenplay by Ketti Frings; based on a novel by June Truesdell
Cast: Robert Cummings, Wendell Corey, Sam Jaffe, Douglas Dick, Suzanne Dalbert, Sara Allgood, Mickey Knox
Paramount Theater

(87) MOTHER IS A FRESHMAN
Twentieth Century-Fox, March 12, 1949　　　　Directed by Lloyd Bacon

Produced by Walter Morosco
Screenplay by Mary Loos and Richard Sale; based on a story by Raphael Blau
Cast: Van Johnson, Rudy Vallee, Barbara Lawrence, Robert Arthur, Betty
Lynn, Griff Barnett, Kathleen Hughes, Eddie Dunn, Claire Meade, Marietta
Canty
Roxy Theater

(88) COME TO THE STABLE
Twentieth Century-Fox, July 28, 1949   Directed by Henry Koster
Produced by Samuel G. Engel
Screenplay by Oscar Millard and Sally Benson; story by Clare Boothe Luce
Cast: Celeste Holm, Hugh Marlowe, Elsa Lanchester, Thomas Gomez, Doro-
thy Patrick, Basil Ruysdael, Dooley Wilson, Regis Tomey, Mike Mazurki,
Henri Letondal, Walter Baldwin, Tim Huntley, Virginia Kelley, Louis Jean
Heydt, Marion Martin
Rivoli Theater

(89) KEY TO THE CITY
MGM, February 2, 1950   Directed by George Sidney
Produced by Z. Wayne Griffin
Screenplay by Robert Riley Crutcher; story by Albert Beich
Cast: Clark Gable, Frank Morgan, Marilyn Maxwell, Raymond Burr, James
Gleason, Lewis Stone, Raymond Walburn, Pamela Britton, Zamah Cunning-
ham, Clinton Sundberg, Marion Martin, Bert Freed, Emory Parnell, Clara
Blandick, Richard Gaines, Roger Moore, Dorothy Ford, Pierre Watkin,
Nana Bryant, Victor Sun Yen, Marvin Kaplan, Byron Foulger, Edward
Earle, Jack Elam, Frank Ferguson, Alex Gerry, James Harrison, Frank Wil-
cox, Shirley Lew, Bill Cartledge, Helen Brown, Dick Wessel, Donna Hyatt
Loew's State Theater

(90) CAUSE FOR ALARM
MGM, March 30, 1951   Directed by Tay Garnett
Produced by Tom Lewis
Screenplay by Mel Dinelli and Tom Lewis; from a story by Larry Marcus
Music by Andre Previn
Cast: Barry Sullivan, Bruce Cowling, Margalo Gillmore, Bradley Mora, Irving
Bacon, Georgia Backus, Don Haggerty, Art Baker, Richard Anderson, Reg-
is Toomey, Kathleen Freeman, Margie Liszt, Carl "Alfalfa" Switzer, Rob-
ert Easton, Helen Winston, Earl Hodgins, Bonnie Kay Eddy
Palace Theater

(91) HALF ANGEL
Twentieth Century-Fox, June 16, 1951   Directed by Richard Sale

Produced by Julian Blaustein
Screenplay by Robert Riskin; based on a story by George Carleton Brown
Cast: Joseph Cotten, Cecil Kellaway, Basil Ruysdael, Jim Backus, Irene Ryan, John Ridgely, Therese Lyon, Mary George, Gayle Pace, Steve Pritko, Edwin Max, Art Smith, Jack Davidson, Roger Laswell, William Johnstone, Lou Nova, Harris Brown
Roxy Theater

(92) PAULA
Columbia, July 16, 1952   Directed by Rudolph Mate
Produced by Buddy Adler
Screenplay by James Poe and Jerry Sackheim; story by Larry Marcus
Cast: Kent Smith, Alexander Knox, Tommy Rettig, Otto Hulett, Will Wright, Raymond Greenleaf, Eula Guy, William Vedder, Kathryn Card, Sidney Mason
Loew's State Theater

(92) BECAUSE OF YOU
Universal, December 4, 1952   Directed by Joseph Pevney
Produced by Albert J. Cohen
Screenplay by Ketti Frings; story by Thelma Robinson
Cast: Jeff Chandler, Alex Nicol, Frances Dee, Alexander Scourby, Lynne Roberts, Mae Clarke, Gayle Reed, Billy Wayne, Frances Karath, Morris Ankrum
Capitol Theater

(93) IT HAPPENS EVERY THURSDAY
Universal, 1953 (no New York release)   Directed by Joseph Pevney
Screenplay by Dane Lussier; adapted by Leonard Praskins and Barney Slater from a book by Jane S. McIlvaine
Cast: John Forsythe, Frank McHugh, Gladys George, Edgar Buchanan, Palmer Lee, Regis Toomey, Jane Darwell, Dennis Weaver, James Conlin, Willard Waterman, Madge Blake, Sylvia Simms, Harvey Grant, Kathryn Card

Television Shows of Loretta Young

Loretta Young Show—NBC, 1953–1961
New Loretta Young Show—CBS, 1962–63

IRENE BENTLEY

FILMS OF IRENE BENTLEY

Dates are for the New York City release

(1) MY WEAKNESS
Fox, September 22, 1933   Directed by David Butler
Screenplay by B. G. DeSylva; based on a story by B. G. DeSylva
Music and lyrics by DeSylva, Leo Robin, and Richard Whiting
Cast: Lilian Harvey, Lew Ayres, Charles Butterworth, Harry Langdon, Sid
    Silvers, Henry Travers, Adrian Rosley, Mary Howard, Irene Ware, Barbara
    Weeks, Susan Fleming
Radio City Music Hall

(2) SMOKY
Fox, January 1, 1934   Directed by Eugene Forde
Screenplay by Stuart Anthony and Paul Perez; based on a novel by Will James
Cast: Victor Jory, Frank Campeau, Hank Mann, LeRoy Mason, Leonid
    Snegoff, narrated by Will James
Mayfair Theater

(3) FRONTIER MARSHAL
Fox, January 31, 1934   Directed by Lew Seiler
Screenplay by William Conselman and Stuart Anthony; adapted from incidents
    in a novel by Stuart N. Lake
Cast: George O'Brien, George E. Stone, Alan Edwards, Ruth Gillette, Berton
    Churchill, Frank Conroy, Ward Bond, Edward LeSaint, Russell Simpson,
    Jerry Foster
Mayfair Theater

INDEX

369

385

387

390